PRAISE FOR

A Bakery in Paris

"Aimie K. Runyan whips up a feast of a novel, full of the warmth and heart characters give each other during two despairing periods of French history. Recipes for boulangerie classics remind us of the power of simple ingredients, artfully assembled. Lisette and Micheline walk their own unique paths to happiness, fighting for their independence and finding loves that support their true selves. As delicious and satisfying as a perfect cup of *chocolat chaud*."

—Kerri Maher, internationally bestselling author of
The Paris Bookseller

"This captivating story is a tantalizing blend of history and culinary inspiration, weaving a poignant dual narrative that links two women to one Paris bakery. From the pivotal moment of the Commune of Paris uprising to life in the aftermath of the world wars, Runyan provides a mouthwatering journey through French history with delicious baking recipes sprinkled throughout the narrative. This book is sure to satisfy your senses, so don't miss out on this delicious read!"

—Stephanie Dray, *New York Times* bestselling author

"Two remarkably strong women—one under siege during the War of 1870 and the other struggling in the aftermath of World War II—both find strength and hope within the walls of a tiny Parisian bakery. With meticulous attention to rich historical detail, heartfelt characters, and a page-turn tale that's peppered with recipes, Aimie K. Runyan has the perfect ingredients for a most satisfying work of historical fiction."

—Renée Rosen, *USA Today* bestselling author of
The Social Graces

"An often heart-wrenching and always heartfelt exploration of two difficult periods in French history and two courageous women who exemplify the lasting legacy of the human spirit. Baking is a science, literature is an art, and Aimie K. Runyan's *A Bakery in Paris* is an absolute treat for historical fiction fans!"

—Gabriella Saab, author of *Daughters of Victory*

"*A Bakery in Paris* is a delicious novel that will have you hungering not only for French confections but to turn the next page. Set in two tumultuous wartime periods in Paris, Aimie K. Runyan weaves a spellbinding story of family, friendship, love, self-discovery, and the power of healing through cooking. Connected through time by family recipes, Runyan will delight the senses of every reader as they follow along the emotionally charged journeys of each endearing character."

—Eliza Knight, *USA Today* bestselling author of
Starring Adele Astaire

A Bakery in Paris

ALSO BY AIMIE K. RUNYAN

The School for German Brides

Across the Winding River

Girls on the Line

Daughters of the Night Sky

Duty to the Crown

Promised to the Crown

A
BAKERY
IN PARIS

A Novel

❋

Aimie K. Runyan

wm

WILLIAM MORROW
An Imprint of HarperCollins*Publishers*

A BAKERY IN PARIS. Copyright © 2023 by Aimie K. Runyan. All rights reserved. Printed in the United States of America. No part of this book may be used or reproduced in any manner whatsoever without written permission except in the case of brief quotations embodied in critical articles and reviews. For information, address HarperCollins Publishers, 195 Broadway, New York, NY 10007.

HarperCollins books may be purchased for educational, business, or sales promotional use. For information, please email the Special Markets Department at SPsales@harpercollins.com.

FIRST EDITION

Designed by Chloe Foster

Eiffel Tower art © The Noun Project / Alena Artemova

Library of Congress Cataloging-in-Publication Data has been applied for.

ISBN 978-0-06-324771-0

23 24 25 26 27 LBC 5 4 3 2 1

To my Jeremy,
who planted the seeds for this book in
the earliest days of our relationship.
I couldn't ask for a better partner,
a better road trip captain, or a better friend.
Here's to many more years of
snuggle-reading on the couch.
I love you.

A Bakery in Paris

Chapter One

LISETTE

Come away from the window, Lisette. I don't want anyone knowing we're up here."

Maman sat in her chair, needlework in hand since breakfast, though I doubt she'd made more than a dozen stitches in the three hours since, but it gave her hands company as she fretted. We lived on the Place Royale, one of the oldest neighborhoods in the heart of the city. After the Revolution, it was known as the Place des Vosges, but with the reinstatement of the monarchy, it was the Place Royale once more. Some of the oldest and wealthiest families in Paris lived here, and Maman was certain that if the Prussians took Paris, our neighborhood would be a prime target for their cruelty, while I thought she attributed more importance to our neighborhood than it deserved. There was no strategic advantage to invading our peaceful little corner of Paris, aside from the riches they could plunder. It didn't seem enough to me, but Maman was convinced that if they breached the walls of Paris it would mean our heads. Despite Maman's concerns, Papa would not retreat to the country as our neighbors had done. For weeks, he refused to think the Prussians would succeed in getting as far as Paris. Now that it seemed likely that they would, he said he would not abandon our home to the invaders, even if it meant risking our lives.

Our manservants, Gustave and Philippe . . . would they defend us against the mob when the Prussians invaded? More likely they would betray us if they thought they could save themselves. For this reason, Papa distrusted them and anyone else of the working class. The defeat at Sedan and the rumored displacement of the emperor made this possibility, once seemingly absurd, now entirely probable.

"Are you worried, Papa?" little Gislène asked from Maman's side.

"Not in the least. The emperor will have the Prussians well in hand before long, mark my words," Papa said as he paced the floor.

Antoine, my little brother, nodded enthusiastically from his chair where he'd spent the last hour reading one of our father's favorite tomes. He longed to follow in Papa's footsteps so badly, I wondered he didn't stitch himself permanently to Papa's side. Gislène, the baby, was curled up next to Maman on her settee. Maman's precious little poppet, complete with gold ringlets. It wasn't hard to understand Maman's preference for her, and she was sweet enough I couldn't begrudge her the attentions that preferment afforded.

I was the oldest. Born a girl when they had so desperately wanted an heir, and too strong-willed to be a pet to Maman. At first, I think they viewed me as a bit of an experiment in child-rearing. They practiced their parenting skills on me—with much help from a string of governesses, of course. But it was ten long, disappointing years before their precious boy was born. I think they rather grew to resent me during that time. Once Antoine was born, followed soon after by Gislène, that resentment grew into a usually comfortable indifference. In Antoine they had an heir, and in Gislène they had their sweet, biddable beauty. I was pretty enough, though red-haired and freckled, which made Maman lament for my marriage prospects. It was lonely at times, being the overlooked child, but it had the chief virtue of affording me a measure of independence that more attentive parents wouldn't have given a young woman of twenty-one.

"I'm going to take a nap," I announced, rather than claiming my usual spot on the side chair with one of the dry tomes of which Maman approved. Books on decorum and the running of a house, mainly.

"Is that the best use of your time?" Maman asked, always keen to exude more interest in my goings-on than she felt.

"Give her some peace, woman. These are trying times," Papa chided. My lips parted in surprise for a fraction of a second. He was rarely one to use his breath to come to my defense.

"A sudden headache, Maman. I'll be right as rain come suppertime, I'm sure."

She breathed a disappointed sigh as though a midday nap were somehow a moral failing. If it were, it was one she succumbed to at least once a week, but it wasn't worth the grief to mention it.

"Take this list to Marie for the marketing before you go up then," Maman said, handing me a scrap of paper marked with her elaborate script. "I hope Nanette has shown her how to do it properly. I don't want the shopkeepers swindling us any more than they already are."

Our newest kitchen maid had just been hired on a few months before, but Maman had taken little interest in training her up, so the job had largely fallen to our elderly cook and myself. Thankfully, Marie was smart and willing, and all too happy to take orders from me instead of my parents.

I refrained from shaking my head and left, the slip of paper in hand, without another acknowledgment.

The kitchen always felt like a completely different country to me, the way it contrasted with the rest of the house. It was bright and airy, owing to the doors that opened onto the back courtyard. Unlike the rest of the house, which was littered with fussy, expensive knickknacks of Maman's choosing, each item in the efficient kitchen had a place and purpose. Each spoon, knife, and mixing bowl had a designated spot on a hook, shelf, or drawer and anyone privileged enough to gain admittance to Nanette's kitchen risked inciting her wrath if a single utensil was mislaid. Gleaming copper pots hung from the walls, or else sat bubbling on the massive cast iron stove that dominated the room, most often laden with soups and stews. As a child, I used to pretend the massive stockpot was a witch's cauldron and the rows of spice canisters were secret ingredients the benevolent witch—sweet Nanette—had spent a lifetime collecting and preserving. Coriander wasn't simple coriander, but rather the trimmings of fur from a very rare species of bat collected on a full moon. Oregano was moss of a yew tree blessed by benevolent fairies, and so on.

Nanette enjoyed the novelty of my presence in the kitchens at first. When my curiosity grew into a serious interest, she didn't shoo me away, but taught me her trade as she would have her own daughter. I learned at her elbow, my little red journal with gilded pages in hand, constantly taking notes. I gave the excuse I was reviewing my lessons in the privacy of my room, and it seemed she was happy enough to believe the fib. On the rare occasion Maman wondered where I was, Nanette and I enacted a plan. The maids were regularly bribed with biscuits and cakes, often of my own making, to come to the kitchens and alert me so I could sneak up the back stairs to my room and come down to her summons from the main staircase after brushing off a healthy coating of flour from my dress. But when I became old enough to go out in public with Maman, my presence wasn't reliable enough for me to be a consistent help in the kitchen. As Nanette grew older, it had become clear to me that she needed a dedicated assistant, and so it came to be that Marie was taken on.

Marie was already working on preparations for the evening meal. She moved with a practiced efficiency that betrayed the hard truth that as soon as she'd been tall enough to see over the edge of a stove, she'd been forced to spend most of her time behind one.

"Maman has marketing for you," I said, placing the list on a clean area on the worktable.

"Of course she has," she said, wiping her cheek with her hand before turning her attention back to the simmering pot. She realized the breach of etiquette and looked at me wide-eyed. "I mean, of course, Mademoiselle Lisette. Right away."

I waved dismissively at the faux pas. Maman probably was entitled to any abuse poor Marie could throw her way. "Is everything all right?" I asked. "You don't seem yourself." Her face looked paler than usual, and there were beads of sweat on her brow, presumably from the effort of working through some sort of injury.

"It's nothing, mademoiselle. Don't worry about it." She took a step toward the simmering pot on the stove and her face betrayed that she was in pain.

"Nonsense, I insist you tell me. I can fetch a doctor for you."

"No need for that. I twisted my ankle this morning. I slipped on the moss in the courtyard. It hurts something fierce, but it'll be well enough in a few days. I've bound it as tight as I can with a rag. No doctor would be able to do more."

Nanette joined us from the opposite end of the kitchen. "That's what that clatter was this morning? I thought you told me an alley cat had knocked over the washboard I'd left out to dry. Why would you make up stories?"

"I didn't want to get sacked. I got back to work as soon as I could stand."

"Child, I don't know how many times I have to tell you, I won't send you packing for a trifle like that. If I did, I'd be back to doing the job of two until I could convince Monsieur Vigneau to hire a new girl. It took me twenty years to convince him the first time. And that was with our little Kitchen Mouse here badgering him at every turn for the last five."

"I'm sorry, Nanette, I won't do it again."

"Well, you can't do the marketing in such a state. I'll have to do it for you." Since the war broke out, we'd trimmed the staff back to its barest levels and there was really no one to spare for the task aside from me.

"Your parents will have my hide if I allow it," she said. "I'll make do, really."

"They'll never know I was gone," I pressed. I could almost feel the warm September sun against my face and would have gladly traded the sooty air from town for the stagnant air of the house for any price. I was nearly mad to be confined there, no matter how fine the carpets or how lavish the furniture and trappings.

"It's not safe for a well-born girl such as yourself to be out in public unescorted just now, mademoiselle. You'd be risking your life."

"So, you'll lend me a dress. That way I won't be conspicuous at the market. Marie will take a rest in my room. We're not too far from the same size. They expect me to be napping until dinner, which is exactly what you should be doing."

"I haven't a spare," Marie explained. "I've been saving for another, but I've only been here two months . . ."

"Never mind that. You can wear one of my nightgowns and I'll wear what you have on, if you don't mind."

Marie looked as though she wanted to object but restrained her reluctance behind clenched teeth. She was clearly using every bit of her will to manage her pain and she hadn't the strength to argue. She moved the soup to the cooler side of the stove and wiped her hands on her apron in resolution.

I let her lean against me as we took the back stairs up to my room. Mine was the closest to the stairs and thankfully the easiest for her to retreat from if someone were to come looking. I fervently hoped no one would take an uncharacteristic interest in my whereabouts.

As we exchanged clothes, she spewed advice about which shops to frequent and how much to haggle at each. Though having provisions delivered had been the custom, the war with the Prussians had sent everything into a tailspin. We had to go in search of what we needed, hoping to find the ingredients to cobble together meals. I prayed I would remember the details Marie prattled off, but it seemed unlikely. I'd just have to do my best and hope I didn't pay so much for the weekly supplies that Maman would accuse poor Marie of malfeasance.

Marie's dress smelled of sweat, grease, and stale flour. I was glad I'd had cause to lend her a nightgown so the smell of it wouldn't permeate my sheets. The nightgown could be laundered before I needed it again, but the sheets would have to wait another week. I'd have to sprinkle them with a bit of my jasmine perfume before I slept that night. It would be all I could do to bear the smell on the dress as I walked in the great outdoors, let alone on my sheets in the confines of my bedchamber as I tried to sleep. Impulsively, I took the bee bottle from my vanity, and put a dab of the scent behind each ear. It wouldn't cover the smell, but it would be enough to distract me from it. I gathered a few coins and banknotes from my own cache in case I had to visit a shop where Papa didn't have an account.

I looked at my reflection in the glass and winced. The smell aside, Marie's dress was stained and shabby and I felt as though I looked as worn and wan as the fabric that had seen more use than it should have been called to. I snuck out the back court-yard exit as quickly and quietly as I could. Officially, since the siege, I was only allowed one daily constitutional in the Place Royale, preferably in the shade of the arcade so as not to exacerbate my freckles. The grassy square was transected by Stabilise walkways; a mixture of sand, gravel, and whitewash just like in the gardens at Versailles. I'd traversed each footpath a million times in the past month, and each time I heard the grating *crunch-crunch-crunch* of the coarse soil under the soles of my kid boots, I feared I was one step closer to madness. It was with a breath of relief that I escaped onto the cobblestones of the rue de Rivoli and the rest of Paris.

Before the upheaval, I loved to sneak away and lose myself in the bustle of the city. It likely wasn't the safest thing for a young woman to do alone, but I had usually been able to persuade a housemaid to accompany me and give me a wide berth. I loved to ramble about the long winding avenues, made even wider and more accommodating during the recent tenure of Baron Haussmann as prefect. Papa despised Haussmann's grand apartments, along with so many of the changes made since the emperor began renovating Paris with the zeal of a discontented housewife, but I recognized the charms of the wrought-iron balconies and the convenience of having roads wide enough for carriages to pass one another.

Despite the temptation, I wouldn't let myself wander aimlessly that afternoon, no matter how much my soul yearned for it. I managed to procure most of what Marie was meant to buy at the butcher, though the supply looked scarce compared to the months before the war. The fromagerie had barely any stock at all, and Maman would have to do without her favorite camembert from Normandy. Papa would simply remind her, in his less-than-diplomatic way, that war called us all to make sacrifices and that hers was comparatively easy to bear. The shelves at the dry goods store were sparse, but not entirely empty.

I gave my list to the shopkeeper, who looked from it to me and gave me a once-over. He said nothing but set about gathering up the goods Maman had requested. Nothing seemed out of the ordinary. Some coffee and flour, a few odds and ends. He was able to gather the entirety of the list in a few minutes' time and brought the items to the counter where I waited.

"Who d'you work for?" he asked, head cocked to the side, as though still assessing me.

"The Vigneau family on the Place Royale," I said. "You can add this to their account."

"You're not the regular girl," he said, now crossing his arms over his chest.

"No, Marie turned her ankle and I've come in her place," I explained. "She wasn't in any condition to walk so far."

"And how am I supposed to know that you're not trying to get free food and charge it to one of my best clients' accounts?" The color in his face was rising and I knew his temper must be close to the boiling point. It would be for me to diffuse it.

"If it's a problem, sir, I can settle the bill in cash this once. I can have them send you a note if I have to come in the future." I reached into Marie's pocket where I'd stuffed a few bank notes. "Will this do?"

"A hundred francs? Are you mad? How in God's name would a kitchen maid come across a hundred francs?" I felt my stomach sink. I hadn't thought about how it would look for a servant to be carrying such a sum.

"The mistress of the house . . ."

"My dear girl, whoever you are, I know enough of Madame Vigneau to know she would no sooner trust a new servant with a hundred francs than she would spit in the emperor's eye."

"Is there a problem, Monsieur Levesque?" A young man in a National Guard uniform approached the counter. His hair was the color of polished bronze, and his eyes were a startling blue. He couldn't have been more than twenty-five years old but had the commanding presence of one who had been in uniform for years. *Monsieur Levesque*. Of course. We hadn't had a maid in my lifetime who hadn't complained of his sour nature.

"Ah, Monsieur Fournier. This—woman—claims to be in the employ of the Vigneau family. And in possession of a large sum of money. It's clear as day she's a thief and a liar."

"Those are weighty accusations, monsieur. Have you any proof of wrongdoing aside from her having money?" The guardsman, rather a tall man, stood to his full height as if conveying the seriousness of the charges.

"No, but since when does a kitchen maid have a hundred francs in her pocket? It can't be through fair means." The shopkeeper crossed his arms over his chest as if his pronouncement was enough to settle the matter.

"You should have been a detective, Levesque. It might have suited you better than being a shopkeeper."

"Are you saying I'm ill-suited for my job, monsieur?" His arms dropped to his sides, and he took a step closer to Monsieur Fournier. A bold move considering how easily the guardsman could set this man in his place.

"I think a shop-keep who isn't willing to sell goods for ready money needs to consider how he runs his business."

Levesque snapped his mouth shut.

"The total is three francs, *mademoiselle*." The last word was dripping with disdain. I felt the color rise in my cheeks at the gross overpayment I had offered him. I found a ten-franc bill and slid it across the counter to him. He gave me my change and stared at me with daggers for eyes as I loaded the wares into Marie's marketing basket. I nodded and exited back onto the street. I exhaled in relief, glad I was nearly finished with my outing, having learned a valuable lesson in how far my ignorance of real life extended.

"Hold on then," the National Guardsman said when I was ten paces from the shop.

"How may I help you, Monsieur—?"

"Fournier," he reminded me. "Théodore Fournier. You can help by telling me why you're pretending to work as the Vigneaux' hired girl and what has happened to Marie."

"So you believe Monsieur Levesque," I said. "Why didn't you arrest me?"

"I don't believe him exactly," he said. "And Levesque is a proper bastard. I wouldn't give him the satisfaction of letting him think he'd found a criminal."

"You think I'm a criminal?" I asked.

"No, but kitchen maids don't carry hundred-franc bills." He grabbed my hands to look at them. "They don't have hands that have clearly never seen a drop of dishwater. Nor are they in the habit of wearing jasmine perfume. What's more, that dress is Marie's. I want to know what's happened to her."

I looked down at the stained dress and then to my hands that were free from the callouses and blisters of an honest day's work. I cooked when my schedule allowed, but I didn't have to ruin my hands scrubbing the pans after I had finished. My disguise had been woefully incomplete. "You're an observant man, Monsieur Fournier. Marie is well," I assured him. "She lent me her dress as I didn't have anything suitable."

He cocked his head, considering my story. He didn't dismiss me out of hand but wasn't fully convinced of it either.

"But what is your connection to the house? How do you know Marie?" I stared at him, wanting very much to turn the question to him. How had he come to know sweet young Marie? To recognize her dress so readily?

I took in a deep breath. There seemed no sense in withholding the truth from him. "I'm the eldest daughter of the house."

"Ah, bored little rich girl taking the day off to see how the poor get by?" he asked, his jaw tightening as he spoke. He said the word *rich* as though it were a curse.

"No, it was as I told Monsieur Levesque. She turned her ankle, and she wasn't well enough to do the marketing and I was the only one who could go in her place. I thought dressing like a servant would be safer."

"You're not wrong on that score," he said, his face softening a bit. "It was foolish for a girl like you to go out alone."

"But not foolish for Marie? She can't be much older than I am. What right have I to send her to run errands that I wouldn't be willing to do myself?"

He paused a moment. "If you truly believe that, there may be hope for us yet. All the same, let me walk you home. Were you finished with your marketing?"

"I had one other errand, monsieur," I said. "I don't mind walking alone. It's not far."

"I'd feel better if I stayed with you," he said. "What's more, you could yet be lying, and I won't know the truth until I see you walk through the door of that house."

"Very well," I said. "If I may be so bold as to turn the question on you, how are *you* connected to Marie?"

"She's from my neighborhood in Montmartre. I've known her since she was a girl. Her getting a position in a posh house on the Place Royale was the talk of the place for a good week."

I considered his words. It was likely true that a job as a kitchen maid in a house like ours was a dream come true for many in that part of town. It was a great deal of work, but there was plentiful food and a warm bed at night. Many had it worse, and it hardly seemed fair.

My reverie was cut short as we reached my desired stop. "Just here." I pointed to the fabric shop that still looked resplendently well-stocked. People had less care for muslins and silks when a wolf was growling at the city door. He took the marketing basket and held my provisions as I placed my order.

"Let me see the blue linen there, please," I said. The shopkeeper handed me the bolt of fabric. It was thick and durable, and not unpleasant to look at. Sturdy, but wouldn't be too rough against the skin. And it would stand up to a good washing, which was imperative. I nodded my approval. "Five yards of this. And another five of the green." I had him gather up good thread and the buttons needed to make a plain but serviceable dress from each.

Methodically, the shopkeeper cut the length of fabric and collected the notions. This time I waited for a total before removing money from my pocket.

"Don't you have a seamstress for that sort of thing," Fournier commented as we began to walk back in the direction of the Place Royale. "I thought they brought samples of imported fabrics from the orient to your house, took measurements, and other such folderol."

"It isn't for me. Clearly Marie is in need of a new dress." I gestured despairingly to the dress I wore. "I thought the blue would do nicely for her."

"Maybe more mistresses should be forced to wear their hired girls' dresses. What about the other cloth?" His voice had softened, taking on the tone of a conversation instead of a schoolmaster scolding an unruly pupil.

"I needn't tell you that war is upon us, monsieur," I said. "It seems that having something sturdy to wear would be prudent."

"You're wiser than your upbringing would usually permit," he said, staring off as he considered my words.

"You don't care for the wealthy, do you?" I said.

"How can one care for a cancer eating away at the very

marrow of our society. No, I don't care for the rich at all," he said, his teeth grinding for a moment before he controlled his rancor.

"Those of us who were born to it have no choice in the matter," I reminded him.

"No, and those who are born to it are generally given an education that prohibits them from doing something of use with their riches that would be of benefit to their fellow man. And so, the cycle continues."

"We do our charity work, monsieur," I said, thinking of the hours Maman forced me to spend making up baskets of food for the less fortunate. It was important work, but always done in the company of tedious people.

"Yes, in plain sight so everyone can see how magnanimous you are. Do you honestly think a basket here or a few coins there is enough to solve the hunger gnawing away at the city? No. There needs to be real change." His words were laced with the fire of conviction.

"I can't disagree," I said. "It always seems as if my mother does just enough charity work to absolve her conscience."

"And so it always is with your lot. But you seem to have more gumption than many of them. Maybe there is hope, after all," he said, echoing his sentiment from before.

"I'm glad I meet with your approval in some estimation at least," I said, surprised to find the statement was true. "You are passionate about your cause."

"It's not just mine. It's the cause of every man, woman, and child who must work for a living. Don't fool yourself into thinking it's anything less."

"I don't doubt it," I said sincerely. "Though I'm not permitted out all that often, it's plain to see that the poor are suffering."

"You'd be kept from seeing most of it, wouldn't you?" he asked, more to himself than to me. "But at least you see it. Many turn a blind eye when faced with it."

Not for the first time, I felt useless. Of course my upbringing had been manufactured to prepare me for a life of being ornamental, but I felt myself spilling over the edges of the mold that had been carved out for me.

"I want to help," I said. "Truly."

"I believe you," he replied. "But it's not help in the form of charity baskets and alms that's needed. We don't need reform by inches. We need revolution."

"Hasn't that been tried?" I asked, keeping the irony from my tone. "Or do you wish for the guillotines to return to the Place de la Concorde?"

"No. Unlike many of my compatriots, I am not a violent man. I abhor it, in fact. But there are times when the only solution to the problem at hand is force. The working people of Paris deserve to have a say in their own lives."

"What can be done?" I asked. "What can we do?"

"We resist," he said simply. "We rally the people to the cause and remind them who has the boots on their necks."

"You make it sound so brutal," I said.

"Because it is," he said.

I thought of the way my parents spoke to the servants, to anyone of lower rank, and knew he was right.

We reached the gate to the servants' entrance to the back

courtyard where the staff accepted deliveries and such. I produced a key to open it, waving it once I'd turned the lock.

"See, legal admittance, good sir. Now if you'll excuse me, I have a kitchen maid who will lose her post if she's discovered napping in my bed."

"You are a surprise, Mademoiselle Vigneau. I hope you surprise me again by coming to hear a talk next Tuesday at Les Halles. It might prove rather interesting to you if you truly want to help."

"I'll think about it," I said, glancing down at my feet.

"I hope you will."

He handed me my basket and walked back into the streets of Paris without another word. I stood and watched a moment as he grew smaller, then disappeared. I didn't know who this man was, not truly, but found myself churning with envy. He had a depth in his convictions I'd never experienced, nor could I ever hope to equal.

Chapter Two

MICHELINE

I sat straight upright in bed, the nightgown that had once been Maman's now doused in sweat. It was a solid minute before I realized the air-raid sirens had been in my dreams and that I didn't have to drag Noémie and Sylvie down to the cellars of our little two-story building to wait out the bombing. The war had been over for months, but the nightmares made it feel as though it never ceased.

I looked over at little Noémie who had crawled into my bed at some point in the night. Her red ringlets framed a face that was better suited for a gallery in the Louvre than our apartment above a bistro with peeling dark-green paint in the far reaches of Paris. She took deep even breaths and looked as though the war was the furthest thing from her mind. A long-forgotten ghost of a memory that would only come back as a twinge of sadness, rather than a tidal wave of grief. I couldn't take solace in much, but Noémie's innocence was my safe haven. I would have given my very life to protect it.

"Nightmares again?" Sylvie asked from her bed on the opposite side of the room.

"Yes, go back to sleep, darling," I bade gently. I'd hoped that it was just before dawn, but my bedside clock told me it was still the middle of the night.

"We'd all sleep better if you'd move into Maman's room, you know," Sylvie said, covering her head with her pillow. "I've half a mind to take it for myself if you won't." Her voice was muffled by the pillow, but even the thick puff of goose down didn't dampen her vitriol. She was twelve, soon would be thirteen, and grew more challenging with each passing day. I sighed and tried to take solace in that too. I was just her age when the war broke out and hadn't had the luxury of being a difficult teenager. Noémie, at the tender age of eight, was more restful company.

Part of me should have been grateful Sylvie had the chance at a proper adolescence, but the raising of her was left to me, and she seemed determined to make up for my lost opportunity, even if it meant driving me insane in the process.

"You will not," I said, summoning the authority of a sister seven years her elder. "It is Maman's room and will remain so until she comes home."

Sylvie shot me daggers. Twelve-year-olds really were a pestilence. She'd done the hard work of coming to grips with Maman's disappearance, where I was not yet able. It had been different with Papa. His death records were conclusive. Killed in action near Sedan. We'd all accepted the news of his death with grief, but without the burden of uncertainty. It was a rare family in Paris that hadn't lost a father, brother, husband, or son to the war. Others had waited for years for their loved ones to be released from prisoner-of-war camps in hopes something would be left of the man they'd sent off to war. If a family had only been called to sacrifice one, they were counted among the lucky.

Maman's story was harder to accept. We hadn't the means to leave Paris early in the war, and soon it was too late to escape, even if we'd had the money. She'd been scrupulous about keeping us safe. Religiously checking the oilcloth that covered the windows for any gaps that might let out a glimmer of light. Never letting us leave the apartment alone under any circumstances. Always choosing the routes to the market with the least chance of meeting a German patrol. She was vigilance personified.

But one day, almost two years ago, when she went to trade her ration coupons for groceries, she never returned.

There had been no air raid while she was gone. There had been no exceptional upheaval in the streets that day. But she disappeared all the same, and we were left behind to make sense.

The woman who always left us, cloistered for our safety, with the words *"Stay here safe and sound for me, my darlings, so I may run my errands with an easy heart and come home all the sooner,"* left just after the midday meal on a reasonably calm Tuesday in June and never came home. The city had just been liberated from German control and we'd begun to breathe a bit more freely. We didn't realize what a mistake that was.

I swung my feet out of bed, careful not to stir Noémie as I stood, and exited to the little parlor. School wasn't for hours yet. The girls could sleep, and I could tend to the mending long before I saw to their breakfast.

Maman and Papa had never been wealthy, and if they had left any money behind, apart from the few hundred francs I found tucked away in Maman's drawer, I never found it. When I went to the bank to inquire if there was anything in their account, even with Papa's papers in hand, they would not help. Papa had worked in a factory for a good steady wage, while Maman took odd jobs and tended to us.

We were more comfortable than most in the neighborhood, however, as we owned our little building. I didn't have to worry about rent, which was a blessing I remembered each night when sleep eluded me. It was just a small apartment over a little bistro, but it was ours. We took in a modest rent from the people who ran the restaurant, which had helped my parents through lean times and kept us afloat now, but only just. I took in mending to help ease the strain on our finances. I also took in washing. I minded children while their mothers ran errands. Anything to earn a few *sous* to keep bread on the table and the wolves from the door.

I took a blouse from the mending basket and fixed the torn cuff in less than a quarter of an hour. I'd finished the three other pieces in the failing light the night before, so the lot was ready to return. Madame Dupuis had sent mending weekly since she'd learned of our plight. Some of the skirts she'd sent for hemming barely needed a half-dozen stitches, but she insisted on paying me as though I'd spent a full hour to repair the entire garment. A few times I wondered if she hadn't torn the clothes herself to have a reason to send them to me, for I couldn't imagine a sedate matron of seventy-odd years being so hard on her things. She had a girl come to do the heavy cleaning, and she didn't venture out much at all. Whatever her motives, I remembered her generosity as well in my prayers, even when my soul felt too broken to make them.

I looked through the basket and every last piece was now in perfect repair. I cursed my own industriousness, for it left me with nothing to do.

I loathed nighttime.

Nighttime was *almost* the hardest.

The very worst was on those rare occasions when I slept through the night and woke up in the morning, refreshed only for the sinking feeling to return to my stomach as I remembered Maman was gone. For a little while on those mornings, it felt like losing her all over again.

It was too easy to get lost in the abyss of my own thoughts. Reading, which used to be a great pleasure of mine, could not keep my mind from wandering.

Wandering to the fear that lurked in every dark crevasse. Wandering to the ache I felt when I thought of Papa. Wandering to the longing I had for Maman to come home and take charge of things again.

These children were hers, not mine.

I loved them to distraction. I wanted nothing but the best for them. And that meant being raised by their mother and not their nineteen-year-old sister.

A part of me, a part I loathed, was so angry at Maman for

leaving me like this. For leaving me to raise the girls on my own. Her children. Perhaps even at the cost of never having a family of my own. I would be twenty-nine when Noémie was out on her own. I wouldn't be in my dotage, but it wasn't exactly young for starting a family.

I should have been free to plan my own life now that the war was over. Bridging the gap from childhood to womanhood and exploring the opportunities that once seemed boundless. University? Career? Family? We weren't wealthy, but I would have had *some* choice in the course of my life. But now, I didn't even have the luxury of *considering* what I wanted.

I stopped myself. Every day, the most important choice I had to make was what was best for the girls. And what Maman would have wanted for them if she couldn't be here to raise them herself. But one day she would come home. There was nothing the authorities or well-meaning friends could say to convince me she wouldn't.

I had to ignore these thoughts. They would lead to no good place. The only thing for me was to play the cards I was dealt the best I could.

As had become my custom, I went to the little kitchen where Maman had spent so much of my childhood toiling over the stove and sought out my comfort in flour, butter, salt, and water. The scent of sugar still hung heavy in the air from three decades of Maman's famous *palmiers*. I'd have given anything to have one of them right then. The rationing was easing, little by little, and I was able to procure some of the delicacies—and staples—that we'd been without during the war. I cried actual tears the first time I was able to buy a sack of real white flour of considerable size, and the grocer seemed equally relieved to have stock on the shelves.

I spent my youth at Maman's apron strings and committed the recipes I'd learned at her side to the depths of my memory as I had my lessons and my catechism. I recalled not only the ingredients and Maman's careful instructions but remembered with vivid detail the first time we made each of them together. I remembered her gentle guidance and loving tutelage. I could evoke the memory of what dress she wore for each recipe. Whether she was wearing rose water or the special jasmine perfume Papa had given her for her birthday when I was a girl. Tonight, my offering to the gods of sleep would be *chaussons aux pommes:* apple slippers. I recalled that Maman had worn her green apron the day she'd taught me, and donned it over my nightdress. The pastry dough was a simple one, but like all good things, it took time. As I mixed the ingredients, I let the rest of the world fall away.

I couldn't take on the world, but I could take on this humble ball of flour, butter, salt, and water and I could make something from it. And it was the closest thing to a comfort I had.

Chapter Three

LISETTE

SEPTEMBER 2, 1870

I rushed into the kitchen, all but flinging the market basket at poor Nanette's head.

"Lord, I was ready to have the *gendarmes* out hunting the streets for you. What took you so long? Were you held up by bandits or did the Prussians get you?" Nanette hurried to put the items where they belonged and separated what she needed to complete the meal we were due to eat in less than an hour. She'd be hard-pressed to get the meal on the table on time, which was a cardinal offense in Papa's book.

"The National Guard," I said. "A shopkeeper guessed that I wasn't a servant."

"It was foolish to have you go. I should have done it myself. And your mother informed me we're having a guest for dinner. She's going to murder me with her favorite crochet hook if the meal isn't perfect. And Marie too. Poor thing fell asleep in your bed, and I didn't have it in me to wake her."

The look on Nanette's face was grim. Marie had been exhausted from her suffering, not to mention the weeks of unrelenting toil beforehand to set food on our table.

"What's left to do?" I asked as the last of the supplies were shelved. "I can help."

"I don't see that I've much choice. Can you get the tarts ready? If we get them in the oven before the first course, they'll be ready by the time you've eaten. But work fast. It'll be the crochet hook for all of us if you're late too."

"In a trice," I said, springing over to the canisters where Nanette kept the flour and sugar. I'd made Nanette's tart crust so many times I could do it in my sleep. I slipped into a side room and changed back into my dress so that a housemaid, sworn to silence, could run Marie's dress to her in my room. I donned the apron Nanette had reserved for my use and got to work. While I enjoyed trussing a roast and fussing with stews well enough, baking was where my heart was. In truth, the pastries and tarts that earned Nanette so much praise had been my own handiwork more often than not for the past eight years.

I had the tart shells in the oven before long, while Nanette fussed over the pheasant I'd brought back from the market and prepared vegetables. Her hands were a blur as she seasoned and chopped her way through the contents of the marketing basket. I prepared the fillings for the tarts; apple, which was Papa's favorite, and pear and almond cream for Maman. Clearly, we were expecting special company if we were preparing both. I focused on the almond cream first. It was the fussier of the two—being Maman's preference it would be—and the apple tart was far more forgiving.

Before long, Marie hobbled in, her face white with pain with every step.

"Sit," I ordered, pointing to a stool in the corner. "You can tell me what to do from there."

"Thank you," she said. "I crossed paths with your mother on the way down."

I blanched. "She didn't question you about being out of the kitchens?"

"I don't think it occurred to her that I wasn't where I should be. I was able to walk normally while she was in view, though I'm paying for it now, sure enough. She says I'm to style your hair and help you dress for dinner."

I blinked in surprise. Maman usually didn't trouble herself with my appearance and trusted me to style my own hair well enough. "Promoted to lady's maid already," I said, offering a wink. "Good work. I don't suppose she said why she's orchestrating a grand dinner as the city is prepared for battle, did she?"

"Important company," she said, her tone dry. "A certain Gaspard d'Amboise, if that means anything to you."

"A family acquaintance," I said, refraining from heaving a sigh. "Good family and all that. I can see them putting on a good table for him, but I don't see why Maman is sparing a thought for my *toilette* for the occasion."

"Don't you?" Nanette said. "You've got twenty-one years to your name. Old enough to be interesting to a man. I'd wager a month's pay they're thinking to marry you off."

"I can't imagine Gaspard taking an interest in me. He probably sees me as a child. He's obsessed with court life and social standing. He'll want an elegant and refined wife."

"Or a young one he can mold to his liking," Nanette said, pointing at me with a wooden spoon for emphasis. "I'd be on my best form tonight if I were you. If you displease the great Monsieur d'Amboise tonight, 'high dudgeon' won't begin to describe your mother's wrath."

"Don't I know it," I replied. I slammed a wooden spoon down on the table harder than I'd intended. Monsieur Fournier spoke of how the poor weren't masters over their own lives, and I realized I knew something of that.

"And on that score, you'd better get dressed. I can finish the tarts on my own. If you see Gustave, tell him he's going to act as footman tonight and serve the meal. It'll look grander than poor Marie hobbling about."

I nodded and ascended the stairs, letting Marie use me as a crutch as she needed. The poor thing needed a week off her feet, but it was one thing among many I couldn't give her.

We selected the smartest dress from my wardrobe, which was limited given my lack of interest in sewing and Maman's usual indifference to my appearance. It was a cornflower-blue silk that Papa had gifted me last Christmas before. Its only embellishment was a bit of fringe at the bust and some delicate bows at the sleeves. It was elegant enough for dinner at home, if not as ornate as Maman might have preferred. Though she'd not been trained as a lady's maid, Marie made quick work of my hair, pinning it into a loose chignon with a few curls at the fringe to soften the effect.

"A proper lady," Marie declared once she finished. "No one would know you were making tarts in the kitchen a half hour ago."

"Just as well for my neck. Not to mention yours and Nanette's," I said with a shiver. "I have a small gift for you, by the way. As a thank-you for lending me your dress."

I produced the fabric and handed it to her. "You deserve to have a new dress. I hate to think of the trouble it must be to launder a dress when you haven't another. And you may keep the nightgown as well. I've got plenty of others."

"Very thoughtful of you," Marie said, casting her eyes down. It probably felt like charity, which a proud girl like her would be reluctant to accept.

"Consider it a bonus for a job well done. And I'll see about getting you an afternoon off so you can sew it in peace."

Marie's face brightened slightly. "Thank you, Lisette. It's a rare employer who is so thoughtful." She realized she'd made a misstep in addressing me by my first name, but I wasn't going to correct her.

"Perhaps more of them should walk a mile in their servants' shoes. Or dresses in my case," I said. The guardsman's words echoed in my ears.

She nodded and hobbled her way back to the kitchens. I was left to go down to the sitting room where Maman and Papa were waiting for Gaspard. When I entered, I was surprised to see Gislène and Antoine absent from the room. Gislène was young to dine in company, but usually persuaded Maman to allow it, and Antoine was getting to the age where it was good practice for him to partake in adult conversation, if only as an auditor.

"The children are dining in the nursery tonight," Maman said, anticipating my question. She looked me up and down and sighed. There was nothing to be done about my red hair or freckles, but it was coiffed well and I was dressed as well as my wardrobe would allow.

"It wants something," she said, as much to herself as to either Papa or me. She removed the teardrop pearl necklace that she wore at her throat and placed it around mine. She still had enough jewelry on that the one necklace wouldn't be missed, though her hand flitted to her throat fleetingly as if she felt exposed. She took a pace back and looked me over once more. "Much better. But you're in need of some new clothes. You've only got the one evening dress and the rest of your wardrobe could do with freshening as well. We'll have the seamstress in for a fitting before the week is out."

"Do I really need new gowns?" I asked. "After all, the city . . ." I gestured to the window I'd been chastised for looking out earlier.

"This foolishness won't last forever," Maman said. "There's no sense in acting like it will."

"Your mother is right. You should have some pretty new things befitting a girl of your station," Papa said, his glance as appraising as Maman's. He turned to her. "Don't neglect the shoes and jewelry and all the other trappings, Ernestine."

"Of course not," she said. "Though shopping isn't an easy task these days. I'm sure we can manage it somehow."

Papa nodded in satisfaction. If anyone was equal to finding ways to spend money on satin slippers and ruby earbobs in the midst of a war, it was Maman.

Philippe entered the sitting room and announced d'Amboise's arrival. He greeted Maman and Papa graciously, as the old friends that they were. When he came to me, he bowed deeply and lingered as his lips brushed my gloved hand.

"Mademoiselle Lisette, you have grown into a lady," he said, his face breaking into a broad smile. He was a tall man, well-built with dark hair and a pleasing countenance. He wore the uniform of the Versaillais—the troops that served the emperor. Or had done, if the reports were true. D'Amboise was perhaps ten years my senior and so focused on moving upward in society, I was surprised that he remembered my name. Or indeed, that he ever really learned it in the first place.

"It happens all too fast," Maman said, affecting an air of a mother clutching to the last moments of my girlhood. It was the height of restraint that I didn't roll my eyes at her. "And to think she's of an age to start a family of her own. It's a reminder of how fleeting life is."

Subtlety was not my mother's gift.

"Very well said, Madame Vigneau. I confess it feels some days as though life is passing me by faster than I realized. One day I was a child with my life before me, the next I am in my thirties and have neglected to think about creating a family of my own."

Nanette had been right. Maman had set her sights on d'Amboise for me, and he seemed all too willing to consider the alliance. And Papa would be in favor. D'Amboise's parents had money and position, even superior to his own. In their eyes, I couldn't aspire to more. From the number of medals on his chest, it was clear he was a man of great ambition, which was exactly the sort Papa preferred.

Philippe opened the door to the dining room, ready to serve the first course. It was a rich carrot soup that would be restorative against the autumn chill. As always, Nanette had seasoned it to perfection and made sure that it wasn't so substantial that we wouldn't want to eat the rest of the meal. She planned every course to complement the next with the skill a master composer used to move between movements in a concerto.

While Maman, Papa, and Gaspard spoke of the war and the emperor's troubles, I thought about Nanette bustling around the kitchen downstairs making sure the next course was ready in time to send up, but not ready so far in advance that it would have time to cool. I thought of Marie hobbling around trying to be useful when she ought to have been resting her ankle.

I thought of the National Guardsman who worried for Marie.

I wondered if his concern went as deep as affection.

An involuntary pang jolted my stomach, and I pushed the thought from my mind. Monsieur Fournier was a novelty. After being too long imprisoned in our townhouse, I found him positively captivating. He might as well have been from another world altogether.

"Don't you agree, Mademoiselle Lisette?" a voice said.

I snapped back to attention. Maman would lecture me for this later. She hated my propensity to daydream, and I could admit it made for awkward moments when I let myself drift at the wrong time. And clearly, this was one of those times.

"Yes, we're all quite sure the emperor's forces will surely be able to rout the Prussians before winter. And what a pleasure it will be to have all this unpleasantness behind us," Maman supplied.

"Quite right," I chimed in. "It will be better for everyone when it's all over." A wanting response, but at least it was something that would appease Maman.

"Are you very keen on politics, Mademoiselle Lisette?" he pressed. I couldn't tell from his tone which response he might prefer. Of course some men might want a wife to share his interests, but others merely wanted a compliant wife who would nod her head as needed. I felt as though I were being interviewed for a position on his household staff. It just happened to be that of wife instead of housekeeper, maid, or cook.

"It's hard to find the time to study them properly," I lied. "I've so much to get on with, learning how to run a household. But I can certainly see why they fascinate you, Monsieur d'Amboise."

Maman's head crooked, almost imperceptibly, and she shot me a small smile. The answer was the right one.

When at long last the desserts, the tarts of my own making, had been served and cleared away, Papa invited d'Amboise to his study for cigars and cognac while Maman and I went back to the sitting room for an Armagnac, Maman's favorite brandy.

"You need to pay more attention at mealtimes," Maman said after a long, uncomfortable silence. "You managed to acquit yourself well, but it could have been embarrassing."

"Yes, Maman," I said. "I was surprised he sought my opinion."

"Well, you must be prepared for the unexpected, mustn't you?" she said, likely parroting something she'd read in a book on comportment.

"Yes, Maman," I said, sipping my brandy and glad of its warmth.

We sat in silence for ten minutes more. It seemed to stretch on for hours, but I knew better than to ask for an early reprieve. I would have to stay until d'Amboise took his leave and pretend I was happy to be there. I thought about engaging Maman in conversation, but every time I thought of a topic, I dismissed it. For her part, Maman seemed content enough to stare into space, whether lost in thought or devoid of it, I couldn't tell. It was probably better I didn't know.

Papa and d'Amboise emerged from the study; the smell of tobacco wrapped around them like a mantle on their shoulders.

"I am so sorry that I cannot stay longer this evening," he said, Maman and I rising to accept his farewell. "Tomorrow will be a busy day with an early start, and I must meet the day and my duty head-on."

"Good man," Papa said, clapping him on the back.

"I shall look forward to seeing you again very soon, Mademoiselle Lisette. It has been a distinct pleasure."

I nodded wordlessly, holding my breath until I heard Philippe close the door behind him.

Maman collapsed on her settee, Papa joining her after he'd refilled his glass with cognac.

"You're to be congratulated, Lisette," Papa said. "D'Amboise has asked for your hand, and I've given my consent."

"What?" was all I could stammer. I wasn't surprised at the

result. It was what Maman wanted, and she wasn't used to brooking disappointment. But I *had* expected that d'Amboise would want longer than the space of a dinner to make his decision. I immediately wondered what defect in his personality would cause him to marry with such alacrity.

"D'Amboise is a solid man. Even-tempered, good family, not given to vice. It's a good match," Papa said.

"He barely knows me," I said. "How can he possibly be certain that I'll make him happy?"

"Oh, don't be daft, girl," Maman said. "He doesn't expect you to make him happy. He expects you to be his wife. To run his house and bear his children and to stand by his side at court. I hope you haven't filled your head with silly romantic thoughts. You haven't been reading novels, have you?"

"No, Maman," I said. I didn't point out there were none in the house, at her insistence, nor that I'd had no way to acquire any if I'd had a mind to.

"Good," Papa said. "He's hoping for a summer wedding, but of course, with the state of things, he understands that setting a date isn't practical just yet."

"I don't see why," Maman said. "It's not as though we're going to rent out Saint Sulpice and invite half of Paris. Why not go to the *mairie* and have it done?"

"He's from an old family, Ernestine. They believe in doing the thing properly, you know." Papa shot a warning look that let Maman know he was at the end of his patience.

Maman sighed. "As long as the thing happens. We should have him to dinner as often as possible, so we keep her fresh in his mind. We don't want him getting distracted in the months before they walk down the aisle. And I'll do what I can to extol the virtues of a spring wedding to Germaine d'Amboise. Surely six months will be enough time for her to plan a sufficiently elaborate affair."

"If he's so easily distracted, perhaps he isn't a good choice," I said, trying to sound dispassionate. Maman would not appreciate a tear-filled plea. A logical argument would be just as likely to fall on deaf ears, but it would earn fewer reprisals.

"Nonsense. Gaspard is a steady sort of man. He approached me about meeting you, you know. Your mother has you worried for naught. You should be happy, Lisette. He'll make you a good husband. And you'll have a grand wedding to look forward to. Fit for Marie Antoinette if your new mother-in-law has her say about it," Papa said, patting my shoulder.

"As long as I make a better end than she did," I said, trying to keep my tone light.

"As long as the d'Amboise family foots the lion's share of the bill for it," Maman said, ignoring me. "We have two other children to think about. Germaine doesn't have that concern, seeing that Gaspard is an only child."

"Calm down, Ernestine. We've money enough to provide for the little ones and still give Lisette here a proper send-off into married life. See to the dresses and all the frippery as soon as you can."

"Very well," Maman said, though not mollified. "I'll send out for the seamstress in the morning."

Maman and Papa continued to discuss the wedding as though I were not in the room and as though the matter didn't concern me. As if it weren't the most significant event in my life to date, or perhaps ever. I left the room without taking my leave, and from the sound of the conversation as I walked away, they didn't even notice my absence.

I considered climbing the stairs to rid myself of the silk dress and seek the comfort of my linen nightdress but found myself going down to the kitchens instead. Nanette and Marie were scrubbing dishes and making preparations for the next day's meals. They were dead on their feet, but the next day would be harried if they didn't put in the work now.

"Well look at you," Nanette said. "My little Kitchen Mouse looks like a proper lady. How was the visit with Monsieur d'Amboise?"

I opened my mouth to speak but found no words. I merely flung myself into her arms and wished, not for the first time, that my own mother had cared for me a fraction as much as this woman did.

Chapter Four

MICHELINE

At last, the sun crested over the horizon in the east, and the dawn had arrived to chase away the shadows. Since Madame Dupuis just lived in the next building over, I took the risk of leaving the girls unattended to return the mending in the morning hours before the girls would go off to school. The old woman was an early riser and would have already cleared away her breakfast dishes by now. I hated leaving the girls alone, especially given the circumstances of Maman's disappearance, but it was far more practical to leave them behind on quick errands such as these. Even so, I scrawled a note for them so they wouldn't worry. I checked the lock once before I went down the stairs and twice more to be sure. I couldn't bear to face Maman if something happened to them on my watch. I placed two of the *chaussons aux pommes* in a small dish on top of the mending as thanks to Madame Dupuis for her business and extravagant overpayment.

With the basket on my hip, I descended the stairs, prepared to navigate the early breakfast crowd in the bistro below by making myself as small as possible. Our building had been built in a time when the shopkeeper and the resident above were invariably the same person and having the staircase to the apartment inside the eatery was a convenience rather than a hindrance. Since we weren't the ones running the restaurant, the girls and I made pains to exit quickly and quietly during business hours so as not to interfere, but I realized the familiar hum of conversation was absent. Where once silence had been calming and restful, it was now only a portent of bad tidings. It was always silent before the bombs fell. It was always silent before the Germans knocked on a door. It was silent when afternoon became evening and slipped into night and we realized Maman wasn't coming home.

I set down my basket on one of the empty tables. Usually on a Thursday morning by this time, they were opening for the breakfast service and had been baking for several hours. There ought to be a small crowd on the little terrace with their coffee, baguette or *croissants*, butter, and jam. But no one was seated, though a regular customer I recognized peered in the window, shrugged, and kept walking. The sign in the window read "Open" as I read it from the interior and the doors had not been unlocked.

"Hello?" I called.

I was greeted by silence.

I felt the familiar ball of dread bunching in my stomach, and I grabbed the back of one of the empty chairs to steady myself.

For most of my childhood I was barred from spending much time in the bistro. It was a place of business and Maman and Papa didn't want our presence to be an imposition on the tenants when they were serving their clientele. I'd been allowed to help prepare it for new tenants on the few occasions when the previous ones had moved on, but aside from that, the place was as foreign to me as the inner sanctum of the Opéra Garnier or the National Assembly. It was a place of work, other people's work, and I had no place in it.

But, in my mother's absence, I was the de facto landlady, and I was within my rights to be here if I thought something was amiss. If the tenants weren't open for business, they wouldn't earn money. If they couldn't earn money, they couldn't pay rent. If they couldn't pay rent, we couldn't eat. It was very much my place to be here now.

"Hello?" I called again, walking down the short hallway to the kitchens.

Silence.

The kitchens were tidy, but empty. The smell of yesterday's supper still hung in the air, but every cooking implement was tucked away. The pots and pans, which ought to be filled with good things and simmering on the stove, were hung on the walls in their designated place. The cupboards were stocked with mixing bowls, baking sheets, and casserole pans that were older than I was, but still perfectly serviceable.

I stood at the top of the stairs that led down to the storeroom and cellars but couldn't bring myself to descend. If there was any room in this bistro that I knew, it was the infernal cellars. I spent too many nights clutching my sisters and praying we would see the dawn. I wouldn't go down there unless my very life depended on it. If there was any indication of where the tenants had gone, it wouldn't be there, anyway.

I noticed a note tucked on the kitchen counter under an empty dish.

Have moved to Lyon to be with family. Best of luck to you.

No other explanation, no warning.

The rent we depended on would not come next month, and I would have to find a way to replace that income.

I walked back to the front of the little restaurant and was tempted to sit and have a good cry. But there was no time. I had to find new tenants, though I had no idea how. That had always been Maman's undertaking. I knew what Maman had charged for rent but didn't know if that was still a fair price. And as they'd given no notice, I hadn't squirreled away extra money in case it took some time to fill the space. I'd been foolish, and I'd not make that mistake again.

I shook my head, demanding grace for myself. I hadn't spent lavishly. A new coat for Sylvie and new shoes for Noémie had been indispensable. A few peppermints or the odd hair ribbon for the girls was the closest thing to an extravagance that I'd indulged in. Even if we had back every *centime* from those little splurges, it wouldn't have made a difference. And Maman would have wanted the girls to have a treat now and again. I did too. They'd missed out on enough of their childhoods to be deprived of every small pleasure.

I calculated the money I had left in my little tin upstairs. Enough to feed us for a week? Two?

I remembered the task at hand and gathered up the basket of mending again. I stepped out to the street, checking the lock three times before stepping down onto the cobblestones.

Chapter Five

LISETTE

SEPTEMBER 6, 1870

Flour, water, butter, egg white . . .

I recited the litany in my head to stave off the near-lethal boredom as I stood for the dressmaker. I retained it all in my head so I could transpose it in my journal later. Reciting recipes was my only defense against madness as I endured endless fittings draped in silks, satins, damask, and velvet that week. A trousseau in the making, and I felt barely a participant in its creation. The dressmaker, a sullen woman named Madame Lacombe, directed her questions at Maman, and it was just as well because I had no patience for it. I thought of Nanette's recipes in my head as the pinch-nosed seamstress bustled about while Maman barked her orders.

As they swirled around me, I envisioned the endless maze of food stalls at Les Halles, the belly of Paris, and how I longed to go there and select my own ingredients for a meal. I thought of the thousands of Parisians who walked those aisles and wished to be among them.

I wanted to know the anonymity of being in the crowd.

I wanted to breathe in the air laced with the salty tang of meat hanging in the butchers' stalls. The earthy scent of fresh vegetables still crusted with the dirt of the farms that grew them. The cacophony of perfumes from sweet fruits that begged to be made into pies. The bread that was the very backbone of the Parisian diet.

I wanted to be in a place that was so utterly and completely humming with life.

And I wanted to know what Monsieur Fournier had to say about the future and what he would say to the crowds assembled to hear him and others at Les Halles. Maman, Papa, and Gaspard could cling to the hope that the reports had been exaggerated, but the papers had declared that France had entered the Third Republic. That didn't bode well for the emperor or our kind. But it boded very well for Fournier and his cause.

Maman, arms folded over her chest, surveyed as the dressmaker finished with the day's fitting.

"I am going to have coffee with Madame Poirier this afternoon," she proclaimed as the dressmaker scurried away. "I want you to use your time profitably."

She walked over to the bookcase and removed a well-worn tome on decorum she'd forced me to read a dozen times or more. "Read this. I will ask you questions at supper. If you cannot answer them well, I will be displeased."

"Yes, Maman," I said, knowing I could give her a full recitation of the entire tome from the table of contents to the index if she wanted.

She grunted and left the room to ready herself for her outing.

I tucked the book in my pocket and hurried to my own room. I had spent my few alone hours sewing in secret, crafting a plain dress from the green fabric I'd purchased the week before. I was nothing like a gifted seamstress, but with the help of a pattern, I was reasonably proficient with straight, uncomplicated lines. Without question, this was the most ambitious project I'd tackled. And as I looked in the mirror, I wasn't displeased with my handiwork. I looked like a well-dressed peasant woman off to do her marketing. I did not look like the daughter of the great Ernestine and Firmin Vigneau. For that, I was pleased.

I dashed down the stairs to the kitchens where Nanette and Marie bustled preparing the soup and roasted lamb for supper.

"Oh, have we taken on another housemaid?" Nanette asked, wiping the beads of sweat from her brow. "Where did you get that getup? Surely not from the snooty dressmaker your mother brought in."

"I made it myself," I said, jutting out my chin. "I bought fabric last week."

"And don't I know it," Nanette said, gesturing at Marie who was now wearing a dress made from the blue fabric I'd given her. She was a far more skilled seamstress than I, and she looked striking in her new clothes. "She's trying to act humble, but she's been strutting like the Queen of Sheba when she thinks I'm not looking. You've turned her head properly, you have."

"I'm glad of it," I said, remembering the condition—and odor—of her old dress. "She deserved a new dress."

"There's many worse off than our Marie who need one too, make no mistake," Nanette said. "But still, it was a kindness. But where are you off to dressed like a common peasant girl?"

"Les Halles," I said, trying to appear as though it were an everyday occurrence.

"What foolishness are you about?" Nanette said, looking up, her hands stopping in their methodical kneading of the bread dough. It was the first time in my recollection I'd seen her stop in the middle of her work. I pictured her stirring a bowl of batter in her sleep.

"I'm going to Les Halles," I repeated. "I've always wanted to go. How can I cook if I don't know how to choose my own ingredients?"

"Do you know what sort of folk convene there, Kitchen Mouse?" she asked.

"Almost all of Paris shops there," I said.

"Including the worst miscreants the underbelly of this city ever spat out. It's no place for you." Nanette stood to her full height, and I could see she was considering blocking the door.

"I'll be fine," I said, grabbing one of the marketing baskets from a hook. "I'll not make the same mistake of carrying too much money this time. I won't be of much use to a robber. And I can get you what you need from the market."

"No, you won't have much money, so all that will be at risk is your neck. The ruffians of Paris and the Prussians to boot. But if I can't persuade you to stay home where you belong, bring back an aubergine and some green beans. Only if they look fresh, mind you."

I leaned over and kissed her cheek. "Only the freshest for you."

"Be safe, mad girl." She shook her head and returned to the kneading as I turned to the door.

I headed in the direction of Les Halles. I'd driven by it in a carriage numerous times, but never dared to venture there on foot or unaccompanied. But I was trying to pass as a peasant woman, and peasant women did not travel with the protection of chaperones. It was a twenty-minute walk from the graceful homes on the Place Royale to Les Halles, and I tried to walk as though I were not out of bounds and countermanding my parents' orders to stay in the house. This was the farthest I'd wandered before, and I felt a tinge of fear in my gut. But I wouldn't turn back now and give anyone the satisfaction of thinking I was a coward.

It was ten minutes into the walk when I heard footsteps behind me, oddly in time with my own. Closer. Closer.

I felt a bead of sweat drip down my neck. I fought to keep my breath even. I fought the urge to run. Too much of my life had been spent in the sitting room with dry decorum books and needlework to have any prayer of outrunning anyone with a notion to catch me. I cursed the conventions that kept me in a gilded cage like a canary and just as helpless when the cat came calling.

"Mademoiselle, mademoiselle, where are you off to?" A

low voice grated like spikes on cobblestones behind me. "Why don't you stay awhile?"

I kept going, pretending to be deaf to the man's words. I refused to look back. I didn't want a face to put with the words. In my mind's eye it was a long, grimy face, framed by lank greasy hair. The mouth would be a thin slash of pasty white lips curled over yellowing, putrid teeth. I quickened my pace, but hopefully not so much he would decide to give chase. But the footfalls behind me grew louder and louder until I could feel the fetid heat of his breath on the side of my neck.

"I asked you to stay awhile," he said, the words slow and rattling like the hissing of a snake. "Not very polite, are we?"

I will not show fear. I will not let this foul man see that I am terrified of him.

And I was.

I felt long, bony fingers slide around and catch me in the crook of my elbow, and I felt a scream rise in my throat, but it lodged there, an unmovable stone.

"Unhand her," a voice demanded. I couldn't see where it came from, and I was too terrified to move my head to find out.

The hand gripped tighter around my elbow.

"You can have what's left of her when I'm finished," he snarled.

"Don't make me ask again," the voice said. Monsieur Fournier appeared in view, emerging from one of the alleyways. Behind him, two others followed, looking keen to keep their friend from trouble. One was a waifish woman in a dress, washed paper-thin over years of use, who looked all too happy to take on trouble headlong. The other was a man dressed in a priest's cassock who bore a stern expression as he crossed his arms over his chest. I wanted to breathe, but the vagrant kept his grip on my arm.

Monsieur Fournier and his companions took a few steps closer. I would have run toward them if the man hadn't tightened his grip.

"We have no wish to harm you," the man dressed as a priest said. "But if you don't release the lady, you will leave us no choice."

"Lady?" the man said. "I don't see a lady. There probably isn't a soul who would miss her. Why spoil the fun? It looks like you've got one of your own to share as it is."

Monsieur Fournier removed a pistol from the waist of his trousers and pulled back the hammer by way of response.

I felt the iron grip at the crook of my arm fall away.

"Selfish," he muttered. I heard his footsteps hasten off down the alley but couldn't bring myself to look back. I did not need a face to illustrate my nightmares.

I closed the distance that separated us and threw myself into Monsieur Fournier's arms. I didn't care if it was improper. I didn't care what his friends thought of me. I wanted nothing more than to feel safe in that moment, and his arms were the only place that could offer that solace. His arms felt as safe and secure as Nanette's kitchen. I let myself linger in his scent—soap tinged with gunpowder and a familiar trace of cloves somehow—and felt my heart slow to a more comfortable cadence.

"Off on another stroll?" Monsieur Fournier asked. I felt a chuckle rumble in his chest, my cheek still pressed against his waistcoat. His hand stroked my hair, in a tender gesture I'd only felt a handful of times in my youth—almost always from Nanette. "Is Marie's ankle still unwell?"

"It's doing much better," I said, finally composing myself and stepping back a pace from him. I tried not to shudder at the wet splotches I'd left on his uniform. "You asked me to come last week, remember? Well, I'm here. I came to see you speak."

"I never thought you'd come," he said. "I see now it was foolish to goad you."

"I'll say," the priest said in a tone closer to a growl. "Did you want to see this young lady hurt? What were you thinking, Théo?"

Monsieur Fournier shook his head. "She's going to be all right now, and I'll make sure she gets safely home after the rally. And you and Pierrine can make sure for me that she stays out of harm while it's underway."

Pierrine looked me up and down and harrumphed. I didn't know who this woman was, nor what relationship she had to Monsieur Fournier or the priest, but she looked none too pleased.

"I'm not a child minder, Théo," Pierrine said, a gravelly tone to her voice I hadn't expected.

"Nor is Mademoiselle Vigneau a child," Monsieur Fournier said, his tone warning. "But she is . . . unused to the harsher realities of Paris."

"So you said, Théo. Do you really think it was wise to bring her here? Who knows who she might talk to. What trouble she might bring about. Don't just think about yourself. Think of the cause."

"Have some faith," Monsieur Fournier said, flicking his friend's snow-white collar. "I expect better from you, Sébas. Mademoiselle Vigneau, these are my two dearest friends, Pierrine Desrosiers and Père Sébastien Cadieux. They're usually far more polite than this."

"I wanted to hear what he had to say," I said, trying to speak without wavering, but I was still haunted by the grip of the miscreant's fingers on my arm. "I don't mean to cause trouble."

"We'll see," Pierrine returned with an incredulous snort. "Just stick close. If we get separated, I'm not going looking for you. And old Jacquot won't let you get away a second time."

"Vile piece of filth," Sébastien growled.

"Now now, *mon père*. Hate the sin, love the sinner," Pierrine teased.

"I'm a mortal man and a flawed one at that, Pierrine. I should be able to find pity for all troubled souls in my heart, including old Jacquot, but I confess I cannot." He tensed visibly at the mention of the man's name.

"You'll forgive us. We like to tease the good father more than we ought. It's hard to take him seriously as a man of the cloth since we knew the mischief he caused as a boy."

"Yes, most priests don't serve in the areas where they were raised. I am one of the unfortunate few who have to suffer the reminders of my misspent youth," he said with a dramatic eye roll to his friends and a conciliatory glance at me. "So are you going to go incite the good people of Paris to another revolution or not, Théo?"

Monsieur Fournier led us to the main entrance to Les Halles where hundreds of people, men and women, young and old, poor and bourgeois, milled around and bartered for their mutton and potatoes. The smell of the foodstuffs mingled with the sweat and grime on the people in the crush. The cloying vapor of cheap scent and low-grade tobacco hung in a toxic cloud over their heads.

There was no podium, but Monsieur Fournier had no need of one. He stood atop a wooden crate, and people turned to hear him. They were arrested by his presence and the din of the crowd began to hush. His bronze hair shining in the sunlight; his dark blue uniform cut an impressive figure against the dappled gray stone of the market building.

"*Citoyens!* The hour is upon us. The emperor has failed, and we have the republic we've been demanding for decades. Now is the time to claim Paris for the workers. The elite have had their time. The elite who treat workers as though they are the shells of cockroaches beneath their feet instead of treating them with the respect they deserve. We keep the country running while the wealthy reap the rewards. The people leading us to defeat at the hands of bloodthirsty Prussians are holed up in their lavish rooms in the palace without a second thought for the maid who spent hours preparing their rooms. The butcher who provided the meat for their next meal. The cook and kitchen maids who would toil to cook it but who would never get so much as a taste of the efforts of their own hand."

I thought of Marie and Nanette who made separate, inferior meals for the staff. They didn't starve, but they had cheaper soups and stews with rough bread they baked once a week while my family and I dined in splendor.

"*Citoyens*, the workers are the lifeblood of this country. We deserve our daily bread at prices we can afford. We deserve fair wages for honest work. We deserve competent protection from the foreign invaders. We deserve to live in a clean city that doesn't sicken our children. More than this, we deserve the respect and honor of those who lord over us. For without the sweat of our brow, this great country of ours would cease to be. But this will never happen. Kings, queens, and emperors will never see us as being worthy of more than the crumbs from their table. They have convinced themselves that we are lesser beings, unfavored by God, and that we ought to be grateful for the charity they bestow upon us. They don't see the truth, or else are afraid of it: that we, the people, hold the power. And the day we choose to seize it will be a great day of reckoning once again. That day is at hand, *citoyens*. The day to take up arms against the tyrants and to reclaim this country as our own."

I stood, Father Cadieux at my right and Pierrine at my left, and felt a frisson down my spine. Théodore spoke the truth, unembroidered and from his soul. I felt that spark from every man, woman, and child who had stopped to listen to him. I looked at him; his golden hair shining in the amber light of autumn, his profile proud and self-assured. This was a man who could convince the people to follow him into hell itself if he took a notion. And it might come to that.

The crowd burst into an exuberant rendition of *l'Internationale*, the lusty workers' hymn sung to the tune of *La Marseillaise*, which had become the anthem of dissent. They were a people united by a common dream: A Paris of the People.

And in an instant, I knew the Paris of my father, of Gaspard, and all their kind was going to come to an end. They would not hand over the city without bloodshed. They'd sooner see it as a pile of ashes than turn it over to the very people who kept it running for them.

But these people had had enough. I could see from the hunger in their eyes, the tatters of their clothes, and the grime on their cheeks that the day of reckoning was upon us.

Things would have to change, or Paris would burn.

And I found that I wouldn't mourn if it did.

Sometimes greatness had to be born of the ashes.

Chapter Six

MICHELINE

Madame Dupuis ushered me in to her apartment with the warmth of someone welcoming an old friend. She walked with a cane, but she never allowed it to detract from her graceful comportment. She somehow managed to glide, despite being dependent on the stick for support. Though I had to be fifty years her junior, perhaps more, she made me feel awkward and gangly.

"Come have some coffee, my dear," she said, paying no mind to the mending that I attempted to show her. She gestured for me to set it near the doorway to her bedroom. Her hired girl would be by later to put it all where it belonged, she assured me, and trusted all was in order. She showed far more interest in the apple pastries, which she placed on two fine china plates as if she were serving them to de Gaulle himself. She paid no attention when I insisted that I'd intended both pastries for her.

She served the pastries and coffee in the parlor, larger than our own, and more finely furnished, though certainly not grand. It was clear she had some means, but it seemed she preferred to keep her life simple. She'd grown up on the butte and had seen no reason to leave for a grander apartment in the center of town.

She took a bite of the pastry and her eyes lit with a youthful joy. "You have your grandmother's gift," she said. "And her mother before her. Your mother was a fair hand in the kitchen too."

"What I know, I learned from her," I said.

She looked thoughtful for a moment, considering the pastry before her. "But she didn't think to keep open the bakery, though so many in the neighborhood loved it. Depended upon it even. Though I suppose I must admit the bistro does some good as well." She was—or had been—a regular diner at the bistro, usually giving them her custom once a week. She felt it her duty to support us where she could.

"Maman rarely spoke of the bakery," I said, embarrassed to know less of my own family history than a kindly outsider. It had been a bistro or restaurant of some sort my entire life and it was hard to imagine it as anything else. I wondered if it was a source of disappointment that Maman had dropped the torch and let the family business fade away. "I gather it was a well-loved place."

"Oh yes. Your grandmother and great-grandmother were famous, in this neighborhood at least, for their baking."

I wasn't surprised by this. I had a handful of faded memories of my grandmother, and they usually involved food and the kitchen. I wondered if Mamie and her mother came to it because of their passion for it, or if, like me, they'd found comfort in the precision and attention to detail that drove out everything else.

"Something troubles you, my dear," she said, placing the pastry aside, with a slight air of reluctance. "Tell me what it is, and we'll set it to rights."

I narrowed my eyes in thought. "You very well might be able to help me, Madame. It seems our tenants in the bistro have moved on. As you know, we rely on the income from renting the place to keep things going since . . . well, since Maman went away." I stumbled over the words, feeling my heartbeat twinge as I spoke them. "Would you know of anyone looking to rent?"

"That is an interesting question, my dear," Madame Dupuis said. She sat back in her chair, sipping her coffee as her eyes glazed over in nostalgia. "Perhaps it is time to be creative. You needn't find another restaurateur. It was a bakery for half a century before your parents got the idea to rent it out when your grandmother retired. Your grandmother and I were the best of friends, and I would walk from school to the bakery with her every day after school."

"You were friends with Mamie?" I asked. I'd never known the two women had any real connection at all aside from living in the same corner of Montmartre. Mamie had passed just before the war broke out, and it was just as well. She hadn't had to see her beloved Paris under siege. She'd moved to warmer climes in a little village in the south after she retired but had always come back to visit.

"Oh, yes. Great chums. Your great-grandmother Lisette was never rid of me. She always set some *sablés* aside for the two of us, no matter how busy she was. And a glass of cold milk too. We would sit in a little chair behind the counter and have our treat and I thought it was the most wonderful place in the world. We were very poor at the time, and your great-grandmother always had a spare loaf of bread that 'she just couldn't persuade anyone to buy.' People aren't like that anymore."

"It's a shame more people aren't," I said. The war—both of them, really—had made people harder, somehow. "Maman never said why she didn't care to continue on with the bakery."

"It's likely that it just wasn't where her heart was. And I admit it was a loss for the neighborhood. But your maman did her part for those in need in other ways. There was never a mother who needed child minding if your mother knew of it. Never a child who went without a coat if there was a bit of wool to be had."

The past tense rattled me. "I know," I said, forcing my voice not to quiver.

She reached over and patted my hand, but did not correct herself or offer a platitude, for which I was grateful.

"So you find yourself in need of tenants," she said, looking pensive.

"Yes," I said. "We depend on the income with Papa gone and Maman . . . missing."

A shadow passed over her face at the mention of Maman. "Of course, of course . . . But I have another thought. Why not reopen the bakery? You have a lot of your great-grandmother in you. You might be a great hand at it."

"I look like her?" I asked.

"No, that would be that precious baby sister of yours. I'm

not talking of hair, eyes, and complexion. I'm speaking of fire and spirit. You're an industrious girl and you'd earn a lot more baking than you do mending."

"I don't have the skills to run a bakery," I admitted. "I can make a decent *boule* and a few of the simplest pastries, but with the war and all, we didn't have the ingredients for Maman to teach me anything really challenging."

"This is true. Many a thing fell between the cracks these past few years. Far graver things than your culinary education. But that's easily remedied. There is a fine baking school near Les Halles. You shall go and get a proper education and we'll have a bakery in the neighborhood again. It will be a good thing for all of us."

"But I haven't the means to attend a school of any kind, let alone something as grand as you propose," I protested. "And there's the question of minding the girls and putting food on the table."

"The girls are in school now. You can study when they do," she said. "As for the rest, you needn't worry. I'll see to your school fees and will keep the larder full for the duration of your course."

"I couldn't accept such an offer," I said. "It's far too generous, Madame. And my family isn't one to accept charity."

"It's not charity," she said. "It's repayment for years of free *sablés* and bread when we had need. Or an inheritance if you prefer to think of it that way."

"I—I don't understand," I stammered. "You're not ill, are you?"

"Fit as can be," she said. "But I have no children, nor even

any nieces or nephews to look after in my will. In this arrangement, I'll have the fun of seeing my legacy do some good before I pass on. It seems a fine reward for a life well-lived. I
couldn't ask for more."

"I don't know—" I began.

"Think of it logically. If I gave you some money, I'm certain you'd spend it prudently, but no matter how you econo-
mized, you'd deplete your funds in time. Two years, perhaps
three? If you go to school, you'll have the tools to earn a living yourself."

"The proverbial man with a fish," I said. "But with breads
and pastries."

"Yes, a bit more complicated than learning to fish too," she
said. "But a worthwhile endeavor. I'll make a call to the school
this very day. In the meantime, I'll give you some cookbooks
that you might get started with. Heaven knows I don't have the
stamina to spuddle along in the kitchen much anymore, and
they'll be of more use to you. I suspect your mother had a few
of her own. You're a smart girl and can follow instructions.
Might as well see if you enjoy it, no?"

"I suppose," I said, uncertain. Schooling alone would be a
huge undertaking while making sure the girls were well cared
for. Running a bakery felt even bigger. Even a small enterprise
would mean long hours and backbreaking work.

But as I considered my alternatives, getting a job in a factory
or hoping to cobble together a living with odd jobs, the bakery
seemed like the best alternative.

"Come, take these," Madame Dupuis said, pointing to a
shelf of cookbooks of various sizes and descriptions with the

tip of her cane. "Have a bit of a go in the kitchen this morning while the girls are in school. You might surprise yourself."

"Very well," I said, collecting the books. Impulsively, I dipped down and kissed the kindly neighbor on the cheek. "If nothing else, I might have a nice treat for the girls when they come home."

"That's the spirit," she said. "And you'll remember your old neighbor with a sample of your handiwork now and again, I'm sure." She shot me a wink that seemed incongruous with the dignified woman I knew.

"Naturally," I said, feeling a smile tug at the corners of my mouth. I could see a glimmer of the child scrambling behind the counter awaiting her coveted biscuits and milk. I loved that my great-grandmother, a woman who'd died when I was an infant, but I'd heard much about from my mother and grandmother, had given the woman before me a few happy memories in a childhood that had been marked with privation. I had no idea if I would be equal to the task of training up as a baker, but I knew I owed it to her to try.

Chapter Seven

LISETTE

SEPTEMBER 6, 1870

After he spoke, Monsieur Fournier rejoined us in the crowd. It took him a few long minutes to find us as he was stopped to shake hands and accept the praise of nearly everyone he passed. Another speaker, far less charismatic, had taken to the soap-box, but the crowd was still enraptured by Monsieur Fournier's words and those under the spell of his rhetoric could not let him pass unacknowledged. When he reached us, I could feel the heat radiate from him. An energy, a passion, that emanated from him when he spoke about this cause, so beloved to him. We set the example, focusing our attention on the new speaker, who, while a pale imitation of Monsieur Fournier, held up the same beliefs and rallied the crowd to the same great ideal.

Taking back Paris for the people.

The speaker, a slight man in a tattered suit with hair the color of dishwater, spoke until the shrill of a whistle split the air like an axe through dry wood. The thunderous sounds of hooves followed. Father Cadieux's eyes flashed in terror.

"It's the Versaillais. Get her out of here before we're all run down."

Monsieur Fournier's face blanched. "Keep Pierrine safe," he barked to Père Cadieux and pulled me away from the crowd. We dipped into an alley, not unlike the one the cretin Jacquot had scurried down, and hid behind some crates. He placed his hand over my mouth to prevent me screaming, though I felt no fear from him. Only from the arrival of the royal troops.

"They will scour every street and alleyway in the vicinity of Les Halles looking for agitators. If they recognize me, I'll be shot on sight and probably you too for good measure," he said in tones barely above a whisper. The sounds of shouts and screams and utter chaos from the crowd a few streets away nearly drowned out his words. "We cannot run, but we must move silently and be ready to hide at any moment. Can you do this?"

I nodded. He removed his hand from my face.

"I won't scream. I wouldn't scream," I assured him, my voice just as hushed as his.

"Good girl," he said. "What shoes are you wearing?"

I pulled up the hem of my new plain dress to reveal the sturdiest boots I owned. They were usually reserved for horseback riding when we retreated to the country but seemed far more practical than the slippers that Maman had me wearing most days.

"Thank God you have some brains in your head," he said. "I just might be able to get you home alive."

For the next hour, we skulked in the alleyways, skittering and hiding like mice when a torch was shone in their direction. We didn't speak, but Monsieur Fournier took my hand in his and gave it an encouraging squeeze each time we were forced to conceal ourselves from passing troops. The walk that should have taken perhaps twenty minutes tripled in length, as cautious as we had to be.

Monsieur Fournier guided me down yet another secluded alleyway, and I could see the worry was ebbing from his face as we entered a small neighborhood park where we could take a respite under the cover of some obliging trees.

"Are you all right?" Monsieur Fournier asked once we were well out of view.

"Perfectly well," I replied, though still catching my breath. "I wasn't expecting the thrills of the afternoon to involve being chased down by the Versaillais on horseback, but it didn't overshadow the rest."

"I was a fool to taunt you into coming," he said. "Sébas was right. It was foolish and selfish in equal measure."

"Nonsense. I couldn't be gladder that I had the chance to hear you speak."

He turned to look at me. "You're daft," he said. "Those men would have killed you for being seen with me."

"But they didn't," I said.

He paused and breathed. After a few moments, he finally seemed able to accept that we'd escaped unscathed.

"They didn't," he agreed, tentatively wiping a tendril from my brow. "You are quite remarkable, aren't you? I thought Sébas was right to chastise me at first. That you were too delicate a flower to withstand a trampling at Les Halles, but there's more to you than he thinks. You're stronger than you seem at first glance."

I had cast my eyes downward, unused to such unreserved praise, but they fluttered back to meet his gaze.

"No one has ever called me strong before." I felt breathless at the admission. Coming from anyone of my limited acquaintance, his wouldn't have been a compliment. It would have been censure for words or deeds deemed too bold or independent for their sensibilities. But from this man, I sensed that strength and fortitude were virtues he prized.

In a moment of pure recklessness, I placed my hands on his chest and stood on my toes to press my lips against his. I'd never kissed a man before, nor had I dreamed of being so forward as to claim my first kiss before it was offered, but there was precious little in that moment that mattered to me less than propriety.

I steadied my racing heart and tried to read his face. Had I offended him? Did he think less of me for being so free with a man I barely knew?

He tucked his finger under my chin and lifted my lips to his. He kissed me, at first tentatively, then hungrily. I found my enthusiasm matched his and he pressed me against the rough bark of a tree, secluded from view. His hands wandered up from my waist to the curve of my breasts. I felt a fire rise inside me, so much I ached.

"God, I want you," he moaned as I touched him.

I was, like most girls of my station, largely ignorant of what went on in the marriage bed, but I now had a better idea of what he meant.

My mouth opened and closed like a fish gasping for air. I could find no words to respond. I knew what a lady should say when a man who was not her husband spoke with such familiarity, but I could not bring myself to rebuke him. It was as though I'd been wandering the desert, dying of thirst, and he appeared before me as the most glittering oasis, a blessed respite from my arid existence.

He kissed me again, this time tender and slow.

"You are a wonder," he said, finally taking a breath.

"I don't want to stop," I said, still gripping his shoulders. "I know I should."

"God, you tempt me, but we've flown too close to the sun for one day. I won't take any more risks with your reputation. You deserve to do things properly."

I could have argued that it felt perfect enough, but I just wanted to absorb the warmth of him pressed against me. After a few moments, he pulled away.

"I need to get you home," he whispered. "I've kept you out far too long."

He stopped and plucked a red rose from one of the bushes. "An apt symbol," he said, presenting it to me. The symbol of the socialist party. The symbol of true love. For him, they were one and the same. For this man, his politics represented a deep love for his people—for all people.

I rose up to kiss his cheek. "The loveliest gift I've ever received," I said.

"Somehow I doubt that," he said. "With parents like yours who can afford to give you the moon itself."

"It was the first given of love, and not obligation, nor with the taint of expectation," I said. "I thank you. Truly."

He held me in his arms just a moment longer, and we found our way back to the roads leading to the Place Royale. My head was bursting with a million things I wanted to say, but everything seemed too trite when I thought about how to put my feelings into words.

"You were incredible, you know," I said, fumbling. "When you spoke to the people. They listened to you. They were enraptured. They looked as though they would have followed you into battle at that very moment."

"Against your own people," he reminded me.

"No," I said flatly. "I'm not one of them. I don't want to be one of them. I don't think I ever have."

"You say that now, but there will be a day when you miss that gilded cage of yours, little canary. You might like the idea of forsaking your family now, but what will you do the first time you have to scrub a floor or make the evening soup?"

"I've made soup more times than I can count. I'm far more of a kitchen mouse than a canary," I said, thinking of Nanette's endearment.

He arched his brow. "I find that surprising that your parents allow it."

"It's easy to get away with things when your parents don't pay attention. Our cook Nanette has been more of a mother to me than my own."

He shook his head, incredulous.

"You still don't believe me, do you?"

He didn't speak, too much a gentleman to contradict me.

"Come now, it's time I took you home." He took my hand in his, brushed his lips gently across my knuckles, and hurried back to the bustling streets in the heart of Paris to find his friends. I watched his long strides for a few moments and looked up at the façade of my parents' home and found the pit of dread growing in my gut as I walked the steps to the rear courtyard to enter once more.

I ignored Nanette's chiding about my tardiness and the absence of the vegetables she'd asked for and went to the pantry. I remembered that roses could be made to root again if soaked in a solution of honey and cinnamon. Nanette rolled her eyes as I dipped the end of the cutting in honey and rolled it in precious cinnamon powder. I scavenged one of her disused herb pots and planted the flower so that it too might have a second chance at life.

Chapter Eight

MICHELINE

I'd never cooked in a kitchen other than the modest one in our apartment. To have the room to spread out and work was a luxury I wasn't used to, but it would be a welcome change from the cramped workspace I'd learned in. The kitchen wasn't particularly posh, but it was well laid out and equipped with every pot, pan, baking sheet, and mold I might ever need.

I arranged the armful of cookbooks Madame Dupuis had given me; the *Larousse Gastronomique* was a massive thing, but the others were less daunting. I looked in the refrigerator, the most modern addition to the kitchen, to find, mercifully, that they'd left behind some butter and eggs and other perishables they wouldn't have been able to transport with them. The rationing might be easing, but shortages were still a reality, as were my limited funds.

But most of the dry goods like flour and sugar would be kept in the cellar. I stood at the top of the stairs and willed one foot to go before the other.

Micheline, you're being daft. It's a cellar. You'll be fine.

I tried not to think of the dozens of times we huddled in the cellar, sometimes with the tenants and their patrons with us. But usually, it was the middle of the night. Maman huddling with Sylvie in her arms and Noémie in mine. We kept a reserve of food and blankets there as well as a few of Maman's most important treasures.

There were nights the bombs were so close, I was certain we'd not survive to see morning. Or worse, some of us would, while others wouldn't. What would the girls do if Maman and I were killed? Would someone have been kind enough to care for them? Would they end up in some horrid orphanage? It was impossible to think about for more than a few seconds at a time, but the threat always loomed over us. And never more closely than when we were in this wretched cellar.

I took the first step down and felt the familiar vise grips around my gut. With every step it was harder to breathe, but I forced myself to move downward. My hand shook as I reached up to pull the cord to turn on the light bulb over my head.

There was flour and sugar along with other dry goods. I couldn't hope to carry the heavy bins up the stairs myself, so I would have to transport up what I needed in smaller containers as the need arose. There was a dust-covered bottle of vanilla extract, expensive and hard to procure these days, which I tucked in my pocket. The room had been kept in good order by the tenants, and they'd left the brown leather trunk with

Maman's supplies alone as we'd insisted. I'd thought a dozen times about coming down here to gather up Maman's things and take them back upstairs but had never been able to bring myself to do it.

It had been Maman's task, and like so many others, it remained undone.

I opened the trunk and peered inside. A photo of Papa was on top. With every air raid, Maman would remove the photo from the worn leather trunk and set it on top, so we could see him watching over us. An angel of deliverance, she called him. There was also her rosary which had a tarnished silver crucifix with intricately patterned silver beads that had been in the family for generations. I watched dozens of times as Maman took a bead between her thumb and forefinger, rubbing it gently as she whispered her prayer. She would exhale and move on to the next bead without ever flickering her eyes open. Hail Marys, Our Fathers, and Glory Bes in rapid succession. I put the rosary in my pocket and would say some prayers for Maman later that night.

Deeper in the trunk, there were papers of varying importance: birth certificates and such that I'd have to go through carefully later. Not in the confines of the cellar. In the depths of the trunk, I came across a battered old book. It was bound in red leather with gilded scrollwork embossed in the cover and gilt-edged pages. I flipped it open to find old, scrawling handwriting. Recipes and notes from a quick glance.

I was going to thumb through the book but felt my heart rate speed up and my chest constrict. Too much time in the cellar. I filled some empty tins with sugar and flour. It would be enough to experiment with. I stacked the old recipe book on top of the tins and ran back upstairs as quickly as I could with my arms full. I'd have to sweet-talk the girls into helping me bring the rest of Maman's things when they came home from school. I don't think either of them hated the place as much as I did. Of course Sylvie would roll her eyes at me, but I could scarce draw breath without eliciting that response from her.

I took the loot to the kitchen and flipped open the recipe book. I didn't know whose book it was, but it showed enough signs of use that clearly the original owner knew her way around the kitchen. One of the first recipes was for *sablés*—Madame Dupuis' favorite. The recipe seemed simple enough compared to some that Maman had taught me that it seemed like a reasonable place to start.

I took one of the heavy mixing bowls, a thick pottery affair that would have withstood the wrath of the German army if, God forbid, they'd ever come knocking, and creamed together the butter and sugar. It was slow, methodical work and I found the muscles in my shoulders lowering as I melded the creamy butter with the sugar. I felt my jaw unclench as I carefully added a spoonful of the vanilla. My fingers became more supple as I added the yolk of an egg. My breathing deeper as I combined flour and salt.

I rolled the dough into cylinders, wrapped them in parchment. The recipe called to let the dough chill in the coldest part of the cellar for an hour, but as we'd purchased a refrigerator for the bistro before the war, I spared myself another trip down the stairs. We didn't have the luxury of a refrigerator upstairs and I would enjoy the convenience of having access to one until new tenants were taken on.

Or until Madame Dupuis got her way, and I turned this place into a bakery.

As I waited for the dough to chill, I wiped the nonexistent dust off the counters and took stock of what was there. I wouldn't need much in the way of equipment to bake the usual staple breads and pastries. Ingredients were becoming easier to come by, week by week, which was a mercy. But it would take months to learn the trade and become licensed.

As I wiped down the counters out front, I could see the faces of Madame Dupuis and my own grandmother at the age of eight, the same age as Noémie, bouncing in through the front door and giggling all the way to the edge of the counter that swung up on hinges to allow admittance for the staff. I could see two small chairs and a tiny table, set each day as if for an elegant tea party, with *sablés* and rich, cold milk for the two girls, famished from a busy day of growing up.

The vision was so vivid, it stole my breath. This had been a place of joy, though it had known its share of tragedy too. It was meant to be a hub to gather in celebration and in mourning. To eat, to restore the body. To restore the soul.

Within an hour, the kitchen glistened. The tenants had treated the space as they would have their own home, and I blessed them for it. Perhaps they sensed, as I had, that this was a building that had seen much and commanded the respect of an elder.

I retreated to the kitchen and removed the cylinders. I brushed them with beaten egg and rolled them in coarse sugar. I sliced them into thin rounds and let them bake in the warm oven. I could have tidied the kitchens further or organized the cupboards, but I found myself glued to the massive oven waiting for the fruits of my labors. In ten minutes, they were the precise shade of golden brown described in the recipe.

I let them cool and admired how even and precise they were. The aroma of butter and sugar hung in the air, and I felt my stomach rumble. I skipped the midday meal most times, trying to save food and money to ensure the girls had a proper dinner meal at night. I was usually able to ignore the pangs of hunger, but today was one of the times it was harder. On days where I couldn't bear to skip my luncheon, I begrudged myself every bite of whatever meager sandwich I put together. I cursed my own lack of restraint.

But the ingredients for these humble cookies had been left behind by others. There would be plenty left for the girls, even if I sampled my handiwork. I hesitated, but I allowed myself to indulge. I couldn't very well feed my first attempt at baking to others without ensuring I'd not made some terrible gaffe, like swapping sugar for salt or some such. As I sank my teeth into the sweet, buttery biscuit, I was filled with warmth. It tasted as fine as any *sablé* I'd sampled in my youth, but more than that . . . for the first time in six long years, I felt the strange sensation of hope rising within me.

I found a small plate and arranged a half dozen as artfully as I could, locked the shop, checked the door three times, and dashed to Madame Dupuis' door.

She didn't appear surprised to see me, nor did she seem

taken aback by my offering. She ushered me into the parlor and poured us each another cup of coffee. I protested as she placed one of the *sablés* on the saucer next to the cup, but she silenced me with a wave of her hand.

"You took my advice," she said, taking her seat. "An auspicious start to any endeavor."

"The recipe is from an old book that I found among Maman's things," I explained. "This recipe was the first I turned to, and since you mentioned *sablés* this morning, it seemed a good place to start."

"Good," she agreed. "Better to start with *sablés* and have some success than to begin with a *croquembouche* and get discouraged."

I chortled at the idea of taking on the monumental undertaking of a tower of cream puffs enshrouded in caramel. It was the centerpiece of the most elaborate weddings, and only attempted by master bakers.

"Don't laugh, my dear. The day will come. Now let's see what you've done with these."

She took a small bite and leaned back into the back of her plush, green velvet chair. Her eyes fluttered closed for a moment, and I began to wonder if she was asleep.

"My dear girl, that recipe book you found was your great-grandmother's. I'd wager all I own that this was her very recipe. These are a marvel, child."

"You think so?" I asked. I considered telling her what I'd seen in the bakery, the sensation I'd felt when I'd eaten the simple biscuit, but I didn't want her to think I was going daft. It was clearly the mental wanderings of someone who'd indulged in too little sleep and too few calories over the course of months.

"You'll begin classes next week. I've already seen to it," Madame Dupuis said in a tone that would brook no argument. Nor was I truly in a place to be able to refuse her offer. "Monsieur Rossignol suffers no fools, but I am sure he will not find one in you."

SABLÉS

→>—<←

This is one of the first recipes Nanette taught me from her native Brittany. A simple butter cookie that is always one to chase away gloomy skies and low spirits. She always kept a supply of these in the larder for me as a child. In this instance alone, I am pleased she's never acknowledged that I've grown up.

Prepare a medium-hot oven. Beat one cup good butter and one-half cup sugar together until light and fluffy. Add two egg yolks and one teaspoon of liquor infused with vanilla and mix well. Add two cups flour in and mix gently until the dough comes together. Lesson learned: don't overmix.

Shape the dough into a log with a three-inch diameter. Let the dough rest in the coolest part of the cellar so the dough will be firm enough to retain its shape. After the dough has rested three hours, brush the log with butter and sprinkle with coarse sugar. Cut out round cookies from the dough log and place on a baking sheet, spaced out from each other. Beat one egg yolk in a small bowl. Use a fork to make a crosshatch pattern on the cookies. Brush the tops of the cookies with the beaten egg yolk. Bake the cookies until they're a lovely golden color.

Best served with milk, tea, or Nanette's good *chocolat chaud*.

Recipe notes: consider glazing with chocolate or caramel for something new.

Chapter Nine

LISETTE

I'd gone to hear Monsieur Fournier speak twice more in the days after his speech at Les Halles. I learned which streets to avoid and how to walk in a way that would attract less attention from scoundrels like old Jacquot. It didn't make me impervious to harm, but I felt like my newfound wisdom made me a bit less vulnerable.

We managed to sneak a few kisses after his fervent speeches. The speeches themselves were powerful enough to awaken a passion I never knew existed within me. But more than that, I found that being in his presence made me a bolder, more principled version of myself. But Monsieur Fournier, I suspect chastened by Father Cadieux, did what he could to keep me at arm's length.

He pulled away from our embrace and shook his head, as if

trying to rid his thoughts of me. "Let us get you home and to your fine supper of quail and braised cucumbers, shall we?"

"No quail on the menu tonight. Nanette and I are making chicken in cider with carrots and a rum cake."

"You help your mother with the menus?" he asked.

"I help Nanette and Marie in the kitchens, though I know you don't believe me. Let me prove it to you. I'll cook for you. Name the date." I stopped, placed my arms akimbo, and waited for him to challenge me.

"You want to cook for me? Alone? In my flat?" he asked. "You wouldn't risk your reputation like that."

I blinked, realizing the impropriety of what I'd suggested. No matter. I wouldn't back down and have him think me as prim as he'd imagined me to be. "Where else?"

"You are surprising, Mademoiselle Vigneau," he said, repeating his sentiment. "And I thought I was at a stage in life where nothing was left to surprise me."

"Well, I'm glad I was able to prove you wrong, Monsieur Fournier. A life without surprises hardly seems worth living."

We reached the corner of the Place Royale, where I would be safe to return home, but where his presence would be suspect. "Very well, I will come collect you in this very spot Monday next at midday. You can tell your parents you're going to church services. We'll make sure to say hello to Sébas so it isn't a total fabrication."

"You may depend upon it," I said, conjuring more bravado than I felt.

For the next two days, I pondered a menu. I wanted something to prove my mettle, but nothing so elaborate that he would think me pretentious. I would please him far more with a hearty *pot-au-feu* than all the dishes with their fiddly sauces and intricate seasonings. Nanette's onion soup would be impressive enough and the ingredients easy enough to procure from our own supplies, despite the shortages we were all suffering.

"If your mother knew I was letting you pinch that block of *comté*, she'd have my hide. Or worse, my job. Do you know how hard it's been to come by cheese in the last month?" Nanette hadn't been able to pry my plans for the day, but she'd guess correctly that she wouldn't approve of what I was up to and was trying at every turn to dissuade me. She knew too well that old Jacquot was not the only man of his sort lurking in the alleyways of Paris.

"I don't need the whole thing," I reasoned. "And it's not like she keeps inventory of the kitchens. She probably hasn't been in this room in ten years." I'd selected a few onions and eggs from the larder and mixed together a blend of pepper, allspice, nutmeg, and cloves to transport to Monsieur Fournier's flat.

"Just you watch. Today will be the day she decides to take notice. I don't like this one bit."

"Don't fret, Nanette. It's my neck she'll wring, not yours."

"Not hardly, Kitchen Mouse. She might be furious with you, but it's me who'd take the blame. It's easier to sack the help than to disown a child."

"I wouldn't allow it," I said. "Please, Nanette. You know yourself what they have planned for me. A lifetime of duty to a man I couldn't care less about. I'm just asking for a little taste of freedom before I'm locked away."

"They're marrying you off to a very eligible man, who's

kind, good-looking, and wealthy. They're not locking you in the dungeon."

"I don't see much difference," I retorted.

"I hope you know what you're doing, girl. If you were my daughter, I'd not let you flit about and let that young Monsieur d'Amboise get the idea that you weren't the steady sort."

"You wouldn't marry me off to a boor like that," I said.

"I'd take him myself if he'd accept the hand of a dried-up old woman like me and don't think I wouldn't. Remember, all this," she said, gesturing broadly, "goes to your brother once your father is gone. The man your parents chose has money and position. You won't starve. You'll be able to live like this the rest of your life."

"That's precisely what I *don't* want, Nanette. I know my life here is comfortable, but it isn't *mine*. Not really. I'm not free to make a single decision for myself and I'm tired of it. I'm tired of my mother only taking an interest in me when I can be useful as a pawn for her. I am tired of only being a problem to be taken care of for my father. I want a few choices. I don't think it's much to ask."

"No, but it may be just enough to cause you grief, Kitchen Mouse. Just be prudent."

I reached over and kissed her cheek. "I promise, Nanette. You've always been a mother to me, and I won't do anything foolish—for your sake."

She shook her head, her eyes betraying the sadness she felt. "You'd better check on your bread if you don't want to take a lump of coal with you."

I dashed to the oven where the bread, a hearty *pain de cam-*

pagne, had baked to a perfect golden brown. I'd made my share of loaves before but had taken special care that this one would be perfect, both in form and flavor. The sweet, earthy aroma filled my nostrils and caused my stomach to rumble in anticipation, despite having eaten a decent breakfast.

Nanette peered over my shoulder to see my handiwork. "What say you, Madame Éscoffier?" I asked, turning to present her the loaf as if I were a student at one of the fine academies waiting for inspection.

"You've outstripped me in baking, Kitchen Mouse. I have to concede to superior skill when I see it." Marie looked over with admiration as well.

"Next, sauces," I declared, offering her a brazen wink.

"Not in this lifetime, child. You might be able to outstrip me with your breads and pies and what have you, but the day you outclass my velouté or espagnol will be the day the devil himself needs a woolen overcoat down below. Now get on with you, if you must go, or else stay and we'll eat that lovely thing, the three of us."

"That sounds like a better plan to me," Marie chimed in.

"I'll make one just for us tomorrow, I promise," I said, placing the bread in the basket and wrapping a shawl around the shoulders of my plain dress. The seamstress had brought a number of the dresses my mother had commissioned already. Each was masterfully crafted, and the fabrics were nothing short of sumptuous. They fit beautifully, and I knew how fortunate I was to have one serviceable dress, let alone a dozen beautiful ones. But when I put them on and looked at my reflection in the mirror, I didn't recognize the young woman staring back at me. She was an elegant creature, fit for ballrooms and fine parties. She wasn't the girl who had run downstairs at every opportunity to learn the ways of the kitchen. She wasn't the girl who preferred the smell of fresh baking bread to the finest bottle of scent.

True to his word, Monsieur Fournier was waiting at the corner where he'd left me the week before. He smiled at the sight of me and reached out to grab my marketing basket.

"I hope you're wearing your sensible shoes," he said. "We've a walk ahead of us."

"Of course," I said gesturing to my brown boots. But I scoffed inwardly, realizing the folly in not having asked him where he lived. Surely within the walls of the city, but it was a large place. "What *is* your neighborhood?"

"I have a flat on the rue Norvins," he said. "In the eighteenth."

"Montmartre?" I asked. We ventured out into the country for the summers, but I'd seen precious little of Paris outside of the gentler districts in the center. As rough as the area around Les Halles could be, it was nothing compared to what I'd heard about the outer *arrondissements*, Montmartre, La Villette, and Ménilmontant. The stories made the market area seem as safe as Maman's parlor.

"Yes indeed," he said. "It will be a solid hour on foot."

"I'll be glad of the exercise," I said. "Too long cooped up makes a body restless."

"Trapped in a gilded cage, are you?" he said. "And no doubt, your parents have a tomcat in mind to rid them of their canary?"

I shuddered at the image but did not answer.

"Very well," he said, extrapolating the truth from my silence. "We'll have no mention of such things this afternoon. The door to your cage is open this once and you should enjoy the fresh air."

"I will," I said. Though the autumn air was brisk, the sun was warm and restorative and I loved the feel of it on my face. I could hear my mother's voice in my head bemoaning my freckles and the numerous times she thrust a parasol in my hand or a hat on my head that would practically engulf me. She'd tried making them fade with dozens of different ointments and potions peddled by every charlatan in Paris. When none of those worked, she tried covering them with cosmetic powders and creams with only marginal success. It was only through a series of earth-shattering tantrums that I'd kept her from trying to bleach my hair from red to blond. But today, I would feel the sunshine on my face, and I would be unabashed as I reveled in it.

The hour walk seemed to pass in mere minutes in Monsieur Fournier's pleasant company, the topics of our conversation ranging from politics, to family, to the city we both loved. Here on the outskirts of town, the buildings didn't soar to five and six stories as they did in the heart of Paris. Most streets were lined with shops that had only one or two stories above them for apartments. Monsieur Fournier's flat was on the second story above a shop that looked to have been abandoned for quite some time. He escorted me inside, and I was surprised at the coziness of it. There were books on every available surface, but it was clean and warm. The kitchen looked like it hadn't been touched in ages. Perhaps not since Monsieur Fournier took up residence.

"You'll forgive me," he said, opening cupboards for me to inspect the scant collection of kitchenwares in his possession. "I find it easier to grab my humble meals from a brasserie or a street vendor. I'm not much use in the kitchen."

"Not to worry," I said, donning the apron I'd tucked in my basket. "You can light the stove, so it won't be midnight before we have our luncheon."

He nodded and set to work with the kindling and matches he kept by the stove. He was proficient enough at the task, likely owing to the need to warm the place or to brew an occasional pot of coffee, even if he ate elsewhere. I pulled the largest pot from his cupboard and set to work chopping the onions. He didn't speak but observed my movements as I assembled the soup and set it to simmer.

"You weren't playing fun, were you? You do know how to cook."

"You haven't tasted anything yet," I countered. "It might be vile."

"Doubtful," he said. "Your movements have the efficiency and grace that can only be born of years of experience. You didn't learn how to handle a knife last week."

"No," I said. "I was six. I'd been begging Nanette to let me help her in the kitchen so often she finally relented. I sneak away to help her and to learn at her elbow whenever I can."

"An odd pastime for a girl of such gentle circumstances," he said. "I figured most girls on the Place Royale wouldn't be able to give their cook's name if they were asked."

"Perhaps not, but Nanette has been with the family, well—longer than I have. She was always kind to me. Greeted me with a biscuit or a sweet whenever I toddled down to the kitchens. She was the only person who didn't seem indifferent to me. And the more I watched her work, the more I was convinced that what she was doing wasn't just cooking, it was sorcery in a saucepan."

"You're surprising," he said.

"You say that often. I'm sorry to shock you," I said. "I know you hold steadfast to your ideas of what a girl of my birth should be like."

"On the contrary, I'm always glad to have my faulty presumptions challenged. It's better than walking through life convinced of a false truth."

"If only more people were comfortable having their views challenged, the world might be a better place. And to return the gift of candor, I confess I didn't peg a National Guardsman to be a scholar," I said, gesturing to one of his many piles of books.

"Not a scholar," he said. "I never had the right name, connections, or funds for university, but I read. I read whatever I can get my hands on. Sense and nonsense together, and I try to parse one from the other."

"A scholar all the same," I said. "The university is just one path to deeper understanding."

"Are you a reader, Mademoiselle Vigneau?"

"When I am permitted to. I can read, quite well, but my mother won't allow my sister and me the freedom to read what we like. She finds that too serious an education makes for an unbiddable wife."

He moved to one of the piles and selected a book, one written by Marx. "Take this and sneak it into your room. Read when you can. If the words I spoke last week were impactful, then this will inflame your soul."

"That sounds . . ." I couldn't find the word. *Dangerous. Exciting. Forbidden. Foolish.* I couldn't speak any of those aloud. "You should call me Lisette," I finally said, keeping my eyes on my work.

"And you should call me Théodore. Théo would be even better."

After it had been left to simmer and the flavors fully blossomed, I ladled the soup into bowls and topped each with a slice of the bread and good *comté* cheese and placed them in the oven to melt and brown for just a few moments. I placed the rest of the bread on the table and put Théo's soup in front of him. I watched expectantly as he took his spoon to break through the layer of cheese and bread and to the bubbling soup below. He waited a moment for the steam to subside and took his first spoonful.

"I'm so terribly sorry," he said.

"Whatever for?" I asked. I took a bite, and it tasted as it always did. "I don't think there's anything wrong with it."

"No. I'm sorry that your parents paid so little mind to you. You clearly spend most of your life in the kitchens to be able to cook this well."

"I do," I admitted. "It's the only place where I feel real solace."

"You have a true gift," he said. "And it's a pity your parents look down on it. You have the talent to be one of the best chefs in Paris. Or better still, a force to feed the hungry of the city. I think that's far more noble than whiling away your hours over tiresome treatises on housekeeping or needlework in a parlor."

"I actually like needlework," I replied. "But you're not wrong. I hate being idle."

"And thank heaven for it," he said. "You're more than an ornament and deserve to be treated as something more than a decoration."

I blinked furiously, willing the threatening tears to remain at bay. No one, not even Nanette, had ever said as much. In her defense, Nanette knew what my parents had intended for me and likely felt helpless to change the course of my fate. Especially if that course meant that I'd be well cared for all of my days. But there was more to life than elaborate dinners and fancy dresses.

"I've offended you," he said.

"No," I managed to squeak out. "It's the loveliest compliment I've ever had. Truly."

His soup bowl empty, he stood and held out a hand to me. I rose and put my hand in his. He pulled me close to his chest and held me there as he'd done in the park near Les Halles. At first his hands remained still, but then he began running them down my sides.

"I'd give anything that you'd been born the daughter of a butcher and a seamstress. That we were of the same world." His words were halting, as though he couldn't take in the air he needed to speak them properly.

"Théo, I'm standing here in your arms. I hardly think we're the proverbial bird and fish."

He took a step back and cradled my face in his hands. "Are we not, my lovely?" he breathed. "I could be killed for this."

"I wouldn't stand for it," I said. From somewhere deep inside me, I found the courage to take a finger and trace the side of his cheek. I could see the resolve break in his eyes. He lowered his lips to mine, and I was lost.

Or else, I was found at last.

As I felt the warmth of his body join mine, I was oblivious to all thoughts of duty, obligation, and honor. All that mattered, all I had room for in my soul, was Théo.

Chapter Ten

LISETTE

SEPTEMBER 12, 1870

Though it was the middle of the afternoon, I drifted off to sleep in Théo's arms. His embrace was warm, and I felt so secure in his arms, slipping into my most vulnerable state seemed as natural as the reddening of autumn leaves.

"My lovely, will you be missed?" he asked sometime later. The light coming through the window was beginning to wane.

"Yes," I admitted. "I'll be expected at dinner."

If I didn't leave soon, I'd have to sprint home and would have to race to make myself presentable for the table. I groaned at the prospect. Mother had begun quizzing me on various points of decorum, entertaining, and housekeeping. She was bound and determined to atone for long years of neglect by cramming twenty-one years of parenting into a handful of months.

Théo walked me as far as the square by Place Royale and left me with a kiss that was too forward for public view, but I found myself completely indifferent to the stares of passersby.

"My darling, you know how I feel about you, but we shouldn't do this again. I will treasure this day for the rest of my life, but truly, I don't wish to cause any discord between you and your family. I simply can't provide for you the way they can."

"How can you say this?" I asked. "After . . ."

"Because I love you more than I love my own happiness," he said. "Please. Do this for me."

I felt the tears well in my eyes, but I fought to swallow them back. I wouldn't let him see me cry. "I have to go," I stammered, and rushed off toward the house.

I hurried into the courtyard where Marie was waiting, her face white.

"Your ankle?" I asked. "Do you want me to fetch a doctor?" All thoughts of Théo vanished in concern. Nearly all, at any rate.

"No, that's much better, Miss Lisette. But you need to hurry. Your mother has been looking for you and our excuses are getting shoddy."

I squeezed her shoulder as I passed and slipped by her into the kitchen. "Thank you for getting her off my scent."

"Four and a half hours you were gone," Nanette said. "And I've had to make excuses to your mother for three of them. Child, if you pull this again, I'll tell your mother what you've been up to my very self. Do you understand me?"

"I'm so sorry, Nanette. I—"

"Just spare me your poetry about young love and change

out of that ridiculous dress and into one befitting your station before your mother comes in here breathing fire. I won't have her burning my soufflé."

"Here," Marie said, thrusting a dress in my hands as she liberated me of the marketing basket. "I sneaked it out of your room an hour ago."

"Thank you," I muttered, heat rising in my cheeks. I couldn't feel guilty about the fleeting moments I'd spent with Théo, but I regretted that it had to come at the cost of any difficulty to Marie and Nanette. Lord knew they worked harder than anyone in the house and had no need for anyone to make things worse.

I ducked into the storeroom and allowed Marie to play at lady's maid, helping to slip from one dress to another. She'd selected a moss-green afternoon dress in satin that wasn't horribly ornate, but like the most basic of the dresses my mother had commissioned for me required help to get in or out of. Even my dresses forced me into a childlike dependence, and it made me want to rage in a tantrum like a two-year-old wailing about the odious injustice of being forced to eat one's supper before sweets or having to take a nap. I felt just as powerless to effect any real change about the course of events.

I raced up the stairs, thinking of a million excuses for my absence, each more pathetic than the last.

"There you are, girl. I thought the gypsies had carted you off," my mother said as I entered the parlor. She looked me up and down and I was worried she'd be able to read the truth on my face as clearly as if Théo had written a missive of love on my forehead with a red wax pencil. She pursed her lips and stood, arms akimbo, before pronouncing, "I was right about the green, it makes your complexion look sallow. Don't wear it when Gaspard comes calling."

I exhaled a long sigh that bore with it the weight of the Herculean effort it took to not roll my eyes. "Yes, Maman."

"The dressmaker has been waiting a quarter of an hour," Maman said, dropping her hands down to her sides. "Let's not keep her waiting any longer."

"More?" I said, incredulous. "I've enough dresses to see me through ten lifetimes now as it is."

"But you haven't a wedding dress," Maman countered. "She's here for your fitting."

"Fitting?" I asked. "Surely, she hasn't made it already?"

"I chose the fabric and the design last week," Maman said. "We want it ready in case plans change for the better. We don't want to risk delaying the wedding just for want of a suitable dress."

I thought of the rainbow of silk, satin, and taffeta in my wardrobe upstairs. Certainly, one of those would have done well enough had Gaspard come knocking at the door wanting to rush off to church in the next fifteen minutes. What Maman would have given if he burst in that moment to do that very thing. But there would be no convincing her that I could get married in anything that hadn't been designed for the occasion.

"You didn't consult me?" I asked. "For my own wedding dress?"

"Why?" she asked, her tone dispassionate. "You have no interest in such things nor, much to my great sorrow, have you much of an eye for it."

"But I thought . . ."

"Never mind. Next thing, you'll be wanting a say on the groom as well. These aren't decisions for a young girl to make."

"Fine," I said, walking past her to the room where Madame Lacombe had been kept waiting. She exhaled as she saw me, not bothering to conceal the look of annoyance on her face from me. I wasn't her client, Maman was, so she felt no need to act as though I were more important to the proceedings than a fitting dummy.

Maman followed me in, and Madame Lacombe's face immediately brightened. The presence of the coin purse that would pay her cheered her greatly.

"I know you will be pleased, Madame," the seamstress purred. "We have spent hours and hours on this gown and the young mademoiselle will be exquisite. It is one of my finest creations."

"That's what I'm paying you for," Maman said without humor. "Let's see it."

One of Madame Lacombe's assistants set to work opening her mistress's trunk while Madame Lacombe motioned for me to stand in front of the arc of mirrors Maman had acquired to make a proper fitting room of the space. I stared off into space as they removed the dress Marie had hastily tied me into minutes before, lifted three massive petticoats over my head, followed by a skirt of heavy silk with a full bustle and long train. Once it was in place, they set to work strapping me into the bodice, cinching my corset as tight as they dared, despite my stifled gasps of protest, before buttoning it all together.

They turned me to the mirror, and I took it all in. It was

crafted of the finest candle-glow silk with delicate gold embroidery at the hem, cuffs, neckline. There was a thin gold silk sash at my waist to accentuate the efforts they'd made to tighten my corset beyond the bounds of all decency. It was the most gorgeous creation I'd ever seen in my life. I doubted even our recently exiled Empress Éugenie had ever owned a gown among hundreds of Worth creations that suited her as well as this one suited me.

I looked like a bride.

A beautiful one.

And I never wanted to run from a place more in my entire life.

I stood in place, trying to look as serene as I could muster as they pinned the hem and fussed with the fit of the bodice. I controlled the shaking of my hands, though I wasn't entirely successful. I tried reciting Nanette's recipe for *choux* pastry in my head, but images of my afternoon spent entangled with Théo kept creeping into my brain. I was, completely and totally rationally, afraid that Maman would be able to hear my thoughts and I strove to keep them chaste as the dressmaker flitted about.

"It should do," Maman pronounced as the dressmaker and her assistant stood aside for her to inspect. "The off-white makes her hair less . . . well, less. And the freckles too. And you've given her a waist and hips. That will remind Gaspard what he's getting."

Not one word about the flawless artistry of the gown. Only a few words to comment on how this gown, which probably cost more than the entirety of our household staff earned in a year, was able to mask some of my—numerous—flaws.

"It's a masterpiece," I said to Madame Lacombe, addressing her for the first time with more than a simple yes or no.

The woman's face split with a smile. It was such an uncharacteristic expression for her, it looked almost uncomfortable. But work of this caliber deserved to be praised.

"Let's get her out of it. Gaspard will be here before long to dine with us. Wear the pink and save the green for after the wedding."

"The green complements her eyes so beautifully," Madame Lacombe said, for once daring to contradict Maman.

"And does nothing to tame her hair and freckles. Do as I say," Maman bade.

I hurried off, wrapped in a dressing gown, hoping Maman would think to send someone to tend to my buttons and laces. My hair. If one curl sprang loose in front of Gaspard, Maman would grouse about it for weeks.

I went to remove the pink evening gown from the wardrobe. Maman wasn't wrong to choose it, for it was one of the lovelier pieces in my new trousseau. As I opened the doors, I saw the green dress I'd made tucked toward the back, likely by Marie acting in stealth during my fitting. I pulled it out and held it to my nose. Théo's scent, so unapologetically and purely masculine, still lingered there, tinged with the scents of the kitchen and his apartment. Soap, nutmeg, onion, soot, bread, and wood fire were all embedded in the fibers of the dress as they were in my soul.

And I would have to let Théo go.

There was nothing I could say, nothing I could do to make a future possible for us.

I dressed for dinner with Marie's harried help as she stole time between making the soup and tending the beef. She styled my hair with pearl beads that probably cost more than a year's worth of her wages. She placed a hand on my shoulder as she finished, and I squeezed it in appreciation.

The girl reflected in the mirror was lovely, but I scarcely recognized her.

I took a few moments to collect myself. I crossed to my window, which was said to have a prize view: directly down onto the Place Royale. I couldn't see much of the city beyond the square at all. Others in my place might have appreciated the finely manicured lawns, the impressive fountains, or the lush cluster of trees at the perimeter and center. To me it looked like a cloister where I was condemned to spend my life locked away from the world. Or worse, a prison yard. And in the center of it was an imposing statue of Louis XIII, whose smug face had always irritated me. But now, after hearing Théo's impassioned speeches, I knew his likeness came to represent something even more foul than I'd been able to understand before.

I shook the thoughts from my head, lest they get me into trouble at dinner, and descended the staircase to dine with my parents and Gaspard but looked forward to it with the same cheer as a hanging. Gaspard had already joined them in the drawing room and positively beamed when he saw me come into view.

He bowed and kissed my hand, the very picture of courtly manners.

"A trinket for you, my dear." He opened a small box, painted red with gilt design around the edges, to reveal a massive emerald ring encircled by diamonds and set in a thick gold band. He placed it on my ring finger and the weight of it was oppressive, though it had little to do with the gems and metal. The weight of promises was far greater than common minerals could ever be.

Maman wasn't so vulgar as to take my hand and examine the ring, at least not while Gaspard was present, but she could assess its value with a jeweler's discerning eye at twenty paces and looked as satisfied as a house cat in cream. Her look said it all: *Good fishing, girl. You reeled in a big one.*

We went into the dining room and were served course after course of sumptuous food prepared by Marie and Nanette. I should have had a hand in it as well and my cheeks burned as I recalled how I'd spent my afternoon. I tried not to think of it, thinking my sins would somehow paint themselves on the dining room walls if I pictured them too clearly. Papa and Gaspard spoke of the mounting tensions in town, Maman filling in with her ideas for the wedding at odd moments. I didn't speak a word during the meal, and it seemed my conversation wasn't missed.

It seemed an eternity later when Gaspard took his leave with a dutiful kiss on the back of my hand. There was no stirring of emotion or even the tug of duty and loyalty when he was near.

"Well done, tonight," Maman said as Gustave closed the front door behind Gaspard. "Quite charming, for once."

I considered pointing out that I'd not spoken more than a few syllables at dinner and, worse, had paid precious little attention to the conversation. But I held my mouth closed, deciding it was better to accept her praise since it was so rarely bestowed.

She finally took her chance to examine the ring, her gasp

audible as she held it up to the candlelight for a closer inspection. The green and translucent gems bounced rainbows of light on the walls as she angled my hand to catch the soft glow of light.

"I never thought you'd land such an eligible match, I admit it. And he seems smitten. I just hope you can keep his attention long enough to see the thing done. But if he does not, at least we have this as a bit of insurance, don't we?"

The bile rose in my throat, but I managed a weak nod.

"I'm positively knackered, Maman. I hope you don't mind if I leave you to sit alone in the parlor this once."

"Not at all," she said. She crossed the room and poured a generous measure of cognac in a crystal glass. "Take this with you to your rooms. You've earned it."

I accepted the glass and walked up the stairs, hoisting my dress so I didn't fall square on my face.

Once in the confines of my room, I set the cognac on my dressing table and set about removing the decadent pink satin and freeing myself from my rigid stays.

I put the gown back in the wardrobe, grateful to have freedom of movement and more air in my lungs. In the back, carefully hung by Marie, I saw the simple green linen I'd worn to town that very day. I touched the linen in one hand and the pink silk in the other. One was flawlessly smooth, made to glisten under candlelight. The other was sturdier and was a garment in which one could . . . live a life.

I knew how the cool satin felt against my skin. How luxurious and effortless the fabric was to wear.

But one spill, even a few droplets of water, could spoil it irrevocably.

I knew the linen was stiff and scratchy.

But it would withstand long hours in a kitchen and long walks in the city.

It would withstand summer sun and winter snows.

I released the satin and slipped into the linen. I couldn't spend my life like a china doll on a shelf.

I was the linen, and I was meant to live life.

CRÈME PÂTISSIÈRE

->-<-

One of Nanette's staple recipes for her lovely desserts. Especially good in her *Religieuses*. Maman prefers pastry cream infused with lemon, while Papa prefers currants. I find the chocolate to be particularly appetizing.

Put the yolks of six eggs and two spoonfuls of sifted flour in a stew pan. Add gradually to it three cups of boiling cream and a pinch of salt. Then put it on moderate fire, stirring until it begins to thicken. Remove from heat and continue to stir so that it may become smooth. (Note, do not rush the stirring or the cream will remain lumpy.) Replace on the fire for ten to twelve minutes until it is done.

Nanette has made variants of the *crème pâtissière* infused with vanilla cloves, citron peel, chocolate, mocha coffee, chocolate, currants, and rum.

Recipe notes: Experiment with flower essences, cinnamon, and tea infusions and various blends of the above.

Chapter Eleven

MICHELINE

I felt sweat beading up on my forehead as Chef Rossignol stood over my shoulder and watched, hawklike, while I attempted for the third time to make a passable pastry cream. It was the first day of classes and I was already a failure. I'd tossed out the two previous batches. Good sugar, eggs, and milk wasted. I knew for certain I'd measured each of the ingredients accurately, but try though I might, I couldn't get the cream to thicken.

On the first attempt, the cream was watery. On the second, it was too foamy. This time? It separated and the fats were solidifying away from the rest of the mixture.

"Mademoiselle, you cannot think this is the way a *crème pâtissière* should be," Chef Rossignol said, hands clasped behind his back. The other students were now openly watching as I toiled and failed.

"No, Chef," I said. "Not in the least."

"Then I expect you to learn this before next class," he said.

"The *crème pâtissière* is the cornerstone of many recipes you will be required to master. If you cannot produce a passable *sample*, there isn't much I can do for you. You will stay until you get it right."

He stalked back up toward the front of the teaching kitchen and mercifully began berating someone else's poor attempt.

I took a quick glance at my wristwatch, one that had been Maman's, but she hadn't worn the day she went missing. I reasoned she wouldn't object to my borrowing such a valuable object given that I was trying to keep track of the girls and their school schedule. It was already three in the afternoon. If I didn't leave within the next fifteen minutes, the girls would arrive home from school before I did.

I didn't want them alone in Montmartre where anything could happen to them. I didn't want them to get into mischief while I was away.

I didn't want them worried that I wasn't coming home.

I began whisking the damned cream more vigorously, willing it to come together.

"Turn the temperature down," a voice whispered.

The young man at the next station over averted his eyes back to the front of the room, lest Rossignol suspect he was aiding a fellow student. I'd only been in class for one session, but I knew he expected each of us to find the answers to our quandaries on our own. If the young man had been caught giving me pointers it would have ended badly for both of us.

I glanced over to him. He was tall and thin with a mop of brown curls framing his face. He had serious hazel-green eyes that were now locked on the instructor as if his very life, and not just his marks, depended on it. He didn't seem the type to hiss bad advice in my ear, so I did as he suggested and turned the knob on my stove lower. Gradually, the mixture came back together, and it looked less like a clump of melted candle wax and more like something fit to eat.

One by one, the students were being dismissed as their offerings were deemed acceptable. The tall boy with the curls among them. Chef Rossignol circled back to me, arched a brow in surprise at the pastry cream that finally resembled human food, and sampled with a small spoon he kept in his breast pocket.

"Not bad," he admitted. "Next time, worry less, cook more. You'll waste less time that way. Both of ours."

He walked off without another word.

I dashed out into the hallway, not caring that the other instructors and a few of the office ladies shook their heads disapprovingly at my unladylike display.

If I left now, I'd only keep them waiting a quarter of an hour. It wasn't much time for them to panic. I tried not to let my mind wander to the possibilities that might befall them, two unsupervised girls in an unforgiving city. It would cause my lungs to constrict upon themselves and would only serve to slow me down further.

"Where's the fire?" a voice called. The gangly boy.

"Montmartre," I said without irony. "I have to get home. The girls are alone."

"Hold on, I can drive you," he said. "It will save you loads of time."

I stopped in my tracks. He wasn't wrong. At this time of day, the public transport, such as it was, was slow, and the surface traffic was manageable. But could I trust this boy? Yes, he'd been helpful with the *crème pâtissière*, but that didn't exactly establish his character.

"I promise to get you home safely to your daughters," he said, holding up a hand as if taking a solemn vow. "I swear on my copy of the *Larousse Gastronomique*. My name is Laurent Tanet."

I sighed. "Thank you," I said, trying not to sound as beleaguered as I felt. "I'm Micheline Chartier, pleased to make your acquaintance."

"Likewise," he said, opening the door from the school to the parking lot. "That was rough in there. You deserve a good turn."

He opened the door to his Peugeot 202. It was definitely built before the war, and had its share of dings and scratches, but had been meticulously cared for and when he turned the key to start the ignition, the engine sounded robust and healthy. I gave him my address and he headed north from the center of town toward the butte.

"A gift from my father," he explained as we pulled out onto the streets. The area near Les Halles was always busy, but he navigated the traffic with confidence. Most young men in their early twenties, which is what I estimated him to be, couldn't afford a car at all, even one that had been well used for the better part of a decade. "He was so happy I made it back alive, from the front, that when I told him I wanted to come to Paris to study cooking, he signed me up himself and handed me the keys to the car."

"How generous," I said, without irony. I was glad I wasn't

the only one who was receiving a helping hand. I could only imagine too well the relief of a father whose son had managed to survive the terrible war. A car and an education seemed like easy gifts if one could afford them. I knew if Maman was waiting for me at home, she'd never lift a finger again. All she'd need do is dote on the girls and advise me from the comfort of the sofa. God, how I wished I could ask her questions. Even more than I wanted her to hold me in her arms and tell me I wasn't failing the girls, I wanted to ask her so many things.

"Rossignol was putting you through your paces today. He likes to do that with the new students," he said.

"Wasn't today the first day of courses?" I asked.

"Of the baking and pastry course, yes. Many of the others, myself included, have taken some previous classes with him. I just finished a three-week intensive course on sauces," he explained. "It was a good way to learn the way he thinks. We figured that since I was coming from Lamballe, I might as well take several courses while I'm here."

"Ah," I said, realizing how woefully underprepared I was. I didn't know a hollandaise from a béchamel, and that was considered elementary compared to baking. "A Breton. And far from home."

"Yes," he said. "And I miss it, but Paris is enchanting. I never got to visit much as a boy. No finer place to learn the craft of baking, though."

"No," I agreed. "No doubt you'll be the pride of Lamballe when you return."

He laughed and glanced at me as he drove. "Have you always wanted to bake?"

I glanced down at Maman's watch. We were making good time. If they had to wait for me, it would only be a few minutes now. I felt the knots in my stomach loosen and I was able to pay attention to his questions.

"No," I said honestly. I could have invented a history that involved a childhood dream of a bakery filled with *mille-feuilles* and intricate fruit tarts. Baguettes and *boules* by the dozen. But I saw no point to subterfuge. "I'd never considered it before last week. My neighbor . . . convinced me to try it. The girls—my sisters—depend on me to make a good living."

"Sisters," he said. "That makes some sense. You seem awfully young yet to be a mother." There was something akin to relief on his face, but I chose to ignore it.

"I might as well be," I said.

"The war," he said simply.

I nodded. I explained how Papa had died early in the war and my attempts to find Maman.

"Things were the shambles for so long," he said. "I don't wonder you haven't had much luck."

He didn't, as so many others had done, remind me that if she hadn't come home by now that she wasn't likely to return. He didn't urge me to move on or to give up my inquiries. I appreciated that in him more than I could voice.

It wasn't long before we reached our little apartment. I was surprised that, instead of idling in front to let me out, he parked the car and came around to open the door for me.

"This is where you live?" he asked.

"Well, the apartment upstairs, yes," I said. "If all goes well, the shop below will be a bakery once I know what I'm doing."

"I have to see it," he said, following me in. His eyes gleamed as if I was showing him Dallayou or Stohrer or one of the grand bakeries of Paris. Clearly, he was looking through the rose-tinted glasses of potential. I explained about the defunct bistro and Madame Dupuis' grand plans.

"She's right," he said. "It's what this place was meant to be. I bet it was a hub of the neighborhood back in its glory days."

"She claims it was," I said. I wondered if he felt what I had when I cleaned the shop last week.

"You'll make something wonderful out of this place," he said with a confidence I envied.

"I hope you're right," I said. "It seems a crazy undertaking, but I can't think of what else to do. The girls need to be provided for."

"Who is this?" Sylvie's voice boomed as she entered the building. Noémie was hard on her heels. I rolled my eyes . . . the child was too bold by half and there was no convincing her to defer to adult authority. Her teachers claimed she was a compliant enough child, but I rarely saw proof of this at home.

"This is Monsieur Tanet," I said, deciding to keep things formal. "We're in baking school together. These are my sisters Sylvie and Noémie."

"How fun!" Noémie exclaimed. "Baking cakes all day long and chatting with your chums."

"It's not like they sit around *eating* cake all day," Sylvie countered. "Baking is a lot of work."

"That it is," Laurent agreed. "Hot stoves, kneading dough, long hours. It's not for the weak of spirit."

"It still sounds like more fun than sums," Noémie said. "I hope you'll learn to make *clafoutis* soon. It's my favorite."

"With blueberries?" Laurent asked.

"Blackberries," she said without hesitation. "And Chantilly cream."

"That is my specialty, young lady. Perhaps I can make some for you. If your sister will permit it, of course," he said, turning his glance to me.

"If you show me how it's done," I said. If he was going to weasel his way into Noémie's affections with butter and sugar, I was going to reap the benefits of it too.

"You have an accord, mademoiselle," he said, making an exaggerated bow and doffing his cap. Noémie dissolved into giggles while Sylvie stood, arms over her chest, unimpressed by Laurent and his overtures at friendship.

"What's your favorite?" Laurent asked, turning to Sylvie. "We can't have you left out."

She opened her mouth, presumably to spit vitriol at an undeserving Laurent, but then her eyes darted to my wrist. "You're wearing Maman's watch," she spat. She tore up the stairs to the apartment before I could say a word in defense. My eyes followed her up the stairs and I stood dumb for a moment.

"I'm sorry," I finally managed to mutter. "She's been difficult ever since . . ."

"Don't apologize for a child who misses her parents," Laurent said. "There are too many like her. On both sides."

"Amen to that," I said. "I just hope I can survive the raising of her."

Laurent put a hand on my shoulder. It was the first time in over a year that anyone aside from Sylvie, Noémie, and occasionally Madame Dupuis had touched me. I was surprised at the warmth that spread over me, much like when I'd taken my first bite of the *sablé*. "I've only known you for a short while, Micheline, but you're capable. Even when pitted against the wiles of a willful girl. I have faith in you."

I wished I felt the same. I wanted to speak the words aloud, but just cast my eyes downward.

"Mademoiselle Noémie, I should be on my way, but you have my word that I will teach your sister how to make blackberry *clafoutis* before long," he said to her as if Sylvie's temper hadn't just exploded like the blackest, angriest thundercloud over the shop.

"With Chantilly cream?" she asked.

"Naturally," he replied. "An extra helping for you." She smiled and ran up after Sylvie, more giggles trailing behind her.

"And you can manage her when she gets overexcited from all the sugar?" I asked wryly as I heard the apartment door close behind her.

"Indeed I can," he countered with a wink. "I'll do with little Noémie as I do with my brothers and take them to run laps around the park until they're ready to sleep for a week. That way, you can get a much-needed rest. Have a good evening, Micheline. I'll pick you up for class in the morning."

I blinked.

"I insist," he continued. "If you have a ride, you won't be rushed. If you aren't rushed, you'll be in a better frame of mind for class. It's the least I can do."

"Least you can do?" I said. "You aren't beholden to me for anything."

"I know," he said. "Perhaps I'm banking it for the future."

I fumbled around in my head for a reason to reject his offer. I ought to say no. I shouldn't trust a man I'd barely met. But I couldn't find the words.

"Thank you," I said, gently shaking my head. I could always formulate a reason to turn him down in the future. But saving valuable time and not rushing to catch a bus and ending up drenched in sweat was too tempting to resist.

He took my hand in his and brushed his lips against the back of my hand, an old-fashioned gesture, but one that suited him.

"It will get better," he assured me. How he could surmise this, I didn't know.

But I wanted to believe him.

Chapter Twelve

LISETTE

I stuffed all I could into the simple valise I had for my personal items when we took summer trips into the country. I was tempted to throw in clothes at first but realized that the miles of silk and muslin would be of no use to me on the rue Norvins. I took a few of my more practical things: wool and tweed that would withstand wear, my sturdiest boots, a hat or two that weren't too ostentatious. I grabbed what little jewelry I had so that I could sell it if times grew dire. I took my recipe book and the tome Théo had lent me. I left behind the books on decorum.

I grabbed every *centime* to my name, which I never thought was all that much, but after my encounter in the dry goods shop, was worth considerably more than I'd realized. I took my silver-plated brush and mirror set and wrapped them carefully in a skirt. They could be sold, and I could replace them with something made of wood for a fraction of the cost. I took the massive emerald engagement ring that Gaspard had given me and left it on the dresser, however, as that was not mine to take. I felt a twinge of regret, knowing it could provide a cushion against the uncertain times that lay ahead, but did not want to be accused of thievery.

I surveyed the room and considered its contents. There were beautiful things that I'd prefer not to leave behind. But as I scanned my belongings, I thought only of what was serviceable and what might fetch a price. Everything else would be dead weight as I tried to flee. My case was already heavier than it ought to be if I wanted to leave in a hurry. I snapped it shut with a prayer that I wouldn't regret anything I'd left behind. The last thing I grabbed, perhaps foolishly, was the flower that Théo had given me. I couldn't leave it behind before it had its chance to take root.

I considered writing a note, but it would take time I didn't have to lose. I tossed on my heaviest coat, though the weather didn't justify it, knowing I'd be glad of it in winter along with a couple of good scarves and a hat I couldn't fit in the bag. I was sure I looked like a madwoman dressed as I was, but I didn't care. I would care even less if it meant I was properly warm in winter.

It wouldn't be long before Maman sent a maid to come help me dress for dinner. I had to stop lamenting the artifacts of my life I'd be leaving behind and get out before I was discovered. I raced as quickly as I dared down the back stairs to the kitchen where Nanette and Marie were bustling about in preparations for the evening meal. Nanette saw how I was dressed and saw the bag in my hand. There was no need for her to ask where I was going or why I was fleeing.

"I hope you know what you're doing, Kitchen Mouse," Nanette said, shaking her head sadly.

"I don't," I admitted. "But I know I can't stay here. I can't live the life they have planned for me. I know what you think, Nanette, and I can't."

"Just be safe, you idiot girl," Nanette said, wiping her cheek with the back of her hand, but barely breaking cadence as she chopped garlic for the sauce.

"Take care," Marie said. I wasn't sure how to read the look on her face—something between pity and disbelief—but she didn't look poised to dissuade me. I kissed Nanette on the cheek, squeezed Marie on her arm affectionately, and offered up a hope that Maman wouldn't trace my disappearance back to them.

I rushed out into the darkening sky of the autumn evening. I kept to shadows as I walked in the pristine streets of the Place Royale where I might be recognized. Once I was out of the immediate area of my home—my parents' home—I walked as briskly as I could out in the haloed glow of the gaslights. The evening would soon grow into night and the streets of Paris would become a much more dangerous place. There were more men like old Jacquot waiting in the alleys.

I tried not to sprint so my energy wouldn't flag before the long trek was completed. I tried to look assertive and purposeful, but any thief or criminal skilled at his trade would know it was an act. As I approached Montmartre, the streets grew more narrow, crooked, and steep with every pace northward. This was not the civilized Paris with the elegant boulevards in the center *arrondissements*. This was the everyman's Paris, paved with the sweat, blood, and bone of unending toil.

When I at last reached the maze of streets leading up the butte, I realized I'd paid far too little attention on my walk to and from Théo's apartment when I had been there three days prior. I could hardly tell one street from another and wouldn't know what to ask if I were brave enough to ask anyone for help. *You couldn't have bothered to look at a street sign? You came all this way and have no idea where to go.*

I noticed people looking at me with suspicion as I bustled along, hoping I didn't appear as lost as I felt. The coat, while far from elegant, was finer than most people had in this district of the city, and it was two months too early for such a heavy garment, as the pooling sweat of my underarms would attest to.

A voice sneered behind me. "A bit far from the palace, aren't we?"

Pierrine.

I was both relieved and dismayed. I knew from her tone that she loathed me, but she was someone who could help me find Théo. Someone who might not wish me well, but who wouldn't wish me ill. I hoped.

"A bit, yes," I said. I could have bitten back with something witty, but it seemed like a poor time to test her patience.

She was wearing a tattered dress that left little of her enviable figure to the imagination. She was supple and curvaceous where I was lean and lanky. She had the shape men craved. Had Théo partaken of her charms? I cast the thought aside, knowing that course of thought could come to no good end.

But with her rich brown hair and soulful blue eyes, it was hard to imagine any man who would resist her.

"Decided to see the slums, have you?" she said. "You ought to have come in the daylight. The rats scamper out at night." She glanced around the street, and it was plain in her expression she was referring to the human vermin that scurried about after the lamplighter had done his job for the night.

"I left in a hurry," I said, not wanting to tell her the full truth. She looked at my valise and was able to surmise enough. "Can you tell me the way to Théo's?"

"Does he know you're coming?" she asked, crossing her arms over her chest.

"Are you his butler now?" I asked. I wasn't in the habit of addressing people in so brusque a manner, but Pierrine didn't seem the sort to appreciate flattery or cajoling. I doubted few in Montmartre would play the social games that were compulsory in the Place Royale.

She rolled her eyes and started walking. I assumed I was meant to follow her, but even if she had no intention of showing me the route to Théo's apartment, I'd be no more lost than I was now.

We arrived ten minutes later, thankfully before night settled in earnest. At the door, she held out her hand expectantly. I widened my eyes.

"My time isn't free," she explained. "I could have picked up company for the evening if you hadn't pulled me away."

I blushed, realizing what I'd pulled her from. I wasn't sure if I ought to apologize, or if it would just make matters worse. I took some coin from my little purse and placed them in her outstretched palm. Her eyes widened in turn. I'd given too much. I'd have to learn to calibrate the value of a *sou* here. Clearly money went further here than in Place Royale.

She hastily pocketed the money before I had the chance to realize my blunder and ask for some of her windfall back. "He's a decent man, you know," she said, crossing her arms over her chest again. "He's not like the simpering vipers that live in the posh parts of town."

"I'm well aware," I said, thinking of Gaspard. "It's why I've come."

She opened her mouth, perhaps to protest. Perhaps to champion Théo. But she snapped it shut and turned to disappear back to the labyrinthine streets of the butte.

I knocked on the side door, hoping against hope that Théo was home. Hoping the sound of my knock would carry up the stairs. He descended some minutes later, looking disheveled.

"What in God's name are you doing here?" he asked. "How did you get here?"

"I walked," I said.

His face went white, and he hauled me up the stairs. "I hope you have a good reason for risking your life walking across the entirety of Paris alone. You've come too close to danger in the past not to understand how dangerous it can be for a woman alone."

"I couldn't stay, Théo," I said. "I simply couldn't. I went home after . . . everything, to be fitted into a wedding gown to marry the most conceited popinjay in all of Paris. I'm equal to a great many things, but I am not equal to spending the rest of my life miserable. And I would be."

Théo rubbed his face and crossed his arms over his chest, much like Pierrine had done.

"I was foolish," he said. "Foolish to indulge in an afternoon with you. Foolish to plant these thoughts in your head. I thought you understood that it was all a passing folly."

"Is that all it was for you?" I asked. "Is that all *I* am to you?"

He blanched. "Lisette, don't do this."

"No, Théo. If I truly mean nothing to you, I'll leave now. If you want me to go home and face my mother's wrath and marry Gaspard, be man enough to say it."

"I ought to lie. I ought to say that you were nothing more to me than an amusing conquest so that you'll go home where you belong."

"But you can't," I pressed.

"I won't drag you down in the muck with me. I couldn't live with myself. You have a life of comfort waiting for you there. With me there will be toil and sacrifice. You deserve better than that."

"A life without love holds no room for comfort," I said.

"And a life without bread on the table and soup in the kettle leaves little room for love," he said. "You might care for me now, but how many cold nights and missed meals will cure you of that?"

"I can work," I said. "I can help make a way for us. You won't have to bear the burden of being breadwinner alone. In case you've forgotten, I'm something of a baker myself. I can win us bread aplenty."

Théo sat in his chair by the fire and motioned for me to sit in the one beside his. I joined him and took his hand in mine.

"Lisette, there aren't words to express to you how much I want you to be mine, but I would spend the rest of my life hating myself for making you live like this," he said, motioning to his apartment.

"It's a bit small," I allowed. "And could use a woman's touch, but it's warm. It's dry. What else does one need? I don't need Versailles or the Louvre. I don't need a posh townhouse in the Place Royale. I have always felt lost in my parents' home, save when I was in the kitchen. I don't know what I can say to convince you, but it's the truth."

Théo buried his head in his hands, deep in thought. "I can't turn you out. A better man would have the resolve to walk you home, but I confess I'm not the man I should be."

"But you're precisely the man I want," I said. "And I won't leave that for all the chateaux in France and all the gowns in the empress's wardrobe. None of it means a whit."

Théo looked up and took my hand in his. "Then stay," he said. "I can't offer you much, but what I have is yours."

TARTE AUX POMMES

⸻⸻

One of Nanette's favorites to make in the autumn near harvesttime. The earthy, wholesome flavors evoke the harvest. A small slice is a wonderful capstone to a hearty meal. I find it one of the great comforts when the world seems bleak.

Make recipe for puff pastry in advance and keep in a cool spot in the cellar. Roll and shape into a tart pan and let bake without fruit for ten minutes. Set aside. Note: press pastry well into tart pan, or it may slide down the edges.

Slice twelve good Pippin apples, add to stew pan with a cup of water, a quarter pound of sugar, and the juice of a lemon. Boil until the apples are cooked through and drain in a sieve. Brush the bottom on the tart shell with apricot or other marmalade. Place boiled apples in baked tart shell. Reduce the syrup made from boiling the apples and use it to glaze the tart. Add tart to hot oven to get a golden sheen.

Top may also be glazed with caramelized sugar or apricot marmalade.

Recipe notes: experiment with a cherry glaze.

Chapter Thirteen

MICHELINE

On a day without classes at the academy, I stood in line at the prefecture as I had done every month since Maman had gone missing. That wasn't entirely true. It was every week for many months. Daily in the days after the Germans had been routed and we felt safe approaching any government building. Just as I would for going to Mass, I wore my best dress and my good hat. I did this for each of my trips to the prefecture, hoping it might help in some small way for them to take me seriously.

"*Bonjour*, Mademoiselle Chartier," the secretary greeted me. "So very nice to see you again."

Is it really? Is it pleasant for you that my mother is still missing, and I have to come to you begging for help to find her?

I wanted to glare at the woman, but none of this was her fault.

I simply offered her a weak smile.

"The prefect will be free in a few moments. Have a seat in the usual spot if you don't mind."

I inclined my head to her and stalked off to the small grouping of chairs outside the prefect's office. It was a farce to her. A game. The usual chair. The same questions. She thought I was being ridiculous. And perhaps I was.

So many people in my position had given up by now. They accepted the truth, mourned their loved ones, and rebuilt their lives.

I envied them. I envied the peace they would eventually find.

But I simply couldn't let go of the hope that Maman was out there. Somewhere. And so, I came to the prefecture every month in hope of news. The prefect, Monsieur Ouimet, was a rotund man with no hair on his head, but a rather flamboyant moustache. He'd served at the tail end of the first war, never having seen much of the fighting. He'd been too old to serve in the second. He was one of the lucky ones, though none of the men of that group would claim it. They wore a shroud of guilt on their shoulders, and it weighed mightily on them. I was certain he'd taken the post as prefect, not for the prestige of the vital service he provided, but as a way to atone for the heinous crime of having . . . survived.

"Mademoiselle Chartier," Monsieur Ouimet called from his office door after a few moments.

I entered his office, Spartan and efficient as it always was. So little seemed to change. The only variable was the color of his tie. Often blue, sometimes green. Red when he was in a particularly feisty mood. The rest of the room was as immutable as the face of a marble statue. He gestured for me to sit.

"You're looking well, mademoiselle. I trust you're here to inquire after your mother once again?"

Once again. I gritted my teeth.

"Yes," I said. "Have there been any new developments?" I asked.

A familiar sadness washed over his face. As it did every month. "I'm afraid not," he said.

"Has anything else been attempted?" I asked. "Any new searches?"

This is where he would assure me that he was still searching. That he was using every bit of his influence to help locate her. This time, he didn't look me in the eye. He laced his fingers and leaned over his desk.

"Mademoiselle, it pains me to say this, but there are hundreds of thousands of people who went missing during the war who will never be recovered. Soldiers and civilians alike. I have tried everything in my power to push the search for Madame Chartier in front of everyone who might be able to help. But after all these months, there can be precious little hope that she will be found."

"I refuse to believe this," I said, sitting taller in my chair. "You promised me you would leave no stone unturned."

He finally looked up at me, set down his pen, and laced his fingers. "Not a single pebble has been left undisturbed, I assure you. I wish I were able to give you the news you want to hear, my dear. Truly. But the fact of the matter is that your mother was very likely killed by one of the occupying troops and they never identified the body before it was interred. There would be no way to trace her now, even if resources weren't so limited. There is nothing more I can do. We have made the difficult decision to list Madame Chartier as presumed dead."

"You promised me," I repeated. I felt the tears spill over my cheeks and my hands begin to shake. "You promised me you'd find her."

"I promised you I would do everything in my power to find her, and so I have done, mademoiselle. I can't express how grieved I am for you, but it may be time to accept the reality that she isn't coming back."

I shook my head, unable to speak.

"I understand you have sisters who are minor children. Are they well cared for?"

"Yes," I spat, any kindness dissipating from my voice like water evaporating off a red-hot skillet.

"You do know that the welfare of children is a chief priority of ours. If they would be better off placed with a family . . ."

"No," I said. "Save your efforts for orphans in need. I can imagine your *limited resources* would be better spent on them."

I felt my chest tighten. He couldn't think that I wasn't providing well enough for the girls. I couldn't have them taken away. I couldn't fail my mother so entirely. I had to master myself once more.

"The girls are well cared for," I assured him, forcing myself to lower my voice to the tones of someone who wasn't on the verge of wringing the neck of the man who sat across from her. "Fed, clothed, clean, and educated."

He looked mollified. "I wish I could be of more help," he said. "I truly am sorry."

"You might help me access my parents' bank accounts," I said. "A reserve of money *would* help matters."

"I'm afraid a presumption of death won't be sufficient for that," he said. "The custom is to keep the assets frozen for seven years. After that time the next of kin, being yourself, can file for access to their estate."

"Seven years?" I stammered. "The girls will be grown by then. That will be of no help to me."

"I do think the government will make special provisions because of the war in the coming years," he said. "But until such provisions are made, there is nothing more I can do."

Nothing more I can do. His litany of *I am doing everything under my power* had been replaced. There was no longer any room for hope, in his view, and that truth skewered me like a bayonet.

I wanted to hurl the paperweight from his desk straight at his head. To tell him he couldn't give up his search for her. But it would serve no purpose. He was a good man, and a kind one. He'd done more than his duty to me and my family. There were others that deserved his time and attention as well.

"I understand, monsieur," I said, standing from the uncomfortable wooden chair. "Thank you for all you've done."

"Many families in your situation find comfort in holding a small memorial service," he said, standing in turn. "It would be my honor to attend if you arrange for such an event."

"That is extremely kind of you, Monsieur Ouimet," I said, my tone softer now. "But you misunderstand. My mother is not dead. I will find her, even if you cannot help me."

He exhaled slowly. "I wish you the best of luck."

"But . . . ?" I said, reading his unvoiced caveat.

"Do what you must, but don't waste the rest of your life seeking for her. I knew your mother, you know. And it's not what she would have wanted."

I nodded and left the prefecture without another word.

I took my time as I walked back home through the labyrinthine streets of Montmartre. The girls would be at school for another three hours, and it was so rare that I had the opportunity to simply wander. There were traces here and there of the German occupation. Damage to a few buildings. Divots in the roads. The worst the Germans left behind was the haunted look in people's eyes. I remembered that the neighborhood had been a friendlier place in the years before the war. There had been more smiles. Less suspicion. But the war had taken that from us.

And I couldn't imagine getting it back.

When I reached home, I found myself in the bistro's kitchen. I'd left the red journal on one of the shelves and had no time to revisit it in the days since I'd begun my baking school. I took it and sat in one of the wood-and-woven-wicker chairs from the restaurant that had been relegated to a corner of the kitchen, I imagined for the weary chef who needed a break from toiling behind the stove. I gently flipped through the yellowed pages.

It did, in fact, belong to my great-grandmother Lisette. And though it was clear the purpose of the book had been to collect her recipes, she added fascinating bits about her life and her struggles in the pages in between her notes about bread and pastries. I let myself have the luxury of losing myself in her story. I felt myself enmeshed in her tale, as though her life was playing out in the very room where I sat. Indeed, many of the moments she recounted took place in this very space. I wondered if Madame Dupuis even knew all of Lisette's story. I would have to share with her over coffee and pastries to see what she knew of the remarkable woman who had made this place what it was.

What it was meant to be.

After some time, I stood and turned to the cabinet and assembled the ingredients for one of the simpler recipes: an apple tart.

The pastry was fiddly, but when I wasn't under the steely gaze of Chef Rossignol, I was able to breathe. I was able to focus on the recipe and my great-grandmother's words. I measured and blended the flour, butter, and sugar carefully. I mixed slowly and deliberately, not feeling the pressure of having a passable tart ready at the same time as my classmates. Not fussed about what the chef might have to say about my technique. Surely, I held the spoon in precisely the wrong way. Certainly, the temperature in the room was too warm to produce a crust just as it should be, according to the laws and dictates in the world of the pastry elite.

But here, in my great-grandmother's kitchen, none of that mattered.

What mattered was that I would be home when the girls finished school.

I would be able to greet them with kisses on their cheeks and inquiries about how their days had gone.

And there would be a warm, flaky apple tart for dessert.

They wouldn't care if the crust wasn't fit to be included in a culinary textbook. They wouldn't care if the apples weren't at the exact right stage of ripeness.

They cared that they were loved. They cared that their sister was doing what she could to make their lives a little sweeter.

As I pulled the tart, perfectly golden brown, from the oven, I knew that nothing mattered more than this. Not even Rossignol's approval.

Chapter Fourteen

LISETTE

SEPTEMBER 17, 1870

How were you able to secure it all so quickly?" I asked, smoothing my hair. I looked at my reflection in the new looking glass, now framed with wood instead of silver, and sighed with resignation. I then shook myself. It was my mother who loathed my freckles and frizzy red hair. I had never longed for my sister's blond ringlets and porcelain skin. I might not be the fashionable girl Maman had longed for, but I wasn't her concern any longer. She still had Gislène as it was. In ten years, my cherubic baby sister could make the most enviable marriage in Paris. And she was such a sweet, biddable child, there was no doubt she would. Provided Maman and Papa's fortune held out and that her looks didn't bloom and fade prematurely, she could aspire far higher than I ever could have done.

"It helps to have friends in high places," Théo said, pointing skyward and making a lazy sign of the cross.

"Sébastien fixed it?" I asked.

"He's a fair hand with forgery. He didn't want to attest that you were an orphan as it would be too easy to prove otherwise and have the marriage nullified. So he forged a letter of consent. They would have a harder time proving the letter wasn't in their hand."

"Forgery. An unusual skill for a priest, wouldn't you say?"

"Sébas is an unusual priest," Théo countered. "And thank God for it. He took his vows to heart and actually seems to care about saving souls instead of amassing coin for Rome. And he seems to like you, so he was willing to take some liberties with the official paperwork to see us married."

I rolled my eyes. The amount of trouble—and expense—it took to be married, either by the mayor or in a church, was exasperating. Letters of consent from the bride's parents, the banns, the fees to the church or the mayor. It was no wonder that so many of the working class chose to forgo the formalities and simply declare themselves married, whether blessed in the eyes of God and the State or not. Théo, however, was not willing to let me spend the rest of my days as his mistress and insisted on a proper church wedding. "What's to keep them from challenging the veracity of the consent letter?" I asked.

"Ah, it happens. Parents change their mind if they think they got a raw deal from the groom and his family. They claim letters are forged all the time, so the courts are wary of those sorts of assertions. And the church doesn't much like parents pulling

their consent from a wedding that's already been consecrated."
He walked up behind me and kissed the nape of my neck and
rubbed his hands along my sides and up to my breasts. "Or
consummated."

"That it has been," I said with a laugh. We'd spent more of
the last three days tangled up in his bed—our bed—than we
had out of it.

"Well then, let's to church before I claim my rights as your
husband again before the deed is done," he said, continuing the
trail of kisses along the side of my neck. I turned to break the
embrace before I all-too-willingly allowed him to make good
on his threat.

"To church," I agreed.

"And a lovely bride you make too," he said, tucking my arm
in his as we headed down the stairs to the little courtyard.

I wore a traveling dress in hunter green wool that I'd always
been fond of. It was worlds away from the cream silk confection my mother had commissioned for my wedding to Gaspard.
But it, along with most of my new finery, had been left behind
when I left in haste. And I found I missed none of it.

For just a moment, though, I despaired that the beautiful
gown Maman commissioned might never be worn. It was too
lovely to crumble away in a cupboard somewhere. She'd have
grander plans for Gislène, and it was out of the question that
she would have her precious poppet in a dress ten years out of
fashion, so there was no chance Maman would tuck it away for
her. I hoped Maman would sell off the gown to some wealthy
bride who hadn't the time to have something bespoke crafted
for her.

But the idea of wearing the gown as I walked arm in arm with Théo down the rue Norvins seemed as ridiculous as wearing a bathing costume on an expedition to the poles. We walked to the church Saint-Pierre-de-Montmartre where Sébastien served. I knew little of the place, other than it was, at over seven hundred years of age, one of the oldest churches in all of Paris. There had been campaigns to restore the church to its former glory, but the efforts had been too small in scale to really prevent the decay of the church. It seemed the powers within the church preferred to spend their money on newer buildings rather than preserving ancient ruins. Despite the cracks in the walls and the lingering smell of must not quite covered by the centuries of incense and candle wax, the church was lovely in its imperfection.

Père Cadieux waited for us just inside the door, the usual humor gone from his face. "I will speak to the bride before the wedding," he said.

Théo nodded, releasing my arm as though he'd expected this request.

Père Cadieux led me to a room off the side of the nave of the church. From the look of it, the small windowless room served as his office. It was crammed full of books and had papers strewn everywhere. I'd never thought of him as a man to abide clutter, picturing his personal areas as sparse and monklike, but it seemed he was a man of letters like Théo with a collection of books to rival Papa's.

He gestured to a seat across from his desk.

"I know this is unusual, but I wanted to speak with you, away from Théo, before I perform the service," he said. "I want to hear from your own lips that you have thought this through. What you're giving away and the hardships you are taking on. Your parents would accept you back with open arms, I'm sure."

I barely stifled a snort of derision. My parents would be furious with me . . . if they'd even noticed I'd left.

"I'm fully aware of the consequences of my marriage, *mon père*," I said. "This is the life I want. I want to be of use, I don't want to be an ornament to a husband who views me only as a decoration or a plaything."

"Call me Sébas. Everyone does." My eyes widened at such an invitation from a priest. "Your feelings are understandable, but the Prussians have reached the city walls. Things are going to become increasingly hard, especially in our part of the city. I don't doubt that you can deal with your own share of hardship, but this will be a test for all of us."

"I'd rather face the Prussians at Théo's side than anyone else's," I said. "And I intend to work hard and be a good wife to him. And be of use to the neighborhood if I can be."

"Théo is lucky to have you," Sébas said. "And I know you're no wilting flower. I just hope you don't come to regret your decision. It would break Théo's heart."

He spoke with such sincerity; I could sense he was incredibly effective at his work. I felt compelled to live up to the standards he set for us. I worried I would fail him.

"You're a good friend, Sébas," I said, stumbling over his name. "I won't let him down."

"I believe you," he said. "And a free piece of advice?"

"Of course," I said.

"If you want to be of use to the neighborhood, don't consider your efforts to be like charity work. They won't appreciate it."

"No," I said. "I don't want to look over the neighborhood from an ivory tower. I want to be a part of it."

"Then you've won half the battle," he said, a smile finally working at the corner of his lips. His eyes flitted past my head for a moment, and he looked pensive. He placed a silver rosary in my hands. It was heavy with intricate etchings on the beads. I imagined feeling the prayers with each bead as I rubbed them between my thumb and forefinger. "Please accept this gift. It belonged to my mother, and she would be glad to know someone as kind and good as you has it now. I truly wish you every success. Come now and let's have you married."

I rejoined Théo, and breaking from tradition, we walked down the aisle together. Pierrine stood in one of the pews on the left of the aisle, Marie next to her. I'd managed to send word to her and Nanette of my upcoming wedding, but it would have been impossible for them both to sneak away, so Marie was sent as her intermediary. The kitchen and her little bedroom behind it were the radius of Nanette's world, and she was happy with the state of it. A voyage to Montmartre would have been like crossing the Atlantic for her these days. Marie was the logical choice to serve as representative, especially as she knew Montmartre well. She'd grown up here, which explained how she'd come to know Théo. Logic aside, my heart ached not to have Nanette there. I didn't mind having a small affair or a simple dress, but Nanette's absence was a loss. Though she'd never have been able to attend the wedding if I'd married Gaspard. She'd have been busy overseeing the team of cooks Maman would have hired to orchestrate a wedding feast.

A few men clad in the uniforms of the National Guard stood in the pews to the right. There was no fanfare or fuss. No women daintily dabbing lace handkerchiefs at tears that didn't truly exist. I didn't feel dread or fear as I marched down the stone aisle. With my arm linked in Théo's, I felt like I wasn't facing the future alone.

Sébas recited the vows he'd uttered countless times before to hundreds of couples before us. This time was different, because he loved the groom like a brother and had far more of an interest in the happiness of the newlyweds than he ever had before. And it seemed the promises were spoken, and we walked back down the aisle just as quickly as we'd arrived.

Sébastien ushered us to a side office where we would officially sign the papers necessary to legalize the union. A National Guardsman by the name of Fabien signed as Théo's witness and I handed Marie the pen to sign as mine.

"I'm afraid we're not having a luncheon or anything as elegant as that," I said to her when she wrapped her arms around me in congratulations.

"I couldn't stay as it is. Nanette is covering for me. She's becoming quite expert at it," she said with a laugh.

"She's learning new tricks, the sly old dog," I said.

"Ah, I never much liked that expression. An old dog can learn tricks aplenty if she spends time with young pups."

I snorted at the comparison. "True enough."

"She wishes she could be here," Marie said. "But her leaving would have attracted too much attention. She didn't want to spoil things for you."

I nodded. "I wish things could be different."

Marie cast her eyes down a moment. "No matter how upset she might have been at your leaving, she loves you."

"I know," I said, hugging her again. "Will you send that to her for me?"

"Of course," she said. "She sent a gift as well."

Marie produced a small velvet pouch from her handbag and placed it in my hands. I loosened the strings to find Gaspard's obscene ring inside. It was a massive oval emerald encircled in diamonds that gave it the look of a flower set in a thick gold band.

"What—?" I began and couldn't finish the sentence. Théo too looked at the jewel in my hand in astonishment.

"It seems Captain d'Amboise pitched quite a fit of pique when your parents told him you'd gone off. He hurled the ring in the fireplace. One of the maids told us and Nanette fished it out herself. She thought it might make things more comfortable for you."

I opened my mouth to protest.

"No," Marie said, holding up her hand. "Nanette said you'd balk and gave me strict orders not to hear a word of it. The ring was his engagement gift to you. You left it behind for him, and he refused to take it back. It's rightfully yours. Nanette wants you to have it. With her blessing too."

I bowed my head, not knowing what to say. "She's been a better mother to me than my own."

"You'll see her again," Théo promised. "She's not chained

to the stove, nor are you prisoner in Montmartre. I'll see to it myself."

"You chose well," Marie said, looking to Théo. "I've known your Théo for quite some time. I'll say there aren't too many men who are worth throwing away a fortune for, but I think he may be one of them."

"You're right, Marie," I said. "I'm one of the lucky ones."

"You always have been," she replied. "Now I'd best run before Nanette runs out of excuses for me."

"At least she'll have fewer to concoct with me out of the house."

"One of the few comforts she'll have in it," Marie said, kissing my cheek.

"What do we do with this?" I asked Théo, holding up the ring.

"Throw it in the Seine for all I care," he said. "Sell it for pin money if you like. Just promise me not to wear it. I strive to be an enlightened man, but the only ring I want you wearing is the one I gave you."

I looked down to my left hand at the simple silver band he'd placed on my finger some minutes before. It didn't have the sparkle and luster of Gaspard's offering, but it had come with a great deal more love.

"You, my darling husband, have a bargain."

MADELEINES AU CITRON

→>·<←

A favorite treat after lessons as a girl, a favorite decadence with tea or coffee of an afternoon as a woman. Nanette's are light as a pillow. I still work to make mine the same. There is something deceptively simple about these little cakes, and they require a respect one would usually reserve for a grander dessert.

Grate the peel of two small lemons over nine ounces of sugar. Add it to a stew pan with eight ounces of sifted flour, six whole eggs, four egg yolks, two spoonfuls of brandy (I prefer cherry brandy to raise the flavor of the lemon), and a dash of salt. Mix thoroughly but do not overmix (note: do not mix after an argument with Maman or they will be heavy and stick to the molds). Clarify ten ounces of butter, careful to skim off all the milk fat, and use the butter to thoroughly coat the Madeleine molds. Do not skimp. Mix the remaining butter back into the batter. Fill the molds with the batter and cook in a gentle oven for twenty-five to thirty minutes.

Recipe notes: experiment with orange, anise, and currants. Perhaps chocolate.

Chapter Fifteen

MICHELINE

I pulled the *Madeleines* from the oven and placed the burnt lumps on the wooden chopping board at my station. The best success of the day was that I managed to keep my tears in check. The rest was a disaster. The exterior of each little cake was hard and almost black in color. From the way they felt when I turned the mold, I had a sinking feeling that the dough in the middle was raw.

The oven was too hot.

The dough was overworked.

I was a disgrace.

Rossignol's round of inspections finally brought him to my station. I didn't dare avert my eyes to the left where Laurent would be waiting with a batch of *Madeleines* the perfect shade of golden-brown and an expression of pity for me and for the affront against God, man, and the great Carême himself that

I'd managed to summon in the innocent ovens of the culinary school.

He cut into one of the cakes, which was, as I feared, dangerously undercooked. He did not, as was his custom, sample a piece. It was just as well, for the sake of his health and his plumbing.

"Please see me after class, Mademoiselle Chartier," he said, then moved on to Laurent who earned generous praise.

This was it. He was going to toss me out of the academy, likely after making me swear an oath to never again enter a kitchen, and I would have to start all over again. I'd have to explain to Madame Dupuis that I had failed and had wasted her money. The heat rose in my cheeks as I thought of how mortifying that conversation would be. She'd trusted me. The girls depended on me. And I had let them all down.

The rest of my classmates filed out once Rossignol had assessed the last of the cakes.

"I'll wait for you," Laurent whispered as he moved to exit with the others.

I shook my head. "No, it's fine. I'll take the bus," I said. I was facing a lecture from Rossignol that would likely leave marks. To cry in front of total strangers would be embarrassing, but to cry in front of Laurent was truly mortifying.

He wanted to protest, but Rossignol was approaching my station, and did not seem the sort to suffer delays with much patience.

The vast academy classroom, with its oceans of countertops, armies of utensils, and fortified wall of ovens, was finally empty. Rossignol slid a stool in front of my station and sat. He was a short, spry man, and sat with an uncharacteristic informality, one foot hitched on the rung of the stool, his posture stooped ever slightly.

"Chef, I am so—" I began.

"Mademoiselle, I didn't detain you after class to hear your apologies," he said. "You pay attention in class, do you not?"

"Yes," I said. Thinking of my red notebook, rapidly filling with notes, that could attest to that.

"After thirty-seven years in this business, I could tell if you were not. So you needn't apologize. You have made me no offense."

"But my *Madeleines*—" I said, gesturing to the offending lump on the cutting board.

"Were an unqualified disaster," he admitted. "This I know. I also know that Hélène Dupuis, who does not issue compliments liberally, sings raptures about your *sablés* and says she's never tasted the like of your *chaussons aux pommes*. I also know you hold a whisk like someone with twenty years of experience in the kitchen. I also know I've rarely met a student with determination to match yours."

I cast my eyes downward. "If I may, Chef . . . then why did you ask me to stay?"

"To ask you a simple question, mademoiselle. Do you want to be a baker?"

"Of course, Chef. Why else would I be here?"

"Because Hélène Dupuis is a hard woman to refuse. And because you are in a difficult position that no one your age should be forced to deal with."

There was no pity in his voice, for which I was grateful, only resignation. Clearly Madame Dupuis had apprised him of my situation. I felt both relieved that I didn't have to explain it, and deeply discomfited that she had divulged my history to a man I didn't know. Did he accept me into the academy out of charity? The thought of it was too much to consider just then, or I would have melted into a puddle before him.

"I'll ask you the question again, Mademoiselle Chartier. Do you want to be a baker?"

I could not answer him. I realized because I didn't know the answer myself.

"Better," he said. "An honest response. But until you figure out the answer for yourself, I will be of little use to you."

"Yes, Chef," was all I could think to reply.

"Until the day you can answer that question with a resounding yes, you will never be a success here. I suggest you take some time to examine what it is you want. But if you wish to continue, practice at home at every opportunity. Dégas did not become a master sculptor because he thought about clay a great deal. He made art. And so too, must you."

"Are you kicking me out?" I suspected bluntness couldn't possibly do me any harm. A few direct words couldn't make him esteem me less than my baking already had.

"*Non, mademoiselle*. We begin the next course in two weeks' time, however, and I hope you will use the respite wisely to consider whether this is truly the path you wish to take, or if you're merely humoring your kindly neighbor's whims. If the latter is true, the uncomfortable conversation you will be forced to have with her will weigh less on your shoulders than the knowledge that you're wasting her money and your precious time."

Without another word, he stood from the stool and padded off to some inner sanctum of the building where I would likely never gain admittance.

I gathered my things and rushed out to the enclosure where people waited for the bus. Even two years after the liberation of the city, the transportation system wasn't back to its pre-war levels, and I hoped it wouldn't be too horribly long before there was another to Montmartre. I'd been spoiled by Laurent's generosity with his time and his vehicle and wasn't precisely sure what the bus schedule was. But I was glad Laurent had listened to me and not lingered. A bus came, finally, and I would arrive back at home with an hour to spare before the girls returned home for the day.

I hadn't been kicked out of the academy—yet. It was something to be grateful for. I would live to bake another day.

But I was a disappointment to Rossignol. I would be to Madame Dupuis if I were brave enough to tell her how poorly I was doing. The girls didn't care so long as they were loved, but they would care very much when there was no food on the table.

I felt the pricking of tears at the corners of my eyes. Rossignol's lecture had been humiliating. Not because he'd been cruel or demeaning. Worse. It was humiliating because he was right.

I had to *really* choose the life Madame Dupuis had offered me if I wanted to be successful. If I simply let myself go through the motions, simply took the path of least resistance without *choosing* it, I would never get anywhere. I would never be happy.

When I descended the bus and walked the two blocks back to the apartment, I was never gladder to have an hour to myself before the girls came home. I craved the solitude of an empty house if I could not have the tranquillity of a mind at peace. I should have locked myself in the kitchen and mastered the *brioche*. I should have busied myself with laundry or cleaning at the very least. But I sat on the sofa and curled up with Lisette's journal.

She ran a bakery here for decades. She'd seen so much here. She'd been a beloved fixture in the neighborhood. As I read through her pages, the recipes and blotted-out notes and her reflections about cooking and life, I tried to absorb her wisdom and her enthusiasm. The bakery was her passion and her joy, and I had to find a way to make it mine.

Chapter Sixteen

LISETTE

OCTOBER 4, 1870

Madame Fournier, you look pensive this morning," Théo said, joining me in the kitchen where I had bread baking for our little breakfast. He'd spent an hour of the early morning repairing a broken pipe in the lavatory. The cold mornings wrought havoc on the plumbing, but at least he was handy enough with small repairs that we were able to keep the place running without too much trouble. Our landlord, Monsieur Thébault, wasn't the most attentive caretaker and expected us to do most of the maintenance ourselves.

I'd made a good deal at the market for some apples that were on the point of spoiling and turned them into apple butter to slather on the crusty bread to make a hearty breakfast. Later, I would use the rest for a tart for after dinner. I'd managed for the past month to keep the household running on nothing more than Théo's modest wages from the National Guard. I wanted to wait until times were truly desperate to sell any of the items of value I'd confiscated from my room, and so far, we'd eaten well enough and kept warm.

But winter was hard on our heels.

As a child, I thought of happy Christmastides snug in the townhouse on the Place Royale, feasting on roast goose and watching the snow drift lazily down onto the rooftops. I'd had no idea how brutal winters were for the rest of Paris.

"I suppose I am," I said.

He came behind me and wrapped his arms around me. "How can I fix it?"

He asked this question whenever my mood seemed less than buoyant. I could see the worry in his furrowed brow. I knew he was imagining that I was unhappy. That I was coming to realize how much I'd sacrificed to become his wife. That worry was at the core of every move he seemed to make these days. There was no convincing him that I was perfectly happy in our little nest. No convincing him that I'd never spared a thought for the trappings of my old life.

"Nothing" was my typical response. And it was true. He'd proven himself to be a kind and loving husband beyond my loftiest expectations. But I couldn't lie to him. "I'm worried about the coming months," I admitted. "And I do precious little to help beyond keeping house."

"That's some small task, is it?" he asked. "For a man who has lived alone as a bachelor for ten years, I know what work you've taken off my shoulders. Not having to worry about scrounging up a dinner or laundering my breeches has been of more comfort than I can express to you. I can come home now and actually experience an hour or two of leisure. I can't remember being able to do that since I was a boy."

"And I am gladder of that than I can put into words," I said truthfully. "But with winter coming, food is going to become more and more expensive. We can get by comfortably now, but I'm able to buy less and less each week with the marketing money. I'm able to stretch things, but how many weeks will it be before it simply isn't enough? Three weeks? A month?"

Supplies in the city were growing scarcer as we were being choked out by the Prussians. Versailles's efforts to protect the capital had been largely ineffective. Those who had means had fled to the provinces before the city was sealed off. A few, like my parents, cloistered away and stockpiled resources. They wouldn't have cared if the poor died in the streets for want of food. In their minds the poor somehow *deserved* their fate, and it could not possibly have anything to do with the obscene disparity between the haves and the have-nots. Marie was kind enough to relay messages so I knew how they fared, but was even kinder in keeping my location a secret from my parents. They were searching for me, though the siege complicated their efforts. I was too precious an asset to let slip through their fingers. They did not yet know I'd married a National Guardsman and rendered myself without value to their social pursuits.

"We'll find a way, my love. Trust me," he said, wrapping his arms around me tighter.

"I do, Théo. I do. But I want to *do* something. I want to be a boon to you, and not just a responsibility."

I could see the conflict within him. His instinctual desire to protect and provide for me was warring with the modern ideas of the woman who was capable and strong that he espoused as part of his philosophies.

"I don't know what to say, my love. I don't want to see you taking up as a seamstress or some such and coming home exhausted every night. Not for the sake of a few *sous*."

"I'm a lousy seamstress anyway. I can mend passably well and embroider some, but I'm not equal to any real sewing." The dress I'd made was serviceable enough, but it had taken me so long to make it, there was no conceivable way I could sew quickly enough for others to turn a profit.

"Don't fret about it, darling. Really. We'll make our way through this winter and all the others to come. Just take care of me as beautifully as you have been and let me take care of you. But if old man Thébault comes round, do have him look at the pipes. I'm no plumber."

"Rent is due, so it's more likely than not," I said with a roll of my eyes. The roof might cave in and Thébault would be none too pressed to have it repaired, but he was prompt as the dawn when rent was due each Tuesday.

I stifled a sigh and leaned into his kiss as he left for his duties. In truth, I loved keeping house for Théo. I loved making the little apartment feel like a home. But there was only so much to be done in an apartment with four small rooms.

I went to the lavatory to inspect Théo's handiwork and to see if he'd left behind a mess from the repair work that needed attending to. All seemed in order, but there was still a small pool of water around the sink that was cause for concern. It seemed to have stopped, but I worried it was seeping into the disused shop below ours. Though we had no control over the shoddy plumbing, and no one had rented the shop in years, it would be an earful from the landlord if any damage was done.

The keys to our apartment worked for the shop as well, so I descended to see if the leak had caused problems below. The scent of dust and neglect were overpowering as I pushed open the door stuck from so many years of disuse. There was a thick coating of dust on every surface and a dingy gray film over the glass display cases. I wasn't sure what enterprises had used the space in the past, but Théo claimed it had been vacant in the ten years he lived above it. The lavatory in our apartment was on the northwest corner of the building, so I trekked to the back of the shop, leaving footprints in the dust as I walked. There was a decent-sized kitchen below the area where the lavatory pipes would have leaked.

Sure enough, there was a small puddle on the floor, but the flow from upstairs seemed to have stopped.

Against the wall stood a mop that probably dated back to the great revolution and bore the eighty years' worth of grime to prove it. I grabbed it and ran it along the floor, knowing full well I was just smearing dirt on the floor, but I was at least sopping up the water to avoid it causing damage.

"What's going on down here?" a voice called from the front of the shop.

Thébault. Damn. I'd hoped to have the mess cleared before he had a chance to see it.

"It's just me, Monsieur Thébault," I called.

The old man, ruddy-faced like a beet and stout as a fire plug, clattered into the kitchen, his expression dour.

"Your rents don't include this space, Madame Fournier," he reminded me unnecessarily.

"No indeed," I said. "But your plumbing leaves much to be desired and I thought you'd appreciate me tending to the leaks before the whole building floats away down the Seine."

"That husband of yours has been murder on my plumbing," he said. "I don't know what he does, but it's a damned nuisance."

"Monsieur, these pipes look like they date back to the times of Joan of Arc herself. They cannot help but leak. They're old and in need of replacing."

"Balderdash," he said, somehow growing even redder. "If you and that husband of yours were proper caretakers for this building, the pipes would be sound and in good working order."

"So you say as I stand mopping a floor in a shop that sits vacant under your care so that it won't sustain damage, sir?"

"You've quite a tongue to talk to your landlord with such cheek. I ought to turn you out for it."

"And best of luck finding anyone to rent it. There isn't a soul in Montmartre who doesn't know the condition you keep this poor building in."

"Well, you'll be out soon enough as it is. I'm selling the whole damned place and you and that husband of yours with his cockamamie ideas can find some other hovel to roost in. But until it sells, you keep this place clean, mind you. And rent due as usual, or I'll have you in the gutter."

I grit my teeth at the odious man's words but took the money he was due from my apron pocket and thrust it in his hands. "Every *sou*, on time, as has been the case since Monsieur

Fournier took tenancy," I said. "You know as well as I that Monsieur Fournier has been a model resident of your property for years and I will be the same. I also know you enjoy feeling affronted, Monsieur Thébault. I truly hope the tenants in your other buildings are better able to oblige you."

He shook his head in disdain and left the building without a parting word.

I looked around the kitchens, larger than ours upstairs by a wide margin, and continued my attack on the floors with the ancient mop. When they were passable, I went upstairs to collect a few rags and a bucket of hot, soapy water to take my assault to the rest of the surfaces in the shop. Within three hours, it looked like something resembling a respectable place of business.

And all the while, Gaspard's ring sparkled upstairs in a drawer, useful only as protection against hard times.

But as the fangs and claws of winter approached, I began to wonder if it might be better to make some plans before they were made for us by the capricious hand of fate.

Chapter Seventeen

LISETTE

OCTOBER 8, 1870

A bakery?" Pierrine asked, hands on her hips and looking dubious.

"A bakery," I confirmed. "There isn't one right in the neighborhood, and it will make things a little easier for the people living here. A shorter walk for their bread will mean more time for paid work or rest."

Near the Place Royale, bakeries were plentiful. Almost one on every corner it seemed. Montmartre had its share as well, but they were scattered about and not always as reliable as those in the *beaux quartiers*.

"It will be a good thing for the families here," Sébas agreed. "An extra twenty-minute respite isn't nothing. I think you'll do well."

"It's backbreaking work," Théo argued. "But given that

things are in such disarray, getting you licensed will be a simpler matter than usual."

"I make no claims that this will be a grand enterprise," I said. "I'll only sell bread at first. Long *flûtes* that bake quickly. Some *pain de campagne*. Perhaps twenty loaves a day to start with the hope of expanding to fifty in time."

"Best to start small," Sébas agreed. "You can expand as you get a handle on how to run a business."

"Hopefully you can stick it out," Pierrine added. Her tone implied that she was highly doubtful of that outcome.

"You think I'll tire of it," I said. "But I want to give it a try. I won't gouge the people like some of the others do, trying to work their way around the pricing laws. Fair prices and good bread."

"Well, if you manage to make it work, it will be a good thing for the people, and I can give no business venture higher praise than that," Sébas said.

"And we own our home, thanks to you," Théo said, wrapping an arm around me. "That won't change, no matter what happens with the bakery. Have you thought of what to call it? Boulangerie d'Amboise after the man who footed the bill?"

I'd gone with Théo into one of the finer quarters of town to ensure Gaspard's ring fetched a fair price, which it did. The emerald was of exquisite quality, and the circlet of small diamonds was flawless. I hadn't expected d'Amboise to skimp on such a gesture—not one so visible to the outside world—but I hadn't expected such extravagance. The bauble was as useless to me as a woolen overcoat in the Sahara, so I had no regrets about letting it go.

"Haha," I said, jostling him with my elbow. "But it's not a bad thought. What about Boulangerie Le Bijou? His ring did cover the bill, after all."

Théo laughed. "The only gem in this place is you, but it has a nice sound to it. You can use what's left of your windfall to have a sign made, among other things."

"Flour, yeast, eggs, sugar . . ." I said. "And we should paint the outside a lovely shade of green to match the ring that bought the place."

"The ingredients may prove more costly than the building," Pierrine said. "Especially with the Prussians still choking us off. And you'll soon learn that the millers who supply your flour are closer to bandits than proper merchants."

"We'll find a way," I said. "Paris has seen harsh winters before. We'll get through this."

"We will," Théo said, though I knew he wasn't as optimistic about my success as I was.

"Good luck," Pierrine said with a wave as she crossed to the door. "You're going to need it."

Sébas rolled his eyes and followed her out to the street.

"You'll get used to her," Théo said, claiming a broom that rested against the wall and sweeping the area near where he stood. "She isn't the bad sort. She's just had a hard life. Harder than most."

"Oh?" I asked, wiping down the counters with a wet rag.

"I grew up with her. Sébas and I both did. She married well. Far above her station. Her parents were so proud. Spent all they had to give her a proper wedding and all. As soon as she gave the bastard a son, he cast her out. He thought women from the slums were hardier and would produce stronger children, but he didn't want the boy to grow up under the shadow of such a low-born mother. He's made up stories about how the child's mother was the daughter of a British duke and died in childbirth. Pierrine has been erased from the picture altogether and she has to make her own way."

"That's awful! He can really do such a thing?"

"Nothing easier for a rich man to do than cast off an unwanted wife. He had money and friends enough, no one said a word. The only thing worse he could have done was to have had her locked away in the Salpêtrière with the other unwanted women of Paris. He spared her that, but she has few ways to make a living. She's had to resort to the worst of it."

I gasped with understanding. "Couldn't she find less—disagreeable—ways to make her way?"

"None that pays so well. She's clinging to the hope she'll be able to persuade the courts to give the boy back, but that's almost impossible. Unless the boy's father and all his blood relations die, she has almost no claim on him."

"How brutally unfair," I said.

"It is," he agreed. "So just remember, you represent the class she hates. The class that used her like a brood mare and set her out to pasture. Try to be understanding."

"She deserves that and more," I said. "I wish I could help."

"We all do," Théo said. "But the situation seems rather hopeless. None of us has the means to do much. And she's proud. She wouldn't accept help if we offered it, most times."

"Sébas gave me similar advice," I said. "But he was talking about the neighborhood at large."

"He's a wise man, though I'd never tell him so to his face. No one likes to feel like the object of pity. You'd do well to heed the warning."

"I will," I said. "But if I can be of use, I want to try."

Théo wrapped an arm around me and pressed a kiss to my temple. "I know you do. It's one of the things I love best about you. I have to get along to my duties. Don't work too hard."

"I assure you, I will," I said with a wink. He shook his head and went out onto the cobblestone street, leaving me behind in the empty shell of a building I hoped to transform into a thriving neighborhood hub.

I stopped to survey the progress we'd made. It would take another few days of elbow grease to make the shop presentable, but where others might see dirt that needed to be scrubbed away and scarred counters that needed to be polished, I chose, whether bravely or foolishly, to see potential.

BRIOCHE: THÉO'S MOTHER'S RECIPE

➤➤◄◄

For all my mother's training, I was not prepared for the elements of married life that women of other stations become expert in as soon as they can walk and take orders. I worry my husband will never eat properly again so long as I am mistress of our kitchens. Today I attempted to make *brioche* for Théo using his beloved mother's recipe. The way he waxed poetic about her *brioche*, I thought it would please him to have this taste of home in the midst of all the turmoil that surrounds us. I realize now I should have started with something less dear to him. Mercifully, he didn't break a tooth. My only consolation now is that his expectations are lowered and any efforts I make in the future will be an improvement. I'd never had occasion to make *brioche* with Nanette, and this has been a lesson in humility.

Soften a half pound of butter. Crumble a quarter ounce yeast cake and stir in one tablespoon warm water. In another bowl, stir one tablespoon sugar and a pinch of salt into two tablespoons cold milk. Sift a half pound of bread flour and make a well in the center. Add yeast mixture and one lightly beaten egg. After working in a little flour, add the sugar and salt mixture, add in another beaten egg. Work the dough until smooth and stretches easily. Mix a third of the dough with the softened butter, then the second, and finally the remaining dough to the mixture.

Put the dough in a large bowl, cover with cloth, and let rise in a warm place until it has doubled in volume. Separate the dough into three pieces, knead lightly, and let rise again. Let rest in a cool place for a few hours. Shape and bake.

Recipe notes: Knead less, handle dough more gently, and bake about half as long.

Chapter Eighteen

MICHELINE

The rain in Paris is a remarkable thing. It can be light and refreshing, a gentle mist to wash away the dirt and grime of the city. Other times, the world turns gray and the rain, more ice than water, chills the very marrow of your bones. It's the sort of day for *soupe à l'oignon,* piping hot coffee with thick cream, and *brioche* laden with preserves or drizzled in chocolate. Maman's *brioche* was better than any I'd sampled from any bakery, but I'd never mastered it on my own.

Maman assured me it had taken her a while to master it herself and she had promised to walk me through it until I perfected it, but first the war cut off such dear ingredients, and then she went missing. Another part of her legacy that would be forgotten. I wondered if Sylvie and Noémie even remembered the taste of her *brioche.* Like the scent of her perfume and the softness of her touch, it was fading from our memories more and more with each passing day.

In the beginning, the girls and I would tell stories about what we wanted to do first when Maman came home. Noémie wanted to sit in her lap and have Maman read from the tattered collection of fairy tales they so loved. Sylvie wanted to spend a day wandering hand in hand with Maman in the various parks in town, dotted with stops at cafés for treats and a cup of *chocolat*. I had wanted, more than anything, to learn her recipe for *brioche* and to enjoy a thick slab of it, lightly toasted, with my homemade lemon curd and a cup of tea. We each had the little things that reminded us of Maman, and her *brioche* was mine.

The girls were at school, and it was a day off from the academy. One of the days I reserved for practicing in the kitchen in hopes of finally achieving a measure of success under Rossignol's watchful eye, though with each passing day I grew more convinced of my complete incompetence in the kitchen when the man was present. I decided to see what Lisette had to say about *brioche*, so I looked through her recipe book, flipping through the pages until there was a mention of it. Certainly, someone with her background would have tackled this kitchen staple with some aplomb, though after reading her entry on the topic, I was reassured that I was not alone in my struggles with the fussy recipe. I read over her recipe a few times and decided I ought to try her version before I fussed with something from Carême or the *Larousse Gastronomique*.

I realized I was short on eggs and would need to go to the market before I could bake. I dreaded going outside in the frigid sleet, but knew I'd be glad for more practice in the kitchen. There was a little épicerie a few blocks away. It was scarcely more spacious than a broom closet, but was always

well stocked, orderly, and run by a good man who always
tried to maintain fair prices even when things had been at their
worst. I was drenched by the time I reached the shop, despite
my raincoat and umbrella, and lost no time finding the eggs,
butter, and a few other necessities. I was glad I wasn't in need
of flour, for a five-pound bag of flour would have been a ten-
pound glob of paste in the bottom of my marketing basket by
the time I returned home.

Now laden down with my supplies, I turned to walk back
home. I considered whether fighting the wind for possession
of my umbrella was worth the struggle, but decided that if it
spared me a few drops, I ought to at least try. The rain had
picked up, and within a block, I was wet through to the skin. I
was about to break into a run and pray I wouldn't slip on the
slick cobblestones when I heard a smart rapping on the window
of the up-and-coming café I passed.

I turned to see Elodie Firmin, a classmate of mine, wave from
the window and then dash to the door.

"Micheline Chartier!" she exclaimed. "Come inside until the
storm passes. You'll catch your death."

"I need to be getting back . . ." I started.

"Nonsense. The old merry band from school is all here.
Come have a bite with us."

I calculated the pocket money I had left in my pocketbook.
Precious little. I didn't take a *centime* more from Madame Dupuis
than I absolutely had to. Any extra expense felt like I was mis-
spending charity money, though she'd be affronted if she knew
I thought that way. I could afford a coffee and a quarter of an
hour to allow the rain to abate, though I'd lament every *sou* spent

and have to keep myself from glancing at the hands of Maman's watch every few minutes.

Elodie was joined by Françoise Perrin and Anne-Sophie Martin, the group of girls I'd lunched with at school. We'd earned our baccalaureates in May two years before and Maman had disappeared in June. We'd all had grand plans for our futures, defying the reality of the world we were inheriting, and could not be persuaded of our folly. Elodie and Sophie were waiting for their beaux to return from fighting with the British, while Françoise, the most bookish of us, planned to study at the Sorbonne. My plans had been more modest, as I didn't have a beau returning to me, and while a university program was appealing, I was hesitant to suggest it to Maman in case it would be too great a strain on our resources. I knew we needed me to earn an income but had hoped there might be a way for me to take a course or two while I worked.

But all those plans of mine were long gone.

I'd left my umbrella in the canister by the door and my coat on the rack, but I was so wet I'd left a puddle in my wake. The waiter who approached our group looked at me as if I were a stray dog who had wandered in from the street.

"Just a coffee," I said to him as I pulled out the chair next to Elodie's. The waiter walked off looking as though I'd sent him to the depths of South America to collect the beans himself.

The girls had circled around two of the tiny café tables, both of which were laden with food. An early lunch from the looks of it. Salad greens, soups, a small beefsteak, fried potatoes, some sort of chicken-in-pastry dish, all languished half-eaten as the girls reminisced. My stomach gave a rumble, despite having had a good breakfast, and I hoped none of them heard.

"Oh, it's just absolute serendipity that you crossed by here," Elodie said as I took my place.

"Or a likely coincidence since I live two blocks north of here," I said, trying to keep the sarcasm from my tone. She was given to flights of fancy and a dash of the poetic that could sometimes become grating. Françoise shot me a knowing glance as she sipped from her coffee cup.

"We've been chatting about you nonstop since we got here, haven't we, girls?" Elodie continued as if she hadn't heard my little barb.

Anne-Sophie nodded enthusiastically. "We've missed you terribly. It just hasn't been the same without you."

I almost blurted out that they knew where to find me. That they would have been welcome to come chat over coffee in my kitchen any afternoon they liked. They could have knocked on my door to go for a stroll on the butte like we'd done so many times in the past. There were a million things we could have done, but they hadn't expended the effort, though all of them were in better situations to reach out than I was. But as was so often the case with unfortunate circumstances like mine, people inadvertently shy away from those affected. As if my mother's disappearance was a resurgence of the Spanish flu and was somehow catching.

"You always were the sweetest thing," I finally managed to say.

Anne-Sophie beamed.

"How have you been getting along?" Françoise asked. She

didn't name the elephant in the room, but at least acknowledged its presence.

"Fine," I said. I was glad it was the truth. As hard as it was,
I *did* feel as though I was learning to make my way in a world
that didn't fully make sense. I was probably making more mistakes raising the girls than I would ever dare to admit, but I had
to hope they were getting fewer as time went on. "The girls are
growing too fast, as you might expect. But it's . . . fine."

"We're so glad to hear that," Elodie chimed in. "Such a
horrible thing to have happen. Your mother was the kindest
woman in the whole neighborhood."

Anne-Sophie had lost her father and Françoise a brother, but
neither had endured the loss of both parents.

"I'm still searching," I said, bristling at the use of the past
tense. The registry office might have given up, but I had not.
"I'm confident they'll uncover where she is before long."

The girls looked at me with a mixture of disbelief and pity.

"Living people are harder to find than dead ones," I pointed
out. "Living people move about. Dead ones can be counted
on to stay where they are."

It seemed like sound logic to me, though no one else seemed
to agree with it.

Françoise cleared her throat. "Micheline, do you truly think
that the authorities will be able to find her if they haven't already?"

"I do," I snapped. "I have to."

Françoise looked as though she wanted to argue the point
but, wisely, stayed silent. The subject moved to Elodie's impending nuptials. Anne-Sophie's recent ones—and the little

arrival expected to come before the end of the year, paired with a good-natured joke about the timing of the cart and the horse. Françoise glowed about her studies and seemed just as happy as the other two. She'd decided to specialize in classics and was thrilled to be up to her ears in Latin and Greek.

They had the futures I'd hoped for them, and I was delighted they found their happinesses. That they'd had the luxury of figuring out what they wanted. That they had the freedom to pursue it. Truly, these were kind, good girls who deserved better than having their adolescence marred by war and it was wonderful to see them doing so well. But even the best, most noble part of my soul wasn't able to curb the pang of jealousy that bored into my gut like a blade.

After my quarter hour was up, I excused myself with the excuse that I needed to return home with my groceries. The girls seemed sad for me to go but hopped back into their cheerful chatter when I was a few paces from the table. I handed some coins to the much put-upon waiter and reclaimed my coat and umbrella. The rain was letting up and the rest of the walk was far better for having stopped.

I considered going upstairs to take a hot bath, but decided I'd do better to start the *brioche* so it would have time to rise and bake before the girls came home. I opened Grand-mère Lisette's journal and turned to the page where she lamented her poor skills with *brioche*. Though she wrote the words more than seventy-five years before, I felt an affinity to her that I hadn't felt to anyone since Maman went away.

I lost myself in butter, yeast, sugar, and flour. Following Lisette's instructions and forgetting Rossignol's barking orders and the pressures of the Academy to become the next Carême. The dough came together as though it were fit for a textbook on pastry making.

Why was it my attempts in class were such utter failures?

It didn't seem like much time before I pulled the warm, perfectly golden-brown *brioche* from the oven. I sliced it to find the interior was dense and rich, just as it should be. I lightly toasted three pieces, slathered them with lemon curd I'd made myself the week before, and began boiling water for a good cup of bergamot tea.

"I'm starving!" Noémie said by way of greeting as she burst through the bistro's kitchen doors just as the tea was finished steeping.

I smiled, glad she'd been spared the reality of that particular sensation. All of us, even Sylvie as young as she was, would have given up their rations for Noémie. I had done as much, more than once, putting my helpings on the girls' plates when Maman wasn't looking.

"Help me take this upstairs," I said, kissing her on the cheek. "We can be refined ladies and take afternoon tea in the parlor."

"We have a parlor?" Sylvie asked, more than a bit churlish as she plunked her stack of books on the counter.

"What would you call the area where we keep the sofa?" I said, planting a kiss on her cheek before she was able to dodge me.

"The two-meter gap between the kitchen and the bedrooms," she replied, sticking her tongue out.

"It has a sofa and end tables, doesn't it?" I asked, thrusting a small platter with the *brioche* in her hands and three small plates in Noémie's. I gestured for them to go up the stairs and followed with the tea.

The girls sat on the sofa looking eagerly at the *brioche*. I served them each one of the lemon-curd coated slices with a flourish and a cup of the bergamot tea. Two lumps of sugar for Noémie, a splash of cream for Sylvie, neither for me. Each took their plates and took their first bites with less decorum than I might have liked, but an enthusiasm that fueled my pride.

"It's so good," Noémie declared before she'd bothered to swallow.

"Just like Maman's," Sylvie said before taking a second bite.

Just like Maman's. Beautiful words. Painful ones.

I had no idea if I'd be able to replicate the recipe for Rossignol. No idea if I truly had the skill or the desire to run a bakery, even if it was the only of my meager choices that would offer the girls a good life. I had no idea if I was doing right by the girls.

If they saw how hard it was to be mother and father to them sometimes.

But right then, as they sat devouring the *brioche* with unvarnished glee, I could enjoy one of the moments where it wasn't hard at all.

Chapter Nineteen

LISETTE

DECEMBER 18, 1870

The storeroom was a cheerful, well-ordered space, though in the past two months that was by virtue of being mostly empty. I looked into my reserves of flour, hoping to find it magically replenished, but found the pile of remaining flour so meager I nearly had to climb in the wooden bin to scrape out the contents I needed. I'd be able to make a few more loaves today, but nothing like what I needed to fill the need in the neighborhood.

We'd been told to ration our customers, which I could understand, but I wasn't sure what to do when there was nothing left to ration.

People had come to depend on Le Bijou, and to disappoint them grated at my very soul. But as a poet was of little use without ink, so a baker was of little use without flour. The Prussians had sealed us off, and there was precious little to be done for the rumbling bellies of Paris.

Defeated, I stood in the little courtyard on the east side of Le Bijou and swept the cobblestones clean from the dust that had accumulated overnight. I pulled my shawl tighter against the bracing winter air and watched as my warm breath danced away on the wind. It was too cold for people to take their meals and refreshments out of doors, so the three small round tables and featherlight rattan café chairs we had for diners were packed away in the cellar to protect them from the weather.

It was early yet, and though I was ready for my onslaught of early morning customers, few had come. As the Prussian siege continued relentlessly, fewer and fewer of my patrons had gainful work that roused them out of bed with the sun. Fewer and fewer had the coin necessary for their daily bread. And simply, there were fewer and fewer of us. The artillery fire took some, starvation took the rest. Théo and I were growing leaner with each passing day.

Théo had left for his duties before dawn, and I was surprised to see him approaching just two hours after he'd left.

"Home already?" I said, kissing his cheek. "Let me get you a bit of bread and some jam for breakfast."

Most mornings, he left without breakfast. I usually skipped it, thinking that if he had to work on an empty stomach, I should be strong enough to do the same. I'd take one of the loaves from the stock, even though it meant a customer would go without.

Théo returned the kiss, then swept me up in his arms and buried his face in my hair. "No time, my love. I had business nearby and was hoping for the chance to see your lovely face for just a moment."

There was a tremor in his voice that only a wife would recognize.

"What's wrong, dearest?" I pulled away so I could read his face, but his eyes remained downcast.

"We had a complaint about a foul smell coming from an apartment and were asked to come investigate. We found Monsieur DuQuay . . ." His breath rattled as he struggled to remain master of himself. "There wasn't a scrap of food anywhere to be found. He just faded away."

He wasn't the only one slowly starving, and it would become worse if I could not at least provide bread for the neighborhood. Living without meat was a hardship. Living without bread was an impossibility.

"He was a good man," I said, stemming my tears for Théo's sake, though they begged to be released in a torrent. The old man had been a favorite of Théo's, and he was sure to feel this loss particularly keenly.

"He deserved a better end," Théo said, clearing the emotion from his voice. "I must be going, but I needed to hold you just a moment before I face the rest of the day."

I pulled him in for another embrace, then forced him to wait just a moment as I fetched a portion of bread for him to take along. "This is for *you*," I insisted. "You will be of no use to this neighborhood if you make the same end as that dear old man."

He nodded and hurried off down the cobblestoned streets, back to the duty at hand. And as soon as he crossed paths with a hungry mouth, the paltry breakfast would be dispensed with.

How many paces would that take? A few hundred, if we were lucky. I grabbed my broom and returned to the courtyard to finish my sweeping.

I thought of the kindly man, who always doffed his cap when he passed me in the street. The last time I remembered seeing him was two weeks before when I had been sweeping the courtyard just as I was then.

"Good morning, Monsieur DuQuay," I called, recognizing the familiar figure of the affable widower who lived up the road. He took his constitutional each morning as faithfully as Sébas attended mass.

He nodded to me but did not offer me a cheerful greeting as he usually did. He was usually accompanied by his faithful liver-and-white spaniel, Maximus, but this morning grief took its place by Monsieur DuQuay's side instead of the beloved companion.

The dog wasn't old, having been a gift from a neighbor with a litter of pups shortly after Madame DuQuay's death a few years before. Théo told me the old man had scoffed at the gift at first, but slowly he'd come to find some solace in the dog's companionship until they'd become inseparable.

It could have been sickness. Goodness knew that dogs younger than Maximus had died from inexplicable illnesses all the time. It could have been an accident with a cart and horse, but Maximus was always tethered on a leash out of doors. But I knew in my heart it was desperation.

At first it was the horses. The old, sturdy carthorses of the shopkeepers were first to go to the slaughter, then it was the gleaming thoroughbreds of the upper class. Those who hadn't fled the city like fleas off a dog doused in lye soap. Now, where once the streets of Montmartre had been abundant with cats and dogs, both friendly and feral, they had become scarce.

Beloved pets like Maximus had been sacrificed to keep their masters from starving. Which was, I reflected, perhaps a kinder end for them than starving to death themselves while their owners watched, helpless to do anything for them.

For a week, Monsieur DuQuay made his morning constitutional up and down the street alone, only nodding at my greetings.

And then I stopped seeing him altogether.

And more would fall. Especially if I wasn't able to find flour.

"Dreaming of your ivory tower, Princess?" A voice, dripping with disdain, snapped me from my reverie.

I turned to see Pierrine coming along the road from the west. She wasn't usually out of a morning, but perhaps one of her—clients—had kept her occupied all night.

"Hardly," I said, wishing I could avoid the encounter with the surly woman altogether. But in a sense, she wasn't wrong. I thought of our summers in Normandy where the wheat fields seemed to go on forever. I thought of the fifty-pound bags of flour in the storeroom at Maman and Papa's house, and how I'd taken them for granted, and would have given anything for that abundance again.

"More practical worries at the moment. Like how to get flour when the whole blasted city is sealed off like a leaky water pipe."

Pierrine's expression shifted from accusative to pensive in a beat. "You and the rest of the city to boot," she said.

"The suppliers have next to none," I said. "Not for any price."

"There are always ways," Pierrine said. She took me by the elbow and tucked me inside. "If you're willing to play a little fast and loose with the law, I might be able to help."

I thought about that a moment. Nanette had always impressed the importance of following rules and being a model citizen, but if ever there was a time to loosen my grip on my moral code, this might well be it. "What do you have in mind?" I asked.

"I know someone," she said. "Someone who might be able to get you what you need."

"Fine," I said. The black market was becoming bolder and bolder, not quite advertising their services, but coming closer than they had dared to before.

On a given day, I would go through two hundred pounds of flour, which was just enough to bake enough simple country loaves. There were no pastries or cakes yet, which were not missed, for the prose of bread was needed far more than the poetry of fine layered pastries with English cream.

"Lock up shop and bring your coin purse, Princess. And leave everything else of value behind if you want to keep it," she said. She looked me up and down, appraising. She eyed the dust from the storeroom on my front. "Put on a fresh apron if you have it. You want to look poor, but not desperate."

I complied. My green dress was beginning to show signs of wear, and no one would confuse me with a woman of means, but I had three aprons and was always able to keep one clean enough to be presentable. I'd never flipped the sign to "Open," so all I had to do was latch the door. So many businesses were shuttering these days, no one would notice mine.

She nodded her approval, and once again, I found myself trailing her down the endless maze of streets that made up our corner of the city.

Ten minutes later, she knocked at a door which was opened by a squat man with rotting teeth.

"Ah, Pierrine," he said, his expression knowing. "Always a pleasure to see you, love."

"And you too, Horace," she purred. Her voice had gone up two octaves and everything about her seemed *softer*.

"You know how much I enjoy your company, my dear, but I'm afraid I'm too busy today to enjoy your charms properly. Do you think you could come back another time?"

"Oh, you rapscallion," she said, a blush actually rising on her cheeks. She leaned closer to him. "I didn't come about that, though you know I'm always happy to 'keep you company' as it were. I came here to introduce you to my friend Lisette here. Lisette, this is Monsieur Horace Mercier, a man of many resources."

He looked me up and down, no doubt finding my attire a bit dowdy for one in Pierrine's profession.

"Oh, a redhead is always a treat," he said. "But if I haven't the time for you, dearest, I haven't the time to make the acquaintance of your charming companion, now have I?"

"She's not . . ." Pierrine winked. "She's looking for someone to supply her with flour for her bakery since the more 'official channels' have dried up."

"Oh well, then. That I can see to. Step inside, lovely ladies, step inside."

Pierrine glanced back at me, her girlish façade slipping in favor of a grimace for my benefit for the briefest of moments.

He led us to a room in a cellar that was stockpiled with goods of every description including a whole wall of fifty-pound bags of flour.

"A baker, are you?" he asked. He took one of my hands in his and inspected it. I fought the urge to pull it back, but Pierrine shot me a warning look. "New to the trade by the looks of it. You ought to consider your friend's line of work. A lot less strenuous for a lot more pay."

"I don't think my husband would approve," I said, taking a step back once he released my hand.

"Husband? More's the pity," he said. "Never mind then. But yes, flour I can get you, dear lady. How much do you require?"

"Two hundred pounds a day, every day except Sunday," I said. "But if you can't manage it, I'll take what you can get if the price is right."

"Two hundred pounds a day is a tall order," he said. "But I think I can manage it for one as lovely as you."

"How much?" I asked, feeling the air in the room becoming oppressive. I wanted to run from the foul place, but I needed this man's help too much.

"Forty francs a day," he said. "A special bargain since you're friends of the lovely Pierrine."

"That's more than twice what I paid from my usual supplier." I did the math in my head. With the rules on pricing, I'd scarcely break even on each loaf.

"And for the others I charge sixty francs," he said. "And I promise you, madame, that no one else in the black market will be able to make you such a deal. They're extorting people. Eighty francs or more for the same amount of flour. It's positively criminal."

"And your prices are not?" I asked, finding some courage.

"I'm merely reacting to the conditions of the market, madame. I'm a businessman, not a saint."

"I'll say that," I said, crossing my arms over my chest. It was tantamount to robbery, but I saw no other choice.

"It's up to you. Just say the word and I can have two hundred pounds delivered to you every evening so you're prepared for your morning's travails, or you can take your chances elsewhere."

I looked to Pierrine who simply gave me an impassive look. This wasn't her problem; she'd merely offered me one solution to it.

"Very well," I said, opening my purse and looking to fish out the bills. Hopefully the siege would end, and I'd not need to rely on the thief for too long. "One week. If I need you longer, I'll let you know."

"Of course, of course," he said. "Put your money away, dear. I'll collect payment later. Expect my men there at dark."

Naturally, after dark. An operation like this couldn't operate in the daylight.

Pierrine and I exited back onto the street, and I felt the knots unfurl in my gut. Most, but not all of them.

"Why do I feel like I've just sold my soul to the very devil?" I asked to no one in particular.

"Trust me, if you don't repay him, he'll be worse than three devils to you," she said. "But it's better than starving."

I thought of old Monsieur DuQuay and couldn't argue.

"Just do me one favor and don't tell Théo where the flour came from, will you? The National Guard doesn't think too fondly of the black market. They don't have to be as pragmatic as the rest of us. They have the luxury of having ideals."

"Sacred, I assure you," I said. I couldn't admit to Théo what I'd done. Even if it was for the good of the neighborhood, the shame would be too great.

Pierrine left me with a mock curtsy at the corner of rue Norvins, and I continued to the shop. Normally at seven in the morning, there would be a queue formed and anxious if I'd left the shop closed. It was closer to eight now, and there was only one customer waiting. She bought one of my last *pains de campagne* and she had to count out every last *sou* to do it.

I wished I could have tucked a little jar of preserves or a slab of butter in her basket, but our own stores were dangerously low too.

It wasn't long before my shelves were bare, and I had to close the shop for the day. A restlessness settled over me. A common enough sensation for one like me who always yearned to be active, but never before did it seem to seep into my soul so profoundly. People were starving and I could do nothing to feed them. And entangling myself with Monsieur Mercier only made my nerves even more raw than circumstances already had them.

I scrubbed, swept, and tidied every nook and cranny of the shop and our apartment, but even after every surface gleamed like the polished marble floors of Versailles, I didn't find a sense of peace or calm.

But later that evening, not long before Théo came home for the night, and Mercier's men delivered four massive sacks of flour to load into the bins, I could take some solace in the knowledge that at least for tomorrow, there would be bread for a few more mouths in our little corner of Paris.

Chapter Twenty

MICHELINE

I stood at my station next to Laurent and focused on the gentle, almost imperceptible ticking of my mother's watch on my wrist. Tick. Tick. Tick.

I'm here. All is well.

I let the thought wash over me like warm, perfumed bath water. I could smell it. Jasmine. Maman's favorite scent.

I'm here. All is well.

It was the third week of class, and I had succeeded only in climbing toward the middle of the class. Just above reprisal from Chef Rossignol, but below his notice. Laurent was faring better. His breads had earned praise more than once, which was an unequivocal badge of honor among the students.

Today was *brioche*. I read Grand-mère Lisette's recipe backward and forward until I memorized it. It hadn't been her most successful recipe, as indicated by various notes she made in the margins. But she'd tried it over and over again, and finally mastered it.

I could do the same.

I had Lisette's journal in my dress pocket. I wouldn't need to consult it, but it was good to have it as a talisman all the same.

The ingredients were already in place, the recipe neatly printed for each of us.

I picked it up, and as usual, it only provided ingredients and vague measurements. We were supposed to divine the rest ourselves and hope we made the mark. Rossignol's recipe, what there was of it, looked similar to Lisette's. Similar enough that I could ignore his and follow Lisette's.

As I heated the milk and dissolved the sugar, I didn't worry about how quickly the others were moving. I added the yeast and watched as it began to gently foam.

"Very good," I whispered as the mixture bubbled to life. "You're doing so well!"

I thought I felt Laurent's eyes glance over to me briefly, probably wondering if I'd run mad, but I ignored it. I whisked flour together with more sugar. Added eggs to the milk and then combined the two together.

As I took the dough in my hands, and kneaded it, I blocked out the sounds of the others clanging dishes and clattering whisks. None of it concerned me. Just the *brioche*.

I felt the hairs on my arm prickle as Rossignol approached. I knew he was watching me, scrutinizing every motion of my hand as I kneaded the dough. But it didn't concern me either. All that mattered was the *brioche*.

I could envision Noémie, sitting down to a thick slice of the sweet, eggy bread. Perhaps with a layer of strawberry jam and a glass of milk. I could see her face, framed with her scarlet ringlets, break into a smile. I could see her satisfied face with red jam in the corners of her mouth as she leaned back in her chair after she finished her after-school snack.

That was what concerned me. And nothing else.

Others milled about as they set their loaves aside to rise. Some paced as they baked.

The room filled with the wholesome fragrance of egg and sugar. I let myself focus on that, rather than giving in to nervous energy.

I pulled my *brioche* from the oven when it reached the perfect deep-golden color and set it at my station for Chef Rossignol to inspect.

He walked up to where I stood, this time not scowling or showing his disapproval. His face was impassive, but at least he didn't look predisposed to hate my work either. It was an improvement.

Rossignol sliced the end from the *brioche* and inspected the crumb and the consistency of the bread. He lifted it to his nose, sniffing before opening his mouth to take a bite.

He looked reflective as he chewed, as though considering the works of Voltaire and not my simple *brioche*.

"*Excellent travail,*" he said, and touched his fingers to the forehead of his brimless chef's hat.

The class collectively gasped. No one had received such praise before. None had expected to.

Laurent waited until we were out of view of our classmates,

then leaned over and brushed a kiss against my cheek. I resisted the urge to put my hand where his lips had been. He'd never taken such a liberty before and while my rational brain had reservations, my heart thudded against my rib cage with reckless joy. The simple kiss had been my first. There had been no time for boys, even if they had been in abundance. If I'd been born a decade earlier, I'd be in the thick of dating and going to parties with boys at the age of nineteen. Maybe even engaged or on the brink of it. But the war had stolen most of the boys my age, and the final years of my childhood along with them.

"You were a marvel," he said, whirling me around in the parking lot. It was the first time he'd held me so close, and I felt my heart thud against my rib cage with such force he must have felt it too. The weeks of car rides to and from the academy, the chats before and after class had created the rich soil from which a resplendent friendship might grow. Perhaps more. From the look that glinted in his eyes, I could tell he wanted more, but I hadn't dared to explore my heart for the answer for myself. Not yet.

"People were staring at you as you worked. I've never seen such determination in my life."

"I practiced," I said lamely. I didn't want to share the secret of Lisette's journal just then. Not to him. Not to Madame Dupuis. I wanted it to be mine alone for just a bit longer.

"Clearly," he said, drawing me closer again. I reveled in the tingling sensation as I enjoyed his nearness. "It's a half day. We should celebrate. Let's cook dinner for the girls together, I promised little Noémie her *clafoutis* after all."

I crashed back to reality. The girls. He had made a promise, and it would be wrong to keep him from honoring it. But spending time with Laurent felt like an indulgence. One I wasn't entitled to.

After years of privation, an indulgence, even one as small as spending time with a classmate, seemed like utter decadence.

And was twice as tempting as any of the confections we made in class.

"That sounds wonderful," I said. I hated to admit it to myself, but I always loathed the sight of him driving off in the afternoons after he dropped me off at home. I enjoyed the free-flowing conversation and his warm way of making people feel at ease. It was a gift that my papa once had, and one I sensed Sylvie would grow into in a few years. God help me.

"We've got plenty of time to do things up properly before the girls get home. It will be a nice surprise for them."

It would be. And to have a hand with the domestic task would feel like one small burden lifted for an evening. But it felt like a betrayal to Maman to think of my labors around the house with any sort of resentment. She'd kept our home immaculately and without complaint for years. I never once remembered her asking Papa for any sort of respite.

I could do the same.

But to have an evening with company and good food would be a healthy thing for the girls. And it wasn't as though Maman had never had a helping hand or moments of leisure.

We hurried to the butcher, where Laurent insisted on paying for a good-sized beef roast. I hadn't had beef since the earliest days of the war, and my stomach rumbled at the prospect. At the grocer's, we gathered potatoes, carrots, onion, leeks, and some fresh herbs to put together a proper *pot-au-feu* and black-berries for the *clafoutis*.

I reached for my billfold, but Laurent brushed my hand away. "Let me do this for you. Please? It would do my weary soul some good to do something for you."

There were volumes unspoken. He knew how hard it had been for me, providing for the girls and trying to give them some semblance of a childhood. He could well imagine the sac-rifices I'd made and the privations we'd endured. And while he couldn't make up for the last two years, he had the means to give us a small taste of what we'd missed.

And how glorious it was to feel, at least in some measure, like someone understood.

Chapter Twenty-One

LISETTE

DECEMBER 23, 1870

I flipped the sign to "Closed" as soon as I sold my last loaf. Given the scarcity of bread, people came from even the furthest *arrondissements* when they heard there were loaves to be had. Especially when they weren't black and coarse, made with whatever horrid substitute for flour could be found. I wasn't going to serve sawdust or dirt to people and charge them money for food that was worse than starving.

With five times the amount of flour and four assistants, I might have been able to meet the demand. It crushed me to turn away a single one of them, but even the great Monsieur Mercier could only procure so much flour, and I was only one woman with a small kitchen.

The coins and bills in the till were cold comfort. If there was no food to be had, it did little good to have even a vault full of cash.

The only security it provided was knowing I could pay off Mercier when the tab came due.

And I was able to tuck away the bread Théo and I would need each day. It was worth paying Mercier's exorbitant fees to send Théo off in the morning with at least a portion of good bread, even if there wasn't much to go with it.

As usual, Théo was off with his duties and I was faced with a day of watching forlorn, dirt-streaked faces peer in the windows, heartbroken to see the empty shelves.

I couldn't bear another day of it, so I bundled up against the bitter cold, hoping by some miracle I could find some meat or anything else that might be suitable for Christmas dinner.

I wandered the streets, almost aimlessly. I headed south toward the heart of town, back toward the neighborhoods I'd frequented as a girl. I looked up at the uniform limestone buildings, the color of fresh cream contrasted with their black wrought-iron balconies and mansard roofs of smelted zinc. Each of them predictable. The businesses on the ground level with a mezzanine. The wealthy on the second floor—the "noble story" with the highest ceilings, most elaborate windows, and largest balconies. The third and fourth floors were more modest apartments for successful tradesmen. Servants had to climb to the top floor on narrow staircases and slept in small rooms under the slope of the gabled roofs with tiny dormer windows to catch a glimpse of the city before they gave in to their exhaustion.

It was hard to think the jumble of buildings and the labyrinthine streets of Montmartre were all part of the same city. They seemed as similar as silk and homespun wool. While there was something comforting about the sameness of Haussmann's planned buildings and grand boulevards, it seemed much less "alive" than the vibrant bustle in the outer *arrondissements*.

And there, in a shop window, I saw the first fowl I'd seen in weeks. A few passersby gazed longingly at the goose who roosted in a box lined with straw in the window. Most of those who paused heaved a sigh of disappointment and moved on. I felt rooted to the spot, unable to look away from the bird who looked like he'd had far more to eat in the past month than the rest of us.

I entered the shop as there was almost no chance I'd be recognized from the time I lived nearby. I didn't think it was one Nanette or Marie ever frequented, nor was it among the few I visited on the day I took Marie's place.

"Excuse me, how much for the goose?" I asked.

He looked at my worn dress and tattered shawl and rolled his eyes.

"Excuse me?" I repeated.

With a heavy air of the dramatic, he breathed in and turned to me. "One hundred and twenty francs, madame. Shall I fetch him for you?"

It was a tremendous sum. Several weeks' worth of flour in good times. But these were hardly good times.

I thought of the time I tried to pay for groceries with a hundred-franc bill, having no concept of what a massive sum of money it was. I wished I'd spent the past few years ferreting away my pin money, but I'd never felt the necessity of being frugal. Part of me thought, at least in some way, that wealth was as intrinsic a part of my makeup as my red hair or my freckles. The sad truth was that had it not been for Nanette and her teachings, it might never have occurred to me to spare a thought for the less fortunate.

But now, I knew what it was to be hungry. Meal after meal of bread alone left me feeling faded and weak, though I tried to keep up a good ruse for Théo. But more than I begrudged the hunger, I begrudged the lack of dignity. The shopkeeper didn't even have the courtesy to treat me like a real person. To him, I was scum, unworthy of his attention, because he was certain I didn't have the means to buy the goods he sold. I felt the weight of the coins and bills in my pockets. There was enough. It would have given me such satisfaction to plunk the money down on his counter and force him to stammer an apology.

But I'd be sacrificing a week's flour money for the satisfaction of one meal. I'd be sentencing Théo and myself to starvation.

"Robbery," I said, and turned to leave the shop. The clerk just scoffed as I left. Though the prices were criminally exploitative, the man reacted as though I were quibbling over a few *sous* too much for a tin of coffee.

I fled back to the streets and wondered how long it would be before some wealthy family from one of the *beaux quartiers* would send a maid to purchase the goose for their Christmas dinner. A man like Papa wouldn't have hesitated to pay what the shopkeeper asked if it meant having a proper meal.

Nanette hadn't sent notes with Marie for me in over a week, though the cold winds and the artillery fire likely made any unnecessary ventures into town a foolish prospect. All the same, I worried and needed the reassurance of laying my own eyes on her. I hadn't seen Nanette in the months since I left to marry

Théo, and my feet led me back to the Place Royale almost involuntarily. What was more, it would give me something to do apart from lamenting the lack of supplies for the bakery and how I was letting down the people in the neighborhood.

The closer I got, the more familiar the buildings became. My breaths became deeper. My shoulders lowered. By the time I reached the periphery of the Place, I knew each cobblestone as well as I knew my own name. Most of the Place Royale was dark and shuttered, just as I expected. The inhabitants of these grand homes had fled ages ago. Many ensconced themselves in their lavish country homes when the troubles began with Prussia these long months ago. They had the luxury of sequestering away from the dangers of the siege while leaving the mere mortals in the city to their fate.

But one light blazed on. Papa and Maman's. Of course Papa was staying and keeping everyone else penned in. I knew he thought he was being valiant. Not showing weakness in the face of the enemy or some such. But he was just pampering his vanity. Putting on an act. For whom, I wasn't sure. The exiled emperor? Whomever would succeed him? Papa himself?

The latter seemed the most likely.

And while we all had indulged Papa's hubris when the Prussians were approaching, the truth was that they were here now, and the city was under siege. He should have taken Maman and the children out of the city while he could. They were just more people that would have to be protected when the city fell.

And fall it would.

It was time to turn back and get home to Théo and the butte, but I kept walking closer until I felt a hand grasp me at the elbow and yank me to the courtyard.

Marie.

"Get in here before they see you," she hissed, dragging me into the kitchen. I acquiesced, and almost fainted at the smell of the stew Nanette was preparing.

I wrapped my arms first around Marie, then Nanette.

"Well, well, the prodigal daughter," Nanette said, turning back to the simmering pot. "Let me guess. Things got hard out on that godforsaken hill to the north, and you regret your escapades and want to come home."

"No. It *is* hard, but that's more the fault of the Prussians than anything else," I said. "No. I just . . . I don't know why I'm here. I suppose I just missed you and Marie and . . ."

I trailed off, looking at the stove as Nanette stirred the massive pot.

"Rabbit stew," she said though I never raised the question. "Took some doing to find meat, but it won't be half bad."

"It smells like heaven," I said, wishing I could be more stoic about the pangs in my stomach. I'd have eaten the whole pot, one teaspoon at a time if given the chance. I kept my hands folded so Nanette wouldn't see them shake. I'd not been able to stop the trembling for the last week and it had come to be an impediment to my chores. I didn't know if it was due more to my hunger or my inability to sleep, but it mattered not as the conditions were certainly interrelated. I did my best to ignore it, but Nanette missed nothing.

Nanette ladled a portion into a bowl and thrust it in my

hands. "Eat," she said in a tone that commanded authority. She'd used it once when I was perhaps six years old and had been too ill to eat for three days. The doctors were flummoxed and told my parents to brace for the worst. Nanette would hear none of it and snuck to my rooms with broth at regular intervals. If it hadn't been for her, I doubt I'd have made it to my seventh birthday.

I sat at the kitchen table. I paused. Théo wouldn't have such a meal that night. I ought to refuse in solidarity. I ought to ask for a portion for him, though I knew Nanette would balk at the idea. Not to mention it wouldn't fare well after an hour's walk home. I felt the tremor in my hands and the pang in my gut. I wanted to assure Nanette I was fine and would eat at home, but the thought of a bowl of stew as a balm against the chill as I walked back to the butte was far too enticing for me.

"Eat," she commanded a second time. I half expected her to brandish a wooden spoon as a warning.

Unable to restrain myself, I ate with an abandon I hadn't experienced before. When I emptied the bowl, Nanette refilled it. When I saw the bottom of the second, I felt sated. I also felt greedy and piggish. Théo wouldn't eat that well tonight. I had been a selfish glutton and I hated myself for it. I'd give him my portion, though it was hardly enough to mention. I tried to will myself to have some restraint, but hunger had a siren song more alluring than any I'd ever dared to imagine. I was compelled like a drunkard to his wine, and I was just as helpless to stop.

"Just as I expected. That dandy National Guardsman of yours can't provide for you."

"That's horribly unfair, Nanette. There isn't food to be had in Paris for ready money and you know it. Not at fair prices," I said, thinking of the plump goose.

"That's the God's honest truth," she admitted. "Poor Marie spends more time trying to find ingredients than she does in the kitchen. She tells me you've been baking."

"Yes," I said. "When I can get the flour. It's small potatoes as far as bakeries go, but it helps feed the neighborhood. And I can practice what you taught me."

"Until a Prussian shell takes the whole damned place down," she said, cursing for the first time since I'd known her. "If this young man of yours had spirited you out of the city, I'd not have a word to say against him."

"My parents haven't left town. How would it be any different if I'd stayed?" I asked.

"Your parents and the children are leaving. Tonight, if the winds are favorable, they say." She angrily banged pots about as she tried to prepare dinner in the midst of her rage.

"What do you mean? How? The city is surrounded by Prussians and they're not letting anyone out. Bribes will get you shot, I hear."

"They're taking off in the middle of the night on some god-forsaken balloon."

"How in the name of all that's holy was Maman able to convince Papa to leave the Place Royale? He was determined to outlast the Prussians or die trying." I'd stopped eating and Nanette glared until I took a few more bites.

"Your sister had a fever and they nearly lost her. It frightened your mother enough that she threatened to leave, with or without your father. With his head on a pike in the middle of the Place Royale if that's what it took. Those were her very words."

The hairs rose on my neck at the thought of Gislène succumbing to illness. Such things were common enough in Montmartre, but the bony fingers of death weren't supposed to reach into the nursery rooms in the Place Royale. Little Gislène, the sweet little golden girl, had almost been a victim of the siege and of my father's intransigence.

Thank God Maman had finally stood up to him. Thank God she thought Gislène was worth it. I looked back to Nanette who was mopping her brow as she attended to the meal. She too looked stretched thin by the siege.

"What about you, Marie, and the others? What are you to do?"

"Fend for ourselves, I suppose," Nanette said. I felt my teeth grind to the point I felt the fine grit of enamel on my tongue. Of course they'd made no provisions for the staff. Théo's diatribes against the wealthy were proven right once more and I hated that my family seemed just as inclined to avarice as the rest of their class.

Nanette banged her spoon against the copper pot forcefully. "They can't spare space in the balloons for the likes of us. Not that you could get me in one. I'd sooner face the Prussians armed with naught but my meat cleaver. They'd get me in the end, but I'd take a few with me, make no mistake."

"I know you would, Nanette," I said, smiling at the image of the valiant woman guarding the kitchens and striking fear in the hearts of the Prussians. "But how will you manage?"

"Oh, don't you worry. I suspect your father hopes we'll stay and guard the house against marauders. If that's what he wants, he can pay the grocer bill for his private standing army when he returns. And I won't spare any expense. If it costs him half a million francs to keep us fed, so be it."

"As well he should pay it, but all of Papa's money won't help if there isn't food to be had."

"Well, we'll have to hope this cursed siege is over soon," she said. "It can't go on forever."

"The Prussians seem indefatigable," I said.

"But the Versaillais are not. Do you imagine that Gaspard d'Amboise your parents picked has much reserve left? They're all gentle born and soft. The Prussians are sturdy boys raised in forests and on farms. Not those fancy city lads and starving factory workers bullied into service. France will surrender soon enough."

"Shhh!" Marie cautioned, finally breaking into the conversation. "That talk is treasonous according to Monsieur Vigneau. He'll send you packing."

Nanette shook her head. "Treason indeed. Your father let poor Gustave go for saying less than that. Loyalty to an emperor without a throne."

"He fired Gustave?" I asked, incredulous. The man had served us as butler for almost twenty years. For a man who spoke so often of loyalty, my father wasn't too quick to show it to those who could garner him no favor.

"No notice. No character reference. Just showed him to the door like a maid who got too close to the heir to the family throne."

I shook my head. "And now they're leaving you all behind."

"Don't mind that. We'll be fine, Kitchen Mouse. It's you I worry about."

"Well, Théo and I can't afford places on a balloon like my parents. And even if we could, I don't think Théo would abandon his post. The people on the butte depend on the National Guard for safety and order."

"So let him stay—but save your own neck. Your parents would have you out of the city in a matter of hours. There isn't a person in that squalid neighborhood of yours who wouldn't take your place."

"But they don't have that choice, do they?" I asked. "They have no means of escape at all." Their faces all rushed into my memory in a blur. There were tall and squat, young and old. But none of them—nary a soul—had Papa's wealth or advantages.

"Which makes you all the more ungrateful for not taking yours while you can. You can play the penitent daughter, face your parents' wrath for a while, and save your skin."

I felt my shoulders sag with exhaustion as I tried to keep up my resolve. I was beginning to feel restored by the ample meal, but now the lack of sleep was causing the room to lose focus. "I can't abandon my husband." I wanted to speak with the conviction of my heart, but I found no force to put behind my words. Nanette pounced on it like a cat on an injured mouse.

"If he's alive when this is all over, you can spirit away back to him. If he finds the wrong end of a Prussian mortar, then you can take solace that it didn't take both of you."

I blanched at the idea of Montmartre in ruins and Théo lost

in the rubble. "Nanette, you can't possibly mean that. I love him."

"Oh, I do mean it. Once you have a child of your own, you'll understand. You'd accept tragedy a thousand times over if it meant sparing your child. And don't you dare cast it in my face that you aren't my blood and bone. You couldn't be more my own if I'd carved you from my own heart and you know it."

I stood and flung myself into Nanette's arms. For weeks and weeks I'd had to be strong. To show a brave face for Théo and to do my part. But with Nanette I was free to fall to pieces.

She pressed a kiss to my cheek, then held my face in her hands. "You'll go with them? Tonight? I'll have Marie sneak up and get one of your dresses and I can draw you up a hot bath to get the slums scrubbed off you. As aloof as your mother is, she may not have noticed you left."

Marie coughed.

"Very well, it's not all that likely, but they'll probably be so grateful to have you back in one piece, it might stave off the temper tantrum. Dinner is in an hour. You'll have time to make yourself presentable. Too thin, but there's nothing we can do for that now. A little rouge at the cheeks and lips to make you look a bit less drawn."

"Really?" I asked. She'd always been vehemently opposed to women enhancing their appearances with color, disdaining my mother's indulgence in the practice.

"I didn't say to paint you like a harlot. I mean to make you look robust and hardy when you see your parents again. You don't want to go before them looking like a common dust-woman."

"Nanette . . ." I started to protest. I'd vowed in front of Sébas, Marie, our whole neighborhood, and God himself to remain with Théo in sickness and in health. For better or for worse. Richer or poorer. We'd been tested more in the early days of our marriage than any couple ought to have been, but it was poor resolve to abandon him at the first test of courage.

I opened my mouth to tell her I had to leave. That venturing back to the Place Royale had been folly of the worst sort. She cut the words off before I could draw the breath to speak them.

"Dammit, child. You're skin and bones. You're starving. If you don't starve to death, you're going to get the grippe or consumption and fade away before winter's out. If I have ever meant a thing to you, you'll go with Marie and get ready. Don't let me live out the rest of my days with your death on my shoulders."

I wanted to protest, but I choked on my tears. I wanted to be strong. I wanted to stay for Théo.

But as I clung to Nanette, I realized I wasn't the woman I'd hoped I was.

I'd not looked at my reflection properly in months. Théo didn't have a mirror, and I rarely bothered with my little hand mirror. I hardly recognized myself as I sat at the vanity, dressed in the soft pink gown made in the most buttery silk I'd ever felt against my skin. The one Maman favored. I was scrubbed clean, dressed for a dinner with the empress herself, and Marie was silently styling my hair by candlelight so as not to alert my parents to my presence before dinner. Marie had clucked as she dressed me, noting how my ribs were visible through my taut skin and how my corset was loose against my frame. Marie had slipped into Maman's room while she was napping and procured a little pot of rouge to bring some brilliancy back to my complexion. My cheeks looked hollow, and my skin looked chalky, though improved by Marie's efforts.

I'd been wasting away for weeks, and I looked like a shadow of myself.

But now I was fed, clean, dressed in fine clothes, and laced with scent from the bottle of jasmine perfume I'd left behind.

Marie squeezed my shoulder and snuck out. Dinner would be in ten minutes, and I would make my appearance at the table as though I'd never left and hope for the best.

Maman and Papa had kept my room much the way I'd left it. They'd gone through the room looking for some clues to explain my departure but hadn't sold off my dresses or the trinkets I'd left behind. They were hopeful I'd return. They'd had people looking for me. They'd alerted the police. Nanette and Marie had kept my secret, and it was only for this they hadn't found me. But even with their silence, had it not been for the chaos of the siege, my parents likely would have found me by now.

But would their spies have recognized me? Would they have seen the privileged girl in the face of the humble baker? It was hard to imagine that they would have seen her in the tired gaze of the woman peddling bread.

I watched the hands of the little enameled clock on the vanity click-click-clicking away toward the appointed hour.

I thought of Théo. I wondered if he'd come home yet. I wondered if he was worried for me. Even more frantic than my parents had been. I thought of Sébas comforting him over too much wine, convincing him it was better I was away and safe. I imagined Pierrine telling him that she knew I'd run off one day. That I wasn't hard enough for life on the butte.

I hated that she was right.

I wanted to be strong enough to face the hardships ahead with Théo. The hunger, the threat of Prussian artillery.

But the thought of another night, willing sleep to come so I could ignore the gnawing pain in my gut was beyond what I could endure.

I was weak and I hated myself for it.

I looked at the clock again and knew I could no longer tarry.

The woman in the mirror looked back at me, and while she was better dressed and groomed, the tiredness still lingered in the green eyes. It would take more than sleep to alleviate it. More than a good meal. It was a weariness that went bone-deep.

I left my room and padded down to the dining room as I had done thousands of times in the years I lived there.

I could envision a dozen different reactions my parents might have to my return. Relief. Joy. Fury.

Indifference.

I stood at the door to the dining room, my hand on the door handle.

I didn't have the courage to return to Théo, but neither did I have the courage to walk through the door.

I could hear animated voices from within the room. They were leaving within hours. This would be the last meal they would take in this house, likely for months, if not longer. For Papa to leave this house, his beloved monument to his own successes, meant that he truly believed the Prussians would be victorious.

It must have cost him dearly to admit as much, but at least the children would be safe. Sweet Gislène and the little rascal Antoine deserved to be safe.

But so did everyone else in Paris.

There wasn't a person in the whole of the city who didn't deserve to sit down to a warm meal and to go to bed that night without fear of a Prussian shell destroying his home and cutting short his life.

There wasn't a soul in Paris—even old Jacquot or the fiend Mercier—who didn't deserve the chance to have a life where they didn't have to work themselves like plow horses simply to have their basic needs met.

That was what Théo was fighting for. It was the cause he'd taught me to believe in.

It was a cause worth fighting for.

Worth dying for.

And so was Théo. I'd made a vow to love him for the rest of my days, and I was not going to forsake him.

I removed my hand from the door handle and sprinted down to the kitchens. I didn't have time to change back into my simple linen dress, so I'd have to return home in the preposterous satin confection of a dress. I would look a fool but would appear less ridiculous than I felt.

Nanette looked up from the stove which she was giving its nightly scrub as I ran in, breathless. She shook her head, understanding what my presence meant.

"I'd never be able to live with myself. Even if I survived the winter, I'd die of guilt. You have to understand that."

Nanette averted her eyes back to the stove and her scrub brush. "I do. I wish I didn't, but I do."

I closed the gap between us and kissed her cheek. "Be safe, please. Don't do anything heroic to save this place, no matter what Papa might wish. Nothing matters as much as you do."

She nodded. "Same thing to you. Don't get yourself killed if you can help it, you wee idiot. There are cats aplenty out there, Kitchen Mouse, and none of them would mind making a meal of you."

"I know that all too well," I said. The months in Montmartre had taught me as much.

"And take your basket with you," she said, pointing her brush to the table where my marketing basket sat. I peered in to find it filled with food from the cellars. Onions, broth, potatoes, salted meat . . . it would feed us for a week if we were careful.

I blinked at her in confusion.

"I know you well enough, Kitchen Mouse. There was no way I could talk enough sense in you to leave with your parents. I can't do much for you, but I can at least do that. Now go before you get strangled on the bank of the Seine before you make it home."

I kissed her cheek and wrapped my tattered woolen shawl around my shoulders. It had to look asinine contrasted with the satin gown, but nothing mattered more than getting home. I hoisted the basket off the table, embracing both Nanette and Marie with one free arm before I rushed out into the night.

The hour it took to find my way back to Montmartre felt interminable, and Théo looked distraught as I crossed the threshold to our apartment.

He scooped me into his arms, and I could feel his ragged breath grow steady as he calmed himself. "My God, Lisette. I didn't know what to think. I thought I'd lost you. I've never been more frightened in my life."

He looked me up and down, arching a brow at the sight of my fine clothes and well-coiffed hair.

"I was lost," I said. "In a manner of speaking. But I'm home now. I'm sorry I worried you."

"You're safe, that's all that matters," he said, placing a kiss on my forehead. "And thank God for it."

"Let me make you something to eat," I said, thinking of the bounty Nanette had provided us.

I made him a hearty meal of onion soup, but had none for myself, still ashamed of my gluttony that afternoon. We prepared for bed knowing that we would at least not starve that Christmas.

We were far luckier than many.

That night, before turning in to bed, I looked out the window to look at the star-studded sky over Paris, scanning to see signs of the balloon that would carry my parents and siblings to safety. I saw a vague shape on the horizon, and couldn't be sure it was them, but blew a kiss, and with it all my wishes for a safe journey.

CLAFOUTIS AUX FRUITS

→>-<←

One of Nanette's favorite uses for small amounts of fruits on point of spoiling when the quantity isn't sufficient to make preserves. Especially well-suited for all sorts of berries.

Sprinkle half a cup of fruit-based liqueur (Nanette favors cherry brandies) over one pound of berries and leave them to soak for an hour or more. Combine one-half cup milk, one-half cup cream, and one spoonful of plain liqueur infused with vanilla. Remove from heat as soon as it begins to boil. Whisk four eggs and five ounces of sugar until creamy. Stir in two spoonfuls of flour until just smooth (lesson learned again: do not overmix). Slowly add the egg mixture to the hot cream (another lesson learned: if you do this too quickly, your eggs will scramble).

Place the fruit in the bottom of a buttered mold and spoon batter over the top. Cook in a medium oven for almost half an hour.

Best served warm with unhealthy quantities of Chantilly cream.

Recipe notes: Nanette usually prepared the dish with cherries. Experiment with currants, blackberries, or blueberries. Consider apricots and peaches. Experiment with marinating the fruits in rum, cognac, or Calvados.

Chapter Twenty-Two

MICHELINE

Cooking with Laurent felt as natural as breathing, especially at home and away from the pressures of the academy. We moved in harmony in the bistro's kitchen, chopping the vegetables and browning the meat. We put it in the oven and Laurent set to work on the *clafoutis*. I looked over Lisette's comments on the subject of *clafoutis* and found that she and Laurent agreed on much. It was a comforting thought.

"You've been cooking a long while," I said. It wasn't a question: he moved with a practiced efficiency that I envied.

"I have," he confirmed. "My mother taught me. I don't have sisters, and with a pack of younger brothers, Maman needed a hand in the kitchen. Papa scoffed at the idea of one of his boys in the kitchen at first, but Maman squelched it quick enough. She needed the help and I was a fair hand at it. It's come in handy more times than I can count. It helped me make friends when I served, that's for sure. A taste of home was always welcome."

"I'm sure it was," I said. "What was it like to serve?"

He grew somber. "Some things are best left unsaid. But suffice it to say, there was a lot more brutality than there was blackberry *clafoutis*."

"That I can only imagine too well," I said.

"We need more flour," he announced, ready to change the conversation.

"In the cellar," I said. My stomach lurched but I volunteered to fetch it. I wouldn't have him see me acting a fool.

I paused at the top of the stairs and forced some air into my lungs. I made my way down, scooped up a huge bin full of flour and ran back upstairs. I placed it on the counter next to Laurent and forced my heart to slow. I placed my hand over the face of Maman's watch and focused on the *tick-tick-tick* it made. Dependable. Even. I wasn't lying in a ball sobbing on the floor of the cellar. It was progress.

"You're white as a sheet," he said. "And shaking."

"I'm fine," I insisted. "I—I just hate the cellar."

Comprehension flooded his face. He wrapped an arm around me and pressed his lips to my temple. "We all have our cellars to contend with."

It was a simple truth. Anyone who survived the war had their scars. And as much as I struggled, I knew my burden was far less than many others. But sometimes, it was hard to be grateful.

Laurent didn't release me. He wrapped his other arm around me, and cradled my head against his shoulder. "You have been so strong for so long. You're doing an amazing job with Sylvie and Noémie. You're finding your stride in class. But it's okay to be weak sometimes. To let down your guard."

I melted into his embrace. I had been in need of this reassurance for so long.

We stood there for a long while. I loved the feel of his arms around me. I loved the smell of him . . . the masculine, earthy scent of his olive oil soap and the tang of his sweat from a day in the hot kitchens enmeshed with the feminine lilt of vanilla and caramelized sugar.

"I'm worried if I let down my guard, I'll have nothing left to cling to," I said.

"You have me," he whispered. "For as long as you want me."

He lowered his lips to mine and I allowed myself, for the first time since Maman had gone, to slip away from the here and now and to luxuriate in a few moments of oblivion.

"The *pot-au-feu* will take a while," he whispered into my ear. "Would you care to show me your apartment?"

I led him by the hand up the stairs and gestured to the small space. The tiny kitchen, the shabby dining room table that spilled into the parlor. The two little bedrooms and even smaller water closet. "It's not Versailles, but it's home," I said with a flourish.

"It's grand," he said, pulling me tight against his chest. "If it's where you live, there is no finer house in all of Paris."

This time, I pulled his lips to mine and drank from them as from a desert oasis. And so it felt. A delicious reprieve after two long years of toil.

"Micheline," he whispered. I felt his hands grow bolder. He caressed my hips and his hands moved down to cup my buttocks. I kissed him deeper as he explored, wanting more than anything to lose myself in him. "Micheline, I want . . ."

"I know," I said, finding the courage to let my hands wander as well. Maman had explained how things were between a husband and wife, at least in basic terms. Some girls at school had taken it upon themselves to fill in the details Maman had thought too indelicate for a girl's ears. I took a step back, laced my fingers in his, and looked to the bedroom doors. I looked to the room I shared with the girls. It didn't seem right to take him in there. I pulled him to the door of Maman's room and hoped the ghosts that haunted it wouldn't come to spoil the moment.

I forced myself to dust the room once a week, and it was clean as the day Maman left. Piece by piece, our clothes hit the parquet floor until we were nestled in Maman's bed, basking in each other's warmth. His mouth became increasingly impatient until he shifted himself on top of me. I gripped on to him as if my very life depended on it. He promised I could cling to him, and cling I would.

The afternoon passed in a blur, the sensations of being with Laurent so novel, yet somehow familiar. We both groaned when the hour came that we had to ready ourselves to welcome the girls home from school.

As I looked in Maman's mirror, the girl—the young woman—I saw reflected back was no different than the one I'd glanced at carelessly that morning. I thought certainly I would look somehow changed after what Laurent and I had shared. As if the truth of what we'd done would be etched on my forehead for all to see. But I looked the same, somehow, despite knowing I was forever altered.

"Beautiful," Laurent said, coming up behind me and wrapping his arms around me. He planted a kiss on the soft curve of my neck, and I felt the desire rise up again.

"Let's go downstairs," I said, reluctantly pulling away. "Or the girls will find us and get an education they're not ready for."

"Excellent point," he said with an expression that betrayed he was just as susceptible to giving in as I was.

If the girls were surprised to see Laurent in the kitchen with me when they arrived home, they hid their surprise well. Perhaps wowed by the abundance of the meal, far grander than we'd had in so long. Perhaps it was my overactive imagination, but as we sat around the dining table upstairs, I thought I could see the glow of health rise in their cheeks. Nourished by the tender meat, perfectly seasoned and slowly cooked. The vegetables, richly flavored from hours in the broth. And it was Laurent who had done it for them.

For Noémie and Sylvie, however, the highlight was the blackberry *clafoutis*.

"With Chantilly cream!" Noémie exclaimed. "You remembered."

"You expected me to forget?" Laurent said with mock indignation. "Mademoiselle, I assure you, I forget nothing when it comes to baked goods."

Both girls burst into peals of giggles at Laurent's comically solemn expression. Noémie was given the first serving, her eyes widening with the first bite. She took two more before she managed to proclaim, "This is the most delicious thing in the whole world."

She didn't shout with glee, but spoke with a reverence usually reserved for Mass.

Sylvie had dug into her portion with almost equal enthusiasm. Though she didn't make any bold pronouncements, she ate with rapt attention.

"You haven't told me your favorite," Laurent said to her. "Anything you like. Your sister and I will perfect it."

Sylvie looked up from her plate to Laurent, then back to the food again. She pushed it away. "I'm not hungry anymore."

She bounded up from her chair and dashed to her bedroom door.

"May I have hers?" Noémie pleaded. I nodded. It was far too decadent for her to have a second helping, but I didn't have it in my heart to refuse her. Not tonight. Laurent looked at her indulgently, sliding Sylvie's uneaten portion before her. I could imagine he'd been a doting brother. Making covert batches of biscuits and slipping them to his brothers between meals when he thought their mother wasn't looking. Of course she knew what Laurent was doing. Of course he knew she knew. But pretending ignorance simply added to the charm of the game.

Noémie finished her sister's dessert and soon looked like she was going to fall asleep where she sat.

"Off to bed with you," I said. She slid off the dining chair and fairly rolled to the water closet to brush her teeth, then to the bedroom where Sylvie would likely be feigning sleep, though she was the biggest night owl of us all. Laurent started collecting the dishes while I tended to the girls. I felt one little weight lift from my shoulders.

I followed Noémie to the bedroom to tuck her in her small

cot. Her feet were dangling over the edge, obliging her to curl up like a cat to sleep. It was no wonder she climbed into my bed at night.

"Darling, sleep in my bed," I told her in low tones in case Sylvie were truly asleep. "You need more space."

"But where will you sleep?" she mumbled, more asleep than awake.

"I'm going to take Sylvie's advice and sleep in Maman's room. She's right. We all need a bit more space, don't we?"

Noémie smiled and burrowed deeper under my blanket. It was a thick quilt Maman and I had made together when she was teaching me how to sew. I loved the thing, with all of its crooked seams and misplaced knots. Maman and I had spent many happy hours on it, chatting about everything and nothing, but it would be Noémie's now. I hoped the love that Maman and I had poured onto it would somehow make up for the love that Maman could not give her now.

Sylvie grunted and turned over in her bed. She'd heard everything and wasn't pleased with me. But the suggestion had been hers in the first place, so she didn't have much room to argue.

I padded softly to the door and closed it behind me, then crossed to the sink where Laurent had made good progress on the dishes. I picked up a clean cloth and began to dry what he'd washed.

"Thank you," I said simply. *For so many things.* I couldn't voice the last words aloud or I would have dissolved into the tears that almost always threatened to burst forth in a torrent.

He set down the dish on the counter and wiped his hands and pulled me into an embrace. His kisses were softer, sweeter, more lingering than they had been before.

"I know it's madness, but I was taken with you from the first day in class. I knew I had to get to know you better," he said when he pulled away. He tucked my head against his chest. "I didn't know if you would be a friend or something more, but I knew somehow that you were meant to be a part of my life. There were many times during the war that I was certain I'd never live long enough to find love and set down roots. When I saw you walk into the classroom, something changed in me. I felt a spark of hope for the first time since those damned Germans crossed our borders. I love you, Micheline, and I want nothing more than to spend my life with you."

I let myself rest against his chest for some time. I'd been too nervous about class to notice Laurent at first. I'd been resistant to letting him closer. Why was that? Fear he would be taken from me like Papa? Go off without a trace like Maman? There was no way he could promise me that harm would never befall him. The only certainty we had was doubt. But Laurent made me want to believe in the future.

"Stay," I whispered into his chest. For weeks I'd tried to ignore my feelings for Laurent. Indulging in daydreams felt like a waste of the energy I ought to be expending on the girls or my studies. But he wouldn't let me brush him aside. He offered kindnesses I was too tired to refuse with no expectation of anything in return, save the occasional pleasure of my presence. I couldn't imagine how pleasurable my company *was* exactly. I felt as thin as used cheesecloth and that my personality sparkled like three-day-old dishwater, but still he wanted to spend time with me. I had tried, for so many months, to deny myself everything for the girls' sakes, but I'd come to the end of my altruism. The girls would survive this act of selfishness, and perhaps come out the better for it.

And if they didn't, I would. And I was beginning to think that was almost as good.

"I'll stay as long as you'll have me," he whispered in turn.

I wondered what Laurent's parents would think of him living with a girl before marriage. What Maman would think. Would Lisette, the first woman to run the bakery below, have been scandalized with such an arrangement?

I found I didn't much care. A time might come when I would, but I wasn't strong enough to refuse myself the enjoyment of his company. His love, his support. Not feeling alone in the world was too precious to push away.

We finished the dishes and crossed the parlor to Maman's room. My room. Our room.

And later, as I drifted off to sleep in his arms, I knew I never wanted to spend another night without him.

Chapter Twenty-Three

LISETTE

JANUARY 26, 1871

I'll be fine," Théo protested from the bed. I held a hand to his forehead, and he was still burning up. Three days with a fever and it seemed to be getting worse instead of better.

"You're not fine," I said. He didn't have the strength to rebuke me. His cheeks, usually rosy with life, were now sallow and chalky. I wasn't sure if he had a bad case of the grippe or something worse. He needed medical attention we couldn't find. He needed medicines we couldn't afford.

Above all, he needed a good meal.

He needed a hearty chicken and sausage stew, thick with the spices and herbs from Nanette's stores. He needed a healthy portion of crusty bread to restore his health.

And we had almost nothing left in our cupboards fit to feed a mouse.

I crossed to the stove to warm my hands, trying to ignore the trembling in my fingers from too many days without a proper meal. The basket from Nanette was emptied weeks ago, and I'd run out of flour from Mercier a week before. I'd rationed it as carefully as I could. I'd reserved as much for Théo and me as I could bring myself to squirrel away, but there were so many hungry mouths, I couldn't bear to hoard more than a few days' worth of ingredients for our own meals.

I hadn't told Théo about my foray into the black market. He wouldn't have approved, but we'd have starved weeks ago without the illicit flour. Not to speak of all the people in the neighborhood who had been able to buy a few extra loaves before the supplies dried up. It had bought them time.

"I'll go out and see what can be found for supper," he said between coughs. "There must be something to be had."

"Don't be ridiculous," I said. "I've looked everywhere. If the city is sealed off, it's foolish to hope that empty shelves have magically replenished themselves overnight. There's no sense in you going out to make yourself sicker to no real purpose."

"I can't bear to lie here while I watch you starve. I was a fool to drag you into this with me."

He'd made similar utterances multiple times a day for the last few months.

"I was free to join you, Théo. And I was free to stay with my parents. I made my choices. And I don't regret them. I'm not a child."

He enveloped me in his arms. "I know," he said. "But this is not the life I wanted for you. Not the life I wanted for *us.*"

"It isn't for us to despair over the lives we're given, but to make the most of them," I said. "And a life without you is no life at all."

I'd told him of my foolish return to my parents' home. I didn't tell him how close I'd come to fleeing Paris. How close I'd come to letting my cowardice get the better of me.

I was ashamed when I thought of how much I'd wanted to leave with my parents and the children.

I assumed Papa would take the family to our country home in Normandy if he was able. In the provinces, food was still plentiful. There wasn't the constant barrage of mortar fire. There was peace and security far beyond what we had here in Paris. And the house in Normandy was self-supporting with abundant crops and livestock. They would eat like kings and queens.

While all of Paris suffered and starved.

I could think of few options, and the one left was about the worst I could envision.

"I'll see what I can do," I said, pulling myself away from the warmth of the stove and wrapping my shawl tight around my shoulders. "Keep the stove going."

I kissed his fevered brow and wondered how long he had left. A few days before the fever claimed him? If we were lucky, a week? The bitter chill of the January winds reached my soul as I pondered how very tenuous Théo's condition was. Fevers were dangerous in good times, but to a body that was already taxed by hunger, fevers were lethal.

Though I felt I'd never completely figure out the maze of streets in Montmartre, I was reasonably certain of the path to get to Mercier's. I gritted my teeth at the idea of asking him for

help. He was making a fortune off the misery of others, probably glad for each day the Prussian siege dragged on. It was a
race to see if Parisian stomachs could outlast Prussian shells,
and I was becoming more and more convinced that there was
no path to a French victory. The only question that remained
was if we could survive long enough for an armistice to be
signed and for the trade routes into Paris be opened again.

I would have to entreat Mercier to sell me more flour on
credit. By the end of last week, I'd sold every last trinket from
the hoard of treasures I'd brought from my parents' house, and
there was nothing left to barter with. Nothing except le Bijou
itself.

And to sell le Bijou would be my very last act of desperation.
A baker was useless without her kitchen, so to sell would be
like a seamstress selling off her sewing machine or a carpenter
selling off his tools to pay for a meal—shortsighted and rash.

I knocked at the foul man's door and half hoped he wouldn't
answer.

"Ah, the lovely Madame Fournier," he said, his voice coiling
around me like a constrictor as he opened the door. "A pleasure
indeed."

"Thank you, Monsieur Mercier," I said, trying to make my
voice less rancorous than I felt. "I won't trespass too long upon
your time, but I am in need of flour."

"Of course, of course. Come in," he said. "I'm always happy
to help my friends, my dear. I can have the men deliver flour
this very evening, as always."

"There is one problem, monsieur," I said, trying not to cast
my eyes downward and appear weak. "I am without funds. I've

sold everything of value that I owned to purchase flour from you over the past few weeks. And with the pricing rules being what they are, I'm lucky to not sell at a loss."

"That is a quandary, isn't it? Why bake at all, lovely one?" he cooed. "When there are more profitable ways to spend time. Not to mention the obvious that you could have saved the stockpile to feed yourself."

"Monsieur, how could I bring myself to do that when the neighborhood is starving?" I asked. "It's the only way I can think of to make people's lot in life a little less miserable during this horrible time. I wouldn't come to you, but my husband is ill. Gravely, I fear, and I cannot bear to watch him suffer if there is anything that might be done. I'll scrub your floors. I'll cook your meals. Anything you require in exchange for some flour. Broth too if you can manage it. You've only to name your price."

I could have belabored how important it was that I bake for the neighbors. Too many, usually elderly like Monsieur DuQuay, had simply vanished. Too many mothers now walked listlessly up the streets with empty arms and hollow eyes. But he knew what was happening as well as I did.

"You truly are an angel, aren't you?" he asked, his voice rasping. He tucked a loose curl behind my ear and I shuddered at the intimacy of the gesture.

"No. I just try to think of others before myself," I replied.

"I believe you, Madame Fournier," he said. "Come with me."

He offered me a gnarled hand and led me up a narrow staircase.

I felt myself tremble despite the warmth from the numerous

fireplaces in the house. I knew precisely how he was going to extract payment, and it took everything not to run and scream.

But pride had no place in the matter when it would mean Théo would starve.

Théo would murder Mercier if he knew what was about to transpire, but his honor would never take the blow. I'd keep the secret from him, no matter what it cost.

He stopped before a door, and I felt a band of iron squeeze over my heart as I expected him to reveal his bedchamber. Instead, I was greeted with the sight of a washroom with all the modern conveniences. A porcelain tub and sinks, gleaming tile floors that had to have been scrubbed that very morning.

I closed my eyes and thought of Théo. I thought of the promises I'd made to Nanette. I promised her I would survive this.

And so I would.

"Wh-what am I to do?" I stammered. I wanted my voice to sound self-assured, but it was too much to ask.

"Draw the bath," he said. "I trust you know how."

I nodded. This wasn't unlike the tub I'd had in my private bathroom at my parents' house. One of the maids had usually drawn the bath for me, but I'd seen her do it often enough that I was confident I could manage the task. I emulated what I'd seen done before and added salts liberally and scent sparingly.

When the tub was full enough I stepped aside waiting for the next order, presumably to undress.

"Come over to me," he bade.

I closed the gap between us, but spoke not a word. Keeping my mouth tightly shut was the only thing that kept the screams stoppered in the bottle.

"Remove my shirt," he ordered. I raised my shaking fingers to his top collar button and unbuttoned the long row of tiny buttons that strained over his protruding gut. I removed the clean, white linen shirt and placed it on a side table. It smelled of musk and good laundry soap and I thought of how rank I must smell.

"Trousers," he commanded. I removed the black freshly-pressed trousers and placed them with the shirt. I averted my eyes so as not to see him standing before me in his underpants and stockings.

"The rest," he said.

I obliged as quickly as I could, keeping my eyes shut as much as possible.

He lowered himself in the tub, letting out an audible moan of pleasure as the hot water made contact with his skin. I stood, rooted to the spot. I focused all my energy on not running for the door.

"Come closer," he said.

Bile rising in my throat, I walked the few paces that separated me from the tub. I decided not to wait for his command and began to unfasten the buttons on my blouse.

"There's no need for that," he said. "Just grab that washcloth and bathe me."

I blinked a few times, then knelt by the tub. I dampened the cloth in the water and began to rub his chest.

"Gently," he said. "Like a mother would wash a babe."

I applied less pressure as I rubbed the cloth across his chest once more. His muscles began to slacken and his breathing grew deeper.

He commanded me to move about to wash his arms. His legs. His back. His feet. I fought the pain in my gut and the wave of nausea I felt at touching this man in ways only the most devoted nurse would endure.

He was like a giant toddler who was just old enough to be compliant in the bath. His eyes would squeeze together in delight as though he'd taken me to his bed. He reveled in the slightest touches the way Théo reveled in my most intimate ones.

In one sudden movement, he stood and pointed to a cabinet. "Dry me," he commanded. I fetched the towel and wrapped it around him. He stepped out of the tub and motioned for me to come closer.

The trembling returned. Now that he was clean, he would claim me. I prayed my humiliation—my further humiliation—would be of short duration. But something told me that a man like Mercier had availed himself of women like Pierrine often enough that he could take his time in deriving his pleasure.

Pierrine. She would know what I'd done. She had her ways of knowing everything.

Would she tell Théo?

And if Mercier had lain with women of her sort, there was no telling what poxes I might take home to Théo. I might be sparing us from a slow death from hunger, only to deliver a painful death from a pox. My limbs shook at the prospect of the risk I was taking. I'd have to find an excuse to keep Théo at arm's length until I was sure I was healthy for him. He would have to learn to forgive me. But even if he didn't, at least he wouldn't go hungry. It was better that he forsake me than to have him die from the illness that had taken hold of him.

I approached Mercier as he bade. He dropped the towel and embraced me. He breathed in the scent of my hair and though he ran his hands up the small of my back, didn't attempt to cup my buttocks or reach around for my breasts. I felt his length grow engorged against me, and I waited for the insistent pull toward the bedchamber. But it never came.

Instead, he wept. I stood there for some minutes, holding him, naked as the day he was born. What pain he was unleashing, I did not know, but it felt more akin to soothing a wounded animal than a man grown.

With a start, he grabbed the towel and wiped his face.

"You ought to go now, Madame Fournier. I can see to dressing myself," he said, clearing his throat.

"But . . . Monsieur Mercier, you'll forgive me, I really must have the flour," I pleaded. "I don't know if I've done something wrong, but I can endeavor to . . . please you."

"No, Madame Fournier. There are women one uses for pleasure, like our mutual friend Pierrine. There are others who are meant to be treasured as wives and mothers. You are meant to be one of the latter. Your husband is a lucky man, and I will not soil you. Go home now and my men will deliver what you require."

I fought back some indignation for Pierrine's honor, but swallowed it back. Théo's health was of far more importance. "I don't understand," I said. "I thought . . ."

"I know, my dear. Don't think that you don't tempt me to distraction, but I wouldn't demean you."

More than you just did.

He bade me farewell and I walked out into the frigid air.

I wondered what pleasure that vile man had derived from me bathing him like a small child. Perhaps he hadn't been loved enough as a child. Perhaps his mother had been the cold sort. But whatever the reason, he was looking for more than physical gratification.

As I walked the serpentine streets back to Le Bijou the tears began to fall, then the sobs. My shoulders shook and I choked on my own spittle and tears, barely able to see the street ahead of me. I would have run the risk of being run down by a carriage were there any horses left in town. I thought darkly that it might have been a mercy to be relieved from my thoughts. As I wept, no one stared. No one noticed. Grief surrounded us like the angry ocean enveloped helpless passengers on a capsized ship. My grief was nothing unique.

The intimacy Mercier demanded of me was far worse than if he'd claimed my body. I could have closed my eyes and let myself drift away from the moment. But there was no closing myself off from what the foul man had forced on me.

Though it was only midmorning when I returned home, I crawled into bed with Théo. He was still burning with fever but wrapped me in his arms as I sobbed. I let him think it was because of the scarcity of food. I would never own the truth of what I'd done.

But true to his word, that afternoon, Mercier's men had delivered not only the flour I'd asked for, but an abundant hamper of foods and some medicines for Théo. And they also bore the news that there had been an armistice. The Prussian siege was at an end.

The betrayal shook me. Had Mercier known we were hours

from the end of our seclusion? Had he hidden the knowledge to take advantage of me? But as the soup simmered and the bread rose for supper, I tried to let my anger keep from spoiling the broth. Théo might not have lasted long enough for the supplies to reach the poorest parts of town. I had to cling to the idea that my humiliation had not been in vain.

CROISSANTS

→>–‹–‹

One of Maman's favorite breakfast staples. Nanette has a knack for always having puff pastry at the ready, which I endeavor to replicate someday. Always start the morning before you plan to serve.

Mix four cups flour, two spoonfuls of salt, one-third cup sugar, one spoonful of yeast, one-and-a-half cups milk, and one cup water. Mix well, place in oiled bowl, and chill in icebox or coldest part of cellar overnight. The next morning, take three-quarters of a pound cold butter and roll between two sheets of parchment. Shape into a square, roughly half an inch thick. Keep butter as cold as you can.

Roll your dough into a square the same width, but twice the length of your square of butter. Fold the butter in the dough and seal edges. Fold the dough-and-butter sheets in half, and then again into thirds. Let dough rest and complete this process two more times.

Roll out the dough and cut into triangles three inches at the base. Roll into the *croissant* shape, stretching the dough as you work. Let rest one hour. Brush the tops with egg whites and bake in a medium oven one half hour.

Let cool one half hour before serving. Serve with butter and any variety of jams, jellies, or preserves.

Recipe notes: consider adding a baton of chocolate in the middle or glazing with a light caramel sauce.

Chapter Twenty-Four

MICHELINE

I woke up in Laurent's arms. The sun was streaming through the window. I didn't remember the last time I'd slept through dawn, and sat up in a panic. Were the girls late for school? Were we late for class?

But my little bedside clock reassured me it was just seven in the morning. Time enough to see the girls fed and off to school and to get to the culinary school on time. I fell back on my pillow and let Laurent encircle me with his arms anew.

"You're beautiful in the morning," he said, brushing featherlight kisses against the side of my face. "And the rest of the day as well."

I shoved him playfully and returned his kisses before sliding from the bed and slipping into my dressing gown to make breakfast for the girls while Laurent dressed. I had *croissants* ready to put in the oven with apricot jam and real honest-to-goodness butter. As long as I lived, I'd never take butter for granted again.

Noémie came padding out of her bedroom as soon as the smell of the baking *croissants* wafted into the parlor. She yawned and stretched with a lack of dignified restraint that reminded me fondly of her babyhood.

"You slept well," I observed.

She flashed a toothy smile. "Your bed is comfortable," she said.

"It's yours now, darling," I said. "And may you have many wonderful nights' sleep in it."

"But what will you do when Maman comes home?" Noémie asked. Her face was solemn. She believed, perhaps even more fervently than I did, that Maman was coming home. She had taken my declaration that she would, one day, return to us as gospel. I envied her confidence. I felt the all-too-familiar lump begin to form in my throat.

"We'll find a solution to that when the happy day arrives," I said. I stooped to her eye level. "I'll sleep on the sofa until we come up with something."

She giggled at the image of me trying to get a decent rest cramped on the tiny sofa that, small as it was, still overpowered the parlor.

"Go fetch Sylvie," I said, ruffling her already unkempt hair. "Tell her breakfast will be ready soon."

She trotted off toward the bedroom, her riot of messy red curls bouncing after her. I'd hardly had the time to peek in the oven to check the progress of the *croissants* when she bounded back.

"Sylvie isn't in the bedroom or the WC," she said, her eyes wide. "She's gone."

"Of course she isn't," I said, wiping my hands on a towel. "She must be hiding from you."

Noémie shook her head. It was true there were few places she could hide, and she'd outgrown childish pranks for the most part, but I wasn't willing to entertain any other possibility.

I crossed the parlor in three long strides and opened the bedroom door. I peered under the beds and in the armoire. Knowing nowhere else to look, I approached the little brown leather trunk at the foot of Sylvie's bed where she hid her treasures. The scuffed trunk was the only small corner of this building I was forbidden from meddling with, and before now, I had always respected Sylvie's right to a small measure of privacy as she entered adolescence. But as I lifted the lid, I felt the dreaded pricking at my skin, and I wasn't concerned with hurting her feelings just then. The pricking sensation always boded ill, and I prayed she left behind some clue about her disappearance.

I sifted through the contents of her trunk; mostly a collection of girlish bric-a-brac from over her twelve years of life. Ribbons and pictures cut out of magazines. Bits of pretty wrapping paper she'd saved from gifts, and various buttons and beads. I'd referred to her as my little magpie, so loath she was to let anything pretty slip from her grasp. The contents appeared undisturbed from the last time I'd managed to peek inside when Sylvie was organizing her treasures. Only one item was missing.

The old leather handbag Maman had given her which contained all her savings.

She'd hoarded away each franc coin Maman or I had given her for her help with mending or for extra chores around the apartment. A special reward for a good report from school. Little remembrances on her birthday and Christmas. She wasn't one to spend the money on penny candy and cheap toys. Only rarely did she spend, and it was usually to buy a small gift for Maman on special occasions. She had probably more than fifty francs to her name. It wasn't enough to go far, but it was enough to get her into trouble.

"Sylvie!" I shouted, hoping to see her emerge from the shadows, cackling at her own cruel joke. I went back to the parlor. No sign of her. I went to check the door at the top of the stairs that led to the bistro. Unlocked. There was no way that I had left it in that condition, and she wouldn't have had the keys to lock it behind her.

"What's wrong?" Laurent asked as he saw my eyes frantically darting around the room, though I knew there was no chance she was there.

"Sylvie is missing," I managed to gasp. I clutched the back of Papa's favorite chair to steady myself. I turned to Noémie, who had tears pooling in her eyes. "You didn't hear anything?" I asked.

She shook her head, a few tears spilling over onto her freckled cheeks. I ran my fingers through the crown of my hair, tempted to pull it out in clumps.

"Get dressed," I ordered her. "We'll search for her."

Registering that I, too, was still in my nightdress, I went back into my new bedroom and grabbed one of Maman's plainer dresses rather than removing mine from the girls' room. Maman's dresses fit me better now than my own clothes did, and she couldn't begrudge me getting some use from them while she was gone. Sylvie would soon fit my castoffs, and it was better to save them for her while there was still wear left in them.

Laurent followed me into the room, his face grave as I dressed as quickly as I could.

"We'll find her, love," he promised. "She can't have gone far."

"We have to," I said, pulling my hair back with a few pins. "Maman will kill me if anything happens to her. Sylvie was always Maman's little *chou chou*."

His face drained of what little color it had left, but he said nothing.

Like everyone else, he probably thought Maman was gone. But he, wisely, surmised that now was not the time to voice his doubts on that score.

Just as we were about to leave I remembered the breakfast in the oven. I cursed my foolishness, thinking a burned-down apartment was just what I deserved for my folly. Clearly, if Sylvie was so upset that she'd run away, I'd been doing something terribly wrong.

I rescued the *croissants* just before they burned, and gave one to Noémie to eat while we searched and wrapped one for Sylvie in case we found her and she was hungry from want of breakfast. I would feed her, then wring her neck. Laurent refused his, and I had no appetite for mine. We thundered down the stairs, where I hoped Sylvie might still be in some corner of the building, but the front door to the bistro was unlocked as well. She'd gone out into the city by herself.

Paris, which could be unforgiving to the innocent.

Montmartre, even more so.

Chapter Twenty-Five

LISETTE

FEBRUARY 12, 1871

Now is the time," Théo insisted, slamming his hand on the scarred table in our dining room. Théo, having regained his health, was now thick in the plans for the rebirth of Paris. He, Sébas, and a number of other *clubistes* had gathered to make plans and drink unhealthy quantities of wine. I couldn't begrudge the extravagance given our months of privation. I'd been able to expand my offerings in the bakery beyond the plain breads I'd offered during the siege and now offered a selection of cakes and *viennoiseries*. I started off with a few modest choices and grew more elaborate as ingredients became more readily available. The customers were glad for a taste of happier times, and I was pleased to provide it for them.

I served the men generous portions of my best breads and pastries in hopes it would keep their indulgence with the wine to a minimum. Pierrine assisted me, though she didn't deign to speak a word to me as she put plates in front of the men. "The emperor's men are entrenched at Versailles, and the Prussians are leaving us alone. We have food in our bellies once again and have relit the fire in our hearts."

"Don't you think it's a bit soon, Théo? People are just getting back on their feet. This sort of thing takes time to plan and execute well. There will be no room for error."

"Can't you see, Sébas? We have to establish a government of the people in Paris while we can. You know that Versailles will regroup before long. Once they chase the Prussians from our doorstep, they'll turn their attentions right back to us and it will be too late. They've elected a pack of monarchists to the National Assembly. If we don't act, we'll have another emperor before the spring gives way to summer."

"Théo is right. We can't give the Versaillais the chance to regroup. We need to act now," one of the men interjected.

A rousing round of cheers went up. They were fueled by the relief of having their stomachs filled properly and the tantalizing prospect of finally having the government they'd hoped for.

"Just make sure you have plans, gentlemen. The Versaillais won't be conquered by a disorganized mob, no matter how noble their ideals might be," Sébas warned.

A few men nodded their agreement, but a few grunted their derision. They saw Sébas as a symbol of the old guard. Those who sought to keep the workers in their place. Those who scoffed couldn't know Sébas very well, else they would have known how subversive his views were. Or perhaps how truly in line they were with what the Church was always meant to stand for and never did.

It wasn't long before the meeting broke up and it was just Sébas and Pierrine left behind. One of the men had shot an inviting glance at her, but she waved him off. She'd suffered like the rest of us during the siege, but without the comfort of regular companionship.

I gave her a glass of wine and a huge pastry and a length of bread with jam as she finally sat. She looked to me as though she wanted to protest, but turned her attention toward the food and ate delicately, though it was clear she wanted to tear into the food like a wolf.

"Why do you always do that, Sébas? Every damn time." Théo downed his glass of claret.

"What do you mean?" he countered.

"Every time we meet, you have to throw ice water on the fervor. Don't you see that you're undermining the cause?"

"Théo, I live and breathe for the idea of a free Paris. But fervor alone won't secure it. We have to be smart. We have to strategize and have a plan. If we just storm Versailles it will be a suicide."

"We stormed the Bastille eighty years ago and came out of it fine," Théo spat, slamming his glass on the table.

"Don't be daft. There were a handful of prisoners. It was a symbolic victory." Sébas sat up straighter and took on the sermon-voice he used when he wanted to command attention.

"A symbolic victory that led to the Revolution." Théo's face grew red as he spoke.

"And the monarchy was back in power how many years

later? Ten? Twelve? Twice now we've had a republic, only to have the president declare himself king or emperor. We want to build something that will last."

"Théo is right," Pierrine interjected. "If we keep reminding our compatriots about how hard this will be, they'll never fight for the cause. We have to keep their spirits up and their blood boiling."

"Hear, hear," Théo said, raising an empty glass to her. I refilled it in haste. "We need enthusiasm as much as we need bullets. Thiers is leading the other side and he's a tired old man. We actually have a chance."

"And you need a plan even more than you need either of those," I said. "I have to agree with Sébas. And more? Thiers may be old, but he's vicious. I wouldn't underestimate that man."

"Lisette," Théo growled. "I thought you were on my side."

"I always am, Théo. Sébas and I want you to win, which is why we're not afraid to tell you the truth. I know what the Versaillais are like. I was to be married to one, remember? I've seen how they think. I know how they act. They have resources we simply do not, so we must be twice as cunning as they are. We cannot afford to underestimate them."

"Well said," Sébas said. "And be kind to your wife. And to me. Don't make enemies where you have none. Lisette and I want this endeavor to be successful as much as you do."

"But the Versaillais are down," Pierrine persisted. "Isn't now precisely the time when we need to act? We won't have this advantage again."

"It may well be," I said. "But our efforts must be well

organized. Meticulously planned. An unruly mob is better at breaking windows than it is at breaking down centuries-old monarchies. What's more, if you act like a mob, you won't win the hearts of the people. Whatever lofty ideals people might have, they crave peace and order more than almost anything else."

"Listen to your wife, Théo," Sébas said. "She's met these people. Lived among them. Use her knowledge, don't balk at it."

Théo crossed his arms defiantly. Not wanting to insult me or deride his friend, but he loathed that we didn't follow his plan with unquestioning gusto.

"Pierrine, let's leave the happy couple to their evening, shall we?" Sébas suggested. Pierrine had finished her food and wine, and cast me a stormy look.

"Plans are all well and good, but nothing will happen without action. Don't let yourselves get mired down with plotting and forget to do the thing, will you?" Pierrine said, her voice dripping with disdain as she went to join Sébas.

Théo nodded and remained silent as his friends departed.

"You're furious with me, aren't you?" I asked.

"I'm tired. I'm going to bed," he said.

"Talk to me," I persisted. "Don't be sullen."

"I'm not in the mood to talk right now. My best friend and my wife think I'm being foolish and that kind of disloyalty is hard to stomach."

I gritted my teeth and stood within inches of his face. *"Disloyal?"* I growled. "Was I *disloyal* when I nursed you back to health? When I fed us when there was no food to be had? Is that *disloyalty*?"

I stopped just short of telling him the humiliation I'd endured to procure him food and medicine, but it cost me dearly to hold my tongue.

He remained silent.

"Very well," I said. "You can think me *disloyal* and a bad wife. But the truth of the matter is, I care more about winning than I do about protecting your feelings. If you think that's *disloyal*, then you deserve to lose."

"You sound like Sébas," he said.

"I've never been paid a kinder compliment. He's been the voice of reason at every meeting you've had," I spat back. "If you have any chance of winning it will be because you listened to him. And men like him."

"It's fucking maddening, you know," he said, resuming his seat. "Always knowing better than everyone else."

"You know what I think? You're both indispensable to the cause. The first time I heard you speak at Les Halles, I was ready to pick up a pitchfork and drive my own father out of Paris on the end of it. We need that fire. We need someone to rally the people. To win hearts and minds. But we also need people like Sébastien with cool heads and logic to determine the best course of action. David didn't beat Goliath by taking him head-on in a fistfight. He used his cunning. And so must we."

"Maddening," Théo repeated, pulling me to him. "The pair of you. It wouldn't be so bad if you weren't both right."

"It's why you love us," I said, sitting on his lap and planting a kiss on his cheek. "You need us both, and you know, deep down, that we're rooting for you. But this is bigger than any one man. It's bigger than Paris. It's the future of the French people. We can't let our pride get in the way."

"I *do* love you," Théo murmured into my neck. "You're right. I'm sorry I was a beast. And I'll apologize to Sébas tomorrow as well."

I returned a kiss, slowly, leisurely. "I love you too, my darling. But the best apology for both of us would be for you to heed our advice and trust that we're always on the same side."

CHOCOLAT CHAUD

→>−<←

Nothing better to soothe the soul. Nanette's special recipe was a special favorite of mine growing up, and she was never too busy to share a cup with me.

In a stew pan, heat two cups milk until bubbles appear. Add six ounces of finely chopped dark chocolate of the first quality. Whisk milk until chocolate is dissolved and mixture is smooth. Bring chocolate to a low simmer, whisking continuously. Stir in a scant spoonful of brown sugar and a small pinch of coarse salt. Pour into cups and serve immediately with a big dollop of Chantilly cream. Garnish with chocolate shavings for company.

Best served at breakfast with bread, butter, and preserves.

Recipe notes: experiment with adding a spoonful of rum, brandy, or other eau de vie *either in the chocolate itself, or infused in the Chantilly cream.*

Chapter Twenty-Six

MICHELINE

The visions of the harms that could befall her flashed like a nightmarish newsreel before my eyes. I couldn't take in a proper breath, but I couldn't give in to the panic that bloomed in my chest like an invasive vine that clutched my lungs.

Laurent was thankfully calmer than I was. "We'll cover more ground if we split up," he said. "Why don't you head south from the square and look for her from there and I'll go north with Noémie?"

"She stays with me," I said, gritting my teeth at the very suggestion of having her taken from me. "I can't lose them both."

"I'll protect Noémie with my life," he said with no bravado. "But Sylvie might not come with me if I don't have you or Noémie with me."

I hated that he was right. Hated that he was capable of being logical in this moment when I could not.

"Let's meet back at the bakery in two hours," he said. "If

we haven't found her, we'll devise a new strategy. If we see a policeman we should alert him, but I think our time right now is better spent searching in the first few hours, rather than filing a report."

I could not argue with his reason. Noémie took Laurent's hand, her expression trustful. She nibbled at her *croissant* as she followed him down the cobblestone street. Concerned for her sister, but willing to see to her own needs as well. I envied her childish pragmatism as much as I envied Laurent his sangfroid.

Right now, I was in possession of neither of those things.

I kept the sobs at bay and tried to keep composed. I'd scarcely be able to find her if I was blinded by tears. I walked the little side streets, looking methodically. I asked a few people if they'd seen a girl of her description on her own, but was usually met with grunts of indifference. I hoped that, if the tables were turned, I would meet the concerns of a stranger with more sympathy.

But would I?

I'd been so concerned with raising the girls and finding Maman that I couldn't be sure that I could shoulder the burden of a stranger as well as my own. Perhaps it was the same for everyone else.

After three or four streets, I was ready to scream with frustration. Searching street by street in an organized fashion seemed logical for finding a missing glove or hat. Sylvie wasn't an inanimate object that would stay immobile in one location. She had no reason to wander the side streets aimlessly. She had no acquaintance there, that I was aware of, and there was nothing else to keep her interest.

But what would interest her? Where would she wander to in her moment of despair?

And at once, I knew where she was.

I ran to the gardens on the other side of Sacré Coeur where Maman and Sylvie had loved to stroll. Maman, in her wisdom, had anticipated that Sylvie would have struggles as a middle child. I had bonded with Maman over responsibility and duty. Noémie was her baby, and was only just preparing to start school when Maman had gone missing, so they were enjoying their long days together. But Sylvie had run the risk of being overlooked. Maman always made sure that she carved out special time, just for the two of them, so Sylvie would understand how important she was to her.

Yet another way in which I had failed.

I saw her, perched on a bench, her arms folded over her chest as she watched birds flying from tree to tree and the early risers emerging for their morning constitutionals. She looked well and safe. But hers was the face of a child who was deeply sad. Grieved. Perhaps more than even me, she missed Maman.

As tempting as it was to rush over to her and sweep her into my arms and sob all over her, she didn't need my hysterics.

I walked over to her, calmly, and wrapped my arm around her. She didn't scoff as she was so wont to do these days. She didn't produce some biting remark. She leaned into me with the unreserved affection of a child.

"How did you think to look for me here?" she asked.

"I remembered that you used to come here with Maman," I said. "And I figured you were missing her."

She snuggled in closer.

"I miss her too," I said. "I'd do anything to bring her back."

"Every day she's further away," Sylvie said. "Every day, more and more, you take her place. First the watch. Now her room. Her dress . . ."

"I wish I didn't have to," I said. "Really and truly. I am just trying to do what's best for you and Noémie."

I could have reminded her that it wasn't my choice. That I wanted nothing more than to have Maman back in her rightful place. But it wouldn't help.

"I know," she said. "But it doesn't make it easier."

"No, it doesn't," I agreed. I nudged her up gently, stood from the bench, and stretched out a hand to her. "Come with me." We had more than an hour before Laurent and Noémie would meet us back at home and Sylvie was in dire need of some maternal attention. I might be a poor substitute, but I was the best alternative she had.

"Where are we going?" she asked.

"You'll see."

A few blocks away was the café where, once upon a time, Maman and I would come for *our* special time when I was Sylvie's age. Before the years of privation and sacrifice. Maman would have a coffee, I a *chocolat chaud*. Sometimes we might have a slice of cake or a pastry if it was a special occasion.

"Two breakfasts with *chocolat*," I ordered as the officious waiter appeared at our tiny table.

I was definitely of an age where I was expected to order a coffee or tea with my breakfast, but I wasn't concerned with appearances that morning. It was an indulgence to be sure. The thick hot chocolate, closer to a cream than coffee in its consistency, was the nearest thing to an embrace from my mother that I could have in that moment. Sylvie and I both needed it.

"I wasn't going to stay away forever," Sylvie said at length after the waiter scurried off.

"Not by choice, perhaps," I said. "But something might have happened to you. Do you think Maman would have left us by choice?"

"No," Sylvie said with a tone bordering defiance.

"I don't either," I said.

"So you think something happened to her?" she asked, her voice growing more tentative.

It hurt to breathe, but I nodded. There could be no other rational explanation. "I don't know what, but she wouldn't have stayed away so long if she were able to come back."

"Maybe she's hurt," Sylvie said. "Maybe she lost her memory. I read about it in a book once."

"Perhaps," I said, not wanting to make light of her fanciful theories. "War brings about strange outcomes. But right now, she isn't with us, and we have to do the best we can without her. No matter how much it hurts. It's what she would want."

Sylvie looked down at her hands.

"I'm sorry I scared you, Micheline. I was just so sad. I used to goad you about moving into Maman's room, but I guess I never thought you would. And Laurent will be coming to dinner all the time now. It feels like a new family. I couldn't sleep thinking about it."

"Is it better than having no family at all?" I asked.

She looked thoughtful for a moment. "I suppose it is," she said. "But different."

"Different isn't always bad," I said. "And I hope in time you'll see that."

"I'll try," she said. "I really will."

"I believe you," I said. "But that doesn't excuse what you did."

"I know. I'll apologize to Laurent and Noémie too. I like him by the way. He makes you happy."

I felt a hint of color at my cheeks. She was far too observant by half. "I'm glad you like him," I said. "He cares for you and Noémie a great deal. But that isn't enough. You're going to do extra chores around the house for a month. Quite a few of them too."

"That seems fair," she acknowledged.

The waiter reappeared with two cups of steaming *chocolat* topped with Chantilly cream along with a basket of breads and *croissants*, butter, and jam. It was every bit as elegant as I remembered from my trips here with Maman.

Sylvie took a sip of her *chocolat*, tentative at first, and then eager.

"This is my favorite," she said. "You need to serve *chocolat* just like this at your bakery."

"Not a bad idea," I agreed. "I ought to hire you as my business manager."

"You can't afford me," she said with a giggle that reminded me of the glorious days before she'd reached this loathsome prepubescent phase. "But I do think the bakery is a lovely idea."

"I'm glad, darling. I think it will be good for all of us."

We finished our breakfasts and walked home with a good quarter of an hour to spare before Noémie and Laurent would return from their search. Since Sylvie was dressed and ready for school, I set her to work sweeping the kitchen while I went in search of something from Maman's room. A little wooden music box that Papa had given Maman for their wedding anniversary some years before. It had inlaid wooden flowers and played a lilting piece from Maman's favorite comic opera, *Les cloches de Corneville*, when opened.

"For you, little magpie," I said, handing her the box. "It was Maman's. It doesn't seem fair that you shouldn't have any token of hers."

"But she's coming back," she said with resolution. "You know she is."

"Well then, you should be entrusted with the care of it until she returns," I said.

She set aside the broom and placed the music box carefully on the kitchen counter, then flung herself into my arms, a torrent of tears.

I held her close, and hoped that things had changed between us. Hoped we understood each other better.

And I knew, with more certainty than ever, that I had to find out what had happened to Maman. For all our sakes.

Chapter Twenty-Seven

LISETTE

MARCH 18, 1871

I heard the clattering of boots on the cobblestones outside. Most of the neighborhood slept, but the ovens beckoned me before dawn to be prepared for the breakfast needs of those in the *quartier*. I had two dozen loaves in the oven with more ready to join them as soon as the first batch had reached a perfect golden brown. I went to the window but pulled back the drapery so slowly I hoped no one would notice. The Versaillais were there. They were marching in straight lines up the butte.

"The cannons," Théo said, having snuck up behind me. "Those bastards are after our cannons."

"Shouldn't Montmartre have some defense?" I asked, shaking my head at the sight of the men in their long pristine blue coats trimmed in red. They looked more like tin soldiers a boy might play with rather than real men going to fight.

"They can't bear to leave the defense to us," he said. "They can't bear to think we're capable of it. We pose a threat to their dominion over us. But the National Guard doesn't have to stand for this. The people of the *arrondissement* paid for those cannons."

"Don't do anything foolish," I said. The two lines of soldiers marching down the narrow street seemed to go on forever.

"Coming from you, that seems specious advice," he said, planting a kiss on my cheek as he slipped into his simpler dark blue uniform coat.

"Whatever do you mean?" I asked, widening my eyes.

"You left a life of comfort and privilege to come bake bread for the most downtrodden souls in Paris. You work fourteen hours a day and seem to thrive on it. And you married me. It seems if either of us is foolish, my dearest darling, it's you."

"Haha," I replied. "Just watch your neck. I didn't sacrifice that life of luxury to be left alone."

"You have my word," he said with a grandiose bow and flourish of his hat. "Stay safe, love. This may get rough."

I nodded and watched him slip out the side door to the court-yard where the three small tables stood, waiting for customers who wouldn't be expected for hours yet.

For two hours, I prepared for the onslaught of the day. *Flûtes, pains de campagne, boules,* even a few cakes and pastries. I would flip the sign to "Open" within fifteen minutes, but things were prepared enough I could sit with a cup of coffee, a piece of bread from a baguette I'd dropped and didn't want to sell to an unsuspecting customer, and a coating of elderberry jam one of the neighbors had traded for bread when she was short of funds. As I took a bite, I reminded myself to slip Madame Courbet one of my best pastries when she was next in the shop. Two *flûtes* hadn't nearly been enough recompense.

Just as I stood to unlock the door, I heard a forceful knocking at the side door that Théo had left a couple of hours before.

Pierrine looked dismayed that it was I who came to the door.

"Where is Théo?" she asked by way of greeting.

"He left two hours ago," I said. "We saw the soldiers and he was worried they were going after the cannons."

"He was right," Pierrine said. "But luckily for all of us, the Versaillais are as useless as they look and forgot the bloody horses they need to haul the cannons off the hill."

"You have to be joking," I said, unable to suppress a laugh. I thought of d'Amboise, arriving in all his pomp to the top of Montmartre only to realize his blunder. How he would conceal his idiocy with bravado. I imagined all those in the upper echelon of the Versaillais were much the same.

"I couldn't make up such a ridiculous lie if you paid me a month's wages to do it," she said. "The brass has sent back a contingent of men to get the horses and the rest are milling around wasting time waiting for them to come back. Are you going to come with me?"

She looked me up and down, daring me to say yes, but fully expecting me not to have the gumption to follow through.

"I was just about to open the shop—" I began.

"You won't have customers today if things go as I expect they will," she said. "You'd do better to come with me and be of use."

"How?" I pressed. "What could I possibly do?"

"What women do best," she said. "Flirt. Puff them up. Feed them the lines they want to hear. Get them to listen to us and make them think that our ideas are their own. Speaking of feeding, bring some of your bread and what have you. Bored men are always hungry, and a hungry, bored man is a dangerous one."

Though Pierrine and I rarely agreed, there was no argument to be found in this. I grabbed my basket and stuffed in what loaves I could carry. And fixed up another for her. I left the best behind, hoping I'd have a chance to open later in the day, but I feared Pierrine's take on how the day would unfold was all too accurate. I saw her glance at the case where I kept the small assortment of cakes and pastries. "Have one of these *croissants*, will you?" I asked in a tone I might use to ask her to help me lift an overloaded trunk.

She waved her hand dismissively. She always looked drawn and hungry, but always refused when she was offered a meal.

"Even if I'm able to open later, they're best fresh. Hate to have them go stale," I pressed. "I can't abide waste, can you?"

She sighed, the rumbling of her stomach betraying how hungry she was. She ferreted away every *sou* to her name in hopes it might be able to sway the judges to let her see little Rémy. She knew as well as I did that it would take more than money to get the judge to countermand Pierrine's husband, but to persuade her of this would break more than her heart. "Fine," she said, reaching her hand out to accept the pastry. She ate as she walked, taking tiny, decorous bites, though her desire to devour the whole thing and several more besides, fairly crackled like the charge in the air after a bolt of lightning. I passed her a small loaf of bread when she finished the pastry but said nothing and kept my eyes forward. I wouldn't insult her by watching her accept my charity. I could hear the crust crack between her teeth, the satisfied sounds of being fed that she couldn't quite suppress.

And there was a pang in my gut. A guilt that I had never known true hunger until the past few months. As a child, if dinner seemed too far off, there was always a bit of bread and preserves waiting for me if I asked Nanette sweetly enough. There were times now I felt positively ravenous after a day's work and was ready to dive into the soup kettle headfirst . . . but I had the comfort of knowing there was soup in it to be had. The hard days of the siege were fading into memory for Théo and me, but not for those like Pierrine. No one should have to starve at the whim of a cruel husband.

I stopped myself.

No one should have to starve.

We walked up the butte, and it wasn't long before we came across the mob of Versaillais troops that seemed to wander the streets aimlessly as they waited for commands from their superior officers. The National Guardsmen were filing in as well, and I could see nervous glances from the Versaillais as the number of the local men assembled grew.

"If they start picking fights with each other, this is going to be a mess," I said.

Pierrine nodded. "A right pissing match it'll be. But I'd lay odds on our lads over those rich prats any day."

"But those 'rich prats' have reinforcements our lads don't," I said, my lips drawing to a thin line. I surveyed the Versaillais troops, most of whom, despite their spotless uniforms and polished boots, looked like they were the brothers, cousins, and friends of our own men.

"The higher-ups might be rich prats as you say," I said. "But not these boys. They're farm boys and factory workers. They joined up for the wages and a better chance to feed their families."

Pierrine harrumphed, but I could see in her face as she assessed the crowd of men, she agreed with me. We edged closer to a band of young soldiers who looked bored, cold, and hungry.

"Looks like the brass have left you poor boys high and dry," Pierrine said to one particularly despondent looking soldier who looked as bored as a schoolboy forced to listen to a dry Sunday school lecture.

"True," he said. "I thought I'd be in for a bit of excitement, you know? Defending the country from the Prussians and all that. Turns out life in the army is just a lot of waiting around for the higher-ups to make decisions."

"They don't care a whit about you working-class boys, do they?" Pierrine continued. "Just leaving you lot to fend for yourselves."

"Not really," he agreed. "It's the same everywhere, ain't it? We might all wear the same uniform, but they dress theirs up with medals and trinkets to remind us they're better than we are."

"How awful," I said, breaking into the conversation. "I bet they didn't even give you a proper breakfast, did they?"

"None of us have seen what you'd call 'proper food' in

weeks," he allowed. "I didn't expect army rations to be my maman's home cooking, but it's pig slop."

"That's no way to treat men in service to the country," I said, opening my basket and offering him a large hunk of fresh bread. "I don't know how they expect you to do your duty if they don't feed you."

"I've wondered that many a time, my dear lady. Bless you for this. You're an angel, you are."

Pierrine winked at me as the man ate hungrily. A few others who'd seen the bread wandered over to see if there was more to be had.

"What's your name, lad?" Pierrine asked as he chewed ravenously. I began parceling out the bread to the eager hands.

"Olivier Lambert," he said between bites.

"What did you do before you joined the army?" I asked.

"I worked my papa's farm, didn't I?" he said. "Not much else for a second son to do. But I knew it would never be mine, so I didn't see much use in staying just to make my brother richer. I don't mean him ill, but a man has to make his own way, don't he? I figured if I joined up, I'd be able to save a plot of land and have a farm of my own one day. Maybe find a girl to settle down with and all that."

"She'll be lucky to have you," Pierrine said. There wasn't the usual rancor in her voice when she spoke of marriage.

"Maybe I'll convince you to come to Poitou with me," he said, looking at Pierrine with an earnest look.

"Not if I talk her into coming to Picardy with me," another voice piped up.

Pierrine cast her eyes downward a moment. They might all mean what they said, but she would never be able to trust them.

"The army was the only way out for me," Olivier said. "But I won't be in this uniform forever."

"It's not the only way. Look at what our men are doing." Pierrine gestured to the National Guardsmen who were organizing in the streets. "They're defending their homes, their women, their children. They're fighting for a new way of life. For freedom from the rich men who treat you like scum beneath their silk shoes. They believe that the common people should hold the power in this country. They believe in the ideals that made our grandparents and great-grandparents take to the streets and set up guillotines."

All eyes were now on Pierrine, and she stood taller.

"Remember who you are and where you come from, lads. It wasn't your General Thiers or the Versaillais who fed you this morning. It was the common women of Montmartre who took the bread from their own kitchens to feed you. Who shared the bread from their very tables, their children's bellies. Why? Because each of you is one of us. Poor, doing what you can for a better life. So I ask you lads, when your generals come back, those gleaming medals on their chests to remind you who they are, with their horses in tow, who are you going to stand with?"

The crowd cheered, and Pierrine glowed with satisfaction. Other women continued to pass out what food they could spare from their larders. My basket was quickly emptied, Pierrine's too. I wondered if I ought to go back to the shop for more when the clattering of horses' hooves shattered the merry bent of my thoughts.

The horses had arrived, and if we did not act soon, we would lose our cannons.

We would lose the only defense of our corner of the city.

SMALL DUCHESS CAKES

⤛⋇⤜

This was a special treat Nanette used to make for me when I'd had a particularly hard day or if Maman had been especially difficult. I'd like to say that one bite was enough to soothe my weary soul, but even the best of cakes cannot do that, no matter how we might wish they could. But I can say that it always gave me the courage to take another step forward.

Place two cups of water and two ounces of butter in a stew pan. When it boils, remove from heat and add in six ounces of sifted flour. Mix well, add in two eggs, a pinch of salt, and two ounces of powdered sugar. Mix again (very well, don't skimp!), then add two more eggs and the peel of a lemon chopped very fine (again, don't rush this, large chunks of lemon peel in a pastry are not pleasant to eat). Roll out onto a lightly floured board and form small cakes. Place three inches apart on baking plate and lightly brush with egg. Bake in a medium-hot oven. When done, remove immediately from baking plate and glaze them with sugar and the heat of a flame. When cool, slit the side and fill with preserves. I always preferred apricot.

Recipe notes: experiment with chocolate in the cake batter, or an infusion of rose water. A chocolate Duchess Cake with cherry preserves would be a treat for Théo.

Chapter Twenty-Eight

MICHELINE

Come back to bed, my love," Laurent whispered in my ear after pulling me back into the bed. I'd seen the girls off to school, watching them round the corner, hand in hand, from the kitchen window with my daily prayer for their safety. Laurent and I had one of our free days from classes. We would usually spend the day practicing whatever recipes were coming up in the curriculum. Duchess Cakes were coming up, and I knew I could use a day in the kitchen to get the hang of it.

But as Laurent stretched out against me, and I felt his length pressing against my side, I knew baking wasn't on his mind. I wanted to protest but found myself far too willing to indulge in a morning embrace in an empty house. Having him close was a comfort that, most days, seemed vaguely surreal and always undeserved.

When we'd had our fill of each other, I disentangled myself from Laurent and kissed him on the cheek.

"Marry me," he said, pulling me close and brushing kisses along the nape of my neck. "Just think how beautiful it will be to wake up like this every morning and know we belong to each other."

A molten bubble of longing rose from my gut, but I could not find a *yes* in my heart to give him.

"We still have weeks of courses left, darling. Shouldn't we wait to think about such things once we have our diplomas in hand?"

"You don't think we can finish our courses while engaged to be married?" he chuckled. "I admit my head will be swimming to know I've finally worn down the last of your reserve, but I think I'll be able to manage a decent *choux* pastry if the need arises."

"Laurent—"

"It would please my mother if we weren't living in sin," he teased, cupping my bare breast.

"And it would please your father if we wait and prioritize our classes," I said. It was a bit of a dirty trick, to invoke the name of the man who had given him so much, but it would buy me some time.

He breathed a defeated sigh and swung his feet off the side of the bed. "To the kitchens?" He lived for the hours we spent together in the kitchen, mastering recipes side by side. I did too, most days.

"I'm off to the Red Cross today, darling," I said as I slipped on one of Maman's old dresses. "Hopefully I'll be back in time to do a batch of practice cakes before the girls are home from school."

His face dropped, but he said nothing. He never explicitly disapproved of the time I spent making inquiries and pestering the registry office, but I could read it in his face. He, like everyone else, thought that she'd already be home if she were coming.

But of all people, I didn't hold it against him. He'd been to the front and seen the horror of it all. He knew better than most people of my acquaintance, the need to cling to hope.

Now that Sylvie had come to a peace with it, Laurent had become a regular fixture in the house, and a valuable one. He related to the girls both like a father and a brother. He noticed their skills and encouraged them. For Sylvie, he bought paints, canvases, and even a small easel that tucked into a corner of our tiny apartment. She was more than a little talented, though I'd been too harried between the academy, cooking, cleaning, and all the other labors that went into raising the girls to notice. Noémie was incredibly skilled with a needle, and managed to pick up some basic sewing and embroidery with minimal instruction. Laurent surprised her with fabrics and threads so she could craft her own little treasures. Her dolls had some of the finest attire in all of Montmartre.

I gave Laurent another kiss and left for the Red Cross with a slight twinge of regret. Maybe my time was better spent with Laurent, but I couldn't ignore the nagging sensation in my chest whenever I thought about Maman. The truth had to be out there. The registry office remained steadfast in their decision to close their search for Maman, so I turned my efforts to the Red Cross. I was nearly as familiar there as I was with M. Ouimet, though met with less understanding and a lot more bureaucracy.

I'd been to this temporary outpost near the center of town that was dedicated to the post-war rehabilitation efforts at least a half dozen times. In the months after the liberation, offices like these were swarmed with people searching for loved ones or in need of other assistance to recover from the effects of the war. Over the months, the swarm became more like a light buzzing. The crowds had been filled with people who found out where their loved ones had fallen in the east. Sometimes there were happy endings where the lost family member was reunited with their family members. Most often, people simply made peace with the fact that their loved one wasn't coming home, and they'd never learn the full truth.

I was ushered to the desk of a woman with a pinched face and a short temper. I'd spoken with her at least three times in the past six months, and she never seemed all that empathetic with the people pleading with her to find information. I could tell that she desperately wanted me to fall in line and become part of that last group and accept that Maman wasn't coming back.

That I would be raising the girls on my own. That I'd be without her guidance and her support for the rest of my days.

The rest of that crowd might be able to accept not knowing the fate of their loved ones, but I was not.

"Mademoiselle, we have your information. We have the photo you provided of the missing person. We are doing everything we can. If we have information, *we* will reach out to *you*."

"You said that on all my previous visits, madame, but I have yet to receive a call or a letter of any kind," I countered.

"The logical conclusion, then, is that there is no information to be had on your mother," she replied. "You can rest assured we're doing all we can to uncover *all* the people who went missing during this terrible time."

"I don't care about *all* the missing people. I care about my mother. I want to know what's being done to look for her. I want to see what has been attempted. Surely you have records I can look over. Something that demonstrates the steps you're taking. If you show me, perhaps I might be able to help."

"That would be impossible, mademoiselle. We cannot allow the public to rummage through our files on a whim. Please do not come back unless you are called for. The time I spend explaining this to you is time I cannot use to serve others."

Others whose cases are not hopeless. She didn't say it, but she didn't have to.

I stormed from the office and flung myself on a park bench. I wasn't tempted to flop over and cry, I wanted to upturn the whole damned thing and scream.

Why could no one find her? Why was it so hard to find answers? Why did everyone on earth make me feel unreasonable for wanting to learn the truth?

I could accept that the past seven or eight years had been filled with so much tragedy that one missing mother was small in comparison with the enormity of it all. Who, truly, had been left untouched? There were villages the world over that lost *all* their men of fighting age. There were entire towns that were razed and that might never be rebuilt. This war had obliterated millions of universes.

But mine was one of them. And it mattered.

The worst of it was knowing that, as unfair as it was to me, it was worse for the girls. I'd had thirteen years with Papa. Seventeen with Maman. More than they would ever have. And they were left with me, inadequate as I was, to take the place of two loving parents. It hardly seemed like a just tradeoff.

I wanted to pull my hair out by the roots and scream into the wind. It wouldn't get me answers, but it made as much sense as anything else. I buried my head in my hands and swallowed it back, however, not wanting to be hauled off to a loony bin and leaving the girls well and truly alone.

"You seem upset," a man's voice said. I looked up from my hands to see a good-looking man, perhaps in his early thirties. He wore a navy-blue pinstripe suit, a gray fedora, and a confident expression. He took a seat on the opposite end of the bench. He pulled a cigarette case out from his breast pocket and proffered me one.

I waved the cigarettes away, not fond of the habit in others and unwilling to adopt an unnecessary expense myself. "It's none of your concern," I said, crossing my arms over my chest.

"Suit yourself, but I might be able to help. I saw you come out of the Red Cross building. Let me guess . . . they're giving you the runaround instead of actually helping."

"More or less," I admitted. It had to be a common tale. The people of the Red Cross were working hard in their various endeavors, but they weren't miracle workers. I couldn't be the only one frustrated with their inaction.

"What's the matter? Sweetheart went missing in the fray?"

I thought of Laurent. What a miracle it was that he'd escaped unscathed.

"Mother," I said. "She went missing just before the liberation."

"Listen, I know they promised you the world in there, but they're barely able to keep their heads above water cleaning up the mess after the Germans left. What you need is a private investigator."

"I don't know," I replied. "That sounds expensive."

"Aren't answers worth it?" He reached into his other breast pocket and removed a pristine white business card and handed it off to me with a flick of the wrist. "Think about it, kid. You can't put a price tag on peace of mind."

He stood, touched the brim of his hat, and sauntered off. I looked down at the card in my hand.

Didier Bodin

Private investigator

There was a telephone number and a nearby address in the corner. I wondered if he spent his time trolling outside buildings like these for people just like me, desperate to find answers. But maybe he was right, that the official channels were simply too bogged down to search efficiently for any one person. Of course sometimes they got lucky, but I suspected that was the exception rather than the rule.

I tucked the card inside my handbag and went home. Laurent was in the bakery kitchen, already on his second round of Duchess Cakes when I joined him.

"The first batch wasn't bad, but I don't think I let them rise quite enough," he said without breaking his rhythm as he stirred the next batch of pastry. "And I don't much care for the filling I used. I think raspberry wasn't the right choice."

"Apricot," I said, pulling down a jar of my homemade preserves from the shelf. "Nothing better. It's like sunshine in a jar."

"Perfect," he said.

I put on my apron and set to work making my own pastry dough. All the while, the business card in my handbag seemed to beckon with each turn of the spoon.

Chapter Twenty-Nine

LISETTE

MARCH 18, 1871

The generals marched up the butte, the sound of the horses' hooves clattering against the cobblestones at a brisk clip.

"Get as close as you can to the cannons," I said to Pierrine, inching my way closer to the nearest of the guns. She looked at me as though I'd sprouted a horn from the middle of my forehead, but quickly followed suit. Other women had come to join us by the cannons. We made no menacing gestures but stood firm.

I felt a familiar hand on my shoulder.

"What do you think you're doing?" Théo asked.

"Defending the cannons we paid for," I said. "And if you want it to happen without bloodshed, you and your men will stand back. Let them fire the first shots."

"At our wives? Our mothers? Our daughters? You expect

us to stand aside and watch? How can you even suggest such a thing?"

"The same way generations of men have asked their women to stay home and tend the hearth fire while our sons, husbands, and fathers are off being shot on battlefields for the glory of some Louis or Napoleon or another."

"Lisette," he said, his tone warning.

"Trust me. Keep your men back. I know these boys. They're good, hardworking young men. They don't want to fire on us," I pleaded.

"But their generals don't give a damn," he said. "And their soldiers will follow their orders."

"If they do, then you and your men can take down the lot and have the papers run them through the muck for being women-murdering villains."

Théo's face grew white as he realized what I was asking. What risk I was willing to take.

"Trust me," I repeated. Agony flashed in his eyes, but he turned to his troops.

"Fall back!" Théo ordered his men. They formed organized lines a few paces behind the cannons and the barricade of women who stood between the emperor's troops and our cannons. Their arms were at their sides. They would not take aim, but they could within seconds. The message was clear: there will not be violence on the streets of Montmartre if the Versaillais didn't fire first, but if they did, retribution would be brutal.

A man, tall with a gray beard and an aquiline nose, rode on a horse to the front of the line of troops that had, in the presence of their superior officers, fallen into an organized formation as our men had done.

I could feel the thud of my heart against my rib cage. I felt my lungs scream for air, but was scarcely able to take a breath.

I wanted more than anything to run to the safety of my shop and our little apartment, but if I did, if we surrendered the cannons to the emperor and his men, our home might never be safe again.

I felt a lurch in my stomach, and though it was far too early to feel movement, I thought of the dearest wish of my heart that seemed to be growing more certain with each day.

A little boy we could call Petit Théo who would be honorable and good like his father, or a darling girl sure to be spoiled by him.

This dearest hope of mine deserved to be raised in a France free from tyranny. A France that heard the voice of its people and listened well.

The general sat taller in his saddle. "Move aside!" he barked.

The women linked arms and blocked the cannons. We did not avert our eyes in deference to the mighty general. We stared him straight in the face and dared him to take what was ours.

"Move aside!" he ordered a second time.

We stood fast.

"Very well, you give me no choice," he drew his ceremonial sword and pointed it toward the crowd of women. "Fire!"

"Coward!" Pierrine yelled. "If you're going to order these boys to fire on women, be man enough to take a rifle in your hand and fire on us yourself."

The men behind him did not lift their arms. They looked to each other and back at us, then to the murderous face of their general.

"Do it!" I shouted to the general. "If you want these cannons, fire the shots yourself!"

The general's eyes focused on Pierrine—then me—and narrowed into slits. "Fire!" he commanded again.

Still, the Versaillais stood down.

"Your men don't want to fire on us," I shouted. "They know these cannons are rightfully ours, paid for by the people. They are for the defense of the city and manned by the National Guard as they should be. Leave us be, and there will be no trouble from us."

"Fire!" he shouted again.

Nothing.

"Fire on these whores, or I'll see each and every last one of you hanged for treason," he barked at his troops. His face was growing dangerously purple, and I secretly hoped he'd collapse of an apoplexy right there in the street and spare us all a lot of grief. I'd have to ask Sébas to hear my confession for those thoughts, but it was probably worth reciting a few rosaries for the satisfaction of seeing him fall on the cobblestones, a victim of his own bloodlust.

I heard a few low growls from the men behind us, enraged by the general's crass insults.

Don't let him bait you. It's exactly what he wants. If you fire one shot, if you make one move toward them, they will be merciless.

"Who do you stand with?" I shouted to the men. "The generals who kept you waiting, hungry and cold, or the women who welcomed you and fed you?"

"Listen to her," Pierrine joined in. "We gave you the food off our tables. We spoke to you as brothers. These generals don't give a damn about you. They'd leave you to freeze and starve and wouldn't spare you a second thought. We're your sisters. We would never forsake you the way they would. The way they have."

Her eloquence struck a chord. The resolve in the men's faces waned entirely.

"Fire, or I'll have your goddamned heads!" the general screamed. He sounded more and more like my little brother Antoine when one of his toys broke.

"No," one of them said. "This isn't right."

"I'm not going to fire on unarmed women," another chimed in.

"They told us they paid for the cannons themselves," another shouted. "I'm not a thief."

"Join us," I shouted. "Join your brothers and sisters in arms and defend what is right. Paris belongs to the people."

A cheer went up among the Versaillais troops. The general, knowing he'd lost, tried to trample his way through the troops and presumably back down the butte to get reinforcements, but the men grabbed the horse's reins and pulled the general down from his mount.

The scene grew chaotic as the National Guardsmen filtered down to join the defected Versaillais troops. The generals and highest-ranking officers were rounded up and were being carted off down the butte. To where, I didn't know, but I was certain their fates would be grim if they resisted their captors.

"You've made your point," Théo hissed into my ear. "Go home and lock and bar the doors. Take Pierrine with you. Don't open the doors for anyone other than me or Sébas. Do you understand?"

I nodded. I'd taken enough risks for Théo's heart to endure for one day. I took Pierrine by the elbow and we slipped through the crowd, narrowly escaping a few skirmishes between the last remaining loyal soldiers and the National Guard.

Pierrine and I slipped in the side of the shop, locked the doors, and shoved what furniture we could against them to secure ourselves inside. I wished we had boards for the windows, but there was nothing for it now.

Pierrine slid down the wall once the last chair was wedged in place.

"I've faced death before," she said. "My husband tried to kill me more than once. I've had men pull knives on me when they didn't want to pay for my company after they availed themselves of it. But I never was so certain I was going to die as I was just then."

I slid down next to her and wrapped my arm around her. "We won today. We kept the cannons safe."

"This won't be the end of it," she said, staring at a spot on the floor, but seeing nothing. Looking to the future that was now certain only in its tumultuousness.

"No," I agreed. "No matter what happens today, the emperor's men won't let us keep the butte without a fight. But today, we won."

"Today, we won," she agreed. "And you were bloody brilliant. I didn't think you had it in you, but those men listened to you."

"And to you," I said.

"What a novel change, having men listen," she said, chuckling without much humor.

I stood up and took another two of my cakes from the display case. Miniature *Gateaux St. Honoré* with caramel and *crème anglaise*. They were some of my favorites, with a harmony of textures. Creamy, crispy, flaky all at once.

"To our victory," I said, handing her one of the cakes. I resumed my place on the floor next to her and felt the weight of the morning press down on my shoulders. I took a bite of the cake and let the sugar, butter, flour, and cream filter into my soul and replenish me.

"I shouldn't," Pierrine said, but took a tentative bite.

"Why not?" I asked.

"I don't like accepting charity," she said.

"It isn't charity," I said, nudging her gently. "It's a woman sharing with her friend. I don't know if you consider me one, but after today, I can't think of you as anything else."

She leaned her head against my shoulder, and I could feel a few tears dampen my sleeve. I pressed my lips to the top of her head. I felt her head grow just a bit heavier on my shoulder as she relaxed.

"I'm not used to having friends," she admitted.

"What about Théo and Sébas?" I asked. "They're good friends to you."

"It's not the same. They see me as a broken soul. Something to fix. Someone in need of saving."

"It's hard to truly love someone who thinks you're lacking, isn't it?" I asked, thinking of my mother. Our situations had been different, so very different, but just similar enough that I could empathize with what she felt.

"I wanted to hate you," she said. "You came in here, gave up everything you had to be with Théo. I thought you'd run back to your parents at the first sign of trouble. That you'd break his heart. I didn't want that for him. But if you didn't run today, I don't think you will."

"I won't," I said. I wouldn't tell her how close I'd come, but I *had* come back. I passed that test of faith at least.

"I'm sorry I've been horrible to you," she said.

"You were concerned for Théo. Nothing wrong with that. I hope that things will be different for us now though."

"I do too," she said. "I've known Théo my whole life. I always felt like a big sister to him. He's a good man and deserved a good woman. I'm glad he found one. It's rare enough these days for the good people to find each other."

"Théo told me a bit about your husband," I ventured. "Not much, but he wanted me to understand . . ."

I felt her stiffen for a few seconds but relaxed once more. "I'm glad he told you," she said. "I'm glad you know, and I don't have to tell you. It's too hard."

"I can only imagine how hard it is. Being separated from your son, especially."

"Little Rémy. Named for his father. I pray for him every night. He's why I go to hear Sébas read the Mass on Sundays. If I wasn't trying to raise the money to get him back, I'd never have . . . well, fallen into the career I fell into. I wouldn't have wanted to disappoint him."

I felt the breath catch in my throat at her confession. How much she adored her son and how much she was sacrificing to get him back.

And how futile her efforts were likely to be.

"You don't disappoint *me*," I said. "Not that my approval should matter a jot."

She lifted her head and bumped my shoulder in appreciation. "I hate it, you know," she said. "The work. The men. I hate it. I just wait for the man who decides that my life is worthless and snuffs me out while he finds his pleasure. It happens every day, right here on the butte, and no one cares."

I thought about the blissful moments I'd spent in Théo's arms and shuddered at the thought of sharing such intimacy with a man I didn't care for. How it felt when I thought I'd have to give in to Mercier. I wasn't so naive to think that some physical pleasure couldn't be derived from the act itself, but to be so vulnerable with a man I didn't know would horrify me. That Pierrine had been driven to it because of her husband's indifference to her suffering was more maddening than I could express in words. And her loss was one I was only beginning to be able to comprehend.

"You'll get your Rémy back one day, Pierrine. I know it in my bones."

"You're more of an optimist than I am," she said. "The judges will never give him to me. He's his father's property as much as I am. And he treats the boy well enough. He just doesn't want me nearby."

"He ought to be made to provide for you," I said. "He can't just cast you aside like a child with a toy he's bored with."

"Half the judges in this town have done the same. And because of what I've had to do to survive, they'll see me as lower than the scum at the crook of the heel of their boots. Honest work for fair wages is the only answer for women. You've been to the clubs and rallies. The bourgeois women talk about the emancipation of women and all that fancy rubbish. What we need is *work*. We need decent jobs and good wages, same as any man. Until that day comes, the rest of these high-minded things won't matter."

"Do you want to come work for me?" I asked. "I can't pay much, but you could learn a trade you can take with you."

"You don't mean it," she said. "I've barely stepped foot in a kitchen in my life. I'll be worse than useless to you."

"I can teach you. You're smart. I won't say the work is easy, but it would be something different for you. And you can economize and stay in the room behind the kitchen to make up for the lousy wages I'll be paying you. It's small, but it's the warmest room in the house in winter. And all the food you need too."

"Including those cakes?" she asked, arching a hopeful brow.

"As many as you like. I'll teach you to make them so you can have them in your own home when you get little Rémy back."

Her eyes shone bright for a moment, but faded just as quickly.

"Théo won't like it," she said. "The added expense and all."

"Leave Théo to me. He won't argue with me when he understands why I need the help." I let a hand flutter to my belly.

"Really?" she asked. A smile flitted to her lips, but didn't meet her eyes. "How lovely. I can't remember the last time I was happy for an expectant mother. Usually the poor woman already has too many mouths to feed or she's a woman like me who can't be saddled with a baby. It's nice to remember that some babies are wanted."

I wrapped my arm around her and pressed my lips to her forehead again. She stiffened, then relaxed. She'd seen so little love in her life, she wasn't sure how to respond to it.

I wouldn't be able to fix the world. I didn't have Théo's grand ideas of even solving the problems of Paris. But I could make Pierrine's life a little more bearable, and that seemed like just enough to get started with.

MILLE-FEUILLE À L'ANCIENNE

→>—<←

Precision is a prerequisite of the *mille-feuille*. There is no room for doubts to enter a single layer, else the whole cake will be a failure. Proceed resolutely, and with no fear in your heart.

Prepare two-and-a-quarter pounds of puff pastry. Cut into rectangles two inches by four inches precisely. If they are not exact in size, the effect will be uneven and unappealing. Place the pastry pieces on a baking sheet, carefully spaced. Place a second baking sheet atop them to prevent excess rising while baking. Bake for ten minutes in a moderate oven. Let cool. If any pieces are less than perfect, try to even them with a hot knife. Barring that, enjoy any broken pieces with afternoon coffee.

Prepare a large batch of vanilla pastry cream. Take one piece of cooled pastry, pipe a thick layer of pastry cream, add a second layer of pastry, a second layer of cream, then a final layer of pastry. Make a vanilla glaze for the top with vanilla cloves, milk, and powdered sugar. Remove one-third of the mixture and place in another bowl. To this smaller batch, add cocoa powder and mix well. Ice the tops with vanilla glaze, and carefully swirl chocolate on top.

You can make one large *mille-feuille* and cut into two-by-four-inch cakes, but I find even the sharpest knife yields results not to my liking.

Recipe notes: experiment with berry-flavored pastry creams to play up the chocolate glaze.

Chapter Thirty

MICHELINE

Laurent, without question, was far better at making *mille-feuilles* than I was. He had a talent for precision that I couldn't match, and I grew frustrated when the edges of my flaky, layered pastries weren't as even as his, nor was the intricate zigzag of the chocolate as well defined. I'd tried a half-dozen batches, much to the delight of Noémie and Sylvie, but they weren't anything like ready for Rossignol. Laurent coached me, but I always managed to flub something small. A small shake of the hand and it all looked a mess.

After another less-than-optimal batch of *mille-feuilles*, I took off my apron, wadded it up in a ball, and tossed it in the corner. For more than a week, I'd thought about the private investigator and his offer to look for Maman. I'd taken his card from my handbag a number of times when no one was around and run my fingers along the raised letters. I'd picked up the receiver to our phone a dozen times and contemplated making the call.

I decided, one day while the girls were at school and Laurent was out running errands, that I'd do better to give in and speak to the man rather than mulling it over day after day. I decided against a phone call, knowing that calls to the registry office and Red Cross had never resulted in more than being shuffled around and ultimately being disconnected.

I trudged to the address on the card and prayed that the man's fees weren't so exorbitant as to be out of the question.

Then again, none of the money in my possession was really my own. It was all Madame Dupuis' generous donations to help fund her unfortunate neighbor girls. Charity.

I pushed the thought from my head and kept walking. If we found Maman, I'd be able to repay her every last *centime*. If we did not, I'd make it up to her in pastries.

Lord willing, perfect *mille-feuilles*.

Bodin's office was in a building off a narrow side street, on the third floor up a dank staircase. His name was painted in the glass portion of the door, which was left slightly ajar. I rapped on the glass with my knuckle twice before entering.

"Ah, the girl with the missing mother. I'd hoped you'd find your way here." Bodin looked up from the papers on his desk, a cigarette smoldering in an ashtray. The room smelled like he hadn't opened a window in months, and I felt like I couldn't quite fill my lungs with enough air.

"Can you help me find her?" I asked.

"I can't make promises, but I can assure you that I'll be able to give the case more personal attention. It's been two years since your mother went missing, yes?"

I nodded, impressed that he'd remembered the details.

"It won't be easy, but I've had stranger luck in the past," he said taking a deep drag from his cigarette. "Tell me all you know that will help me find her."

I recounted everything I could remember about her disappearance, her appearance, anything identifying about her. I gave him one of the last photos taken of her. Though it was several years before her disappearance, it was still a good likeness of her before she'd gone.

"She was a lovely woman . . . much like her daughter," Bodin said.

"Um . . . thank you," I replied, looking down. "So what happens next?"

"Well first, we have to discuss the issue of payment."

I felt my stomach sink. I'd known this was coming but had foolishly hoped that he somehow might forget that small question.

"I'm afraid I don't have much," I said. "I've been left to raise my younger sisters, you see . . ."

"I understand far too well, mademoiselle. These have been hard times for many." He stood from his desk and came around to the chair near mine. "You're a clever girl. I am sure we'll be able to come to an arrangement."

He patted my hand reassuringly. *My God, he's actually going to be able to help.* I felt the tears of relief sting at my eyes.

"I'm so grateful, Monsieur Bodin," I said. "I'd do anything to have Maman back."

"That's precisely what I was hoping to hear," he said. He scooted his chair closer and lowered his lips down on mine. Insistent. Forceful.

His intentions registered with me, and I felt the scream rise in my throat.

What if this is the only way I can get her back? I swallowed back the scream, but only just.

Could I allow this man to take what he wanted if it meant finding her? Surely it was better than doing something like mortgaging the bakery.

Or never finding out the truth.

Bodin placed his hand at my side and worked his way up to my breast. When he cupped it, rough and uncaring, I felt myself recoil. To allow him to paw and grope me where Laurent had caressed me so gently was a transgression I wouldn't be able to atone for. It wasn't that Laurent wouldn't be able to accept a moment of weakness in such desperate times; I wouldn't be able to forgive myself.

I pushed back from Bodin, the chair screeching on the wooden floor. "I can't do this," I said.

He grabbed my wrist. "Come now, I thought you were smart. Don't you want to find your mother?"

I pulled my wrist from his grip. "Yes, but I don't want to lose myself in the process."

I ran from the room and hurried back up the butte to the bakery. Laurent was still not back from his errands and the girls were still safely in school. I got out the ingredients to practice my *mille-feuilles* once more, but once they were all in place, I sunk to the floor, my back against the cabinets and my head on my knees. I let the tears come, let them have me.

One more roadblock in finding her. One more disappointment.

As hard as I tried to keep my expectations in check, each time I raised my hopes, it was only to find them dashed.

And it was like losing her all over again.

I allowed myself to wallow in it for a while. To allow the tears time to stain my cheeks.

When I was finished, I stood and got back to work, trying to make the perfect batch of *mille-feuilles* for perhaps the twelfth time. I tried to push everything from my mind and keep my hand steady. Though one thought kept creeping in, no matter how hard I tried to banish it:

Would I ever be able to accept that Maman was never coming home?

Chapter Thirty-One

LISETTE

APRIL 3, 1871

Three cheers for Citizen Fournier and his new position at the *mairie*!" cheered Sébas, raising a glass of good Bordeaux to the four of us assembled.

"Hear, hear!" Pierrine and I joined in, clinking our glasses.

Pierrine and I had put together a lavish meal with onion soup, a beef tenderloin that had been slowly roasted to perfection, potatoes, carrots, and an assortment of our best pastries. We dined in splendor that night, and I couldn't remember anything Nanette served us ever tasting finer.

The noose had been removed from the neck of Paris, and once more we could breathe.

It had taken time, but the supply of food into the capital was much back to normal. Beyond flour, water, and yeast, we had beef, pork, and fowl again. I knew it was my imagination, but

I could almost feel my body absorbing the goodness from the food and healing all the minor hurts that had been slow to heal during the months of want. With every bite, I felt a pang of guilt, a tinge of regret, for those who hadn't been able to outlast the siege.

Despite her concerns that she would be a poor assistant, Pierrine had proven a fast learner in the kitchen and determined to earn her way. In two short weeks, she had learned a few recipes and was improving in her technique.

More importantly, there was a healthy glow in her cheeks from adequate sleep and food that hadn't been there before. There was still a fire in her gut lit by the anger she bore toward her husband, but it was further from the surface now, and better under her control. She had put on some weight and looked like she had more energy to face the world.

"A real government functionary," I said, leaning over to kiss Théo's cheek. "I don't think even my parents could object to that."

"How disappointing. I admit I got a thrill from imagining how displeased they'd be by me."

"They might approve of a government functionary, but not this particular government," Sébas said with a laugh.

"Oh, perhaps not," I allowed. "But if they were wise, they'd be glad to have friends on the other side."

"Fair point," Pierrine said. "And on that note, I took my afternoon off to speak with a magistrate. They're willing to hear my case next week. If the people are truly in charge, then Bérnard's rank and privilege won't matter as much. With the right judge, I just might stand a chance of getting my boy back. You would let me keep him here, wouldn't you? Until I find something larger for us?"

"Of course," I said, leaning over to kiss her cheek. "We'd love the boy as one of our own."

Sébas looked down at his glass for a moment. "The laws still greatly favor the father in these matters, Pierrine. I hope you won't get your hopes up too high."

Théo shot Sébas a warning look. *Not tonight,* mon ami. *Don't spoil this for her. Or for me.*

Pierrine either didn't notice Théo's glare or chose to ignore it. "I'm aware, but if ever I had a chance, it's now," she said.

"Agreed," Théo said. "It's the dawn of a new day. With Sébas and I giving you spotless character witnesses and with steady employment with Lisette in one of the most honored professions in all of France, you've never been better placed to make an attempt."

"I hope to God you're right. For Pierrine's sake." It was clear Sébas wanted to say more, but stopped short. But it was clear he was worried Pierrine would lose her case and fall deeper into the abyss for the loss. That Sébas held his tongue made me more worried than if he'd voiced his concerns aloud.

Did he think it was hopeless? A year—even a few months ago—it certainly would have been. No court in the world would have awarded a child to its mother if the father made a claim. Added to the reality that he was a man of standing and she had been reduced to working the streets, it would have been worse than hopeless even with her new position in the bakery. Even with Théo testifying on her behalf.

But now, there did seem to be reason to hope. To dream of better things. A world the way it should have been.

But dreams, as we knew all too well, did not always translate into realities.

"We'll all do our part," I said. "And even if the worst should come to pass, Pierrine will know she tried everything. That's a comfort, whatever the outcome."

Sébas looked mollified at my addition, like a father trying not to make promises to a child that couldn't be kept. But Pierrine was right, the time had never been better to plead her case.

"And even if things go badly, Pierrine will be needed here to be a doting godmother to our own little one," I said. I rested my hand on her shoulder and she patted it with her own. She looked up at me with a small smile. I was offering a consolation prize. I knew it would be a long way from raising her own child, but she'd at least have an outlet for the maternal love she had kept pent up for so long.

Théo lowered his glass from his lips and looked at me, eyes wide with comprehension. "Really, my love?"

"Really," I said. "Early days yet, so no cause to crow too loudly yet, but I couldn't keep the news entirely to myself."

Théo stood and wrapped his arms around me. "I don't know what I've done to deserve such good fortune, but I'm not going to question it." Emotion caused his voice to warble as he tucked me under his chin.

"It's because you're a good man, Théo, and for once, the world seems to be favoring those on the right side," Pierrine said, and she squeezed my hand as if to add me to that number.

"This calls for champagne with our dessert," Théo said, standing. "Bordeaux may be a fine companion to a meal, but to celebrate this night, we shall sip the stars."

"Come on, Dom Perignon, let's get to the wine merchant. He'll be closed, but I'm sure he wouldn't mind opening the door to us just this once," Pierrine said. "We'll let the young maman have a rest. Perhaps Sébas can practice his sermon for her. Nothing better for bringing on a catnap."

"Very funny," Sébas said drily. Of course, Pierrine was one of the most attentive members of the congregation when Sébas spoke, nor had she missed a Sunday in years.

As soon as they left, Sébas rubbed his eyes with both hands.

"Thank you," he said, after a few moments of silence. "I didn't want to cast a pall over the celebrations tonight, but I don't want Pierrine going into the hearing thinking that she was assured a victory. Things may have changed, but they don't change that fast. They haven't tossed out the law books altogether."

"Nor the prejudices that brought the laws about," I said.

"Precisely," Sébas said. "You understand better than your husband that hearts and minds aren't changed overnight. No matter how much we might want them to be."

"You're worried," I said. "And not just about Pierrine."

"What gave me away?" he asked.

"You didn't bait Théo at dinner or urge prudence as you normally do," I said.

"You noticed," he said. It wasn't a question. He didn't meet my eyes but fiddled with a few crumbs that remained on his dinner plate with the tines of his fork.

"When you remind him of how perilous our situation is, it's concerning. When you stop altogether it's terrifying."

"I'm glad you're paying attention at least," he said. "Thiers is a determined man. He won't let Paris stay in our hands for long. He has the entire army of Versailles behind him and the blessing of everyone in France who carries influence."

"The army didn't prove all that effective against Prussia," I said, unable to keep the sarcasm from my tone. "Perhaps we'll be just as fortunate."

"The army will be all the more resolved to prove their worth after their defeat. They'll be brutal, too, to save face. And the reality is that the citizens of Paris are not in the same class as the Prussian army, no matter how valiant they may think they are. We don't have the same resources as Prussia. We don't have their firepower. We don't have the organization and planning they have. We may have staved off the Versaillais for a while, but it's only a matter of time before Thiers and his men come back and claim the city back for the oligarchs."

"You paint a bleak picture," I said.

"I'm trying to paint an honest one. I wish I could tell you that the Commune was going to triumph, and that France was finally headed in the direction the Revolution tried to take us, but I confess I can't lie to you and fill your heart with false hope."

"Is it really as dire as all that?"

"Lisette, I hear things from the superiors. The Church would love to see the Commune squelched and they're putting their resources into defeating it. As much as I wish it, I don't see how the Commune will prevail for long. You know these people too. You were born among them. They won't let Paris remain in the hands of the people."

"So what are we to do?" I asked, leaning back in my chair, and wishing that the Bordeaux was palatable to me in my state.

"What we've always done. Survive."

I nodded.

"You must promise me to be prudent. No matter what Théo does. It's not worth risking the baby's life or yours," Sébas said.

"You think it will come to that?" I asked.

"It's only a question of when they will come knocking at the door," Sébas said. He took my hand in his. He tucked his finger gently under my chin to pull my face to look directly at his and repeated, "You must promise me to stay safe."

"I promise," I said. "Though I wish you were wrong."

"You know I'm not," he said. He seemed to remember himself and removed his hands from mine. He sat back in his seat and focused his eyes on the wall beyond me.

"Why the Church, Sébas? You've got the heart of a revolutionary, but you tied yourself to the institution that wants more than anything to keep the monarchy in its place."

"I hoped to be a voice for the people," he said. "People have found solace in the Church, but the Church has failed to be what they need. I hoped to remind my superiors of their true purpose."

"Have you met with much success?" I asked.

"No," he admitted. "The Church is convinced it knows better than the people. My superiors are convinced they know better than I."

"That has to be hard," I said. "Why do you stay?"

"Because I'm more like Théo than I would ever admit to his face," he said, the corners of his lips turning up in a smile. "An optimist. To the point of foolishness. I cling stubbornly to the hope that the Church will finally serve the people as it should."

"I hope you're right," I said. "If anyone can bring about this change, it's you."

"Well, if nothing else, a tumbled-down church in ruins makes for a great place to hide weapons for the cause," he said with a wink. "No one would think to look there. And no one would ever imagine that a priest would house a stockpile, now would they?"

Though he was careful to be humble, especially among the people of the neighborhood, Sébas was a man of incredible intelligence and learning. Théo would have made a great scholar too, had his situation been different. I wondered what these men would have made of the world if they had been born to families like mine. Sébas wouldn't have been constrained to a life as a parish priest. If he'd been called to the Church and wasn't in line to inherit, he could have set his sights on becoming a bishop or even a cardinal. There was no question that Théo would have gone into politics. But had they been born to families like mine, their fervor would have been for causes antithetical to those they held dear. They would have rallied for the preservation of the institutions and systems that kept power in the hands of the elite.

Pierrine, had she been born to a family like mine, would have been harder to cast aside. Her family could have protected her from a wicked husband like Rémy Desrosiers. They would have had connections to help persuade the courts that the child would be better off in the care of his mother's family than in his father's. She wouldn't have custody in her own right, but her family could have fought for her.

If they'd wanted to.

She would have been at their mercy just as she was at the mercy of the courts now.

It seemed hopeless to think of a world where these men could have the riches to meet their full potential, without the riches corrupting the very essence that made them good men. It seemed impossible to imagine a world where Pierrine might live a life where she'd known love and security without being vulnerable to the whims of the men who held dominion over her.

Sébas sensed this, and looked back at me.

"Maybe tonight, Théo is right. It's time to honor what has been won and celebrate our victory, no matter how fleeting it may prove to be." His eyes tried to glimmer with hope, but the spark was shallow.

"You're right." It was my turn to step out of character and breach the unspoken boundary between us. I reached over and squeezed his hand. "Théo is lucky to have you as a friend, you know. You're the embodiment of his guardian angel and conscience all in one."

"It's a bloody lot of work, trying to talk sense to that idiot," Sébas said. "But he's been my best friend since I was able to walk. It seems worth it to try."

"I'm glad you do," I said.

"Glad he does what?" Théo said, bounding in with a bottle, Pierrine hard on his heels.

"Is such a good friend to you," I said, softening the truth with a wink to Sébas. "A good friend to all of us."

"A sentiment to drink to," Pierrine said, fetching glasses. She filled hers, filled to the brim with frothy wine the color of candle glow. "To friendship."

"To friendship," we chorused.

"It's going to turn out, you know," Théo said as we downed our glasses as though he'd overheard the conversation Sébas and I had while they were gone.

"How do you know?" I asked, placing a kiss on his cheek.

"It will because it has to," he said with supreme confidence.

And for a fleeting moment, I let myself believe it too.

CROQUEMBOUCHE

I helped make one of these when Nanette was commissioned to help with the wedding of one of our neighbor girls. Nanette said it was one of the biggest challenges of her life, but I never saw her look prouder when it was finished. I didn't have one for my own wedding, but now I make sure that every bride in the neighborhood, no matter how poor, has at least a small one for her wedding breakfast.

For a traditional wedding *croquembouche*, prepare a large batch of *choux* pastry dough and a very large batch of pastry cream. Using a piping bag, pipe the pastry into one-and-a-half-inch mounds, more than two inches apart. Bake in medium oven for a quarter of an hour. When baked and cooled, take a small knife to the bottom of each pastry and fill each of the baked puffs with vanilla pastry cream from a fresh piping bag.

Make a cone structure from stiff paper on a large board that can be used to transport the *croquembouche*. Make a large pot of caramelized sugar. Working quickly, dip the tops of each filled puff in the caramel and place them around it to create a giant cone of pastry. Reheat the caramel as needed to keep it supple. When the cone is complete, let the remaining caramel cool and create strands of caramel floss with a fork to create a lovely webbing around the cake.

Recipe notes: Can be gently decorated with sugar flowers or even real ones. Experiment with different flavors of pastry cream and perhaps chocolate, lemon, or almond choux pastry. Especially fun to alter the recipe to make bold flavors for the celebration of a wedding anniversary.

Chapter Thirty-Two

MICHELINE

T he *croquembouche* is the queen of all French pastries," Chef Rossignol lectured as he walked the aisle between our stations. "By itself, the humble creampuff is a simple enough undertaking. But to construct a real *croquembouche* is quite another. Your creations must not just look impressive, they must be a delight to the palate. But even more than this, a *croquembouche* must be strong. It must stay intact throughout the marriage ceremony and the wedding meal. It must look as flawless after three hours in the summer sun as it did the moment you arrived at the reception hall to deliver it. There is no room for error."

This was true of a *croquembouche*, but the reality was that Chef Rossignol expected the same perfection from a simple batch of *Madeleines* as he did this all-important wedding cake.

"The *croquembouche* must be as resilient as the love the bride and groom have for one another. This is the most important dessert of the couple's lives together, and I hope your final results show that you have treated this assignment with the respect it is due."

Laurent's eyes met mine, and I saw the longing in them. After six months of sharing our dreams, and my mother's bed, he was ready to build a life together.

My palms grew slick with sweat, and not just because we were waiting for Rossignol to pass his judgment.

It was the day of our final practical exam, and Laurent and I waited at our stations. Our *croquembouches*, the towers of cream puffs encased in a cloud of caramel floss, awaited the scrutiny of Chef Rossignol.

After six months of intensive study for our diplomas in boulangerie and pâtisserie, Laurent and I had reached the end of our course, and our success would all come down to what one man thought about our performance on one afternoon. Laurent's *croquembouche* turned out a bit squatter than mine, but his *choux* pastry was a deeper golden brown. The caramel work on both was flawless. About half the students, some with tear-streaked faces, had been less successful. Several hadn't been able to finish in time and stood next to well-constructed but incomplete towers. Some had *choux* pastry that looked a bit scorched. Others were underdone and their towers had collapsed. The rest of the students had towers that looked every bit as lovely as ours, though Rossignol's critiques often revealed flaws I hadn't known had existed.

When he finally arrived at the station I shared with Laurent, he stood before Laurent's offering first. He cut loose one of the cream puffs from the middle of the tower. Mercifully, it didn't come crashing down. As he bit into the cream puff, the caramel crackled between his teeth. As impassive as he kept his face, there was no ignoring the glint in his eye. For only the second time, he touched his index and middle fingers to the band of his chef's hat in a small salute. Laurent beamed, and deservedly so.

He moved over to mine. I'd read Lisette's directions on *croquembouches*, which were, understandably, not something she'd made often, but she'd made some notes that provided a bit more guidance than Rossignol's notoriously opaque recipes. I'd tweaked the recipe for the cream filling more than anything else. I used three vanilla beans to infuse the cream when he called for two. I added cream to the milk when the vanilla was steeping over the low flame. I strained the custard to make the texture softer. And when the chef wasn't looking, I tipped in just a spoonful or two of rum that I snuck in with a flask just before the mixture cooled. Given my druthers, I'd have experimented with chocolate or cherry fillings as well as the traditional vanilla custard cream, but this was the time to demonstrate that we could produce the basics before we flaunted our hubris by attempting the experimental.

Once more, he removed one of the cream puffs from the conical tower and put it to his lips. The compulsory crackle of caramel was like a fine concerto to me. He paused to consider the flavor, looked down to the creampuff and back to me.

"*C'est une merveille,*" he said. "*Félicitations, mademoiselle.*"

The heat rose to my cheeks, and I couldn't contain a smile. He said my *croquembouche* was a marvel.

Despite the hardships and toil of the past two years, for a moment, it all seemed as though things were—honestly and truly—right in the world. I felt the coils release my gut. I felt my shoulders loosen and my jaw unclench. I took a deeper breath than I'd taken since perhaps before the war began.

Rossignol continued to assess the rest of the towers, but I found I couldn't listen to his critiques with the attention they deserved. All that mattered to me was that I had succeeded. I'd been able to accomplish this without the girls running feral or running myself mad. Of course the financial contributions of Madame Dupuis, and Laurent's help and support, had made the whole endeavor possible, but I'd done my best to make great things of the opportunity they'd afforded me. And, for once, I would allow myself to be proud.

As soon as class was dismissed, we hurried back to the bistro—the bakery—and looked at the place in wonder. We could open as soon as we were ready.

"I'd like to take the lead on breads to free you for pastry work," Laurent said as we sat with a notebook at one of the little bistro tables. "If you don't mind, of course."

"I'd assumed as much," I said. It only made sense to play to our strengths. He made the finest baguettes I'd ever tasted in a time where the quality sold in other bakeries was on the decline. It would be a source of pride to make bread in the old way, before cutting corners with cost and saving time meant more than quality.

"The kitchen is lacking a few of the modern machines that will help us produce what the neighborhood needs," he said. "A kneading machine, for one, will save hours without compromising the quality."

"That sounds expensive," I said, thinking of the modest amount of cash I'd kept in reserve from Madame Dupuis' allowance she gave me each week.

"I've spoken to my father about it, and he's willing to lend us a hand to get our start. We won't need to spend a fortune, but we'd do better to start with a kitchen that's equipped to meet our needs."

"That's very gracious of him," I said. I was already indebted enough to Madame Dupuis, I wasn't sure how comfortable I felt accepting more help from Monsieur Tanet, a man I hadn't yet met. "But are you sure? It's a great deal to ask of him."

"He's proud to help," he said. "He'd saved for this very occasion. He always believed parents should do what they can to set their children up for a good start into adulthood. 'Give them enough to do something, but not enough to do nothing' was always his motto."

"A sound one," I said. I'd already planned to set aside a regular sum for the girls for this very purpose. Whether it was used for schooling, a career, or a family—or some combination of those things—would be up to them. "But he never agreed to provide for me in the bargain."

"No," Laurent said. "But you could think of it as a wedding gift if it makes you more comfortable."

"Wh-what?" I stammered.

"A wedding gift," he repeated. He leaned closer and lowered his lips to mine.

"You know how much I want to marry you. And now that we've got our diplomas and we're going to open the shop together . . . we can have a lovely to-do. My family will come in from Lamballe and we can properly wow them with the splendor of Paris. What do you think?"

My time was up, and I had no excuses left to offer him. I'd pleaded with him to table the discussion of marriage while we were in our courses, but now they were over, and I could offer no good reason to delay further. And there was no part of me that wanted to refuse him.

I simply didn't know how to accept him.

I leaned back in my chair and turned my face away from his. "I—I don't know."

"I thought you would want to," he said. His tone was wounded. I'd hurt him. This man who had never been anything but kind to me. Who'd shared my bed for months and been a father figure to the girls.

But how could I marry? It was a monumental decision, and I didn't have Maman to ask for advice. I didn't have Papa to give his blessing. To marry without them wouldn't feel like a marriage at all.

When I had thought of getting married when I was a girl, I'd always envisioned Papa walking me down the aisle at Saint-Pierre. Maman in the first row, dabbing daintily at her tears of joy. A flowing white dress and a few close friends to wish us well.

All I could envision now was a rushed ceremony where, instead of focusing on the vows, I'd be distracted, hoping the girls would behave. There would be no flowing white gown. I'd have to wear something of Maman's. If there were to be a wedding luncheon, I'd likely end up making it myself.

But none of that was truly of importance.

What mattered most was that Maman and Papa would not be there.

The very idea broke my heart.

"Can—can we worry about getting the bakery off to a good start first?" I asked. "I don't want to take on too much all at once."

"You don't want to marry me?" he said. "Micheline, I thought you loved me."

"I *do* love you, Laurent," I said, feeling not even the slightest hesitation at speaking those words aloud. "It's just so much at once."

"It will be fine," he said. "There's no such thing as too much joy, is there?"

"Joy has been rationed more strictly than butter," I said. "And even harder to find. After more than two years of privation, it's a shock to the system."

"Just be honest with me," Laurent pleaded, his face growing red as he tried to control the fervor of his pleas. "If this isn't what you want, let me know so I can build a life for myself elsewhere. I don't think that's asking too much."

"No it isn't," I agreed. "But all I'm asking for is a little time."

He paused a moment, the color lowering from beet-red back to something closer to normal. "I can be patient," he said at length. "But I won't wait forever."

"I wouldn't ask that of you," I said. "Truly I wouldn't."

"I'd hoped you'd be happy," he said. "I'd hoped this would be one of the happiest moments of our lives."

"I'm sorry, Laurent. I didn't mean to ruin things for you."

"You haven't," he said. "I have. By making assumptions I had no business making. And I am so damned sorry."

He stood up and gathered his things.

"Where are you going?" I managed to stammer.

"My place. You need time to think. I need time too. I'll be back to work at the bakery if you want me, but I can't stay here . . . I may not be old-fashioned, but I can't live with a woman who has no intention of marrying me."

Laurent stood and left the bakery without another word.

I let my head drop to my arms, crossed on the bistro table, and cursed myself. I'd hurt one of the few people on whom I could depend. Who loved me. Who I loved.

And I had no idea how to make it right.

Chapter Thirty-Three

LISETTE

MAY 21, 1871

Sébas rapped smartly on the glass. I was set to open in a matter of minutes, but it was clear he wasn't here for his breakfast. Pierrine wiped her hands on my apron and rushed to flip the locks for him. He entered the shop, his face white as the flour in my storeroom. With the stories of the impending trouble, I wasn't going to risk a shortage again. I'd stockpiled food for the past week and would spend every last *centime* I had to keep us well supplied until there was some sort of ceasefire. I baked plain breads again, and in far smaller quantities.

"What's the trouble?" Pierrine asked by way of greeting. There was no need to suppose he came bearing any news other than ill.

"The Versaillais have breached the city," he said. "The reports are brutal."

Théo thundered down from the apartment, having heard the commotion.

"Surely the barricades will hold them off," Théo said. "We need to reinforce them and rally all the support we can."

"Théo, this is the whole of Thiers's army. They're mowing down anyone with Communard sympathies. I don't think barricades are going to be enough."

"They came in from the west, yes?" Théo asked. Sébas nodded.

"The west has more loyalist sympathies. Of course they had an easy time if they have yet to meet any real resistance. They haven't come to the People's Paris yet."

"Théo," Sébas said. "Do you really think the Commune can hold off the army? How long do you think we can hold out?"

"How can you say that, Sébas? We have Paris under our control. We can't just hand it back over. We can't."

"Think of what you're doing. Think of your wife and unborn child. I don't want to see the monarchy restored any more than you do, but this fight is tantamount to suicide. Don't be a martyr."

"Damn you, Sébas. Every time we come close to winning, this is what the cowards say. You want to shrink away and hide. You don't want to risk your necks for the cause. What use are you if you're not willing to lay down your life to be your own master? If you don't stand with us at the barricades, then get out of our way."

"You can't win this," he said. "Isn't it worth living to fight another day?"

"You wouldn't understand, Sébas," he said. "You're too

mired in tradition. You're a man of thoughts, not action. Go to your church and pray. I'll go to the barricades and fight. We'll see how it all comes out in the end."

Théo grabbed his rifle and stormed out the door without a backward glance at his best friend. Or at me.

"Théo!" I shouted. He didn't break stride as he left the shop, the door slamming behind him.

I gripped the counter, willing myself to stay upright.

"I'll go with him," Pierrine said, rubbing my shoulder. "Maybe I can be of use."

She left the bakery, her pace listless. She'd lost her case with the magistrate once again, and as Sébas had feared, it had broken what was left of her spirit. If she hadn't won when the people ruled Paris, there wasn't much hope for the situation to ever improve.

I stared after them and Sébas stayed rooted in place. We stood in silence for what felt like the space of hours.

"Lisette, promise me you won't do anything foolish," he said at length. "Remember the promise you made to me. Think of the baby."

My hand flitted to my midsection. The little one, aside from causing me uncomfortable mornings, was still imperceptible. Still many months away from coming into the world. What sort of world he would be born into, I couldn't say. Whether Paris would still be standing, I didn't know. But right now, I could only think of his father.

"Of course," I mumbled.

"I'm serious, Lisette. Théo may hate me for speaking reason, but you're more sensible than that. You know I wish it weren't true, but there is no conceivable path for the Commune to make its way forward. Thiers's army is too powerful."

I thought of thousands of men, all like Gaspard, who had spent the last two months plotting their attack on the workers of Paris. How their egos had been bruised, first by the Prussians, then by the Communards. They would be ruthless in their quest to restore their honor. They would come with their *mitrailleuses* and shoot every last person who even appeared to have sympathies for the Commune.

"What am I going to do?" I asked to no one in particular.

Sébas came behind the counter where I was rooted, and for the first time in our acquaintance, wrapped his arms around me. "You're going to survive, Lisette. You're going to be smart and do what's right for you and the child. As much as I want to drag Théo from the barricades by the collar of his own shirt, the thought of you falling into the hands of the Versaillais makes me twice as scared."

I looked up at him, baffled by his vehemence.

"Lisette, this isn't what you were meant for. You weren't meant to suffer like this."

"So you're like everyone else who wants to stuff me into a gilded cage like a canary," I said. "Théo is the only one who thought more of me than that."

I shuddered at my use of the past tense.

"When there is a roving army of vicious cats roaming about, you're damned right I want to put every canary I care about in a sturdy steel cage. But since I can't protect them all, you're going to bear the brunt of it."

"Sébas . . ."

"Lisette, I have to get back to the church, but I need your word that you'll come to me and ask for sanctuary if there is any trouble. Wear your best clothes and put on your best Place Royale manners. Promise me."

Promise me. His constant litany. I opened my mouth and snapped it shut. "Fine," I said. "I promise."

He didn't look completely mollified, but Sébas left me to guard his church from marauders. My stomach sank as I realized that he was warehousing the arms for the Commune. If the Versaillais took the church, they'd have one of our major stockpiles under their control. And they'd blame Sébas for it. And the Communards might, in their blind rage, take down any man wearing a cassock because they assumed he was a monarchist. I wasn't sure which side posed a larger risk to him, the Communards or the Versaillais. Sébas was a man caught between the two worlds and risked being severed in two.

The emptiness of the shop was oppressive. I couldn't breathe under the weight of it. If I didn't find an occupation soon, I'd run mad, but there was no sense in opening a shop when all my customers were either at the barricades or too frightened to leave their apartments.

I found my marketing basket, the one Nanette had given me, and loaded it with all the bread I'd made for the day. I would not go back on my word to Sébastien and fight at the barricades, but I could feed those who did.

I followed Sébastien's advice and put on the pink satin dress I'd worn home after my visit to my parents' house. The May weather was fine compared to the bleak days of January when

I last wore it, and while still impractical, at least it wasn't as ill-suited to the weather. It was impossible to think that such violence could transpire under the gentle rays of late spring. It was the season of birth, of life, but all over Paris, lives were being cut short.

I loaded myself down with every loaf of bread I'd made that morning. Mostly long *flûtes* that were faster to bake and had become my staple in the shop. At first, I went to the apartments of those I knew were elderly and likely suffering as they hid in their homes. Most of them only answered when they heard my voice calling them and telling them there was no cause for alarm. They accepted the bread gratefully, and I hoped it would make the long days of the street fighting more endurable for them.

But once I'd done that, I ventured closer to the barricades. Those who fought for us were likely starving and a bit of bread might help them rally their strength. God knew they would need it. I tore each loaf into thirds and passed them out to whomever I came across. Each morsel was taken with gratitude. I was about to retreat with my empty basket to the bakery when the volley of the *mitrailleuses* grew heavier and louder. The Versaillais were at our doorstep.

Remembering my promise to Sébas, I turned to run to the church as fast as I could without attracting attention.

The Versaillais had spilled into the *quartier* now, and I tried to keep my composure as I walked. I came across two Versaillais with their bayonets pointed at a woman—Pierrine—against the walls of the church. There was no flicker of fear in her eyes. There was no trembling in her knees. Only the fire of defiance. A soldier of some rank—a major perhaps—came up behind them.

"She's one of them, sir. A *pétroleuse*. I'd bet my life on it."

In the days since the Versaillais breached Paris, there had been reports of people—women especially—burning buildings and monuments. Laying waste to the city so they would at least have the satisfaction of leaving Thiers with nothing but a city of ashes to rule over. The reprisals against these women were swift and brutal.

"Well, go on," was all the major said.

"No!" I screamed, but it was too late for Pierrine. They snuffed her out as soon as the major gave his order.

They turned to me. The major cocked an eye at my appearance. I didn't look like the rest of the people of the butte, and it was the only thing that had given them pause.

"She is . . . was . . . my assistant. She was just a baker."

"What sort of baker wears a gown such as yours?" the major asked, drawing his bayonet.

I stood, unable to speak as one of the soldiers grabbed me by the arm and shoved me against the same wall where he'd murdered Pierrine. I was forced to step over her body to accept my fate. The man shoved me so hard I hit my head on the wall. I saw flecks of light and fought to stay conscious as they shouted at me. Their words seemed garbled, and I began to shake.

"Unhand her!" a voice screamed.

Sébas.

I heard the men arguing but could make no sense of their

words. Soon, Sébastien was in front of me, blocking me from the bayonets.

"She was feeding the Communard scum!" I could hear one of them yell. A crowd of Versaillais had gathered though they all looked like blue-and-red hazy figures to me.

"She feeds those who need feeding," Sébas barked. "As the Lord commands us to do."

The men were screaming and motioning for Sébas to step aside. They wanted to finish their job but were loath to kill a priest to do it. I gripped on to Sébastien's shoulders, knowing I would faint if I released him.

Finally, someone ripped Sébas away and I fell to the ground. I felt the prick of a bayonet at my chest. I wished I could be brave like Pierrine and meet my end with such courage, but I felt myself shake as the blade came closer.

The world was swirling, but in a moment, all came into focus and I saw the face of the soldier towering above me.

Gaspard d'Amboise.

He gaped in horror as he recognized me, and at once, all went black.

Chapter Thirty-Four

MICHELINE

Laurent and I graduated from our baking class with special distinction. I kept Lisette's journal in my apron pocket as a talisman during every written exam and practical evaluation. She brought me luck with every lesson, though Laurent reminded me that it was my own confidence that allowed me to move ahead. I'd gotten out of my own way.

And with some hard work to convert the bistro back into a bakery, and a fresh coat of emerald-green paint on the building façade, the bakery was ready to open. Sylvie, whose artistic talents were far beyond what I'd realized, had insisted on painting an Eiffel Tower in the window with the words *depuis 1870* with some of the leftover gold paint. "For the tourists," she explained. "They love the tower and anything pretending to be older than it really is."

None of us could find fault with her arguments and the effect, I had to admit, was charming.

Laurent had inherited his father's head for business as well as his mother's talent in the kitchen, so it seemed natural to go into the enterprise together. And true to her word, Madame Dupuis had arranged everything in the way of paperwork that we would need to open. I was constantly in awe of her generosity, both in goods and in deeds, and did what I could to thank her. It seemed a regular basket of pastries was enough to please her, though she remained rail thin.

I hoped it would become a place that was special to the families of the neighborhood. Where mothers could take their daughters for a special cup of *chocolat* when the world seemed like a burden. Where fathers could bring their sons for a *mille-feuille* after a triumph at school. Where friends could meet and chat over coffee. Where workers could have a quick breakfast to set them up for a hard day of toil. I wanted it to be a place that would become an integral part of the beating heart of Montmartre.

"Le Bijou will be back again, and it seems like all is right in the world," Madame Dupuis said as she came to inspect our handiwork the night before the grand reopening.

"Le Bijou seems like a curious name for a bakery," Laurent said. He'd questioned it when I'd commissioned the new sign but didn't press when I told him the bakery couldn't bear another name.

"I don't know the story behind the name, but I do know it was something of a joke between your great-grandparents. Though they were never wealthy enough to have much interest in jewels, I trust it had some significance to them."

"I'm sure it did," I said. I subconsciously patted the pocket where the worn red journal rested. The truth of the jilted suitor was in Lisette's pages, but for some reason, it didn't seem right to share her private writings with someone who wasn't family, as lovely as Madame Dupuis was. And it wasn't a story I wanted to share in front of Laurent after our tearful row the night he proposed. I snapped out of my reverie and back to the present.

"You'll come here for breakfast every day," I said, gesturing to a few bistro tables I'd chosen to leave in place so people could sit and enjoy a pastry and coffee at their leisure. In fine weather, we'd even open the terrace so customers could enjoy the sun and watch the people walk by on their way to the Place du Tertre. The quaint square where artists, from the great Renoir to the numerous aspirants who were destined to go unremembered, painted the comings and goings of the common man. "I'll make something special for you every morning. And if the weather is foul and you don't want to leave your flat, I'll bring it to your door myself."

She patted my hand and smiled appreciatively. It was a small gesture for me to make, given all she'd done for us, but I wouldn't forget her kindness. As she aged, I'd be there to care for her as I would for my own mother. I'd already said as much to Laurent and the girls, and they agreed wholeheartedly.

"I'd better make sure we have all we need to begin baking tomorrow morning," Laurent said. He kissed my cheek, then Madame Dupuis'. She gave a girlish giggle at the attention. He bounded off with the energy of a hunting spaniel as if it was a three-week pleasure jaunt that awaited him, and not a three-thirty-a.m. wakeup call to begin a day of toil in the kitchens. I admitted that I shared his enthusiasm more than I ever dreamed.

So many times in the past two years, I felt like all my choices had been taken from me, but I now wondered if it hadn't directed me to the path I would have chosen despite all the rocky roads that led there.

"Are you ready for tomorrow?" Madame Dupuis asked. "You must be excited and terrified in equal measure."

"You have the gist of it," I said. "Once things are established, I'm sure I won't be so anxious about it."

"Yes, I think you'll find in this neighborhood you'll never want for business. The trick will be keeping up with demand."

"I hope we manage," I said. "The prospect is daunting."

"You will, my darling girl. You will," she said, taking a seat at one of the bistro tables. "Something troubles you. Why don't we settle it over a cup of coffee?"

"Would you prefer to try Sylvie's *chocolat*? I'm still perfecting the recipe."

"Oh, even better," she said. "There is something akin to magic in chocolate, is there not?"

"Nothing like it in the world," I agreed, setting the cup of thick hot chocolate before her along with a couple of *Madeleines*. I hadn't perfected Lisette's recipe, but they were getting closer. Madame Dupuis took a sip, her eyes closed for a moment in appreciation. "It's perfect," she declared. "It's simply a marvel."

"Did my grand-mère serve *chocolat*?" I asked. There was a recipe in the journal, but I wasn't sure if it was something she would have served in the bakery.

"No," Madame Dupuis replied. "In the beginning, she only sold bread, or so I was told. As time went on, and during my day, she was able to expand her offerings to pastries and cakes, but everything was taken home to eat back then."

"I hope you don't object to the changes," I said. "I thought it would be welcome for people to sit and enjoy their food."

"Naturally," she said. "Things must be allowed to change and evolve, or they will never thrive. Your grandmother changed the menu when she took over. Expanded and experimented. You can honor the history of this place without being constrained by it. Your foremothers would have wanted you to leave your mark here, just as they did."

"I hope that's true," I said.

"It is. And clearly this recipe isn't what has you troubled. Nor the bakery. Not really. Tell me what's the matter and we'll set it to rights."

I took a sip of the *chocolat*, slowly, to bide a few more moments as I worked up some courage. "Laurent has asked me to marry him."

"Oh *félicitations*, my dear. He is a wonderful young man. He's exactly what your mother would have wanted for you."

"How can you know that?" I asked. "How can any of us? She isn't here to tell us what she wants."

"I knew your mother all her life, my dear. I knew what a good woman she was. What a devoted mother she was. She wanted her girls to know love and to find their own happiness. I think that she would see that Laurent and this bakery are precisely what you need to have those dreams realized for you."

"I told him I couldn't give him an answer," I said. "My father has died and my mother isn't here to give her consent. What if she comes back and disapproves of all I've done?"

"She wouldn't," Madame Dupuis said. "It wouldn't be her place to disapprove when you've had nothing to go on but your own instincts and some meddling from your old neighbor. But it doesn't matter. She isn't coming back, Micheline."

The words pierced my skin, my core, my very soul, as though the kindly woman wielded a knife. I waited for her to qualify her words or retract them, but she did not. The silence was nearly as painful.

"You don't know," I said. "She could—"

She raised her hand to silence me. "I *do* know, Micheline." She was not speaking conjecture, no matter how much I willed her to leave me some sliver of hope. "I should have told you sooner, but the truth can be an ugly thing. She was killed by a mob of angry men, hell-bent on getting retribution for feeling impotent for five years. They humiliated, sometimes killed, women who they suspected of collaborating with the Germans."

Tears welled in her eyes as she looked off for a moment, likely recalling the hideous truth of Maman's end.

"But Maman would never . . ."

Her eyes flashed back and locked with mine. The emotion left her voice at once. "Your mother would have done everything in her power to put food on your table. Even at the cost of her own honor. Nothing, not her pride or her dignity, mattered a whit to her compared to you girls. I didn't tell you because I didn't want you to think ill of her. And I never dreamed you'd be so tenacious in your pursuit of her."

I shook my head. How many people had said, or at the very least implied, that my quest was in vain? How many had, in their quiet ways, urged me to give up the search as a bad job and move on with my life?

"How did you know she was . . . collaborating with them?" I asked.

"She told me herself," she said, sadness welling in her eyes. "She hated those thugs with their ugly boots and boorish manners. But they controlled the food supply in and out of the city. She caught the fancy of a captain or major of some sort and let him enjoy her company in exchange for food for you girls."

"How did she never tell me?" I asked. "I wasn't a small child like Sylvie and Noémie."

"She wanted to protect you from it all. She swore me to secrecy, and I respected her wishes, but I see the time for that has passed. I will say prayers that she will forgive me, but I cannot let her absence loom over your head any longer."

"I just can't believe she would do such a thing." I felt my hands shake and what little I had of my *chocolat* trying to resurface.

"I can believe it. Easily. She loved you girls more than she loved anything else in this world. She hated every moment of her debasement, but she wasn't willing to let you and your sisters starve. Especially since she didn't have your father's feelings to consider any longer, God rest him." She paused a moment to clear her throat. I saw the tears glisten in her eyes, but she swallowed them back admirably. "I offered to help so many times, but money alone wasn't enough to get the food we needed toward the end of the occupation. Those barbarians took everything for themselves and shipped what they couldn't eat back to their own country. Worse than locusts. Your mother used the only currency that interested them."

"If I'd known I would have done something to help," I said.

"Like what, child? Would you have offered yourself to the beasts in your mother's stead? Do you think she could have lived with that? No. Blame the brutes who forced her into such a predicament. Blame our own countrymen who were heartless in the face of her sacrifice. Though none of it will bring you peace. But whatever you do, don't blame yourself or your poor mother."

I was helpless to keep the tears at bay any longer. I felt them stream, hot down my cheeks, and I made no efforts to curb them.

"What do I tell the girls?" I asked once I was able to regain my composure. "How can I tell them what happened to their beautiful Maman?"

"You tell them that she died so they can say their goodbyes," Madame Dupuis said. "That because of the war, it took a long time for the authorities to identify her. You can tell them they had no idea what happened to her, only that she was a casualty of that terrible war. Which is the truth. If they must know more when they're older, you won't have said anything that is a lie. That will be important if the truth does ever come out. Which I pray it does not. For their sake and hers."

I crossed my arms across my stomach and rocked back and forth gently for what might have been several long minutes. Trying to keep my ache from ripping a hole in me big enough that my very soul might slip out.

"Thank you," I said when I was finally able to draw breath. "For telling me the truth."

As much as it hurt, it was better to know than to spend the rest of my life wondering.

"I should have told you two years ago," she said, wiping tears away. "But seventeen is awfully young to bear the burden of raising two girls and contending with what happened to dear Eliane. I'd hoped that you would come to accept the inevitable and grieve in your own time. I never dreamed you'd be quite so tenacious. I hoped you'd have a bit of your Grand-mère Théodora in you, but I learned these past two years that there's far more of her in you than I ever thought possible. She would be so proud of you."

I managed a weak smile. "That means a great deal," I said. "I've felt like I'm failing at every turn."

"Mistakes, not failures," Madame Dupuis corrected. "As one would expect from a girl as young as you are now. The important thing is to learn and grow from those mistakes."

"I made a big one with Laurent," I said.

"That boy is mad for you. He'll forgive you if you apologize. He's not the stubborn sort."

"No," I agreed. "He's a good man."

"He is. And you don't need your mother's blessing. You need your own," she said, taking my hand in hers. "And not that it matters, but you have mine as well."

Chapter Thirty-Five

LISETTE

JUNE 10, 1871

I was back in my room in the Place Royale. Nanette was by my side, sitting in a chair, holding my hand. It reminded me of the times she snuck away from the kitchens when I was suffering from some childhood malady.

"Eat some of this good soup, darling. It will help you build back your strength."

I obliged her and took a spoonful of the soup she'd made: a hearty potato and leek bisque that I'd always loved when I was feeling poorly. It was the same comforting blend of flavors I remembered from my childhood, but it turned to ashes in my mouth.

"Think of the babe and eat," Nanette urged. She and Marie were the only ones who knew about the child. It was still early enough that anything might happen, and it seemed unnecessary to tell my parents before I felt the baby quicken. Part of me longed to hold the baby in my arms; whether it was a strapping, serious boy or a willowy spitfire of a girl or whatever God deemed fit for me. I just hoped the little one favored Théo in looks and spirit. His golden-bronze curls and blue-green eyes. His revolutionary fervor.

Part of me dreaded a future, raising the child alone. Maman and Papa would surely cast me out when they found out I was with child. They could hush up my "hasty marriage" to a Communard, but a child would be tangible evidence of how much I'd betrayed them and all they held dear.

The news that Théo had died on the barricades came about a week after Gaspard had carried me from the streets outside of Sébas' church. Nanette had enlisted Gaspard to scour the listings of the dead and missing for Théo's name, and he was able to determine that he'd been killed the same day I'd been hauled here. The same day we lost Pierrine. It was truly the day my world transformed into a place that seemed cold, bleak, and unfamiliar.

But at least I knew with certainty that Théo was gone. His death rent a hole in the depths of my soul, but that horrid truth was still better than not knowing. I'd made a point of writing to Gaspard that I was grateful for the pains he took to find Théo for me. I may have despised all he stood for, but I was not so obstinate as to deny my appreciation for what was, ultimately, a great act of kindness.

Nanette told me I had blacked out from the injury to my head, but Gaspard had personally brought me from the butte to the Place Royale. He'd commandeered a horse and wagon to transport me here, and set the household staff in motion, fetching a doctor and sending word to my parents at their country estate that I was back home and alive. They were home a few days later, bringing a renowned physician and a mountain of food along with them.

There was a knock at the door, and I moved to sit up, but Nanette stilled me.

"Rest," she commanded.

I expected to see Gislène at the door. She'd taken to visiting me in my rooms in the afternoon. She would read to me from novels, a few select titles Maman had decided weren't too scandalous, and we would chat companionably. I'd spent so little time with her before, I felt a small tinge of regret. She was a lovely child, not just in looks and superficial manners. She was caring, attentive, and whip-smart. At the age of eight, she was reading books far more complex than the ones I'd been interested in at that age and was years beyond Antoine in that regard as well. She'd become a delightful companion in my convalescence, and I found myself looking forward to her visits.

But instead of being greeted by the sight of Gislène and her golden ringlets, Nanette opened the door to see Maman there, looking dressed and coiffed for a visit to her deposed Empress instead of her own daughter. Maman looked surprised to see Nanette out of the kitchens, as if she didn't recognize her out of context.

"I was just seeing to Mademoiselle Lisette's luncheon,

Madame," Nanette explained by way of greeting. She looked to me with a slight apology for using the title she was so accustomed to. But referring to me as Madame Fournier would have not endeared her to Maman.

"How very solicitous of you," she said. "A maid could have carried the tray up."

"I don't mind, Madame. I like to see how the young *demoiselle* is doing with my own eyes when I can spare a few minutes. She gave us such a scare."

Maman looked mollified. "That she did."

"I'll leave you two ladies to your business," Nanette said with a slight curtsy to Maman and a nod to me.

"Nanette is devoted to you," Maman said, taking the seat Nanette had vacated.

"Yes," I agreed. "I don't think another family in all of France can say they are as lucky in their choice of a cook."

"Perhaps not," Maman said. "She was attentive to you in ways I should have been."

She knew. All this time we took such pains to avoid her suspecting my time in the kitchens, and she knew. It might have been foolish to underestimate her powers of observation when it came to things under her own roof, but to be fair to myself, I'd been given little reason to think better of her.

"It doesn't matter, Maman," I said truthfully. "It wasn't your way. And I was cared for. I have nothing to complain about."

"Even so, if I'd been a more diligent mother, you might not have run off like you did. When your sister was so very ill, my heart well and truly broke that both of you might be lost to me forever. And when I saw you in a dead faint in Gaspard's arms, I was terrified the worst had come to pass. That thought haunts me." She took my hand in hers. "I've been given another chance to be a better mother to both of my girls and I won't waste the chance. I'm not so foolish as to think I'll be given another."

I sat up in surprise. I'd never, not in twenty years, heard my mother speak of her feelings with such fervor.

I opened my mouth to speak, but she continued.

"I do hope you know that your father and I have always acted in what we hoped was your best interests."

"Yes, Maman." Of course, what she considered to be my best interests also served hers, but I wasn't in the spirits to engage her in an argument. It took all my energy to raise a spoon to my lips these days, and I wouldn't waste what little I had in a diatribe she had no desire to listen to.

"Gaspard, despite what you may feel, is a good man. He saved you. He brought you home to us alive. It's more than your husband was able to do."

"Maman—"

"No, I won't speak ill of the dead, Lisette. And you can be happy you had your little adventure and the chance to experience a bit of the world. I'm just glad you're none the worse for it."

"Thank you, Maman," was all I could think to say. I'd never imagined that Maman had imagination enough to have aspirations that extended beyond the Place Royale. That she spared a thought for the world beyond her little domain.

"The point of my visit is a simple one. Gaspard wishes to renew his engagement with you. Once you've had time to recover, of course. He understands you may not be ready for some time. But he does care for you, Lisette. And that's not something our kind of people get to take into account all that often when they marry."

I stared, disbelieving. Maman was invoking affection, if not love, when it came to the question of matrimony. I had been raised to believe that love and marriage were affairs as closely related as radishes were to the crown jewels.

"When did this all come about?" I sputtered.

"He came to your father last night. That poor man looked as though he'd seen the depths of hell itself. I think with all that's going on he wanted to know there are better times waiting for him in the future. Once . . . well, once the city is back to normal."

Back to normal. Once the bodies were burned or buried. Once the blood of the Communards had been washed from the streets. Once the charred remains of cherished buildings and monuments were cleared away and the workers—what remained of them—began rebuilding the city from the ashes.

"Your father simply told him that he still supports the marriage. That we will encourage you to consider the offer. And I hope you will. He will try to make you happy. That's as much as I could ask for any of my children."

"Maman," I said, sitting up. "It isn't quite that simple. I am with child."

Maman went pale for a moment but calmed. I had been a married woman, and though I would no longer be a fit consort for a prince, there were many among the most elite circles who wouldn't consider me "damaged" for being with child. It was the choice of father that would cause me grief.

"How far along?" she asked.

"Not very. Perhaps three months gone. I haven't seen a midwife to know when to expect . . ."

"I understand," Maman said, rubbing her temples. The cogwheels in her brain were churning as she calculated a way out of my predicament. "That does change things, but perhaps we can find a way. Just rest and get stronger. The rest will sort itself out."

For the first time in my life, my mother lowered her lips to my brow and brushed a wayward curl from my forehead. It felt awkward, and she looked almost pained at the show of affection. She left, and I stared at the door long after she made her exit.

I couldn't be sure if she was simply angling to restore the union she'd so longed for, or if she was genuinely concerned for my welfare. Concerned for the welfare of the child. Her grandchild.

But if it was all an act, the *Comedie Française* was being deprived of one of the greatest talents in all of Europe.

And for now, I would choose to believe it.

Chapter Thirty-Six

MICHELINE

I couldn't sleep. The chill in the sheets beside me was too much. My heart swelled with remorse for how I'd treated Laurent. Worry that he'd never forgive me. But there was little use in staring at the ceiling, so I stood and donned Maman's old dressing gown. He promised he would continue to work with me in the shop but was sleeping in his apartment. His absence in our little rooms above the bakery had been felt profoundly, not just by me, but the girls too. I had to find a way to make it right. There were no words fit to apologize to Laurent, but perhaps there was poetry enough in pastry.

On the terrace was the bush of a fine red rose that had been in the family longer than I had been. It was kept in a large pot on the terrace, and Maman had cared for it devotedly. The owners of the bistro hadn't seemed to mind the imposition of the riotous plant that looked as if it might take over the entire neighborhood if not pruned into submission. I'd taken care of it, just as Maman had done. I clipped it back in the fall, covered it in the winter, and watered it in the spring and summer. The blaze of red flowers had always given me a small delight, but today, the flowers would serve as more than a simple pleasure for the eye.

The moon was heavy that night and bright enough to see by, even without the glow of the streetlamps. I went to the terrace where the bush had resided for decades, armed with my best pruning shears. I clipped a dozen of the fragrant blooms, not quite at their peak. The fragrance, and thus the flavor, would be strongest earlier in the morning, so this endeavor was one for the early hours. I'd always loved the showy fragrance of this particular bush, which curiously had soft notes of honey and cinnamon that harmonized with the floral scent. I took the flowers into the kitchen and trimmed the heads from the stems and dropped each of the delicate pink petals into a pot of boiling water.

Within minutes, the room smelled as though I was in the finest garden in all of France. The color began to fade, and though the fragrance still hung heavy in the room, it was as though the deep pink of the petals had evaporated into the ether. I added sugar and mixed gently. I then took the juice of several lemons and the burst of color, more vibrant than the original, took my breath away. I added pectin with a bit of sugar to thicken the jelly. The final ingredient was a dash of Maman's favorite rose water. She used it so sparingly, adding just a bit to her bath or dabbing it behind her ears before a special occasion. One of so many things she'd left behind.

I poured the liquid into jars and let them cool before moving them to the refrigerator to help the jelly set more quickly.

While the ruby-red jelly set, I began the preparations for Laurent's favorite pastries: *Kouign Amann*. They were a specialty of Brittany, and a reminder of home. The process to make them was much like that of *croissants*, though they would be folded up to resemble a crown. It was familiar work, mixing the butter and flour methodically, and I gave myself over to it. It took hours. Folding and rolling the dough, chilling the dough, and repeating the process so the pastry would puff into layers. When, finally, it was time to bake, I sprinkled my work surface with a mixture of salt and sugar instead of flour. I cut the dough into squares and folded them into a buttered muffin tin.

They came out a beautiful golden brown, and I spooned the jelly on top, petals and all, to form a lovely reddish-pink glaze. As a final touch, I drizzled just the barest hint of dark chocolate over them. Not so much as to overpower the rose flavor, but enough to help it bloom on the palate. It was a small gesture, but I hoped it might be the beginning of an apology to Laurent for my hesitance. But though I hurt him, I hoped he would be able, in time, to understand the origin of my hesitance.

For the past few weeks, he'd come to the bakery to help prepare for the opening, but he now returned to the little room his parents had rented for him in a nicer neighborhood closer to the academy. Despite having the room at his disposal, he'd spent most nights with me in the flat above the bakery before I'd refused his proposal. All of them, actually. He'd retreated there to nurse his wounded feelings, and in the space of those long nights, I realized just how cold the bed felt without him. How accustomed I now was to being able to roll over and wrap an arm around him as a child would cuddle her beloved poppet in the middle of the night.

The girls had wondered where he'd gone, and I was running short of excuses on that score. They had grown to love him, not quite as a father, but something close. Something that would fill the void Papa had left.

Papa. So strong. Invincible in our eyes. He was tall, broad, and jovial. Messy copper-brown hair and a ready smile for his girls. He joined up in the fervor to defend France against the invaders six years before. He promised he would make France safe for us all, but he fell in battle somewhere near Sedan on a bright day in May. I'd spent so much time worrying about finding Maman, that I'd somehow forgotten my grief for him. Perhaps because I'd had more time to grow comfortable with the loss. It was definite that the certainty of his demise had made it easier to accept. But it had set into motion the events that would take Maman from us as well. And as I, perhaps for the first time in months, spared a thought for Papa, I realized how much grief was still in me.

I read in Lisette's journal about how the emperor had been defeated near the same city. How the battles there had changed the courses of both our lives. We'd both seen Paris in her darkest hours, and I wished I could talk to her. To ask her what she had done in her darkest hours to keep from sinking into the abyss of helplessness and despair. But then, perhaps I knew the answer already.

The road forward, for the women on the Vigneau line at least, was carved out in the kitchen. The road forward was paved in flour, yeast, egg, and water. The road forward was cobbled in the kind of love that was kneaded with our bare hands and blossomed in the oven. The road forward was through our little bakery in the heart of Montmartre.

I wanted to travel that road with Laurent. And I didn't think I was too late.

I knocked on the door of his room. It was still an hour or two before I expected to see him at the bakery. I wasn't sure if he'd even be awake, though in my experience he was an early riser. A good trait for a baker.

He opened the door, dressed and ready for the day, though he blinked for a few moments before reacting to my presence at his door as though he wasn't fully awake.

"I brought you breakfast," I said by way of greeting. I had placed *Kouign Amann* in one of the paper takeaway boxes we'd bought for the bakery for cakes and larger pastry orders. I wanted to have a stamp designed so we could put the name of the shop on them. It would be a fun project for the girls to stamp them when we got a new order of boxes in and would be a little extra advertisement for the bakery. But like so many things, there hadn't been time to see to it.

He paused, and for a horrible moment I thought he might shut the door. But he finally exhaled and opened the door wider, whispering a raspy, "Come in."

His room was small, but orderly. He'd left quite a few of his things in the flat above the bakery, but the room looked comfortable and lived-in. His prized copy of the *Larousse Gastronomique* lay open on the table where he took his meals when he ate at home. Always the student, always poring over books.

I handed him the box of pastries. "I'm sorry," I said lamely.

"I know," he said, setting the box on his table and pulling me close. He was fresh from a bath and smelled of clean linen and toasted sugar. I wanted simply to melt into him and forget myself. For hours. Maybe forever.

"Then why did you leave?" I asked, not raising my head from his chest.

"You needed space and time," he said. "I didn't want to give them to you, if I'm honest. I wanted to stay by your side and beg you to marry me. But I knew that if I pressed, you'd just slip further away. I was willing to keep my distance for a while if it meant not losing you."

"Sometimes you understand me better than I understand myself," I said. "It's maddening, you know."

"I don't understand you better," he said. "But I do have the advantage of being able to see you in ways that you cannot see yourself. Micheline, what you've done these past two years has been something akin to heroic. You took over raising two girls and running a house when you were still a girl yourself. You've borne more than you ever should have been asked to."

"It doesn't excuse how I behaved toward you," I said, burrowing my face in his shirt. "You didn't deserve that from me."

"You've had to walk a hard path. If you trod on my feelings in the process a few times, I'll manage well enough." He combed his fingers through my hair, and I felt my heart slow. My breath grew deeper. The very presence of him calmed my soul.

Still ensconced in his arms, he led me to his bed where we could sit. I told him everything Madame Dupuis had told me about my mother's death. I told him that, though I wanted more than anything to marry him, the wedding day would be bittersweet at best. To marry without my parents in attendance was something I'd never imagined.

"My parents will love you enough for all four of them," Laurent assured me. "It won't be the same, but I hope you'll feel a little less alone."

I nodded, wiping the tears from my cheeks. He didn't yet understand what it was to go through life without his parents there to support him. And I was glad he didn't have cause to. But even if he couldn't walk in my shoes, I was grateful he cared enough to imagine how the jagged pebbles felt through the thin soles of them as we ambled down the rocky road of life.

And it was a greater comfort than I had known in many years to know I would walk it with his fingers laced in mine.

Later that night, I took Lisette's journal in hand, and began making entries of my own.

CONFITURE AUX ROSES À LA MICHELINE

›>‹‹‹

I recommend using clean roses from a bush planted with love, best plucked in the light of the full moon.

To make rose jelly, place two cups of water and two cups of rose petals and one spoonful of rose water in a stew pan. Bring to a low simmer and let continue for ten minutes. Breathe deeply and stir gently. Add one and three-quarters cups sugar to the simmering roses and stir to dissolve the sugar. You will see the color has faded from the roses, but don't despair. Add the juice of two lemons to the mixture and watch as the ruby color reemerges. So it is, in many things in life. When things look hopeless, it often takes a small change to set things to rights. Simmer another ten minutes over low heat. Mix one-quarter cup sugar and one spoonful of pectin. Sprinkle the sugar mixture into the simmering roses gently and slowly so the jelly will be smooth. Simmer for another twenty minutes before pouring into jars. Jelly will be loose, but luscious.

Recipe notes: Serve as a glaze with Kouign Amann, *to win the heart of a Breton. Sometimes food is simple nourishment for the body. Sometimes it is nourishment for the soul. Sometimes it is an apology. This time, it must be all three.*

Chapter Thirty-Seven

LISETTE

Gaspard is thrilled, of course," Maman said a few days later. We were sitting in the little courtyard by the kitchen. She'd only been vaguely aware of its existence until she'd found me there in one of the solid wooden chairs resting and helping Marie shell peas for dinner. Though naturally dubious of nature and the out-of-doors, Maman conceded it was a pleasant enough spot to take afternoon coffee. She looked out of place, and I couldn't be sure that she was trying to please me, or simply playing nice until I was delivered to the church.

Maman had conveyed my acceptance to Papa, who conveyed it to my groom-to-be.

"He doesn't mind . . . ?" I asked. My hand floated to my abdomen in wordless acknowledgment of the little life that grew there.

"He was a little taken aback, but not wholly shocked. You

were married, after all. It's the natural progression of things. He swore to me he would provide for the child as his own."

I nodded. Gaspard wouldn't lie about such a thing. And as he would know the babe from the time he was born, the chances were good he'd be able to deliver on his promises.

"Though I think he'd be pleased if the child were a girl. Easier to provide another man's daughter with affection and a dowry than to pass on the bulk of the family fortune to another man's son."

I scoffed. "I'll do what I can on that score." I tried to sip from my coffee, but it was ash in my mouth. I couldn't be sure if the babe was changing my tastes, or if it was that nothing was palatable because I felt utterly numb.

I had agreed to marry Gaspard, though I couldn't even begin to envision a life with him. I couldn't wrap my thoughts around a future beyond a few hours from now. How could I possibly be equal to decisions that would shape the rest of my life?

"And his mother did express one concern," Maman continued, shaking me from my reverie. "The timing of the birth will be questionable."

"I suspected she'd come to that conclusion," I said. "What does she propose? That I sit cross-legged and keep the baby inside for an extra year or so?"

"If you could manage that, she'd be in favor," Maman said with a derisive snort. "But she wants you to wed as quickly as possible."

"In quiet and haste, I assume?" Absconding and marrying in near secret, just as Théo and I had done. But this was even more deceitful. I loved Théo, but had barely spared Gaspard a thought in the whole of my life.

"No, with all the pomp that can be thrown together in short notice," Maman said. "So that no one has a reason to whisper. She's making it known that you were engaged the whole time. Of course, with all the commotion in town, no one has been paying attention like they used to."

"*Commotion,*" I said. The faces of the dead were as clear in my mind as Maman's; she sat before me and they were already forgotten, or worse, villainized, for their simple desire to govern themselves.

She paled in embarrassment at the understatement but continued. "She wants you and Gaspard to take an extended honeymoon at their home in Provence with the excuse that you both need to recover from the . . . difficulties . . . we've all been through. And to tend to their properties. Perhaps a year or two. She's prepared to engage the best doctors and midwives in France to attend to you when your time comes. And when you come back to Paris, the child will be old enough that no one will be able to tell that the baby was born a bit too soon."

"I see," I replied. "Madame d'Amboise was certainly thorough in her planning."

"Oh, absolutely meticulous," Maman said with a smirk that lingered somewhere between ironic and admiring. "If anyone *is* shrewd enough to decipher that the child was conceived before the wedding, you're to use the fear of the violence in the city and your worry for Gaspard as an excuse for 'imprudent choices.' And the great disappointment you both had that your wedding had to be postponed. No one ever need know that your engagement was ever broken. She has more of a romantic streak in her than I ever would have guessed."

"So I am to erase Théo from my story. Forget him completely." I waited for the ache to resurface in my bosom, but there was but the faintest twinge. The pain had been so acute, it was though I couldn't feel it any longer. And that, somehow, was worse.

"Dearest, it's for the best that the baby thinks of Gaspard as his father. That the world thinks of it that way. But as for forgetting him, that is entirely up to you. You're the mistress of your own heart."

Though I'd spent years of my life trying to ignore my mother and her ways, I tried to see things from her perspective. In her mind, a good marriage would save me from ruin and her grandchild from an uncertain future. Pierrine's face flashed before my eyes. There wasn't anything I wouldn't do to spare my baby the heartache that poor woman had been forced to endure.

And I had to think Théo would want me to do the same.

I gathered my thoughts and focused once again on Maman. I'd have to tend to my broken heart another time.

"How neat and tidy the plan is. Madame d'Amboise ought to have a post in the *Assemblée Nationale*. She's wasted in the domestic sphere," I said, failing to bite back all the rancor in my voice. "When is it all to be? I assume she's set the date and seen to every detail, right down to what I shall have for breakfast the morning of the nuptial mass."

I snorted at the very idea that Madame d'Amboise's influence might extend as far as the kitchen Nanette presided over.

"Next Tuesday," Maman said. "Thankfully you already have your dress, and we can see to everything else."

I recalled the lovely silk confection that hung in the wardrobe upstairs. Every detail scrupulously chosen by Maman.

"It is a beautiful dress, Maman. I never told you as much."

Maman set down her coffee cup in surprise. "I'm glad it meets with your approval. You didn't have much time to pay your compliments on the way out the door."

"You and I haven't agreed on much, but I know you were trying to secure a good future for me," I admitted. "And your taste in wedding gowns is unparalleled."

Maman looked mollified. It was true that she worked hard for my benefit and that of the family, self-servingly or not. And her efforts were rarely acknowledged.

"At least you've grown wise enough to recognize what your father and I have tried to do." I couldn't quite read the look on her face, whether she was exasperated or relieved.

"Maman—" I began.

"Why don't we get you back inside," Maman said, clearly not wishing for the discussion to continue along this bent. "We don't want you to get worn out. And besides, Nanette has news for you."

"Do I hear my name?" Nanette said, looking up from the stove as we entered the kitchen.

"I think the time is right for Lisette to know of our scheme," Maman said.

"Ah, well, though it should be your prerogative as lady of the house to choose your own staff, your mother and I have decided that I ought to come cook for you as you settle into married life. If that would suit you, of course."

I flung my arms around Nanette. "Nothing could make me happier," I said.

"Go on now," she said, wiping a tear away with her apron. "You'll be too busy running the house to do much more than bark orders at me anyway, but we thought it might be a comfort for you to have me close by."

"Bark orders indeed," I said, placing a kiss on her cheek. I tried not to see Maman's rueful look. "Will you like Provence? Will you mind traveling so far?"

"Oh, the warmth will be good for these old bones," Nanette said. "And wherever you are will suit me fine."

Maman's cheeks flushed with Nanette's motherly pronouncement. I turned to her.

"But what about you, Maman? How will you get on without the best cook in all of Paris?"

Marie cleared her throat and looked expectantly at Nanette.

"Marie's a fine cook and quick study. The family won't starve in my absence," Nanette said with poorly concealed pride. Marie had finished her training at Nanette's side and had met with her mentor's approval, just as I had done.

"And we'll get you a maid of your own to train up to assist you," Maman promised her. "Now let's go upstairs and get you ready for dinner. Gaspard is anxious to see you."

I wished I could return the sentiment. Lord knew he deserved it. But I felt a sense of dread at the reunion. I hadn't seen him properly since our last dinner before the siege. It seemed so very odd to be reuniting as an engaged couple when so much had changed in the months since we'd last seen each other.

Maman helped me select a dress, one of her favorites in a rather lively shade of lavender that was well suited for late spring. I might have been another bloom in the gardens of Versailles in that shade. But it seemed vulgar. I'd not once worn black for Théo. Instead of wearing my widow's weeds and attending a funeral, as I should have been allowed to do, I'd don a wedding dress and marry another man. Maman actually saw to my hair herself and it looked better than when any of the maids had been set to the task.

"Thank you for Nanette," I said as we admired her handiwork.

"Anything to make your *entrée* into married life easier, darling." The corners of her lips turned up in a smile that did not suit her countenance. *Anything to see the deal signed and delivered, more like.*

I sighed. Maman had softened a bit, but she hadn't changed. Not in any way that really mattered. But for the sake of Théo's child, I'd do as she bid. I plastered on a smile and descended the staircase.

Gaspard greeted me, this time not in uniform, but in his best suit of civilian clothes.

"I didn't think you'd appreciate seeing me in my uniform," he said, noticing how I appraised his appearance.

"That was very . . . considerate of you," I said. Indeed, I didn't think it was something he would have done before the siege. He was so proud of his uniform before I'd left, I didn't think he'd have been willing to part with it for any price.

"We'd have been proud to see you in your uniform, d'Amboise. Damn fine work Thiers has done, ridding the city of the rabble. You ought to be proud." My father, already a brandy in from the rosy hue on his cheeks, raised what was left in his glass to Gaspard.

Gaspard inclined his head to my father, but did not acknowledge the compliment. "To be fully truthful, sir, I think I've had my fair share of uniforms for one lifetime. I'm very much looking forward to a peaceful life in Provence." There was a hunted look in his eyes. He'd seen far too much, and I realized the Provence scheme was as much for his benefit as my own. He turned to me. "I assume my mother told you of her plans?"

"Yes," I said. "Madame d'Amboise has a mind for details."

"You've only seen the smallest tip of that very considerable iceberg," he said, rolling his eyes. "Thiers should have enlisted her and he'd have retaken Paris without spilling a drop of blood. And probably improved on Haussmann's renovations in the process."

"Would that he had," I said, looking away.

"I'm sorry, that was callous of me," he said.

"Never mind," I said, waving my hand dismissively.

"I trust the plan is . . . acceptable to you?" he said. "I know it may be hard for you to be so far away from Paris. From your family."

"Nonsense," Papa interjected. "The change will be good for her."

"It does sound lovely," I allowed. "I've never been further than the Touraine. I've always wanted to travel."

"Excellent. There are so many charming places that are an

easy carriage ride from my parents' home. Our home. While we rest, we can take short excursions as often as it pleases you. And once . . ." He glanced at my midsection. "Well, once things are more settled and you're feeling up to it, perhaps a grand European tour?"

"Gaspard, that does sound wonderful. Exactly what I would wish for my girl," Maman said. But her tone was different. It wasn't the prodding insistence of Papa. She truly wanted this for me.

"It does," I agreed. And though I couldn't keep the tears from my voice, I squeaked out, "I'm more than fortunate that your mother has been so attentive to detail. And that you yourself are amenable to taking on a burden that isn't yours to bear."

His blue eyes searched mine. He took my hand and pressed his lips to my hand.

"My dearest Lisette, I hope to show you in time that it is no burden at all and that I truly hope for your happiness in all this."

Gaspard had arranged to take me for a carriage ride on Saturday before the wedding. Usually, an unmarried couple of our standing wouldn't be allowed to go unescorted, but given that we were to be wed in three days and that I was already in a delicate condition, there seemed little reason to be too guarded with my reputation.

"Try to smile a little, darling," my mother said as she helped me to get ready for the outing. "I know it isn't easy, but Gaspard is trying so very hard. I don't know many men who would go to such lengths for a fiancée or even a wife."

I took Maman's hand. "I know. He is a *good* man. And a kind one. You picked well for me. Even if he isn't Théo."

"You can be happy again, darling. I know this. But you'll have to make the choice to be so."

I embraced her. She meant what she said, I just don't think she understood the enormity of what she was asking of me.

Gaspard arrived promptly, and he escorted me to his carriage. Despite the delightfully warm weather, he placed a blanket across my lap. "The air in springtime can still have a bite to it," he said. "And since you've been unwell, I wanted to make sure you'd be comfortable."

"You're too kind to me, Gaspard," I said as he climbed in beside me.

We rode in silence for some time. Gaspard turned to leave the city, for so many of the roads were impassable and the efforts to rebuild the city were only hampered by traffic.

"I never thanked you," I said. "For saving my life."

"Don't speak the words," he said, growing solemn. "That was the darkest day of my life. That week was the bleakest I've ever faced. I can't tell you the number of times I've awoken in a cold sweat, having dreamt of what would have happened if any other soldier had come upon you. It's quite literally the stuff of my nightmares. But it was really your priest friend who saved you. If he hadn't stepped between us and you, I'd never have had the time to recognize you."

"Sébastien," I said. "Do you know what happened to him?"

Gaspard shook his head. "If he was clergy, he was probably spared by our side. The archbishop didn't do too well in the hands of the Communards though."

"So I heard," I said lamely. There had been so many reports of death, I couldn't register them all in my head. The Archbishop Darboy had been killed as the Versaillais had retaken Paris, and his death had been among the many reasons the Versaillais had taken such swift reprisal against the Communards. We had dared to defy the authority they thought was theirs by divine right.

"The priest begged me to care for you," Gaspard said. "It seems you were rather dear to him."

"He and my husband were the best of friends, though they didn't always agree on things," I said. "Perhaps if Théo had listened to Sébas and been a little more cautious . . ."

"It was an atrocity, what happened," Gaspard said. "I believed so firmly in our cause. That the nobility is charged with maintaining peace and order for the working classes. That they needed our governance to be able to survive and thrive. But our side took things too far."

He grew white with the memories of what he'd seen.

"It wasn't justice," he said. "For every Versaillais to fall, how many Communards paid with their lives? For every monument destroyed, how many homes did we burn? It wasn't justice, it was a massacre of the working class of Paris. And I was disgusted to play any part in it."

"Thank you for that," I said. "They're good people. They work hard and simply want the chance to lead their own lives. Nothing all that extraordinary about what they wanted. It's a shame they'll never have it. I wonder when our dear emperor will be reinstated." There was no keeping the venom from my tone.

"He won't be," Gaspard said with assurance. "The public sentiment, even from the highest echelons of society, is too violently opposed to it. He's cowering away in England, and likely to remain there for the rest of his miserable days."

"I never thought I'd live to hear you speak a word against him," I said.

"I was a soldier, Lisette. I was trained to follow orders without question. But when a man sees what I saw. The mismanagement that led to our failure to push back the Prussians. The utter savagery used against the workers of Paris . . . a man with a brain can't see all that and hold his questions any longer."

"You're beginning to sound like my Théo," I said. I breathed in with pain at the sound of his name spoken aloud.

"He was a National Guardsman?"

"Yes, and a Communard," I said, not caring if it rankled Gaspard's feelings. "He believed that Paris should be run by the people."

"I used to think he was wrong. I don't any longer." He looked far away for a moment, remembering the ghosts of the recent past.

"At least one heart has been turned," I said. "That is a victory at least."

He responded with silence for a while. "I see you don't wear the ring I gave you. I had expected your parents had given it back to you to wear. I returned it so . . . unceremoniously, I hope it wasn't damaged."

I laughed, having almost forgotten the almost obscene emerald Gaspard had given me all those months before. "Your ring is now a bakery," I said. "On a small little street in Montmartre."

"A bakery?" he asked, his tone surprised.

"Yes. It will astonish you to hear this, but I was a baker. When there was flour to be had, at least. Just in a small way. Just enough to help the neighborhood. But it gave me a sense of purpose. A way to help."

"So you *were* feeding the Communards when you were stopped?" he asked.

"I fed anyone who needed feeding," I said, remembering Sébas' words.

"Take me to it," he said, motioning to turn the carriage back north. "I want to see this bakery I financed."

I coached him through the streets, trying to take the route with the widest roads that were less likely to be blocked.

A half hour later, we arrived. Le Bijou still stood, though other buildings in the neighborhood hadn't fared so well.

"We painted it green," I said. "To match the ring. It seemed fitting."

We climbed down from the carriage, and I opened the doors that had never been locked that day. There had been so much chaos on the butte, no one had bothered to pillage a shop of such small consequence.

I showed Gaspard the storefront, then the kitchens where I'd toiled so many hours. There were too many ghosts to take him to the apartment upstairs. I was animated as I showed off the fruit of my labors, and he smiled to see it.

"You created this," he said. "You did more in a few months with next to nothing than I've done with my entire life with every conceivable advantage. God, I envy your satisfaction."

"Gaspard, in truth, this place is yours. I paid for it with the ring you gave me, after all," I reminded him. I rubbed his arm. "And soon you'll have work to do in Provence. I am sure you can do something grand with your holdings there. Something to be proud of."

"You took the token I gave you and made something real from it. I couldn't have invested the money better," he said, surveying my shopfront. "I hope you're right about Provence. I truly do. But are you sure you want to go? This neighborhood is made better by your presence in it. I've never been able to say the same."

"I made a promise to you, Gaspard. I won't go back on my word to you a second time."

"I'm not asking you to do that. I'm releasing you from your promise if you no longer wish to keep it," he said. "I can see the pain in your eyes, Lisette. I didn't want to, but it's there. And it kills me. I don't want to see it turn into resentment. I couldn't bear it."

"Gaspard, there isn't anything left for me here. Truly."

"There is," Gaspard insisted. "You have a neighborhood that needs you more than ever. You have a business and a home. I don't want to take you away to Provence knowing you've left a part of yourself here. If I can't have all of you, I'd rather leave you whole for someone else."

I wasn't able to find words but rubbed my hands longingly on the wooden counter where I'd sold bread to my friends and neighbors.

He swallowed hard.

"I thought as much. I can have your family send your things. I'll explain it all myself. They'll come to understand in time."

"Thank you, Gaspard. I don't deserve someone as good and kind as you. I hope you find a grand lady who will suit your grand plans."

"Hopefully a sweet Provençale who will be content enough with a quiet life. I hope you will be happy here, Lisette. You deserve it. Though I was wondering if I might be so bold as to ask for a parting gift?"

I blinked in astonishment. "I haven't much . . ."

"You have enough. One kiss?" he asked.

I nodded, and he lowered his lips to mine in a chaste kiss. The first he'd dared to claim.

"I wanted so very much to have the chance to love you. But I know now this will be for the better. Be well, sweet one."

I watched as the carriage departed our little street in our little corner of the butte. I expected a pang of loneliness without Théo tromping through the door after a hard day on duty. Without Pierrine whispering idle gossip about a customer after they walked out the door with their bread in tow. Their presence was still there, somehow, and there was still flour, yeast, salt, and water to transform into the staff of life. If I hurried, I could have some *flûtes* ready for the dinner crowd. I went up to the apartment to change out of my silk dress into one of the sturdier dresses I'd left behind. I felt myself breathing easier after just a few moments.

Théo's spare boots, the old ones that let in water in the rain, were still in the corner. His cup, with a half inch of coffee in the bottom, was sitting by the sink waiting for me to rinse it. It didn't seem possible that he was gone. He'd left too much of himself behind to truly be gone forever.

I sat on our bed for just a moment and buried my head in my hands. I'd cried for Théo, but rarely had the luxury to do so in private. At my parents' house, someone was always there, trying to comfort me when the effort of keeping my tears at bay became too much. I would have to learn to endure it, but Théo's presence here was so strong I could almost hear him bounding up the steps now.

I nearly let out a scream when I felt an arm wrap around my shoulders.

"God in Heaven, Sébas. I thought you were Théo for a moment." I rested my head against his shoulder. "I never thought I'd see this place again."

"I never thought I'd see *you* again," he said, tightening his grip around me slightly. "Though for your sake I'd trade places with Théo. I know how much you miss him."

"He should have listened to you," I said, shaking my head. "If he'd been more cautious, he'd still be here."

"No," Sébas said. "They mowed them all down. Hunted them like dogs. Any trials they bothered to hold were farcical. If they'd known he was sympathetic to the Commune, they would have killed him. At least he died on the barricades defending Paris. It was a better death than many got."

"But what was it all for, Sébas? Are we any better off than we were before?"

"I'd like to think so, Lisette. I have to hope that all that sacrifice was for something."

For the first time, I noticed he wasn't wearing his usual robes and collar. He saw my eyes glance to his throat.

"Changes are everywhere," he affirmed. "I couldn't be part

of the Church that sided with those who would massacre the very people that needed their protection the most."

"So I'm not the only one breaking vows," I said with a hollow laugh, thinking of Gaspard, who was well on his way back home by now. "I ought to take some comfort in that."

Sébas returned my laugh and rubbed my shoulder.

"How long will you stay?" Sébas asked. "I thought you'd be well entrenched in the bosom of family life again."

"I was," I said. "But my intended knew my heart better than I did and brought me back. I don't know how I'll plod on alone, but I'll do my best."

"You won't be alone, Lisette. Not if you don't wish it."

He placed a kiss on my forehead, and I led him down to the kitchens to teach him the craft that I loved.

Chapter Thirty-Eight

MICHELINE

Three weeks later I stood in my bedroom. The one I would share with Laurent for the rest of our married days. I wore Maman's best dress, a lovely thing in emerald-green silk with a sweetheart neckline, trim waist, and a full skirt that she'd saved only for the most important occasions. If she had been there with us that day, it's likely what she would have worn to celebrate our wedding. Like so many things these days, I found it comforting and sad in equal measure.

"You look beautiful," Noémie declared, coming over to hold my hand. I bent down to kiss her head, careful not to mess the curls that Sylvie had worked hard to tame into something like a civilized coiffure. I breathed deep. She was freshly bathed and smelled of linden and orange blossom and wore her best blue dress.

Sylvie grunted her agreement, and I decided to take it as highest praise. She still struggled with the reality that I had to fill Maman's place in her life, but she was slowly making peace with it. Some days were harder, and as I stood wearing one of our mother's dresses, preparing to bring a father figure permanently into her life, I suspected this was one of them.

I didn't tell the girls everything Madame Dupuis had shared with me. There wasn't need for them to know the gruesome truth of it all. Perhaps they never would, but certainly not now.

"You look lovely, my dear," Madame Dupuis announced from the door. She had insisted that a bride, at the very least, needed new shoes and a hat for the occasion of her wedding and had taken me shopping. Laurent had watched the girls and she had taken me to one of the nicer shops in the heart of town for a pair of black patent-leather shoes and a simple green silk hat to match the dress, with a bit of loose netting to make it feel just a bit bridal. She slipped a small emerald pendant on a gold chain around my neck, and pronounced me ready to wed, as soon as Noémie fetched the bouquet of red roses that we'd assembled from flowers we'd culled from the bush on the terrace.

I found I wasn't sad to forgo the white ball gown and a formal luncheon. The thought of such excess after the war felt like a mockery to those who were lost, though I knew none of them would likely begrudge us our merriment.

We'd already signed papers at the *mairie* the previous afternoon, but today, at Laurent's mother's insistence, we would exchange vows in Saint-Pierre. Just as Great-grandmother Lisette had done with Théo *and* Sébas. Her second love, while unexpected, bloomed into a romance as all-consuming as the first. Just as Grand-mère and Grand-père and Maman and Papa had done.

Madame Dupuis and the girls walked me the few hundred feet to the church. Laurent was waiting there with his parents and all his brothers.

The priest, a rather dour man who, in my mind, was the very antithesis of the man that had presided over this church in my great-grandmother's time, spoke the timeless vows that he had recited to hundreds of couples before us. And would likely speak to hundreds more before he passed.

It was perfect.

It was still painful.

But as we walked back to the bakery where our new, but already loyal customers awaited their bit of the *croquembouche* we'd made to share with anyone who stopped by that day, it was worth the ache of missing my parents if the end result was that I was married to Laurent.

There was a modest crowd assembled to feast on the golden tower of cream puffs enrobed in strands of caramel. Laurent and I had made it together, and it was finer than either attempt we'd made for Rossignol. Together, we created something greater than we ever could have apart. I knew that by myself, I could do great things, but with Laurent at my side, we would both reach greater heights.

He was a good man who had vowed to raise my sisters as his own daughters. Who, in a few short years, would show how true to his word he was when our own daughter was born. He treated all three of them as though they were the most important beings on the earth.

Save, perhaps, for one.

Chapter Thirty-Nine

LISETTE

JUNE 1875

As was our custom, we closed the shop for our afternoon break after we'd had our midday meal. We gathered up the children to stretch our legs and brush away the cobwebs from a morning spent hard at work. Nanette, who no longer cared to take a stroll of an afternoon, would keep an eye on the shop and put in some extra loaves for the dinner rush. She was happy to take on the duty, since I was always the one to light the ovens at an ungodly hour while she slept until the morning crowd came for their breakfast.

"I want to go see Grand-mère and Grand-père," Théodora said, looking up at us with pleading blue-green eyes the same shade as her father's. She had his copper ringlets and the same conviction when she spoke. I had gotten the dearest wish of my heart that something of her father would live on in her.

"That's a bit far for today," Sébas said. "Little Guillaume would be in tears by the time we reached the Place des Vosges. We can go on Sunday in the carriage. I know your grandmother wants to get her hands on baby Nanette. And to spoil you and your brother with sweets while your maman and I aren't looking."

Théodora giggled. "Clever Papa. We didn't think you noticed."

"Always your first mistake, *ma chère*. Never underestimate how clever your papa is," I said. "Or your maman. I was raised by your grand-mère, and I know all her tricks."

My parents, after a long and uneasy adjustment to my new circumstances, doted on the children. My mother harbored grand aspirations for all of them, but I was determined they would set their own courses in life. Though if my parents saw fit to make the children's situations easier as they grew into adulthood, I wouldn't argue.

"Why not to the park?" Rémy asked. "I saved a bit of stale bread for the ducks." As the oldest, eight-year-old Rémy didn't plead or whine to get his way. He had Pierrine's dark hair and impish expression but was the most serious boy I'd ever known. His father had been killed during the horrible week that claimed his mother as well. With Gaspard's help, we were able to track down little Rémy and raise him as our own. It seemed the least we could do to honor his mother.

"Next time, son. Let's head east," Sébas said.

We walked past the church where he had served for a decade. Théodora was still confused about how her beloved papa could have once been a priest, and still didn't fully understand how it was that she had been lucky enough to have two papas, but she was grasping more and more as the days rushed by.

Not far from Sébastien's former church, the ground had been cleared to erect a new church. A massive basilica that would tower over the butte. A reminder that the elite had won and the workers had been put in their place. We stood and watched the hive of laborers preparing the land for construction. It would be a massive undertaking, and I was glad I'd likely not see it completed in my lifetime.

"Loathsome place," I said, resisting the urge to spit on consecrated ground. "But I suppose the victors must be allowed to build the monuments."

"We don't have a monarchy," Sébas pointed out. "And the sentiment against the violence after the Commune was extreme enough, there likely won't ever be again."

"It's something," I agreed, "I only hope it will last. For their sakes." I glanced meaningfully at the older children and cuddled my sweet newborn daughter to my chest.

Sébas hoisted Guillaume, his miniature in every respect, aloft to get a better look at the city that still bore the scars that had changed our lives forever.

"It will, my love," Sébas said, leaning in to kiss me as Guillaume squealed with delight from his perch on his father's shoulders. "It will because it has to."

And we walked back to the bakery with the green façade, hand in hand. On the little terrace, the rose that Théo had given me was now a sturdy young bush that bloomed reliably and grew heartier with each passing year. I could not help but smile each time I saw it. The first gift that I was given that was born of love, not obligation, and without the taint of expectation. As we opened the door to our little bakery in the heart of Montmartre, the rose's aroma mingled with the earthy smell of baking bread. They blended to create the perfume that, to me, would always be the scent of love and Le Bijou.

PAIN FRANÇAIS

⊹⊱⊰⊹

I have learned all manner of elegant recipes at Nanette's hip, but this is the one that is never missing from the table. The one we rely on to sustain us. Common man or the emperor himself, rarely a meal goes by where a portion of common bread is not present—or sorely missed.

Add to six pounds of flour, two pints of milk, three-quarters of a pound of lukewarm butter, half a pound of yeast, and two ounces of salt. Mix all well together. Knead with a sufficient quantity of warm water. Cover the dough and let rise for two hours. Shape into rolls and let rest on tinned plates over a slack stove. Let stand one hour, then bake in a very hot oven for twenty minutes.

Recipe notes: No alteration needed. Serve often, and with love.

* * *

AUTHOR'S NOTE

A question many authors are posed is "Where do your ideas come from?" Many authors find the question annoying. Largely, I suspect, because the origin stories of their books aren't all that interesting, and they hate disappointing their readers. Most books aren't inspired by anything as dramatic as a bolt of lightning or a stone tablet hidden in the woods. Alas, most of my books start when a friend messages me with a link to an article and says, "Hey, you should write a book about this." In other cases, research for one book leads to an idea for another (e.g. *The School for German Brides* was born from research materials I found for my previous book, *Across the Winding River*).

In the case of *A Bakery in Paris*, right at the beginning of the Covid lockdown I was actively hunting for new ideas. Usually, I have plenty in my back pocket, but none of them felt right. At the time, I was dating a historian and I asked him for his thoughts on a potential new topic. I was keen to break away from the World War II books I'd been doing and wanted to look to a new era for the sake of diversifying my craft. He suggested I look into the Siege of Paris and the Paris Commune of the early 1870s for inspiration. I remembered some of this history from my graduate school days, and, after refreshing my memory, I knew the dashing historian boyfriend was right. And yes, reader, I married him.

For various reasons, *The School for German Brides* was contracted first, so I had to wait a full year to dig into this manuscript. Writers will tell you of the siren song of the "affair book" . . . the book that you want to write because you're supposed to be writing something else. *A Bakery in Paris* was the most alluring affair book of my career, and it was incredibly hard to wait to begin writing this tale. Thankfully, my wonderful editor, Tessa, believed this would be a great follow-up to *The School for German Brides*, as it doesn't entirely leave behind the World War II aspect of my previous work, thanks to Micheline's post-war timeline. But it *does* seek to depart from my previous novels that centered on the conflict itself. The idea was to focus on Paris as it was rebuilding—and reinventing—itself.

Both Lisette's story from the 1870s and Micheline's from 1946 deal with a city recovering from the horrors of war, and also the families that must heal and move forward when the path seems impossibly barred. I wrote the entirety of Lisette's story first, and then moved along to Micheline's. I had worried that the narratives wouldn't flow together without a lot of overhaul, but the similarities of the circumstances in which they lived have such strong parallels that it wasn't as hard as I'd feared to intertwine the story arcs. Originally, there was going to be a third timeline set in the 1990s, but there was such rich material to expound upon with the first two heroines that I couldn't find a way to make the modern heroine live up to her foremothers. Once I let go of the idea of the third voice, the narrative simply worked.

Both Micheline and Lisette, and the rest of the characters that surround them, are all of my creation. There are references to real historical figures, but aside from a cameo from a real Versaillais general, none appear "onstage." That said, many of the events depicted are true. The women of Montmartre held off the Versaillais troops who were waiting for the horses that the generals had forgotten. The Versaillais were dislodged by the National Guard, and that was the beginning of a two-month reign of the common man over Paris. Sadly, their infighting, and a lack of organization and a common vision, meant the Communards would ultimately fall to the Versaillais.

The real plot twist in all this was that though the bourgeoisie and the monied classes disdained the Commune in its time, the bloody and disproportionate reprisals of the Versaillais against anyone even tangentially associated with the rebellion swayed the public opinion back in favor of the workers, who were fighting for fair treatment and representation under the law. Though the Commune was defeated and the Byzantine behemoth, the Basilica of Sacre Coeur, still looms large over the city to remind the people of the power of the elite, France never again saw a monarchy. This rebellion was well and truly defeated, but the people were ultimately victorious.

Also based in truth were the vicious attacks against women

in France who were accused of "horizontal collaboration" with German troops during World War II. When Micheline's mother, a young widow, is desperate to feed her three young daughters, she sacrifices her dignity to keep her beloved children alive. There was little sympathy for the women who were reduced to such measures. Many suffered beatings and had their heads shaved in great spectacles of public humiliation. Others simply disappeared at the hands of their own countrymen who'd had their spirits broken over the course of the long war and were looking to reclaim a bit of their lost pride. This was the fate of Micheline's much-lamented mother, and many other women like her.

Lisette's bakery, Le Bijou, is fictional, but I did search photos of countless Parisian boulangeries for the perfect prototype on which to base my own little slice of Paris. I found a minuscule spot called La Galette des Moulins right in the heart of Montmartre, on the rue Norvins, just off the Place du Tertre. The building is a lighter shade of green than that of the one you see on the cover, and I haven't been able to find out how old the building is, but the tiny little bakery has a courtyard beside and apartments above, just as depicted in the book. With its warm reviews from regular patrons but glaring absence from many travel guides, it was the perfect understated place to set the story.

While much of this novel was written while international travel was impossible, and I had to spend hours on Google Street View (what a lifesaver!), I did have the opportunity to visit Paris between drafts. It was my first return to one of the cities of my heart in more than twelve years. While the trip itself was going to be a whirlwind adventure across much of Western Europe, I would get three days to photograph and absorb the places where Lisette and Micheline lived and loved. The first morning of the trip, we trekked the fifteen-minute hike up the butte from our hotel to the beloved bakery that I'd used as a model for Le Bijou. I'd studied the building from every angle online, but I was finally going to step foot in the place for myself. I planned on buying an obscene number of pastries, a good coffee, and photographing until the owners got annoyed.

When we showed up, the bakery was shuttered. After a quick search on my phone, it seemed it permanently closed about a month before our arrival. I'd checked the opening hours so many times before our travels, but apparently not close enough to our actual stay in Paris. Yes, I cried actual tears in the Place du Tertre for the hole-in-the-wall bakery that hadn't survived the pandemic long enough to experience the boom of the "summer of revenge travel." And there were no other bakeries for blocks and blocks. Of course, in modern times there are multiple cafés and restaurants right in the square, so the average Parisian or traveler won't starve. In Lisette's time, bread was a staple of the diet. Nutritionally questionable or not, people ate pounds of the stuff per day to live. Having to walk a half hour or more to find bread would have been a real burden for the hardest working people in the city. So many times, in both timelines, the *need* for a bakery in that corner of Montmartre is brought up, and the absence of one in 2022 drove that point home for me.

There was something poetic about the bakery having been closed upon my arrival. It was going to be a stellar moment in what was already an incredible trip. But as I stood and resigned myself to taking pictures of the exterior of the storefront and the little courtyard, I sympathized with Madame Dupuis, who knew there was a need for a good bakery in her neighborhood. I truly hope someone opens it again and restores it as a bakery. If said proprietor is reading this? Invite me to the grand opening and I'll bring signed copies of this book for your first patrons in exchange for a hot *pain au chocolat* and a coffee. Or a *tartelette au citron*. Maybe both?

A stone's throw from the now-shuttered bakery is the Église Saint-Pierre de Montmartre, one of the oldest churches in Paris. It's the church where Sébas served as priest, where Lisette married Théo, where Micheline married Laurent, and where countless members of their family, for generations, attended services in good times and in bad. The church, now in the shadow of Sacre Coeur, still stands today and continues to serve the people of the Montmartre neighborhood where Lisette and Micheline lived. It was indeed a warehouse for Communard weapons during the attacks, though I found no proof of a compassionate priest who allowed the munitions to be stored in the place of worship. I'd like to think some of the clergy were sympathetic to the plight of their most needy parishioners, but unfortunately, most sided with the Versaillais, who represented the last vestiges of monarchy and the established order that the Church sought to uphold.

The theme that I found reinforced during my visit to Montmartre was, especially in Lisette's time (but still today), the importance of neighborhood unity. Neighbors looked out for one another. They supported local business and worked diligently to make sure that their little corner of Paris was thriving. This wasn't just an abstract idea. There were neighborhood organizations that worked for the benefit of all residents of the area as well as those fortunate enough to visit. A sign in honor of the "Place de la Commune Libre de Montmartre" dedicated on April 11, 1920, during Madame Dupuis's heyday, commemorates the organization that was charged with making sure that the needs of their small community weren't ignored while the more powerful *quartiers* had their voices heard. This was the very spot where, for a time, the organizers would have met to discuss the matters central to Montmartre and its residents.

The sign is attached to a green wrought-iron fence that surrounds the terrace of the very bakery that inspired Le Bijou, and if you imagine hard enough, you can see the vines of an unruly rosebush that smells curiously of honey and cinnamon.

For book club questions and for further reading, please visit aimiekrunyan.com.

ACKNOWLEDGMENTS

If *The School for German Brides* was the book I labored to write in three-hundred-word chunks during one of the heretofore hardest phases of my life, *A Bakery in Paris* was the joyful one I got to write when life began to regain a sense of normalcy, and as I found the space to process all the hardships of the previous few years. I think both the optimism and the challenges of that period are reflected in this work, and I am so grateful I've had the chance to share Lisette's and Micheline's stories with the world. As with all books, there is a whole host of people without whom the book never would have happened, and I offer them my deepest thanks:

- My talented editor, Tessa Woodward, who has been enthusiastic about this project since the very beginning. I appreciate your vision and I am grateful to have you as a champion of my work.
- My new, incredible agent, Kevan Lyon, who took over

this project and has been a wonderful support. Thank you so much for sharing your expertise and wisdom with me!

- My dear friends from the writing community, Rachel McMillan, J'nell Ciesielski, Kimberly Brock, Heather Webb, Kate Quinn, Andrea Catalano, Jamie Raintree, Jason Evans, and many others for all their amazing support. I am so glad Facebook Messenger exists.

- My dear friends *outside* the writing community, especially Stephanie, Todd (you're in both friend categories, you lucky duck), Danielle, Carol, and Sam for all the encouragement.

- My Author Genie, Kerry Schafer/Kerry Anne King for keeping me on track with newsletters and all the admin duties of writerly life. Thank you for nagging me when I need it!

- The Tall Poppies and the Lyonesses for all their cheerleading and signal boosting. You ladies are a force, and I am glad to be part of these amazing groups!

- All the countless, amazing reader groups across social media who uplift writers' voices and the tireless people who run them: thank you for spreading the word for us when it's becoming harder to be heard!

- My local indie, Macdonald Book Shop, for all their support and prime shelf space in the Local Author section. You make me feel way cooler than I am. And to all the independent bookstores everywhere who champion new and midlist authors as well as the big dogs: we see you and appreciate you!

- JijiCat for the hours and hours spent by my side offering editorial advice while I wrote this book. Thank you for accepting payment in treats and butt rubs. And to Zuri for being extra cute (and fierce).
- The Trumbly and Vetter Clans for being so encouraging of this crazy career of mine.
- My darling kids, Ciaran and Aria, for being remarkable young people who dazzle me every day with their wit, vivacity, and relentless kindness (except maybe toward each other . . . sometimes).
- Of course, my husband, Jeremy, who is the most supportive partner a person could ask for. I appreciate you more than I can express.
- And to all the readers who have taken their precious time to read my work: you have my eternal gratitude. Thank you for sharing your time with me and my stories.